PRAISE FOR SHERRY THOMAS

Not Quite a Husband

"Exquisitely crafted...beguiling mix of complex characters and realistically complicated romance."
—*Chicago Tribune*

"Thomas, who has made a name for herself with her exquisite use of language, deftly switches between past and present in this lyrically written, emotionally captivating story graced by beautifully developed, realistically flawed characters, clear motivation, and descriptions that make late Victorian India spring to life."
—*Library Journal*

"Thomas has quickly become a fan favorite thanks to her wonderful storytelling and her unique ability to get into her characters' minds and our hearts. Her prose has a musical quality that flows effortlessly and lures the reader into the beauty of her words as well as her story. Then add diverse plotlines, engaging characters, depth of emotion, and a sweeping romance—what more co..."

Delicious

"This seductive, magical historical rewards readers with exquisite language, nearly erotic culinary descriptions, and a fairy-tale ending. A delectable treat."
—*Library Journal,* Best Romances of 2008

"A Cinderella story with a compelling culinary twist, Thomas's scrumptious Victorian confection proves impossible to resist."
—*Publishers Weekly*

"Packed with engaging characters, gripping dialogue, a devious plot, steamy sex, and smart writing. This is definitely an author on the rise. Another keeper! Get it!"
—Reader to Reader

"Delicious, delectable, and a mouthwatering blend of *Cinderella, Top Chef* and *Like Water for Chocolate,* not to mention *Chocolat.* [Sherry Thomas] dazzles with her intelligent, compelling story and memorable characters. This well-crafted romance places her among the very finest of the next generation of authors."
—*Romantic Times,* Top Pick!

"Entertaining and thoroughly absorbing."
—Romance Reviews Today

"*Delicious* just about says it all: Sherry Thomas's second novel is a multicourse banquet of delectable storytelling, scrumptious characters, and delightful verbal treats."
—The Romance Reader

Private Arrangements

2008 Romantic Times Reviewers' Choice Award for Best First Historical Romance
Double-nominated for the prestigious Rita Award for Best First Book and Best Historical
Chosen as one of Publishers Weekly's *Best Books of the Year*

"A love story of remarkable depth... Entrancing from start to finish."
—Mary Balogh, *New York Times* bestselling author

"Exquisite, enchanting... An extraordinary, unputdownable love story."
—Jane Feather, *New York Times* bestselling author

"Lively banter, electric sexual tension, and an unusual premise make this stunning debut all the more refreshing. Thomas is a writer worth watching."
—*Library Journal*, starred review

"Thomas makes a dazzling debut with a beautifully written, sizzling, captivating love story. . . . Her compelling tale of love betrayed and then reborn will make you sigh with pleasure."
—*Romantic Times*

"So if you've worried (as I have) about the future of historical romance, just remember two words: Sherry Thomas. Readers, don't miss this one. It's a keeper and be very thankful that historical romance has a new, shining star."
—TheRomanceReader.com

"[A] superb debut, *Private Arrangements* . . . will win readers over with its elegant writing, exceptional characterization, expertly detailed late Victorian setting and exquisitely romantic love story."
—*Chicago Tribune*

"A deeply involving story . . . I loved the complicated plot and the subplot of Gigi's mother and the Duke of Perrin. The author does a wonderful job of re-creating the late Victorian era and her characters are vividly real. This author is definitely one to look for."
—Coffee Time Romance

Also By Sherry Thomas

PRIVATE ARRANGEMENTS

DELICIOUS

NOT QUITE A HUSBAND

His at Night

SHERRY THOMAS

BANTAM BOOKS
NEW YORK

A Bantam Books Mass Market Original

Copyright © 2010 by Sherry Thomas

Published in the United States by Bantam Books, an imprint of The Random House Publishing Group, a division of Random House, Inc., New York.

Bantam Books and the rooster colophon are registered trademarks of Random House, Inc.

ISBN 978-0-553-59244-3

Cover design: Lynn Andreozzi
Cover lettering: Ron Zinn
Cover illustration: Aleta Rafton

Printed in the United States of America

www.bantamdell.com

2 4 6 8 9 7 5 3 1

*To my dear friend Janine Ballard,
who is my story guide, my common sense,
and the wind beneath my wings.
May 15, 2003, has been and will always be
one of the luckiest days of my life.*

His
at Night

Chapter One

The Marquess of Vere was a man of few words.

This fact, however, would astonish all but a select few of his numerous friends and acquaintances. The general consensus was that Lord Vere talked. And talked. And talked. There was no subject under the sun, however remote or abstruse, upon which he did not eagerly venture an opinion or ten. Indeed, there were times when one could not stop him from pontificating on that newly discovered class of chemical substance known as the Pre-Raphaelites, or the curious culinary habits of the Pygmy tribes of central Sweden.

Lord Vere was also a man who held his secrets close.

But anyone so deluded as to voice such a pronouncement would find himself surrounded by ladies and gentlemen on the floor, screaming in laughter. For Lord Vere, according to public opinion, could not distinguish a secret from a hedgehog. Not only was he garrulous, he volunteered the most intimate, most inappropriate personal knowledge at the drop of a hat—or even without a stitch of haberdashery anywhere in sight.

He gladly related his difficulties with the courting of young ladies: He was rejected early and rejected often, despite his stature as a peer of the realm. He gave up without hesitation the state of his finances—though it had been discovered that he was quite without a notion as to how much funds were at his disposal, current and future, thereby rendering his conjectures largely moot. He even ventured—not in mixed company, of course—to comment on the size and girth of his masculine endowment: enviable on both counts, the measurements verified by the experiences of the merry widows who looked to him for an occasional tumble in the sheets.

Lord Vere was, in other words, an idiot. Not a raving one, for his sanity was rarely questioned. And not so moronic that he could not see to his daily needs. Rather, he was an amusing idiot, as ignorant and puffed up as a pillow, silly to the extreme, but sweet, harmless, and very well liked among the Upper Ten Thousand for the diversion he provided—and for his inability to remember anything told him that did not affect his meals, his nightly beauty rest, or the pride and joy that resided in his underlinens.

He could not shoot straight; his bullets never met a grouse except by accident. He rarely failed to turn knobs and levers in the wrong direction. And as his gift for wandering into the wrong place at the wrong time was legendary, hardly anyone batted an eyelash to learn that he was an eyewitness to a crime—without having any idea what he'd seen, most assuredly.

Such an extraordinary idiot had he been in the thirteen years since his unfortunate riding accident that no one not privy to his more clandestine activities had ever remarked on his proximity to some of the most sensational criminal cases of the upper crust, shortly before those cases were solved and the culprits brought to justice.

It was an interesting life, to say the least. Sometimes the tiny handful of other agents of the Crown who knew his true role wondered how he felt about playing the idiot for most of his waking hours. They never found out, for he was a man of few words and held his secrets close.

Of course, no secret remains a secret forever....the beginning of the end of Lord Vere's secret came, quite literally, in an ambush by a young lady of questionable ancestry and equally questionable methods.

A young woman who, in a strange twist of fate, would soon become the Marchioness of Vere, his lady wife.

❧

The rats were Vere's idea. His idea of a joke, to be more precise.

London was emptying at the tail end of the Season. Vere had seen his brother off at the train station earlier in the day; tomorrow he himself was headed for Gloucestershire. There was no time like the beginning of August to appear innocently at a country house to which he might not have been invited—and claim that he had: After all, what was one more guest when there were already thirty of them running about?

But tonight's meeting was about Edmund Douglas, the reclusive diamond mine owner suspected of extorting from the diamond dealers of London and Antwerp.

"We need a better way to get into his house," said Lord Holbrook, Vere's liaison.

Holbrook was a few years older than Vere. When Oscar Wilde had been the country's leading literary celebrity, Holbrook had worn his dark hair long and cultivated an air of intellectual ennui. Now that Wilde had gone off to a disgraced exile, Holbrook's languor was accompanied by shorter hair and a more straightforward display of nihilism.

Vere helped himself to a piece of Savoy cake. The cake was airy and spongy, and just sturdy enough for a spoonful of apricot jam. Holbrook had a way of keeping his hidey-holes—a smattering of properties across metropolitan London—well supplied, so that whenever his agents had to make use of one, there was always good liquor and the makings of a proper tea.

Across the gaudy drawing room—this particular house behind Fitzroy Square had once housed a succession of kept women—Lady Kingsley dabbed a napkin at the corner of her lips. She was a fine-looking brunette about the same age as Holbrook, the daughter of a baronet, and the widow of a knight.

As covert agents, women had the advantage. Vere

and Holbrook must assume personas not their own in order not to be taken seriously—an absolute necessity when one went about inquiring after sensitive matters on behalf of the Crown. But a woman, even one as sharp and capable as Lady Kingsley, often managed to be dismissed on nothing more than the fact of her sex.

"I told you already, Holbrook," she said. "We must make use of Douglas's niece."

Holbrook, sprawled on a red velvet chaise trimmed in gold fringe, filliped the most recent case report lying on his chest. "I thought the niece hadn't left the house in years."

"Precisely. Imagine you are a girl of twenty-four years, well past the age when a young lady ought to be married, and isolated from all the gaiety and amusement of proper society. What is the one thing that would tempt you the most?"

"Opium," Holbrook said.

Vere smiled and said nothing.

"No." Lady Kingsley rolled her eyes. "You would wish to meet eligible young men, as many of them as can squeeze under one roof."

"Where do you plan to collect a houseful of desirable bachelors, madam?" asked Holbrook.

Lady Kingsley waved her hand in dismissal. "That is the easy part, the mustering of manly lures. The problem is that I cannot simply drive up to Highgate Court and present the gentlemen—it's been three months since I leased the next-nearest house and I still haven't met her."

"May I?" Vere pointed at the report on Holbrook's

chest. Holbrook tossed the report his way. Vere caught it and skimmed the pages.

Edmund Douglas's estate, in which he'd maintained residence since 1877, was a manor constructed to his specification. There were hundreds of such new country houses all over the land, built by those with a fortune to spare, thanks to the prosperity of the Age of Steam.

A fairly common sort of estate, yet one that had proved difficult to penetrate. Plain burglary had not succeeded. An attempt to infiltrate the staff had also failed. And due to Mrs. Douglas's ill health, the family rarely mingled with local society, rendering useless the more socially acceptable routes into the manse.

"Have a domestic disaster on your part," said Vere to Lady Kingsley. "Then you will have an excuse to approach her."

"I know. But I'm hesitant to damage the roof—or the plumbing—of a leased house."

"Can't your servants come down with something disgusting but not infectious?" Holbrook inquired. "A case of communal runs?"

"Behave yourself, Holbrook. I am no chemist and I will not poison my own staff."

"How about an infestation of rats?" Vere suggested, more to amuse himself than anything else.

Lady Kingsley shuddered. "What do you mean, an infestation of rats?"

Vere shrugged. "Put a dozen or two rats to run about the house. Your guests will scream to evacuate. And the rats won't do permanent damage to the house, provided you have a rat catcher set to work soon enough."

Holbrook sat up straight. "Splendid idea, my dear fellow. I happen to know a man who breeds mice and rats to supply scientific laboratories."

That did not surprise Vere. Holbrook had at his fingertips a large assortment of bizarre and bizarrely useful contacts.

"No. It's a terrible idea," Lady Kingsley protested.

"Au contraire, I think it is pure genius," declared Holbrook. "Douglas travels to London to meet with his solicitor in two weeks, am I correct?"

"Correct," said Vere.

"That should be enough time." Holbrook reclined back onto his red velvet chaise. "Consider it done."

Lady Kingsley grimaced. "I hate rats."

"For Queen and country, madam," said Vere, rising. "For Queen and country."

Holbrook tapped a finger against his lips. "Funny you should mention Queen and country, my lord: I have just received word of the blackmailing of a certain royal and—"

Vere, however, had already shown himself out.

Chapter Two

Two weeks later

Miss Elissande Edgerton stood before the manor at Highgate Court. Rain pummeled her black umbrella; a cold gray mist obscured all but the driveway.

August, and already it felt like November.

She smiled at the man before her. "Have a safe journey, Uncle."

Edmund Douglas returned her smile. It was a game to him, this façade of affection. *There is no crying in this house, do you understand, my dear Elissande? Look at your aunt. She is not strong or clever enough to smile. Do you wish to be like her?*

Even at six, Elissande had known that she had no wish to be like her aunt, that pale, weeping specter. She hadn't understood why her aunt wept. But whenever Aunt Rachel's tears spilled, whenever her uncle placed his arm about his wife's shoulders to lead her to her room, Elissande had always crept out of the house and run as far away as she dared, her heart pounding with fear, revulsion, and an anger that burned like smothered coal.

So she had learned to smile.

"Thank you, my dear," said Edmund Douglas.

But he made no move to enter the waiting brougham. He liked to prolong his good-byes—she suspected he knew very well how much she ached for him to be gone. She stretched out her smile.

"Take care of your aunt for me while I'm gone," he said, his face lifting toward the window of his wife's bedchamber. "You know how much I treasure her."

"Of course, Uncle."

Still smiling, she leaned in to kiss him on his cheek, controlling her aversion with an expertise that made her throat tighten.

He required this demonstration of warmth before the servants. It was not every man who disguised his evil so well that he fooled his own staff. In the village one heard rumors of Squire Lewis's bum pinching, or Mrs. Stevenson's watering of the beer she provided her servants. But the only sentiment circulated about Mr. Douglas was a uniform admiration for his saintly patience, what with Mrs. Douglas being so frail—and not altogether right upstairs.

At last he climbed into his carriage. The coachman, hunkered down in his mackintosh, flicked the reins. The wheels scraped wetly against the gravel drive. Elissande waved until the brougham rounded the curve; then she lowered her arm and dropped her smile.

Vere slept best in a moving train. There had been times in his life when he'd taken the Special Scotch Express from London to Edinburgh for no reason other than the eight hours of dreamless slumber it offered.

The trip to Shropshire was less than half as long and involved several changes of trains. But still he enjoyed it, probably the most he'd enjoyed himself since his naps on the way from London to Gloucestershire, where he'd spent the previous two weeks retrieving a contingency invasion plan that the Foreign Office had somehow "lost." A delicate task, considering that the target of the plan was German South West Africa—and relations with Germany were strained at best.

He'd accomplished his assignment without a whiff of international scandal. His pleasure at his success, however, was muted. He led his double existence for the pursuit of Justice, not to bail out fools who couldn't keep sensitive documents away from harm.

But even when the cases did feed his hunger for Justice, even then his satisfaction was hollow and short-lived—the feeble glow of embers about to turn into ash—followed by an exhaustion that lingered for weeks.

An emptiness that the deepest, most nourishing slumber could not erase.

The carriage Lady Kingsley had sent for him sped

through miles of rolling green country. He could no longer sleep and he did not want to think of his next case. Granted, Edmund Douglas's general reclusiveness had necessitated an unusual amount of planning, but the investigation was simply another in a career filled with unorthodox cases that local police could not solve, and often did not even know about.

He stared out of the carriage. Instead of well-grazed grassland, still wet with rain but glistening under a newly emerged afternoon sun, he saw a different landscape altogether: crashing waves, high cliffs, moors purple with heather in bloom. A path at the top of the slopes stretched before him; a hand, warm and steady, held his own.

He knew the path. He knew the cliffs, the moors, and the sea—the coasts of Somerset, North Devon, and Cornwall were exceptionally beautiful places he visited as often as he could. The woman who held his hand, however, existed only in his imagination.

But he knew her light, lithe footfalls. He knew her sturdy wool skirt: It shushed softly when she walked, a sound he could hear only when the air was still and the path high, away from the pounding of the waves. And he knew the contour of her nape, beneath the wide-brimmed hat that protected her skin from the sun: He had draped his coat over her shoulders many times, when her own jacket proved inadequate against the coast's cool and variable weather.

She was an indefatigable hiker, a serene friend, and, at night, a sweetly accepting lover.

Fantasies were like prisoners, less likely to stage a revolt if allowed judicious amounts of supervised exercise. So he thought of her often: when he could not sleep, when he was too tired to think of anything else, when he dreaded going home after weeks upon weeks wishing for quiet and solitude. All she had to do was lay a hand on his arm, her touch warm with understanding and care, and he would be all right, his cynicism soothed, his loneliness subdued, his nightmares forgotten.

He was sane enough to not give her a name, or envision her physical likeness down to the last detail—this way he could still pretend that he might yet meet her one day, in some inconspicuous corner of an otherwise harshly lit and overcrowded ballroom. But he *was* weak enough to have imagined her smile, a smile of such perfection and loveliness that he could not help but be happy in its radiance. She did not smile very often, because he was not capable of frequent happiness, even the imagined sort. But when she did smile, the sensations in his heart—like being six again and running into the ocean for the very first time.

This day, however, he didn't want emotions, but quiet companionship. So they walked together, on a path he'd only trod alone in real life. By the time the carriage passed the gates of Woodley Manor, Lady Kingsley's leased estate, he was standing beside her in the ruins of King Arthur's castle, his hand on the small of her back, looking down at the churning foam caps far below.

And there he might have remained a long time—he was quite good at saying his good-byes and hellos while remaining in his reverie—were it not for the sight of his brother before the house waving at him.

That brought him abruptly back to reality.

He bounded out of the carriage, tripping over his walking stick. Freddie caught him.

"Careful, Penny."

Vere had been Viscount Belgrave from the moment he took his first breath. He became the Marquess of Vere at sixteen, upon his father's death. Except for his late mother, a few very old friends, and Freddie, no one ever referred to him by his nickname, a diminutive of Spencer, his given name.

He embraced Freddie. "What are you doing here, old chap?"

Vere rarely thought of himself as heading into danger: His investigations did not require weapons drawn and his public persona offered him protection from undue suspicions. But he'd never had Freddie nearby going into a case.

Freddie was the one single thing that *had* gone right in Vere's life. The anxious boy Vere had once fretted over had grown up to be a fine young man of twenty-eight: the finest man of Vere's acquaintance.

The finest man of anyone's acquaintance, he thought with absurd pride.

Two weeks in the country had reddened Freddie's fair complexion and bleached his sandy curls several shades lighter. He picked up the walking stick Vere had dropped and unobtrusively straightened Vere's necktie, otherwise always set thirty degrees askew.

"Kingsley asked me if I wanted to come visit his aunt. I said yes, once he told me you'd been invited too."

"I didn't know the Wrenworths had Kingsley to their place."

"Well, I wasn't at the Wrenworths'. I left their place last Thursday and went to the Beauchamps'."

And there he should have stayed. The substantial lack of bodily harm in his line of work notwithstanding, Vere would have been better pleased had Freddie not come.

"Thought you always liked it at the Wrenworths'. Why'd you leave so soon this time?"

"Oh, I don't know." Freddie unrolled Vere's sleeves, which Vere not infrequently kept rolled at uneven lengths. "I was in the mood for a different place."

This gave Vere pause. Restlessness was not a trait he usually associated with Freddie—unless Freddie was unsettled about something.

A virgin-meeting-dragon's-teeth scream shattered the bucolic quiet.

"Good gracious, what was that?" Vere exclaimed with very believable surprise in his voice.

The question was answered by more screams. Miss Kingsley, Lady Kingsley's niece, rushed out of the house shrieking at the top of her lungs. And barreled directly into Vere—he had a terrific talent for stepping into people's way.

He caught her. "What's the matter, Miss Kingsley?"

Miss Kingsley struggled in his grip. She stopped screaming momentarily, but it was only to gather another lungful of air. And then she opened her mouth wide and emitted the most demonic screech Vere had ever heard.

"Slap her," he begged Freddie.

Freddie was aghast. "I can't slap a woman!"

So Vere did. Miss Kingsley ceased her shrieking and went limp. Gasping and blinking, she stared at Vere with unfocused eyes.

"Miss Kingsley, are you all right?" Freddie asked.

"I'm—I'm—Dear *God,* the rats, the rats..."

She began to sob.

"Hold her." Vere thrust her into Freddie's kinder, more compassionate arms.

He ran into the house and came to a dead halt in the middle of the entry hall. A dozen or two rats, he'd said to Holbrook. But there were *hundreds* of them, flowing like streams along walls and corridors, sprinting up banisters and down curtains, knocking over a porcelain vase with a loud crack even as Vere stood stock-still, at once revolted and mesmerized by the sight.

"Out of my way!"

Kingsley, Lady Kingsley's nephew, came running, a rifle in hand. At the precise moment he crossed the center of the hall, a small rat jumped down from the chandelier.

"Kingsley, above you!" Vere cried.

Too late. The rat landed on Kingsley's head. Kingsley

screamed. Vere flung himself to the floor as Kingsley's rifle went off.

Kingsley screamed again. "Bloody hell, it's inside my coat!"

"I'm not coming anywhere near you if you don't put down your rifle first! And don't throw it, it could go off again."

"Ahhh!" Kingsley's rifle fell with a heavy thud. "Help me!"

He jerked wildly, a madman's marionette. Vere dashed to his side and yanked off Kingsley's day coat.

"I think it's inside my waistcoat. God almighty, don't let it get inside my trousers."

Vere ripped apart Kingsley's waistcoat. And there the little vermin was, stuck under Kingsley's brace. Vere grabbed it by the tail and tossed it aside before it could twist around and bite him.

Kingsley sprinted out of the front door in his shirt-sleeves. Vere shook his head. More screams came from a room to his left. He hurried toward it and opened the door—and had to immediately grab on to the top of the door and get his feet off the floor as a torrent of rats rushed out.

Lady Kingsley, three young ladies, two gentlemen, plus one footman stood on the furniture above a sea of rats, two out of the three young ladies screaming away, Mr. Conrad joining them with equal gusto and volume. Lady Kingsley, atop the piano, used the music stand to grimly whack away at any rats that dared to climb up to her island of safety. The footman, a poker in his hand, defended the young ladies.

When enough rats had stormed out of the drawing room, Vere helped Lady Kingsley's besieged guests down from their high places. Miss Beauchamp trembled so much that he had to carry her outside.

He found Lady Kingsley standing with one hand against a wall, her other hand on her abdomen, her jaw clenched tight.

"Are you all right, ma'am?"

"I don't think I will need to try very hard to look stricken when I call upon Miss Edgerton," she said, her voice barely above a whisper. "And Holbrook is a dead man."

❦

"'On the highest point of the plateau is the small chapel of Santa Maria del Soccorso, where a so-called hermit keeps a visitor's book, and sells wine. The view from this headland is singularly attractive and imposing, the precipice being absolutely vertical, and the coastline in every direction full of beauty...'"

Elissande saw it clearly: the Isle of Capri, rising sirenlike from the Mediterranean. Herself, walking along its abrupt cliffs, her hair flying in the breeze, a bouquet of wild carnations in her hand. No sound but the sea and the seagulls, no one but the fishermen repairing their nets far below, and no sensation but the clarity and serenity of utter, absolute freedom.

She barely caught her aunt as the latter toppled from her seat in the water closet.

It had been more than forty-eight hours since Aunt

Rachel last eliminated—the effect of an invalid existence. Elissande had wheedled Aunt Rachel to sit for a quarter hour after lunch, with herself reading aloud from a travel guide to Southern Italy to help pass the time. But thanks either to her less than stimulating reading, or the laudanum from which she could not wean her aunt, Aunt Rachel had fallen asleep instead—with the receptacle beneath her still worryingly empty.

She half pulled, half carried Aunt Rachel out of the water closet. In her arms the older woman weighed little more than a bundle of sticks—with about as much mobility and coordination. It was her uncle's specialty to discover what displeased his dependents and to inflict it upon them. For that reason Aunt Rachel's nightdress smelled strongly of cloves, which she disliked.

Which she *had* disliked. For years now, Aunt Rachel had been in a near-perpetual laudanum haze and noticed little else, as long as she had her next dose of the tincture on time. But Elissande still cared—she'd brought an unscented nightdress from her own room.

She gently deposited her drowsy aunt on her bed, washed her own hands, then changed her aunt's nightdress, and made sure Aunt Rachel slept on her right side. She kept careful record of the hours Aunt Rachel lay on each of her sides: Bedsores came easily to someone who spent the overwhelming majority of her time in bed.

She tucked the coverlet about the older woman's shoulders and retrieved the guidebook that had fallen on the floor in her haste to catch Aunt Rachel. She'd lost her place in the book. But that wasn't important. She was just as happy to read about lovely Manfredonia on the Adriatic coast, founded by a hero of the Trojan War.

The book flew out of her hand, crashed against the painting that hung on the wall opposite her aunt's bed—the painting Elissande did her best never to look at—and plunged to the floor with a resounding thud. Her hand went to her mouth. Her head swiveled toward Aunt Rachel. But Aunt Rachel barely twitched.

Elissande quickly picked up the book again and checked it for damage. Of course there was damage: The endsheet had torn from the back cover.

She closed the book and clutched it hard. Three days ago she had taken her hairbrush and smashed her hand mirror. Two weeks before that she'd stared a long time at a box of white arsenic—rat poison—that she'd found in a broom closet.

She feared she was slowly losing her sanity.

She had not wanted to become her aunt's nursemaid. She'd meant to leave as soon as she was old enough to find a post somewhere, anywhere.

But her uncle had known it. He had brought in the nurses, so that she'd see Aunt Rachel cower and cry from their maniacal "medical" treatments, so that she'd be forced to step in, so that loyalty and gratitude, otherwise lovely things, turned into ugly, rattling chains that bound her to this house, to this existence under his thumb.

Until all she had for escape were a few books. Until

her days revolved around her aunt's regularity or lack thereof. Until she threw her precious guide to Southern Italy against a wall, because her control over herself, the one thing she'd been able to count on, was eroding under the weight of her imprisonment.

The sound of a carriage coming up the drive had her gathering her skirts and rushing out of Aunt Rachel's room. Her uncle enjoyed giving her false dates for his returns: Returning early cut short the reprieve of his absence; arriving late dashed her hope that he'd perhaps met with a most deserving end while away. And he had done this before: making up a trip only to take a drive in the country and come home in a mere few hours, claiming that he'd changed his mind because he missed his family too much.

In her own room, she hurriedly shoved the travel guide in the drawer that held her undergarments. Three years ago her uncle had purged his house of all books written in the English language, except the Bible and a dozen tomes of fiercely fire-and-brimstone sermons. She'd since found a few books that had accidentally escaped the eradication and guarded them with the fearful care of a mother bird who had built her nest in a menagerie of cats.

The book secured, she went to the nearest window overlooking the driveway. Oddly enough, parked before the house was not her uncle's brougham, but an open victoria with seats upholstered in jewel blue.

A gentle knock came at the door. She turned around. Mrs. Ramsay, Highgate Court's housekeeper, stood in the open doorway. "Miss, there is a Lady Kingsley calling for you."

Squires and local clergy occasionally called on her uncle. But Highgate Court almost never had women callers, as her aunt was well-known in the surrounding area for her exceptionally delicate health and Elissande's was equally well-known—thanks to her uncle's strategic public comments—as unspareable from the former's sickbed.

"Who is Lady Kingsley?"

"She has taken Woodley Manor, miss."

Elissande vaguely recalled that Woodley Manor, two miles northwest of Highgate Court, had been let some time ago. So Lady Kingsley was their new neighbor. But ought not a new neighbor leave a card first, before calling *in person*?

"She says there is an emergency at Woodley Manor and begs that you will receive her," said Mrs. Ramsay.

Lady Kingsley had come to precisely the wrong person then. If Elissande could do anything for anyone, she'd have absconded with her aunt years ago. Besides, her uncle would not appreciate her receiving guests without his permission.

"Tell her that I'm busy caring for my aunt."

"But, miss, she is distraught, Lady Kingsley."

Mrs. Ramsay was a decent woman who, in her entire fifteen years at Highgate Court, had yet to notice that both of the ladies of the house were quite distraught too—her uncle had a knack for hiring servants who were loyally unobservant. Instead of holding her head high and conducting herself with a modicum of dignity, perhaps Elissande too should have succumbed to vapors once in a while.

She took a deep breath. "In that case, you may show her into the drawing room."

It was not her habit to run from distraught women.

❧

Lady Kingsley was almost beside herself as she recounted her faintly biblical tale of a plague of rats. After her recital, she needed an entire cup of hot, black tea before the greenish pallor faded from her cheeks.

"I am very sorry to hear of your trial," said Elissande.

"I don't think you've heard quite the worst part of it yet," answered Lady Kingsley. "My niece and nephew have come to visit and brought seven of their friends. Now none of us have a place to stay. Squire Lewis has twenty-five of his own guests. And the inn in the village is full—apparently, there is to be a wedding in two days."

In other words, she wanted Elissande to take in nine—no, ten strangers. Elissande tamped down a burble of hysterical laughter. It was a great deal to ask of any neighbor of minimal acquaintance. And Lady Kingsley didn't know the first thing of how much she was asking from *this* particular neighbor.

"How long will your house remain unusable, Lady Kingsley?" It seemed only polite to inquire.

"I hope to make it suitable for human habitation again in three days."

Her uncle was supposed to be gone for three days.

"I would not even think of putting forward such a request to you, Miss Edgerton, except we are in a bind," said Lady Kingsley, with great sincerity. "I have heard much of your admirable devotion to Mrs. Douglas. But surely it must be lonely at times, without the companionship of people of your own age—and I've on hand four amicable young ladies and five handsome young gentlemen."

Elissande did not need playmates; she needed funds. By herself she had a variety of paths open to her—she could become a governess, a typist, a shop woman. But with an invalid to feed, house, and care for, she needed ready money for any chance at a successful escape. Would that Lady Kingsley offered her a hundred pounds instead!

"Five handsome, *unmarried* young men."

The desire to laugh hysterically returned. A *husband*. Lady Kingsley thought Elissande wanted a husband, when marriage had been Aunt Rachel's curse in life.

There was never a man present in all her dreams of freedom; there had always been only her, in glorious, splendid solitude, replete in and of herself.

"And have I mentioned yet," continued Lady Kingsley, "that one of the young men staying with me—in fact, the handsomest one of them all—also happens to be a marquess?"

Elissande's heart thudded abruptly. She did not

care about handsome—her uncle was a very handsome man. But a marquess was an *important* man, with power and connections. A marquess could protect her—and her aunt—from her uncle.

Provided that he married Elissande within three days—or however short a period of time before her uncle returned.

Very likely, wasn't it? And when she'd hosted ten guests her uncle had not invited—a blatant gesture of rebellion such as she'd never dared—and fallen short of her goal, what then?

Six months ago, on the anniversary of Christabel's death, he had taken away Aunt Rachel's laudanum. For three days Aunt Rachel had suffered like a woman forced to endure an amputation without chloroform. Elissande, forbidden to go to Aunt Rachel, had pummeled the pillows on her bed until she could no longer lift her arms, her lips bloody from the bite of her own teeth.

Then, of course, he'd given up on his attempt to detach Aunt Rachel from her laudanum, an evil to which *he* had introduced her. *I simply can't bear to have her suffer anymore,* he'd said, in the presence of Mrs. Ramsay and a maid. And they had believed him, no questions asked, never mind that it was not the first, the second, or even the fifth time this had happened.

At dinner that evening, he had murmured, *At least she is not addicted to cocaine.* And Elissande, who hadn't even known what cocaine was, had been so chilled that she'd spent the rest of the night huddled before the fire in her room.

The chance of success: infinitesimal. The cost of failure: unthinkable.

She rose from her seat. The windows of the drawing room gave a clear view of the gates of the estate. It had been years since she last ventured past those gates. It had been at least twice as long since her aunt last left the manor itself.

Her lungs labored against the suddenly thin air. Her stomach wanted very much to eject her lunch. She gripped the edge of the window frame, dizzy and ill, while behind her Lady Kingsley went on and on about her guests' civility and amiability, about the wonderful time to be had by all. Why, Elissande didn't even need to worry about securing provisions for them. The kitchen at Woodley Manor, well removed from the house, had been spared from the rats.

Slowly Elissande turned around. And then she smiled, the kind of smile she gave her uncle when he announced that, no, he wouldn't go to South Africa after all, when she'd finally come to believe that he truly would, following months of preparations she'd witnessed with her own eyes.

Lady Kingsley fell quiet before this smile.

"We shall be only too glad to help," said Elissande.

Chapter Three

Aunt Rachel showed no reaction at the news: She dozed on.

Elissande smoothed limp strands of graying hair behind the older woman's fragile ears. "It will be all right, I promise."

She laid an extra blanket of soft wool over Aunt Rachel—Aunt Rachel, thin as poorhouse porridge, was always chilled. "We need to do this. It is an opportunity that will not come again."

Even as she spoke she marveled at the remarkable timing of Lady Kingsley's plague of rats, almost as if the rats had known the hour of her uncle's departure.

"And I'm not afraid of him."

The truth didn't matter one way or the other. What mattered was that she should believe in her own valor.

She knelt down by the bed and took Aunt Rachel's small, fine-boned face into her hands. "I will get you out of here, my love. I will get us both out of here."

The chance of success was infinitesimal, but it wasn't nil. For now, that would have to do.

She pressed a kiss to Aunt Rachel's sunken cheek. "Congratulate me. I am to be married."

❦

"We need to get married," said Vere to his brother.

Lady Kingsley had two carriages but only one team of horses. So the ladies had gone off first to Highgate Court, leaving the gentlemen behind to wait for their transport.

"We are still young," said Freddie.

Messieurs Conrad and Wessex played a game of vingt-et-un; Kingsley sat on his luggage, reading a copy of *The Illustrated London News;* Vere and Freddie strolled slowly along the drive.

"I'm almost thirty. And I'm not having any successes."

It was easy to fail when one proposed exclusively to the most sought-after debutantes of the Season, especially easy when the proposals were accompanied by copious spills of punch upon said debutantes' bodices. Vere felt strongly that he should be perceived as a man eager to settle down: the effort lent his role greater authenticity—the poor, sweet idiot too dumb to see that he ought to set his sights lower.

"Let a girl know you better before you propose to her," said Freddie. "I don't see how any woman can fail to love you, if you would but give her a little time."

Thirteen years, and Freddie still spoke to Vere as if nothing had changed, and Vere had remained the same brother who had protected Freddie from their father. Vere had expected the usual stab of guilt; what he had not expected was that he had to turn his face away to hide the tears that were suddenly in his eyes. He'd best take a long sabbatical after the Douglas case—this life was taking its toll on him.

But Freddie's answer did give Vere the opening he'd sought. "Do you think I should propose to Mrs. Canaletto then? She's known me all her life."

"No!" Freddie cried, then immediately flushed. "I mean, of course she does love you, but only as a brother."

"Dash it. What about you? Do you think she also only loves you as a brother?"

"I…ah…um…"

The talent for lies and pretenses that Vere possessed in such abundance had bypassed Freddie altogether. He was no good at prevarications of any sort.

"I don't know for certain," Freddie finally said.

"Why don't you ask her and find out?" Vere said blithely. "I know; we can both ask her at the same time. How could I be sure, otherwise, that she hasn't harbored some great, big, secret tendresse for me all these years?"

Kingsley, bored with his newspaper, came up to ask Vere for a cigarette, and Freddie was spared from having to reply to Vere's question.

But Vere already had answers enough.

The amiability of her guests overwhelmed Elissande. They were so happy to meet her, so grateful that she had opened her home to them, and so delighted to be put up, on such short notice, in the style and comfort to which they were accustomed.

L'affaire des rats had indeed been traumatic, to a one they confirmed to Elissande. But they were younger and of shorter memory than Lady Kingsley. Already they thought it a once-in-a-lifetime experience. Miss Kingsley made fun of herself, of how she'd screamed so unstoppably that if Lord Vere hadn't told her later, she never would have known that he'd had to slap her to interrupt her hysteria. Miss Beauchamp likewise recounted how she had half fainted by the time Lord Vere had come to her rescue and had to be carried out in his arms, clutching at his lapel all the while.

Their gleeful laughter astounded Elissande. They did not seem quite real to her, these rosy, robust young women, so entirely free of dread and fear, as if the thought had never crossed their minds that enjoyment carried consequences and should therefore remain as hidden as misery.

She hardly knew what to do in their cheerful company. So she fell back on the familiar and smiled. They, on the other hand, made a to-do over her. Her teeth, exposed by her smiles, were admired. The pallor of her skin, unsullied by the cumulative effects of riding, boating, and lawn tennis playing, quite envied. As was her tea gown, which Miss Kingsley declared she'd seen on a dummy in Madame Elise's shop on Regent Street, but which her mother had refused to buy for her. Elissande wondered how long Miss Kingsley's interest in fashion would persist if *she* had to wear the latest styles to daily tea and dinner with Elissande's uncle.

"It's a shame you couldn't have been in London this past Season," said Miss Beauchamp. "Oh, all the jubilee fêtes."

"Too many," said Miss Duvall. "My feet were worn out dancing."

"And I must have gained a stone," said Miss Melbourne, who was as slender as a sapling.

"Miss Edgerton, don't listen to Miss Melbourne," said Miss Kingsley. "Every time she takes a sip of water, she vows buttons pop off her bodice."

"My goodness," said Elissande. "Gentlemen must form long queues to fetch Miss Melbourne her beverages then."

The young ladies regarded Elissande in astonishment, then burst out laughing, Miss Melbourne most of all, doubled over with the force of her mirth.

Elissande almost joined them. She didn't, in the end, because laughing herself was even more alien than hearing others do so.

Miss Beauchamp suddenly held up her hands. "Shhh. I think the gentlemen are here."

With that, all the young ladies rushed to the windows, Miss Kingsley pulling Elissande along.

The open barouche had not yet reached the house, but already Elissande's eyes were drawn to one passenger in particular—an outrageously good-looking man, with features of perfect strength, masculinity, and symmetry. His head was tilted back slightly, to better take in the house. And then he turned to the gentleman next to him and smiled with evident affection.

For a moment, she forgot the impossible task that lay ahead of her. A bright pleasure such as she'd never known lit within her, a pleasure that derived from something as inconsequential as the way the afternoon sun fell across the brim of his hat, or the way his hands rested atop the walking stick balanced insouciantly between his knees.

"Come away now," said Miss Kingsley, again pulling at Elissande's sleeve. "We don't want them to see us just standing here like a gaggle of silly schoolgirls."

Elissande allowed Miss Kingsley to guide her to a seat. She had no doubt of his identity—*the handsomest one of them all*. Her heart raced with a burst of nerve-wracking happiness. He rescued young women from plagues of rats; he had lovely friends; he looked like a hero of classical antiquity. *And* he was a marquess, an important man who could shield her aunt and herself.

She felt it. The shift in the tide, the reversal of fortune, the inexplicable thrust of destiny gathering momentum.

This was it. *He* was it. Her three days began this minute.

🍂

The carriage drew up before a three-story stone edifice built in the Gothic Revival style that had been still popular two decades ago. Ivy spread luxuriantly over the front of the house, lending it a greater air of authenticity and age. The windows were true lancets, rather than mere rectangular windows with a façade of pointed arches above. There were even grouted gargoyles to lead water off the steeply pitched roof.

The manor was more than respectable: It was grand. Yet despite its fine, geometric garden, there was something barren in its aspects.

An older country estate, such as the one Vere grew up in, was a hotbed of horticulture and animal husbandry. There was a walled garden that supplied fruits and vegetables for seventy people, a vinery that contributed hundreds of pounds of grapes, and half a dozen specialized hothouses that produced, among other luxuries, strawberries at Christmas and pineapples in January. And while the game park provided pleasure shooting, the duck pond, the henhouse, and the dovecote were entirely utilitarian.

Whereas Highgate Court was but a house and a severely manicured garden in the middle of nowhere. Truly nowhere: Shropshire was a rural and sparsely populated region and Highgate Court occupied one of the emptiest stretches within it.

He had a glimpse of the young ladies crowded around one large window before they quickly dispersed, like birds taking flight.

"I need to get myself a diamond mine," said Wessex, who was always short on funds, in exasperated admiration as they walked into the manor.

"Diamonds are mined?" exclaimed Vere. "I thought they grew in oysters."

"You are thinking of pearls, Penny," said Freddie, patient as always.

"I was?" Vere scratched his head. "Anyway, nice place."

"Everything is Louis the Fourteenth," said Kingsley of the furniture in the spacious and elegant entry hall. And Kingsley knew about such things.

The walls and fixtures of the interior had yet to acquire the patina—indeed, the sensation—of age. But beyond that, one could not fault the sensitive taste of the master of the house, who had succumbed to none of the blatant displays of wealth and glitter Vere had expected of a man of such recent fortunes.

He quickly recalled the scant known facts of Edmund Douglas's life. His father had been either a publican or a dockworker in Liverpool. He'd had two or three sisters, the birth of the last of whom had killed his mother. He had run away from home when he was fourteen, very fortunate timing, for influenza killed everyone else in the household soon thereafter. Eventually he had made his way to South Africa, established a reputation as a brawler, and profited handsomely from the discovery of diamonds.

Nothing Vere knew of Douglas suggested subtlety or restraint. In Kimberley, South Africa, people still remembered the wild, almost orgiastic festivities he'd mounted after becoming a very rich man overnight. Of course—Vere realized for the first time—nothing he knew of Douglas suggested that the latter would become a recluse either.

He glanced once more at the entry hall, noting the passages that branched from it, and then followed the other gentlemen into the drawing room. Once Freddie moved out of his line of sight, he had a direct view of Miss Edgerton, in an eye-catching, buttercup yellow tea gown.

Lady Kingsley had said that she was pretty, with a tremendous smile. She was indeed very pretty, shining strawberry blond hair, light brown eyes—an unusual combination—and the soft, fine, almost melancholy features of a Bouguereau Madonna.

She seemed slightly overwhelmed by the sheer number of men piling into her drawing room, her eyes darting from one gentleman to the next. Then her gaze came to rest on him—and did not move again. After a moment, her lips, very soft, pliant lips, parted and curved, showing off a row of even and notably white teeth. Dimples next appeared, deep, round, charming. And finally, a blaze of giddy, impossible pleasure in her wide, wide eyes.

There were so many things to do when entering a drawing room for the first time. He had to estimate where he might take a spill that wouldn't damage his knees, which curios he could "accidentally" knock over without breaking, and always, when he visited a house in a professional capacity, to mark a way out of any given room, just in case.

This time he forgot everything. He only stood and stared.

That smile. Christ, that smile. He recognized it by the wave of ecstatic joy that all but knocked him flat on his back.

Had he thought himself incapable of happiness on a sustained basis? He was wrong—and how. He could never have enough of this sweet elation. He wanted to splash in it, swim in it, drink it by the gallons, until nothing but bliss pulsed in his veins.

The girl of his dreams. He had met her at last.

❦

Lady Kingsley came forward. "Miss Edgerton, may I present the Marquess of Vere. Lord Vere, Miss Edgerton."

"I'm so pleased to meet you, my lord," said the girl of his dreams, still smiling.

He could barely speak for his gladness. "The pleasure is all mine, Miss Edgerton."

The pleasure, privilege, and stunning good fortune. All his.

He broke his long-standing policy that required him to establish his moronic bona fides immediately, and instead stood some ten feet from her and basked in her presence, saying little as tea and sandwiches were passed around.

But she noticed him even in his silence. Several times she glanced up at him and smiled. And every time she smiled, he felt it, the peace that had long eluded him no matter how many wrongs he'd helped unearth and punish.

All too soon it was time for the ladies to go up to their rooms to change for dinner.

"You are welcome to wander about the house as you wish," Miss Edgerton said to the gentlemen as she rose. "But I would ask that you please do not enter my uncle's study. It is his private sanctuary and he does not wish for it to be disturbed, even in his absence."

Little registered on Vere but the smile she bestowed upon him—she was at the door and actually turned around halfway and smiled directly at him. He drifted from one end of the drawing room to the other, fluffing curtains, rearranging bric-a-brac, and brushing his fingers absentmindedly along mantels and tops of chairs.

Lady Kingsley had to personally come and escort him to Edmund Douglas's study for him to perform a preliminary search. He went through the motions and discovered two hidden compartments in the desk: One of them held a revolver, the other hundreds of pounds in wrinkled, stained banknotes, both of which a man was perfectly at liberty to possess.

Documents crowded the study's copious cabinets. One cabinet contained ledgers relating to the running of the estate. All the other cabinets were devoted to the filing of letters, telegrams, and reports from the managers of the diamond mine, a quarter century of records of the origin and continuance of Douglas's wealth.

Lady Kingsley was waiting for him outside the study—she'd been standing guard. "Anything?"

"Excellent record keeping and completely above-board," he said. "And have I mentioned that it is a pleasure to work with you, madam?"

She frowned. "Are you quite all right?"

"I've never been better," he said, and sailed on past.

Chapter Four

"Is it true that diamonds come from mines rather than oysters?" Vere asked his reflection above the washstand.

Bloody hell.

"Or is it that if you split open a pearl, you find a diamond inside?"

Bugger.

Everything was backward. This was the woman with whom he'd roved the coast of the West Country for more than a decade, the woman who understood his every mood and desire—his haven, his refuge. He didn't care that her uncle was most likely a criminal. He didn't mind that he must now conform his conduct to the limits Society found acceptable. But why, for God's sake, must he meet her on a case, when he could not compromise his role?

As the highest ranking man present, he would be seated next to her at dinner. So they must converse.

Possibly at length. And he must play the part of the idiot, no matter how he wished otherwise.

He pushed his fingers through his hair, the jubilation of the past hour now a jumble of frayed nerves. There was no helping it: He was bound to disappoint her at first. He could only hope that it would be a mild disappointment, and that in her kindness she would overlook it and choose to appreciate his sweetness instead—he portrayed sweetness beautifully, copying it, as he did, from Freddie's character.

When he'd finished dressing, he sat down and tried to compose a better line of inquiry: subtle stupidity, if such a thing were possible. But his mind kept drifting away, back to the cliffs, back to the moors, back to the stunning coasts of the West Country.

The sun was setting, the sky ablaze. The wind whipped her coat and the ribbons on her hat. As he placed his arm about her shoulder, she turned toward him. And how lovely she was, eyes the color of delicately brewed tea, a long, straight nose, lips as soft as a whisper.

Meeting her in person was, he realized with a renewed pang of anxiety, perhaps not quite the unmitigated good fortune he had first believed. She had a face now, a name, a history and identity of her own.

They'd been one for so long. Now they were separate entities, so separate she barely knew him. And it was up to him to return them to that seamless unity he'd loved so well.

In his idiot guise, no less.

❦

"You look well, Penny," Freddie said, as they crossed the entry hall toward the drawing room.

Vere had never liked the way he looked—he bore an uncanny resemblance to his late, unlamented father. But tonight he hoped his looks would do him some good. Tonight he needed every arrow in his quiver.

Lady Kingsley pulled him aside almost as soon as he entered the drawing room. She spoke to him in a low voice and he heard not a single word she said as the crowd parted and revealed Miss Edgerton.

She stood with her back to him, in a dinner gown of pale blue beaded tulle. The skirt was narrowly fitted through her hips and thighs, then flared out in ruffles studded with seed pearls, as if she were Venus, freshly born of the waves, with a froth of sea foam still clinging to her calves.

And then, as if she felt the force of his gaze, she turned around, her gown sparkling with her motion. The bodice of the gown was cut modestly. But even the almost prim décolletage could not disguise the magnificence of her bosom, or the deep cleavage that came as a complete surprise to him, since he'd never before looked below her chin.

His heart thumped. Of course he'd made love to her before, but always gently, and more as a prelude to sleeping in her arms than for its own sake. He'd never imagined she'd inspire an animal lust in him.

Well, on that account he did not mind being wrong.

She smiled. And it was a wonder he did not knock his head on the ribbed vault ceiling—surely he levitated high above the floor.

Someone said something to her. She turned her face toward the speaker. A sharp pain on his forearm made him hiss—Lady Kingsley had rapped him, hard, with her fan.

"Lord Vere!" she whispered, her voice ominous with disapproval. "Did you not hear a word I said?"

"Beg pardon?"

"Look at me when I talk to you."

Reluctantly, he wrenched his gaze from Miss Edgerton. "Sorry?"

Lady Kingsley sighed. "She thinks you are intelligent."

"She does?" A lightninglike thrill zipped through him.

"She is not meant to, *remember*? We have work to do, sir."

❦

His imagination was showing itself to be quite secondrate. How many times had he walked arm in arm with her? Over how many sustained miles? And yet he'd never known that she smelled of honey and roses, nor that her skin gleamed like Vermeer's pearls.

Entering the dining room, however, startled him out of his romantic daze. Above the mantel hung a large and—to say the least—peculiar painting: a fairhaired angel in midflight, black robe flowing, black wings spread, a bloodied sword in her hand. Far below her on the ground, a man lay facedown in the snow, a red rose in full bloom next to him.

Vere was not the only guest who remarked on the unusual and unsettling painting. But the general cheer of the gathering was so pervasive, and Miss Edgerton's person so agreeable, that the guests, to a one, chose to ignore the obvious theme of death the painting evoked.

Miss Edgerton said grace. Vere prayed that Fortune would look kindly upon him. May he walk the fine line between lovable dimness and outright idiocy and walk it well.

"Miss Edgerton," he said, as soup was laid down, "would you happen to be related to Mortimer Edgerton of Abingdon?"

"No, indeed, Lord Vere. My late father's family hails from Cumberland, not Berkshire."

There was such delight and warmth in her voice. Her eyes sparkled. Her attention was wholly and wholeheartedly centered on him, as if she'd waited her entire life for him. He wanted to propose this minute and take her away. Let someone else worry about Edmund Douglas.

At the farther end of the table Lady Kingsley set down her water glass quite loudly. Vere clenched his hand about his spoon and forced himself to proceed. "What about old Mortimer's brother, Albemarle Edgerton. Are you related to *him*?"

This was where her good cheer would first falter. But she would think that he was jesting or had made a silly blunder. She would give him the benefit of the doubt.

Her merriment, however, dimmed not at all. "Not Mr. Albemarle Edgerton either, I'm afraid."

"Their cousins the Brownlow-Edgertons in the next county? You must be related to *them*."

Now there could be no mistake. Now she would see that he was not only below average in intelligence but hadn't a clue of his below-average intelligence. But she only radiated pleasure, as if he'd inquired whether Helen of Troy had been a direct ancestress of hers.

"Not at all, no. But you seem to know them very well. Are they a very grand family then?"

Had she understood anything he said? How could she not react at all? It was human to respond to clearly recognizable stupidity with at least a pause. Where was *her* pause?

"Indeed, I do know them very well. And I was sure you must have descended from one of them. Truly wonderful people; a shame neither old Mortimer nor his brother ever married. And their cousins were all spinsters."

At the beginning of the evening he could not have imagined that he would intentionally tip over into overt asininity. But he had not been able to help himself.

She nodded earnestly. "All the more reason they should have had children."

No pause. No wavering. Not a single sign that she noted his absurdity.

He took a sip of his soup to buy himself some time

to think—and found that he couldn't. His head was in a state of paralysis. This was not how it was supposed to proceed.

And he could not—nor did he want to—understand what it meant.

He took two more sips of the soup, which seemed to have come directly from the Thames, and glanced surreptitiously her way. Her outward poise and perfection slew him. What was wrong with her on the inside? How could she carry on a conversation with him as if there were nothing at all the matter with him?

His eyes lit on the painting behind her.

"The artwork, is it Raphael's *Deliverance of Saint Peter*?" He was going to provoke a reaction if it killed him.

"Do you think so, sir?" she asked evenly, her eyes wide with an admiration he most certainly had not earned.

For a moment he had considered—indeed, nearly hoped—that perhaps she was a dimwit herself. But she'd gone overboard with the flattery of her gaze.

She was angling for him.

It wasn't something that never happened. He was a wealthy, titled man and from time to time a girl with five Seasons under her belt and no other prospects would try her hand at him. But he, fool that he was, had not believed it possible that *she* would join the ranks of opportunists.

"Well, *Deliverance of Saint Peter* has an angel and a man," he said.

She looked behind herself a moment, turned back to him, and said happily, "And so does this one."

Oh, she was good. So very good. Were he truly an idiot he would be thrilled.

Well, he *had* been truly an idiot this night, hadn't he? One smile and he had been ready to pledge his undying love.

How could he have been so stupid? Why had he been so quick to conflate a devious woman he'd known for all of five minutes with the uncomplicated girl of his dreams? They were not one. They had never been one.

Miss Edgerton glanced at him. She smiled again, a smile luminous enough to serve as God's own desk lamp. Almost immediately he felt it—the glee, the exhilaration, the swell of contentment. And in the next second, unchecked dismay.

A childish, illogical part of him did not understand that she was a smooth, clever actress. It saw only the same smile that had made him ecstatic before.

"Won't you tell me more about your friends the Edgertons?" she asked.

Her question angered him—her question, her smile, his stupid inability to separate truth from illusions. He'd never before tormented the women who tried for his hand—they were usually a bumbling lot, dispirited and largely ashamed. Miss Edgerton, however . . . glossy, confident, cunning Miss Edgerton did not require such tender sympathy from him.

He canted forward slightly. "Why, certainly," he said. "I can go on for hours."

He went on for hours—no, days. Decades, possibly. Elissande's face wrinkled and sagged with the passage of time.

The Edgertons of Abingdon, the Brownlow-Edgertons of the next county, the Edgerton-Featherstonehaughs of the next other county, and the Featherstonehaugh-Brownlows two counties over. They were a family with numerous branches and offshoots and Lord Vere was intimately acquainted with every last leaf on the blooming tree.

Or so he believed.

As he traced the descent of the family, not a single person whom he mentioned more than once managed to stay the same. Daughters became sons; sons became grandsons; a couple who'd had twelve offspring suddenly became childless. Women who had never married were subsequently referred to as widows. One particular boy was born on two separate occasions and then died once in London, once in Glasgow, and—as if that weren't enough—one more time five years later in Spain.

And Elissande tried and tried to deny it.

When he'd come through the drawing room door, she had been enraptured. Not only was he handsome, he was *strapping*. She hadn't known until that moment that she wanted some size in a man: He absolutely embodied the part of her knight, her bulwark, her fortress.

He seemed to feel precisely the same way, stopping in his tracks when he saw her for the first time. Then, for as long as they were in the drawing room, he'd looked at her as if she were air, water, and poetry...

And Aunt Rachel's evening sitting in the water closet had proved fruitful! Elissande could not have asked for a more auspicious omen. She'd arrived to dinner vibrating with an almost fearful euphoria, the gongs of Destiny loud in her ears.

He was as handsome up close as he was from a distance, his features impeccably chiseled: neither too rough-hewn nor too refined. His eyes were a beautiful blue, almost indigo in the candlelight. And his lips—goodness, his lips had made her feel shy for no reason she could articulate.

Until they'd sat down at the table and those lips had started to move. He made distressingly less sense the more he talked. And the more distressed she became, the more engrossed she made herself appear and the more brilliantly she smiled—a lifelong reflex she could not stop all of a sudden.

He was her hope. He was her chance. She was desperate for their conversation to right itself, for his blunders to prove but a case of bad nerves. But the request to hear more about the Edgertons—she'd thought that speaking of people he knew and enjoyed would help—what a ghastly mistake on her part. Instead of family anecdotes, he unleashed a skull-scrapingly painful recitation of massacred facts on births, marriages, children, and deaths.

Even so, she'd hoped things might improve, until Lionel Wolseley Edgerton kicked the bucket for the third time, at which point her hope also gave up the ghost.

She smiled at him. Why not? What else was there for her to do?

"Have I told you the Edgertons' motto?" he asked, after a beat of silence.

"I do not believe so."

"Pedicabo ego vos et irrumabo."

On her other side, Lord Frederick coughed, a hacking fit of it, as if he'd choked on his food.

Without a care in the world, Lord Vere rose, strolled to his brother, and struck him a few times between his shoulder blades. Lord Frederick, red-faced, muttered a word of thanks. Lord Vere ambled back to his own seat.

" 'We too have scattered arrows.' Isn't that what the Edgertons' motto means, Freddie?"

"I—I believe so."

Lord Vere scratched himself in his armpit and nodded in satisfaction. "Well, there you go, Miss Edgerton. I've told you everything I know about the Edgertons."

She was glad of the numbness his genealogical treatise had produced in her. She couldn't think. Therefore she couldn't quite feel the horror of knowing she'd made the worst mistake in her life.

But the marquess was not yet through with her. "It has just occurred to me, Miss Edgerton: Is it not somewhat inappropriate for you to be hosting so many of us gentlemen by yourself?"

"Inappropriate? With Lady Kingsley in attendance every step of the way?" She beamed at him, even as she sawed energetically at the venison on her plate. "Of course not, my lord. Besides, my aunt is also in residence."

"She is? I'm sorry. I must have forgotten meeting her already."

"It's quite all right, sir. You haven't met her. Her health is frail and she is not strong enough to receive callers."

"That's right. That's right. So it's just you and your widowed aunt in this great big house."

"My aunt is not widowed, sir. My uncle is very much alive."

"He is? I apologize for my mistake. Is his health frail too?"

"No, he is away."

"I see. Do you miss him?"

"Of course," she said. "He's the heart and soul of this family."

Lord Vere sighed. "I aspire to that. One day I should also like my niece to say that I'm the heart and soul of my family."

It was the moment Elissande was forced to conclude that Lord Vere was not only an idiot, but an idiot of staggering proportions.

"I'm sure she would." She mustered a reassuring smile. "I'm sure you will be a wonderful uncle, if you aren't one already."

He batted his eyelashes at her. "My dear Miss Edgerton, you smile so divinely."

Her smiles were her armor. They were a necessity. But of course, a man like him wouldn't know the difference.

So she let him have another one. "Thank you, my lord. You are so very kind and I'm so very glad you are here."

❧

Lord Vere at last turned to talk to Miss Melbourne on his other side. Elissande took a sip of water to calm herself. Her head was still numb, but the sinking sensation in her stomach was already quite horrible.

"I've been studying your very intriguing painting, Miss Edgerton," said Lord Frederick, who'd been quiet most of the evening. "But I can't seem to quite identify the artist. Would you happen to know?"

Elissande regarded him warily. Idiocy was something that ran in the family, wasn't it? But he'd asked a reasonable question and, as much as she wanted to crawl under a blanket and douse herself in laudanum, she could not leave him without an answer.

"I'm afraid I've never inquired into it." The paintings—there were three on the same theme—had always been there. And she'd always done her best to ignore them. "What's your guess?"

"My guess would be someone from the Symbolist School."

"What is the Symbolist School, if you don't mind my asking?"

Because the Symbolist School could not be explained in isolation—it was related to but distinct from the Decadent Movement, which arose in reaction against Romanticism's unquestioning embrace of nature—Elissande soon became aware that Lord Frederick was very well versed in art, especially art of their time.

After three courses of Lord Vere's escalating inanities, it was a relief and a pleasure to encounter conversation that was intelligent and to the point. When she'd had something of a preliminary grounding in the ideas and motifs of the Symbolist School, she asked Lord Frederick, "What do you think, then, of the symbols in the painting?"

Lord Frederick set down his utensils. "Does the painting have a name?"

"It's called *The Betrayal of the Angel*."

"That's interesting," said Lord Frederick, leaning back in his chair to better study the canvas. "I thought at first that the angel was the Angel of Death. But it is the Angel of Death's express role to take a man's life. So it doesn't accord with a theme of betrayal."

"Do you think the man struck a bargain with the Angel of Death, perhaps, and then the angel reneged?"

"That's an interesting idea. Or perhaps he had no idea what kind of angel she was. Perhaps he thought her the gentle, harp-plucking kind."

Elissande considered it a moment. "Wouldn't such an angel have white wings and a white robe?"

"Yes, she would, wouldn't she?" Lord Frederick

spread his thumb and his index finger along his chin. "Perhaps she transforms? If I were to paint this theme, I might show her mid-transformation, her white wings and robe turning black as she flies away from him."

If *he* were to paint this theme. "Are you an artist yourself, sir?"

Lord Frederick picked up his fork and knife and bent his face toward his plate, seemingly shy about discussing his artistic inclinations. "I do enjoy painting, but I'm not sure I'd go so far as to call myself an artist. I've never exhibited."

She liked him, Elissande realized. He had not been blessed with his brother's Olympian looks, but he was pleasing in both his features and his demeanor—not to mention he was an intellectual giant next to Lord Vere.

"Was Shakespeare any less a poet before he published his first volume?"

Lord Frederick smiled. "You are too kind, Miss Edgerton."

"Do you paint portraits or classical themes or perhaps biblical stories?"

"I have done a portrait or two. But what I like best is painting people when they are outside. Taking walks, picnicking, or just daydreaming." He sounded embarrassed. "Very simple things."

"That sounds lovely," she said sincerely. So much of her life had been spent trapped inside this house that the simple activities Lord Frederick took for granted were infinitely appealing to her. "I would be privileged to see your work someday."

"Well"—his already sun-ruddied complexion acquired an even deeper color—"perhaps if you ever came to London."

His blush further endeared him to her. Suddenly she realized something else: Lord Frederick would do well as a husband for her.

He was not a marquess himself, but he was the son of one and the brother of one and that was almost as good, with the influence of his family and all their connections behind him.

Furthermore, she could trust him to understand a delicate situation. Should her uncle come calling, Lord Vere would no doubt nod and agree that of course Mrs. Douglas longed to return to her own home and, well, here she was, and could he help hand her into the carriage? Lord Frederick, a far more discerning man, would sense her uncle's malice and help Elissande secure Aunt Rachel's future well-being.

"Oh, I shall try," she said. "I most certainly shall try."

Chapter Five

It wasn't a country house party until Vere had mistaken someone else's room for his own. He had plenty of choices. Miss Melbourne would scream loudest, Miss Beauchamp laugh hardest, and Conrad grumble most forcefully.

So of course he chose Miss Edgerton's room.

He had been inside her room already: When the ladies had departed for the drawing room after dinner, he'd left the other gentlemen on the pretense of having to retrieve his special Colombian cigar from his room.

He had taken the opportunity to map the rooms and their occupants. But what he had really needed was a moment alone, which he'd spent in the empty passage, his back against his own door, his hand over his face.

He had lost nothing: How could he lose something that had never existed in the first place? And yet he had lost everything. He could no longer think of his constant companion as she had always been—warm, supportive, and understanding. Now he saw only Miss Edgerton's predatory prettiness, the flattery that gleamed in her eyes as the sun gleamed on a crocodile's teeth.

Now he at last understood why young boys sometimes threw rocks at pretty girls. It was this wordless fury, this pain of shattered hopes.

He was here to throw rocks at Miss Edgerton.

She was seated before her vanity table, her profile to him, combing her hair slowly, absently. As she raised her arm to reach the top of her head, the loose, short sleeves of her nightdress slid down to expose her upper arm and—for one heart-stopping fraction of a second—the curve of the side of her breast.

"Miss Edgerton, what are you doing in my room?" he called from the door he had silently opened.

She looked up, gasped, and leaped out of her chair. Hurriedly she grabbed her dressing gown and belted it tight about her person. "My lord, you are quite mistaken. This is *my* room."

He cocked his head and smirked. "That's what they all say. But you, my dear Miss Edgerton, are not married yet. No such hanky-panky for you. Now run along."

She gaped at him. Well, at least she wasn't smiling.

It had not made him any happier that the rest of the evening she had not come near him, but instead played cards with Freddie, Wessex, and Miss Beauchamp, smiling all too often. The stupid, illogical part of him still wanted her smiles; worse, he felt downright proprietary toward her.

He strolled inside and sat down at the foot of her bed, which brought him face-to-face with the painting that hung on the opposite wall. It was a canvas approximately three feet by four feet, bursting with a single blood-red rose and its razor-sharp thorns. At its edge were the shoulder and arm of a man lying facedown in the snow, one long black feather, next to his lifeless hand—a definite relation to the painting in the dining room.

Vere loosened his necktie and pulled it off.

"Sir!" Her hands held tight to the closure of her dressing gown. "You cannot—you may not disrobe here."

"Of course I won't *really* disrobe, not with you still here, Miss Edgerton. And why are you still here, by the way?"

"I already told you, sir. This is my room."

He sighed. "If you insist, I'll kiss you. But I won't do anything else."

"I don't want to be kissed."

He smiled at her. "Are you sure?"

To his surprise, she flushed. His own reaction was a flash of acute heat.

He stared at her.

"Please leave," she said unsteadily.

"Penny! Penny, you are in the wrong room," Freddie, good old Freddie, called out from the open door.

She fled to him. "Oh, thank you, Lord Frederick. I was at a loss to explain to Lord Vere that he'd made a terrible mistake."

"No, no, I will prove it to both of you," Vere

claimed loudly. "See, I always put a cigarette under my cover, so that I can have one last drag before I go to sleep."

He marched to her bed and, to her strangled yelp, flung back her bedcover. There was, of course, nothing there.

He widened his eyes. "Did you smoke my fag, Miss Edgerton?"

"Penny! This *really* isn't your room."

"Oh, all right," said Vere, throwing up his hands. "Drat it. I like this room."

"Come now," Freddie urged him. "It's late. I'll take you to your room."

He was ready to walk away, but at the door Freddie took hold of his arm. "Penny, shouldn't you say something to Miss Edgerton?"

"Right, of course." He turned around. "Lovely room you have, Miss Edgerton."

Freddie nudged him.

"And I do apologize," Vere added.

With some effort, she wrested her eyes from Freddie. "It's quite an understandable mistake, sir—our rooms are close."

Their rooms were close indeed. He was diagonally across the passage from her. The next-closest guests, Freddie and Lady Kingsley, were each two doors away. Yet another indication of her careful planning, to bump more easily into the marquess she'd intended to bag.

As if to demonstrate that she bore no grudges at his faux pas, she directed at him a smile as serene and graceful as any she'd dispensed this entire day. "Good night, my lord."

He knew very well by now that her smiles had no meaning. He knew she manufactured them the way a forger fabricated crisp twenty-pound banknotes. And he still could not help a new surge of that very old longing.

"Good night, Miss Edgerton." He bowed. "My apologies once again."

&

The height thrilled Elissande at first. A true mountain, so far above the distant plains she might as well be standing on Zeus's own balcony. The air was thin. A bright, harsh sun shone. A black speck circled distantly in the sky. She raised her hand to shield her eyes from the glare of the sun.

But her hand moved only a few inches. She looked toward it in consternation and blinked. A dark manacle bound her wrist. A chain, each link as big as her fist, protruded from this manacle. The other end of the chain staked into the sinew of the mountain itself.

She looked at her other wrist. The same. Bound like Prometheus. She yanked her wrist. It hurt. She yanked harder. It only hurt more.

Panic, rising as fast as floodwater in a basement. Her heart pounded. Her breaths came in short, inadequate gasps. *Please, no. Anything but this.*

Anything but this.

A sharp cry pierced the air. The dark speck grew, sinking rapidly toward her. It was a bird—an eagle, its beak as sharp as a knife, and it was nearly upon her. She struggled frantically. Blood trickled from her wrists. But she could not free herself.

The eagle emitted another shriek, its beak plunging into her belly. In her agony she could not even scream, but only thrash madly.

She woke up still thrashing.

It took a few minutes for the residual terror to pass. With still unsteady fingers, she lit her hand-candle and excavated the guidebook to Southern Italy from her undergarment drawer.

" 'West of the village rises the almost vertical wall of limestone precipice that separates the elevated tableland of Anacapri from the eastern part of Capri,' " she read softly to herself. " 'The only way formerly of reaching Anacapri was by an ascent from the beach of eight hundred rude steps, cut in the face of the rock and constructed probably in times anterior to the Roman rule. Now a finely engineered carriage road leads to Anacapri. The views from this road are most beautiful.' "

🍂

Vere had joined the Douglas case at Lady Kingsley's request. He was willing enough—he owed her a favor for her help on the Haysleigh case—but he was not entirely convinced as to Douglas's guilt. Douglas had been staying at Brown's Hotel both times, when the trail of the extorted diamonds led there. Each time he also traveled from London to Antwerp, where a large number of diamond dealers had been subjected to extortion tactics.

But Douglas had legitimate reasons to visit both London and Antwerp, important centers for the diamond trade. And even Lady Kingsley, who was sure they had the right man, could not explain why someone who swam in diamonds wanted more diamonds.

"One reason is that he has less than we think he does—he must have exaggerated the richness of his find," Lady Kingsley whispered to Vere, after a three-hour examination of Douglas's papers in the latter's study. "The rumor was that the vein was so extraordinary, any bucket of dirt yielded the fortune of a lifetime. But the reality, not quite."

Vere hefted a box of documents back to its proper cabinet. "Perhaps there has been theft by the management."

"There is always that possibility. But if he thought so, he has not gone back in person to check. At least the foreman and the accountants never referenced a visit from him." Lady Kingsley lifted her lantern high so that Vere could better see where the next box should go. "What about the household accounts?"

Lady Kingsley had a special facility for business documents; Vere had come as her valet this night, his main purpose to stand guard and lift heavy items. But she had needed a rest from reading in the scant light they dared, and Vere had taken the opportunity and checked the household records.

"There is not much land attached to the estate:

very little income, and a great many expenses," he reported. "But still, normal expenses. Nothing that would give him a motive for engaging in criminal activities."

"Some do it for the thrill."

"And most don't." Vere adjusted the boxes to sit flush with one another, the way he'd found them. "Did you see anything at all that mentioned artificial diamonds?"

"No, nothing."

The case against Edmund Douglas had begun quite by chance: A suspect the Belgian police arrested for an unrelated matter had boasted of fleecing the diamond dealers of Antwerp on behalf of an Englishman. It had not ranked as a top priority for the Belgian police to investigate what they'd considered an instance of bald braggadocio, though Vere suspected that their lack of concern also had something to do with the fact that the diamond dealers of Antwerp were a community of Jews.

Notwithstanding the apathy of the Belgian police, the equal indifference of Scotland Yard, and the resolute silence of Douglas's supposed victims, the case had somehow managed to pluck Holbrook's notice and subsequently found a champion in Lady Kingsley, whose father had committed suicide when he could no longer keep his extortionist happy.

She'd been doggedly on the case for months, compiling an extensive dossier. And one thing in the dossier that had puzzled Vere from the beginning was the reason the Belgian criminal had given for extorting from the diamond dealers: that they passed off artificial diamonds as the real thing.

As far as Vere knew, while the French chemist Henri Moissan had published on his successful synthesis using an electric arc furnace, no one else had been able to duplicate his results. Synthetic diamonds were not yet a reality. And even if they were, the world was in no danger of running out of real diamonds. The diamond dealers of Antwerp and London had no reason to traffic in man-made ones.

Lady Kingsley left the study first. Vere waited several minutes before heading up the service stairs. The door from the stair landing led out to the eastern end of the house, where the master's and the mistress's apartments were located.

He listened at the door of the master's apartment, then slipped inside. A man's bedroom saw a steady stream of servants to make the bed, clean the grate, brush his clothes, and dust the furniture. It was unlikely Douglas would leave anything particularly important there, but Vere hoped for some insight into Douglas's character.

He retrieved a fountain pen from his pocket and carefully unscrewed it from the middle. The pen held a small amount of ink and could write a few paragraphs, but its true purpose was in the dry cell battery and the tiny lightbulb mounted where the ink chamber should have been.

He swept the apartment quickly with the small stream of light—much neater than carrying a candlestick or a lantern, although the light did not last long and the battery always needed rest. His light came to a stop at the framed photograph on Douglas's nightstand, the only photograph Vere had thus far encountered in the house. He crouched down for a closer look.

It was a wedding photograph of an exceptionally handsome couple. The woman possessed an ethereal, dreamlike beauty; the man, of medium height and slender build, had a similarly refined appearance. On the frame were engraved the words *How do I love thee; Let me count the ways.*

There was something half-familiar about the woman's face. He'd seen it somewhere, and rather recently. But where? And when? He had a good faculty for faces and names. But even if he hadn't, he would not have forgotten a woman with a face like that.

It came to him: the strange painting in the dining room. The angel's face.

Was the bride Mrs. Douglas? If so, it would imply the bridegroom was Edmund Douglas. Of course, it would be ridiculous for a man to display another man's wedding picture on his nightstand. But Vere had trouble reconciling the sleekly, almost delicately handsome man in the photograph with what he knew of Edmund Douglas.

Shouldn't he be heftier in size? If Vere wasn't mistaken, Douglas had been a boxer. And even if he had been a wiry fighter, where were his scars and his crooked nose?

In Mrs. Douglas's room the smell of laudanum was strong and distinct in the air. Mrs. Douglas slept, her breaths laggard, her person so thin as to be almost two-dimensional.

He shone a little light next to her face. Beauty was a commodity of notoriously unreliable endurance. Still, Mrs. Douglas's appearance shocked him. She was a mummified parody of her former self, her hair scant, her eyes sunken, her mouth half-open in her laudanum-induced torpor—a face that would frighten small children were they to come upon her unawares.

But such was the nature of life. All the diamonds in Africa could not guarantee a man a wife who wouldn't turn into a scarecrow in time.

On her nightstand there was also a photograph. A portrait of a very young baby in a tiny coffin, surrounded by flowers and pale lace: a death memento. At the bottom was written *Our Beloved Christabel Eugenia Douglas*.

Vere put down the photograph and raised his light. The next thing he saw gave him a long pause. It was the third iteration of *The Betrayal of the Angel*, painted from a vantage point halfway between the other two. The man lying inert in the snow occupied most of the canvas; at his side, where his blood would have pooled, the dark rose bloomed furiously. Of the angel there was only the sweep of a black wing and the point of a bloody blade at the upper-right corner.

With the tips of his gloved fingers, Vere felt against and under the edge of the frame. There, the release latch. The painting swung outward to reveal a wall safe. It made sense: Mrs. Douglas's ill health gave a legitimate excuse for keeping the servants out, and therefore her room was a better place to hide things.

He pulled out his lock picks from the inside pocket of his waistcoat. Holding the light between his teeth, he set to work, feeling for the pins. After a few minutes or so, the lock clicked and he opened the door of the safe—only to find a second door with an American combination lock inside.

Footsteps pattered in the passage outside. Vere closed the safe, pushed the painting back until it latched, then retreated to the farther side of the bed, stuffing the pen into his pocket as he went.

The door opened. The footsteps headed directly for the bed. He flattened himself against the wall, behind half-drawn bed curtains, willing the woman—the light footsteps belonged to a woman—to come no closer.

She stopped at the opposite edge of the bed. There she stood a long minute. He found it difficult to breathe quietly. Her presence agitated him.

"I won't give up, you know," she said, her voice strangely bleak.

It took a skipped heartbeat to realize she was not addressing him, but her semicomatose aunt.

"It *is* possible, isn't it?" she asked the unresponsive Mrs. Douglas.

What was *it*? What did she *want*?

She leaned down, kissed Mrs. Douglas, and left.

In the morning, Elissande ordered breakfast sent to everyone's room except Lord Frederick's. Then she settled down in the breakfast parlor to wait for the latter to come, so that they might enjoy a leisurely time together.

She would ask him to tell her more about art, and perhaps something about London. She'd listen attentively, nod her head, and take an occasional ladylike sip of her tea. And then—what? She liked Lord Frederick. Very much. But she had no innate grasp on how best to court him, unlike...

There was no point denying it. With Lord Vere, she had not worried at all about the specifics of courting. The only thing that had mattered was that they decrease the distance between them—her whole person had yearned to be closer to him.

Until her whole person had been repelled by him.

Even so, when he had stated cavalierly that he would kiss her—

No, she had felt nothing at all at his inappropriate flirtation, nothing except outrage and disgust.

Lord Frederick appeared at the door. Excellent, her plan had worked. She smiled at him. In the next moment her smile froze. Lord Vere followed him into the breakfast parlor—Lord Vere who had copious mud on his boots and sticks of straw in his hair.

"Oh, hullo, Miss Edgerton," Lord Vere trilled. "I was out for a long walk. Came back and met Freddie coming down the stairs. So here we are—we've brought our appetites and our captivating company for you."

She should pity him: He could not help being an idiot. But the only thing she felt was a burning irritation. His presence was spoiling her carefully laid plans.

"How sweet of you," she made herself say. "And here I was all by myself. Do please fill your plates and sit down."

But how to salvage breakfast? She would need to bombard Lord Frederick with questions about art—his art in particular—the moment he took his seat.

But Lord Vere thwarted her yet again by commencing his monologue while still standing before the sideboard, loading his plate with fried eggs, broiled herring, and buttered muffins. The topic of his dissertation was animal husbandry. Apparently he'd been to an agricultural fair or two and considered himself an authority.

He expounded at considerable length on the Shropshire mutton sheep, its merits and demerits, and then compared it to the Southdown, the Oxford Down, and the Hampshire mutton sheep, the rams of which possessed something of a Roman nose, in his opinion.

Despite her country upbringing, Elissande knew nothing of sheep. But she could just imagine the atrocious mistakes he was making. She still wanted to shake him by the shoulders and ask him how she could possibly have Raphael's *Deliverance of St. Peter* in her dining room when it was a wall fresco at the Palace of the Vatican—part of the architecture of the papal apartment itself.

At some point Lord Vere shifted his focus from sheep to cattle. He had not only attended agricultural fairs, he wanted Elissande to know, but he had seen actual scorecards. "My, those fine animals were put through a rigorous judging—head, body, forequarter, hindquarter. But do you know what the most important aspect of judging a dairy cow is?"

"No, I'm sure I don't, my lord," she said, stabbing her knife into the muffin on her plate.

"Mammary development, Miss Edgerton, worth a whopping thirty-five percent of the overall score. The udder must be very large and very flexible. The teats must be of a nice size and evenly placed. Milk veins, extensive; milk wells, capacious."

He was no longer looking at her face but at her chest. "I don't believe I've viewed a dairy cow quite the same since. Now when I see cows, instead of just saying to myself, 'Oh, look, cows,' I study their udders and teats for their conformity to the principles of animal husbandry—and for the sheer enjoyableness of studying udders and teats, of course."

Elissande could not believe her ears. She opened her eyes a little wider and nodded a little more vigorously. Then she slanted a look Lord Frederick's way, certain that the latter must be frowning at Lord Vere, trying to warn his brother that his speech had quite smashed through the bounds of acceptability.

But Lord Frederick was not paying any attention. He ate slowly, his eyes on his plate, his mind obviously elsewhere.

Lord Vere went on about udders and teats, his gaze fixed to her torso. In his enthusiasm he dropped two forks and a spoon, overturned his teacup, and finally caused a fried egg to land directly onto his own lap, at which point he jumped up, loudly upending his chair. The egg on his trousers flopped to the floor, but not before leaving behind a perfect round of sticky yellow yolk just where no one ought to look.

The commotion finally brought Lord Frederick out of his reverie. "Penny, what the—"

"Oh, dear," said Elissande. "You'd best change fast, my lord, if you don't want your good clothes ruined."

For once, Lord Vere did the sensible thing and departed. Elissande slowly unclenched her hands underneath the table. It was, however, another few seconds before she could master herself enough to smile at Lord Frederick.

"And how are *you* this morning, sir?"

❧

The breakfast tray in his room and the lack of one in Freddie's told Vere everything he needed to know: Miss Edgerton had meant to have breakfast with Freddie, just the two of them.

He could not fault her taste: Freddie was the best of men. She with her plentiful smiles and scheming ways, however, was not remotely worthy of Freddie.

But let her try. He would thwart, foil, and destroy every last one of her plots.

But for now he needed to speak to Lady Kingsley. He slipped a note under her door. She met him five minutes later at the turning of the grand staircase, from which point no one could approach them unobserved.

"I've asked Holbrook for Nye," said Vere.

Nye was a safecracker. After Vere had left Mrs. Douglas's room, he'd changed, written a seemingly rambling note that Holbrook would know how to decode, and walked into the village just in time for the telegraph office to open. On his way back he'd caught a ride on a hay wagon and laid his head down for a pleasant nap after a sleepless night, arriving at Highgate Court as Freddie came downstairs for breakfast.

"Where is the safe? And you still have straw in your hair."

"In Mrs. Douglas's room, behind the dead-man painting," said Vere, running his fingers through his hair. "Do you have the servants' movements?"

"They don't go into Mrs. Douglas's room unless called for. Twice a week Miss Edgerton puts her in a wheelchair and walks her up and down the passage. That's when the servants go in to clean and change the bedding and so on. Otherwise only Miss Edgerton—and I imagine Douglas himself—enters the room."

"In that case, Nye can start working as soon as Miss Edgerton comes down for dinner."

Lady Kingsley glanced up and waved at her niece, who returned her wave before disappearing down the passage, probably to visit one of her friends. "How long will he need?"

"He has opened a combination-lock safe in as little as half an hour. But that was when he could drill. Here he cannot drill."

Lady Kingsley frowned. "Last night when the ladies retired, Miss Edgerton went to Mrs. Douglas's room before she went to her own."

"We must make sure then she doesn't retire so early tonight."

"We'll do that," said Lady Kingsley. "And I can invent a reason to keep her with me for a while even after the ladies retire, but not for too long."

Miss Kingsley reappeared at the top of the stairs. "Lord Vere, could I borrow my aunt a moment? Miss Melbourne simply can't decide what to wear today."

"You do what you can and I will take care of the rest," Vere said with just enough volume for Lady Kingsley to hear. Then he raised his voice. "Of course you may have her, Miss Kingsley. Here, she is all yours, with my compliments."

❦

It was a good talk, about the places in London and the surrounding countryside where Lord Frederick liked to paint. But it was not an exciting conversation. Not that Elissande was overly familiar with exciting conversations, but still she felt the missing spark.

Lord Frederick did not look at her as if he were a

hungry head of cattle and she a fresh, fragrant bale of hay—and goodness, why was she thinking in terms of animal husbandry when she'd never done so in her whole life? Lord Frederick was polite and obliging, but he betrayed no sign of a *preference* for Elissande.

She blamed it all on Lord Vere, especially when he returned much too soon, still wearing the same egg-stained garments. His endless discourse on mutton sheep must have drained all life and verve from Lord Frederick, who'd had to listen to him for God only knew how many thousands upon thousands of hours over a lifetime.

"Penny, you forgot to change your trousers," Lord Frederick pointed out.

"So that's what!" Lord Vere cried. "I got up to my room and for the life of me I couldn't remember why I went. Bother."

Idiot!

"Perhaps you should give it another try?" Elissande suggested, curving her lips and wishing that smiles were arrows. Lord Vere would be more perforated than St. Sebastian.

"Oh, no use now. I'll just forget again," Lord Vere dismissed her idea breezily. "I might as well wait until I change for the shooting. And how is the shooting here, by the by, Miss Edgerton?"

Was he looking at her bosom again? His eyes certainly did not meet hers. "I'm afraid we don't keep a game park, sir."

His eyes remained precisely where they were. "No? Hmm, I suppose we shall have to play tennis."

"I'm sorry, but we lack a tennis court also."

"How about archery? I'm not so terrible as an archer."

Beside him Lord Frederick squirmed.

"With my aunt's health and my uncle's consideration of it, we do not have anything that would produce noise or excitement about. Perhaps you'd like to go for a walk instead, my lord?"

"I already went for a walk before breakfast—do you not remember, Miss Edgerton? I suppose I could settle for a game of croquet instead."

How did he do that? How did he carry on a conversation with her while his eyeballs were firmly ensconced between her breasts?

"I apologize. We do not have the necessary equipment for croquet."

"Well," said Lord Vere, finally exasperated enough to return his gaze to her face. "What is it you do around here then, Miss Edgerton?"

She sent him a smile that should have damaged his vision. "I look after my aunt, sir."

"That is exceedingly admirable, but unbearably tedious, is it not, with no amusements nearby whatsoever?"

She managed to sustain her smile but not without putting some effort into it. How he irked her, like a rock in her shoe.

"Tedium does not enter into it at a—"

She stopped. The dreaded sound: a carriage arriving. "Excuse me," she said, rising.

"Are you expecting someone?" Lord Vere followed her to the window.

She said nothing, wordless with relief. It was not her uncle. She did not recognize the carriage. She also did not recognize the middle-aged, sharp-featured woman in a blue traveling dress who exited the carriage.

"Is that not Lady Avery, Freddie?" said Lord Vere.

Lord Frederick came swiftly to the window. Lord Vere yielded his place.

"What is she doing here?" Lord Frederick growled. He swore under his breath, then remembered himself and turned to Elissande. "I beg your pardon, Miss Edgerton. I did not mean to speak so rudely of your caller."

What a perfect gentleman he was. "You may speak as rudely of her as you wish, sir. I assure you I have never met this particular caller."

"Oh, look. She has brought luggage," said Lord Vere, unperturbed. "Think she's come to stay?"

Lord Frederick smacked his palm against the windowsill, then again begged Elissande's pardon.

"It's quite all right," said Elissande. "But who is she?"

Chapter Six

Lady Avery was a Gossip.

Elissande was not entirely unfamiliar with the idea of a gossip: Mrs. Webster in the village had been one, carrying on about the butcher's wife or the vicar's new gardener. But Lady Avery regarded herself quite above such provincial rumormongers as Mrs. Webster: *She* was a woman of the world with entrée to the very best Society.

With her arrival, Lord Frederick promptly disappeared. To Elissande's mounting despair.

To be sure, she had begun to despair even before Lady Avery's unannounced arrival: Lord Frederick was in no rush to appropriate her hand, while her time, already as limited as Lord Vere's intelligence, shrank second by rapid second.

Lady Avery did not help matters by immediately setting out to grill Elissande on the provenance of the Douglases, and refusing to believe that Elissande in truth knew nothing of her uncle's origins and only a little more of her aunt's.

"The West Cheshire Douglases?" Lady Avery asked. "Surely you must be related to the West Cheshire Douglases."

Was Lady Avery a student of Lord Vere's particular school of genealogical exploration?

"No, ma'am. I've never heard of them."

Lady Avery harrumphed. "Most irregular. Who are *your* family then? The Edgertons of Derbyshire?"

Well, at least this she did know. "The Edgertons of Cumberland, ma'am."

Lady Avery's brows knitted. "The Edgertons of Cumberland. The Edgertons of Cumberland," she mumbled. Then, triumphantly, she cried, "You are the late Sir Cecil Edgerton's granddaughter, aren't you? By his youngest son?"

Elissande stared at her in shock. She'd believed Lady Avery's expertise in gossip to be about as valid as Lord Vere's knowledge of animal husbandry. "Sir Cecil was my grandfather, yes."

"Ah, I thought so," said Lady Avery, satisfied. "Quite the scandal when your father ran off with your mother. And such an unhappy end, both of them dead within three years."

Lady Kingsley, Miss Kingsley, and Miss Beauchamp entered the drawing room. Elissande was suddenly as alarmed as Lord Frederick must have been. Her parents' story had not only been tragic, but also not fit for polite company, as her uncle had repeatedly impressed upon her. What if Lady Avery decided to disclose the less savory details to everyone present?

"Lord Vere says you frightened his brother away, Lady Avery," Miss Kingsley called out cheerfully.

"Nonsense. I've already extracted everything out of Lord Frederick during the Season. He has nothing to fear from me at the present."

Miss Beauchamp sat down next to Lady Avery. "Oh, do tell, dear lady. What did you extract from Lord Frederick?"

"*Well…*" Lady Avery drew out that syllable for a good three seconds, obviously relishing her role as the dispenser of juicy tidbits. "He did see her in June, when she was in town to marry off that American heiress, Miss Van der Waals. And you would not believe this, but they have also met in Paris, in Nice, and in New York."

Everyone looked shocked, including, Elissande imagined, herself. Who was this "she"?

"They have?" Lady Kingsley exclaimed. "What does Lord Tremaine think of it?"

"Well, apparently he approves. The two men have dined together."

Lady Kingsley shook her head. "My goodness, will wonders never cease?"

"No indeed. I asked Lord Frederick if she looked well and he asked me when had she ever *not* looked well."

"Oh, my!" Miss Beauchamp squealed.

Please let it not be. "Does Lord Frederick have an

understanding with someone?" Elissande ventured to ask.

"My apologies, I forgot you do not know, Miss Edgerton. Lord Frederick *did* have an understanding with the Marchioness of Tremaine. And in the spring of 'ninety-three, she was prepared to divorce her husband for him. It was going to be quite the scandal, but the divorce never took place. She reconciled with her husband and withdrew her petition."

"Poor Lord Frederick." Miss Kingsley sighed.

"No, lucky Lord Frederick," Lady Avery corrected her. "Now he can marry a nice young lady like Miss Edgerton here, instead of someone who would forever be referred to as 'that divorced woman.' Don't you agree, Miss Edgerton?"

"I don't think Lord Frederick has any plans to marry me," Elissande answered with, alas, no false modesty whatsoever. "But I do, on the whole, believe that it is more...convenient not to have a divorce in one's spouse's past."

"Excellent," said Lady Avery. "My dear Miss Edgerton, you understand the essence of the issue. One must not be a romantic in this life. Look at the cynics; they were all once romantics."

"Is—is Lord Frederick now a cynic?"

"No, bless him, he is still a romantic, would you believe it. I suppose not every disappointed romantic turns into a cynic."

Such a good man, Lord Frederick. If only Elissande could entice him to ask for her hand, she'd love him so much better than that faithless Lady Tremaine.

In fact, she would be the best wife in the history of matrimony.

❦

Vere needed to be at the house. But when Freddie came to him, wanting some company, he could not refuse. They walked for miles in the country, rowed on one of the meres that dotted the very northern tip of Shropshire, and took their luncheon at the village inn.

"I'm going back," Vere said at the end of the luncheon, rising from the table and yawning. He must know what instructions Holbrook had sent and coordinate with Lady Kingsley on getting Nye into and out of the house. "I need a nap. I didn't sleep well last night."

"Nightmares?" Freddie rose too and fell in step beside Vere.

"No, I don't get them so often anymore." In his last year at Eton, Freddie had to come into Vere's room almost every night to shake him awake. "Anyway, you stay here if you'd like. I'll hire the inn's carriage to take me back."

"I'll come with you," Freddie said quietly.

Vere experienced another stab of guilt. Freddie no doubt wished to stay away for the rest of the day— Lady Tremaine was ancient history, yet Lady Avery still pounced upon him as if he'd freshly waltzed with Scandal. But Freddie had also made it a point always to accompany Vere whenever they were out somewhere unfamiliar.

Vere briefly clasped his hand on Freddie's shoulder. "Come along then."

Back at the house, Vere found Lady Kingsley waiting impatiently for him. Nye would be arriving shortly before the start of dinner. They agreed that Vere would let him in through the doors that led from the library to a terrace on the east side of the house—the side away from the kitchen, and therefore less likely to be seen by the servants.

"And what do we do after I must relinquish Miss Edgerton at night, if Nye is still not finished?" asked Lady Kingsley.

"I'll think of something."

"Make sure it's not something you'll regret," said Lady Kingsley.

Twenty-four hours had yet to pass since he first laid eyes on Miss Edgerton. Little wonder then the memory of his infatuation was fresh in Lady Kingsley's mind. Yet it already seemed impossibly distant to Vere, a time of long-ago innocence.

"I'll be mindful," he said coolly.

Knowing Miss Edgerton's aim, as soon as he concluded his tête-à-tête with Lady Kingsley, he looked for his brother. He found Freddie—and Miss Edgerton—in the otherwise empty dining room, Freddie gazing into his No. 4 Kodak camera, Miss Edgerton, in a most becoming day dress of pale apricot, gazing adoringly at Freddie.

The ardor in her eyes cooled considerably as she noted Vere's presence. "Lord Vere."

Vere ignored the caustic sensation in his heart. "Miss Edgerton. Freddie."

Freddie pulled up the brass button on top of the box camera to cock the shutter. "Hullo, Penny. How was your nap? It's only been"—he glanced at the clock—"three quarters of an hour."

"My nap was superb. What are *you* doing?"

"Taking some photographs of this painting. Miss Edgerton was kind enough to grant me permission."

"Be churlish for Miss Edgerton to refuse you, wouldn't it?" Vere smiled at her.

She smiled back at him, her expression as sunny as his. "It most certainly would be. Besides, I've never seen a camera before."

"I've seen tons of them. And they all do exactly the same thing," he said dismissively. "By the way, Miss Edgerton, Miss Kingsley said the ladies would like you to join them for a turn in the garden."

"Oh," she said. "Are you sure, Lord Vere?"

"Of course. I saw her not three minutes ago in the rose parlor."

He *had* seen Miss Kingsley less than three minutes ago in the rose parlor. Miss Kingsley, however, had been engaged in a game of backgammon with Conrad, her admirer—and had no intention of going anywhere. But by the time Miss Edgerton realized this, it would be too late; Vere would have whisked Freddie someplace safe—safer, at least—from her calculating grasp.

"And she was quite keen on your company," Vere added.

"I suppose I'd best go see her then," said Miss Edgerton reluctantly. "Thank you, Lord Vere. Excuse me, Lord Frederick."

Vere watched her. At the door she looked back. But Freddie was already busy with his next snapshot. Instead her eyes met Vere's. He made sure his gaze shifted obviously to her breasts. She left quickly after that.

He turned his attention back to Freddie. "Fancy a game of snooker, old chap?"

Of course Lord Vere was wrong. *Of course.*

Miss Kingsley and Mr. Conrad, both chortling, told Elissande not to worry. Perhaps it was someone else who had asked Lord Vere to convey a message, and Lord Vere, with his slightly inaccurate memory—a most charitable turn of phrase—had made mistakes concerning both the originator and the recipient of the message.

Miss Kingsley even kindly rose and offered to take a turn in the garden with Elissande, if she was still in the mood for it. Elissande, who had never been in the mood for it, thanked Miss Kingsley profusely and begged that she and Mr. Conrad forgive her interruption and continue to enjoy their game.

By the time Elissande returned to the dining room, Lord Frederick was gone. She did locate him in the billiard room fifteen minutes later, but the room was full of men—everyone except Mr. Conrad, it seemed.

"Miss Edgerton, would you like to join the game?" Lord Vere asked cheerfully.

The other gentlemen chuckled softly. Even without any experience to guide her in the matter, Elissande understood that she could not possibly accept the invitation. It would give Lord Frederick quite the wrong impression of her character—an accurate one, that was, and that would not do.

"Thank you, sir," she said with what she hoped was a lighthearted tone. "But no, thank you. I was only passing through."

She still had dinner, during which she would have Lord Frederick next to her.

Alas, the next blow came precisely then. Lady Kingsley had prepared the seating chart the evening before, since Elissande had never dealt with rules of precedence. Elissande fully expected the seating to remain the same. To her dismay, however, Lady Kingsley produced a new seating chart for the evening, a chart that placed Lord Frederick three seats away from Elissande.

She hardly ate. The squeeze in her throat prevented any kind of meaningful swallowing—a whole day gone by, and she'd made no progress at all. Her uncle's return, edging closer by the hour, was a chill between her shoulder blades, a chill no coat or fire could dispel.

The only silver lining was that Lord Vere had also been seated away from her. A very fortunate thing for him. If she caught him staring at her bosom one more time, she might just brain him with the epergne.

After dinner, the company played charades until quarter to ten. When her uncle was at home, this was usually the time when Elissande would gratefully bid him a good night and escape to the sanctuary of her own room. Last night, the ladies, after the ordeal of the rats, had retired at about the same time. Lord Vere, however, was determined to change things.

"The night is yet young," he said. "Let us play something else."

Miss Kingsley immediately took up his cause. "Oh, yes, do let us. May we, Auntie dearest?"

Lady Kingsley appeared hesitant.

"Oh come, Lady Kingsley," wheedled Lord Vere. "There is no rule written in stone dictating that ladies must be in bed when the clock strikes ten."

Elissande ground her teeth. She seemed to do that whenever Lord Vere made his presence known.

"Quite so. I say we play something else." Miss Beauchamp joined the campaign.

"Well, the decision is not up to me," said Lady Kingsley. "We are here at Miss Edgerton's gracious hospitality."

A chorus of pleas came at Elissande. There was not much she could say, other than, "Of course we can play something else. But what shall we play?"

"How about Pass the Parcel?" asked Miss Melbourne.

"We don't have a parcel prepared," said Miss Duvall. "I say *La Vache Qui Tache*."

"*La Vache Qui Tache* makes my head hurt,"

complained Lord Vere. "I can never remember who has how many spots. Something simpler, please."

"Sardines," Mr. Kingsley suggested.

"No, Richard," said his aunt. "Absolutely not. No one is to run about the house disturbing Mrs. Douglas."

"I know. Let's play Squeak Piggy Squeak," said Miss Kingsley.

Mr. Conrad quickly seconded the idea, followed by Lord Vere. The rest of the guests also voiced their consent.

"Well," said Lady Kingsley, "it's not something I truly approve of, but I suppose with both myself and Lady Avery present, you can't get into too much trouble."

The young ladies clapped to be allowed to stay up late. The gentlemen rearranged chairs. Elissande, who was unfamiliar with parlor games in general, asked Miss Beauchamp, "I'm sorry, but how does one play Squeak Piggy Squeak?"

"Oh, it's quite simple," said Miss Beauchamp. "We sit in a circle. One person is blindfolded and placed in the center of the circle. He is the farmer, and the rest of us are pigs. Someone spins the farmer three times around, then the farmer has to make his way to a pig and sit on the pig's lap. The pig squeaks and the farmer guesses the identity of the pig. If he succeeds, the pig becomes the farmer. If not, the farmer goes on for another turn."

"I see," said Elissande. No wonder Lady Kingsley required two chaperones. For so many unmarried young men and women to be taking turns sitting on one another's laps was, if not outright unseemly, at least a great deal less than decorous.

Mr. Wessex volunteered to be the first farmer. Mr. Kingsley blindfolded him and turned him about not three times but at least six. Mr. Wessex, who'd had a good few glasses of wine at dinner, wobbled dangerously. He stumbled toward Miss Kingsley. Miss Kingsley squealed and put out her arms to stop him from crashing directly into her person.

Mr. Wessex deliberately leaned his weight into her hands. Miss Kingsley squealed again. The other young ladies giggled. Mr. Wessex, suddenly not quite as unsteady, turned and sat down on Miss Kingsley's lap.

"All right, my dear piggy, oink for me."

Everyone laughed, except Elissande. It was one thing to hear the game described, quite another to see it in action. The extent of the contact between Miss Kingsley and Mr. Wessex dumbfounded her. The suddenly risqué atmosphere in the drawing room made her both unhappy and strangely curious.

Miss Kingsley squealed one more time.

"Hmm, yes, I know this little piggy. But a part of me wants to be the farmer for a bit longer yet." Mr. Wessex crossed his legs and mused. "Dilemma, dilemma."

Miss Kingsley laughed silently into her hands. Mr. Conrad forcefully opined that others deserved a turn to be the farmer. Mr. Wessex gave in to the pressure and identified Miss Kingsley, who, as the new farmer, promptly fell into Mr. Conrad's lap and there stayed what seemed endless minutes, pondering her choices.

Good gracious, it was *indecent*.

And Lady Kingsley and Lady Avery allowed it? They did. The two of them sat a little behind Elissande, away from the game circle, Lady Avery talking animatedly, as she always did.

"...years ago, in a game of Sardines, she was hiding and he found her first and squeezed into the cupboard with her. They must have either thought her hiding place impenetrable or entirely forgot themselves. You should have seen her state of undress—and his!—when I went into the cupboard myself. So of course they had to marry." Lady Avery sighed. "I do love a good game of Sardines."

Elissande nearly screamed when somebody suddenly sat down on her lap. It was Miss Beauchamp, who tittered as if she'd been given an unhealthy dose of laughing gas.

"I can already tell it's not a gentleman," she said between bursts of mirth.

"How do you know?" asked Lord Vere, in all sincerity.

Behind Miss Beauchamp's head, Elissande rolled her eyes.

"Silly, sir. Of course I know. My back is cushioned magnificently. I'm quite certain I don't even need this piggy to make a noise to identify her. Such a marvelous bosom could only belong to our hostess. Miss Edgerton it is. Am I right?"

Elissande had to answer. "Yes, you are right, Miss Beauchamp."

Miss Beauchamp leaped off Elissande's lap and ripped off her blindfold. "I knew it."

Now the blindfold went over Elissande's eyes. She was spun, or so it felt, four and a half times to the left and then two and a half times to the right. So she should be facing more or less the same direction as she had when she first stood up from her chair.

Directly across from her was Lord Vere. She most certainly did not want to head that way. She turned tentatively to her right. A little more. Yet again a little more, perhaps? Would that be where Lord Frederick was?

What good sitting on his lap would do, she had no idea. But she'd rather land in his lap, if she must land in somebody's lap.

Gingerly she set out in her chosen direction, her hands stretched out before her. But after a few steps, she stopped. The fireplace had crackled. The sound came from directly behind her, which meant that she was not headed for Lord Frederick.

She made a quarter turn to her left. In front of her someone whistled and to her right a woman chuckled. Did that sound like Miss Kingsley? If she were headed toward Lord Frederick, shouldn't Miss Kingsley be more to her left than her right?

She scooted back a step or two. Was she returning to the center of the circle? She took another two steps—and stumbled backward over someone's foot.

She gasped. And gasped again as a pair of strong

hands caught her lightly by her waist. Deftly he righted her—it was a he; of that much she was sure. She was not built like a bird; none of the ladies present would be able to handle her weight so easily.

"Thank you," she said.

There was no reply, but from somewhere Lady Avery said, "Now, now, Miss Edgerton, you can't simply walk away like that. You were headed for his lap. And no disputes, sir. She *was* headed for your lap. You cannot redirect her."

Lady Avery was in motion, walking about. Elissande could not decide where her voice was coming from. She stood in place, uncertain what she should do next.

"Oh, come, sir. You know what you ought to do," urged Lady Avery.

He apparently did, for he lifted her bodily, as if she weighed no more than a kitten, and set her down not on his lap, but on the chair itself, between his legs.

She swallowed with the alarming sensation of being so close to a man, her thighs pressed against his. There was a physicality to him, a quality that went beyond the mere amount of space he occupied, as if his body would effortlessly engulf hers if she did not take care to preserve herself.

She spread out her hands, looking for the armrests of the chair. But she touched only his hands, bare and warm and already occupying the armrests. She yanked hers away. That motion jerked her body backward against his chest.

She was wrong; it was not that his body *would*

engulf her, but that it already did. She was surrounded by him, by his silent, still presence, while she fidgeted and fumbled, unable to treat their contact with the flirty lightheartedness expected of her.

He touched her again, his hands on her upper arms, steadying her. Steering her torso away from him, in fact.

Perhaps she had stumbled upon Lord Frederick after all. He could, she felt, be depended upon to maintain his sense of dignity and propriety amidst such pointless ribaldry. To help him in that effort, she scooted her bottom forward.

Only to almost fall off the chair. She hurriedly scooted back—directly into him.

She could not even gasp this time. Behind her bum he was, dear God, he was...

Hard.

Her cheeks scalded. Further understanding failed her. She froze in place: She could not think, could not speak, could not move a single muscle to extract herself.

Again, it was he who took charge of the situation, lifting her up, and this time, when she came down, she came down on his lap, somewhat away from the part of him that gave her fits.

But not nearly far enough, not with the sensation of his strong thighs so vivid upon her posterior. Really, whose idea had it been to get rid of bustles?

"What...what am I supposed to do now?" she beseeched.

"Say, 'Squeak, piggy, squeak,'" said someone.

She could say nothing of the sort to the man behind her. It was ridiculous enough under normal circumstances. In this instance it would be just dreadfully wrong. She would have to guess his identity without any other clues.

He seemed rather on the taller side, which would eliminate Mr. Kingsley. And most likely he was not Mr. Wessex, who used a highly aromatic cologne that preceded him. The man behind her smelled only of a whiff of cigar smoke and, beneath that, shaving powder.

"I think Miss Edgerton likes being on this piggy's lap," said Miss Beauchamp, chuckling.

Miss Beauchamp's voice was very close, to Elissande's immediate left, in fact. And to Miss Beauchamp's right had been—

"Lord Vere," she mumbled.

And rose immediately. He started to clap before she even reached for her blindfold.

"How did you know it was me?" he said, still clapping, with a smile so densely guileless that it might very well have been one of hers. "I haven't even squeaked yet."

"A good guess," she answered.

Miss Beauchamp had been correct: She *had* liked the startling, alien, mortifying, but not entirely unpleasurable sensation of being practically in his embrace. But now she was repulsed—by him, by herself, by the blind sensuality of her body.

Revulsion, however, did not stop her renewed awareness of him. Of the softness of his hair when she tied the blindfold for him, the width of his shoulders as she spun him about, the tightness and muscularity of his arms as she stopped him from falling back onto her, so hard did he wobble from her spins.

The game went on, reaching its loud and boisterous conclusion at eleven o'clock, with Miss Beauchamp seated firmly on Lord Vere's lap and both of them laughing as if they'd never had such a good time.

❧

At half an hour past midnight Elissande finally left Lady Kingsley's room. Lady Kingsley had stumbled a step as they'd ascended the grand staircase together and Elissande had caught her. She had not complained of anything, but Miss Kingsley had whispered anxiously to Elissande that Lady Kingsley suffered terrible migraines from time to time and perhaps the jollity of the evening had been too much for her.

So Elissande and Miss Kingsley had sat with Lady Kingsley until the latter at last fell asleep. Then Elissande escorted a continuously yawning Miss Kingsley to her room. She herself yawned too, as she walked toward Aunt Rachel's room at the opposite end of the house.

She stopped mid-yawn. Someone was singing, heartily slurring the rousing chorus of a ludicrous song.

"'Daddy wouldn't buy me a bow-wow! bow wow!

Daddy wouldn't buy me a bow-wow! bow wow! I've got a little cat. And I'm very fond of that. But I'd rather have a bow-wow. Wow, wow, wow, wow.' "

She turned the corner. Lord Vere. Of *course*. He bobbed and weaved and caught himself against the wall just outside Aunt Rachel's door.

" 'We used to have two tiny dogs,' " he sang, " 'such pretty little dears. But Daddy sold 'em 'cause they used to bite each other's ears.' "

She fought to unclench her teeth. "Lord Vere, please. You'll wake everyone."

"Ah, Miss Edgerton. How lovely to see you, as always."

"It's late, sir. You should retire."

"Retire? No, Miss Edgerton. It's a night for song. Don't I sing wonderfully?"

"You sing splendidly. But you can't sing here." And where was Lord Frederick to bail her out this time?

"Where may I sing then?"

"You should go outside if you must sing."

"Fair enough."

He stumbled forward some distance and reached for her *uncle's* door. She sprinted after him and yanked his hand off the door handle. "What are you doing, Lord Vere?"

"But that's the door for going outside."

"That most certainly is not, sir. That is my uncle's room."

"Is it? Beg pardon. I don't usually make such mistakes, I assure you, Miss Edgerton; I normally have the most impeccable sense of direction."

Oh, he did, did he?

"Perhaps you could show me the way out?" he asked.

She inhaled deeply. "Of course. Follow me. And *please* be quiet until we clear the house."

He did not break out into song, but he did not really remain quiet. He talked as he zigzagged beside her. "Was it not the most wondrous fun playing Squeak Piggy Squeak tonight?"

"I've never had a better time."

"And I shall always treasure the sensational memory of your bottom on my lap."

She did *not* treasure the memory of his hardness against her bottom; in fact, she disgusted herself with the flash of heat the remembrance brought to her face. How could she have felt even the remotest quiver for him? Such stupidity as his should have been obvious via touch, unmistakable like a fever. Or leprosy.

She walked faster. Somehow he kept up. "Why do you suppose the memory of your bottom on my lap is more sensational than that of Miss Melbourne's, for instance?"

If she had the least indication that he spoke with deliberate vulgarity, she'd have turned and punched him. Perhaps even kicked him. But he was steeped in that grating obliviousness so particular to him, and it would be like hitting a baby or thrashing a dog.

"No doubt because my bottom is twice the size of Miss Melbourne's," she said tightly.

"Is it? Marvelous. Now why did I never think of that?"

They reached the front door of the house. She unlocked it and led him outside some distance. The moment they stopped, he began to sing. She turned to leave.

"No, no, Miss Edgerton. You can't go. Let me perform for you, I insist."

"But I'm tired."

"Then I shall perform for you under your window. Is that not romantic?"

She'd rather stick sharp objects into her ears. "In that case, I'll stay here and listen."

He sang interminably. Long enough for a Hindu wedding. Long enough for a snail to scale Mont Blanc. Long enough for Atlantis to rise and sink again.

It was windy and chill—the temperature was in the forties. She shivered in her inadequate dinner gown, her bare shoulders and arms prickled with cold. He was loud and drunkenly off-key. And even the night sky conspired against her: no rain to force him back inside into his bed, and too much cloud haze to offer any stargazing.

Suddenly he stopped. She regarded him, astonished: She'd already accepted the possibility that he'd never stop. He bowed—nearly falling over in the act—and then looked at her expectantly. Apparently she was to clap. She did. Anything to get rid of him.

Her applause made him happy and he did not hesitate to tell her so. "I'm so glad to be a source of enjoyment to you, Miss Edgerton. I shall sleep better knowing your life is richer and more beautiful for my voice."

She did not hit him. That was certainly to be the basis for her beatification someday, because anyone less than a saint would have done him terrible injury by this point.

She accompanied him to his door, going so far as to open it for him.

" 'Good night, good night, parting is such sweet sorrow.' " He bowed again and tipped sideways, banging into the doorjamb. "Who wrote that, do you remember?"

"Someone quite dead, sir."

"I suspect you are right. Thank you, Miss Edgerton. You've made this an unforgettable night."

She pushed him into the room and closed the door.

❦

Aunt Rachel was asleep, of course—laudanum let her escape life. Sometimes—a great deal of times lately—Elissande was tempted herself. But she feared the grip of laudanum. Freedom was her only goal. It was no freedom to be wretchedly dependent on a tincture, even without her uncle about to withhold the bottle at his whim.

A night and a day remained to her. Her freedom was no closer now than it had been two days ago. In fact, it was infinitely farther away than it had been during those giddy hours when she'd seen Lord Vere but not yet heard him speak at length. And Lord

Frederick, kind, good, amicable Lord Frederick, was in his own way as unobtainable as the moon.

Her risk-it-all gamble appeared doomed to failure. She simply did not know what to do anymore.

"Go," Aunt Rachel suddenly whispered.

Elissande approached the bed. "Did you say something, ma'am?"

Aunt Rachel's eyelids fluttered but did not open. She was mumbling in her sleep. "Go, Ellie. And do not come back!"

When she was fifteen, Elissande had left once. And those had been the precise words her aunt had whispered into her ear before she walked the five miles to Ellesmere. The branch line at Ellesmere took her to Whitchurch. The regional line at Whitchurch took her to Crewe. From Crewe, she had been only three hours from London.

At Crewe, however, she had broken down.

By the end of the day she had returned home, walking the same five miles to reach Highgate Court a half hour before her uncle came back. Aunt Rachel had said nothing. She'd only wept. They'd wept together.

"Go," Aunt Rachel said again, more faintly this time.

Elissande pressed her hands into her face. She must think harder. She must not let a little obstacle such as her inability to attract a proposal stand in the way. Surely God had not let loose a plague of rats on Lady Kingsley for nothing.

Her head came up. What had Lady Avery said this

evening? She had caught a man and a woman in a cupboard in a state of undress and they'd had to marry.

Lady Avery could catch Elissande and Lord Frederick together, in a state of undress. And then *they* would have to marry.

But how could she do this to Lord Frederick? How could she deliberately entrap him? Her uncle was the one with all the subtlety, all the cruelty, and all the manipulativeness. She never wanted to be like him.

"Ellie," her aunt mumbled in her troubled sleep. "Ellie. Go. Do not come back."

Elissande's heart clenched. Apparently a lifetime spent under her uncle's thumb had not left her untainted. Because she could. She could do this to Lord Frederick. She was capable of using him to save herself and Aunt Rachel.

And she would.

❦

From his room Vere monitored Miss Edgerton's return to hers. After the light under her door disappeared, he waited five minutes before venturing into the corridor, tapping once at Lady Kingsley's door as he passed.

Mrs. Douglas slept. He unlatched the painting and swung it out of his way. Lady Kingsley arrived in time to hold the light for him while he re-picked the lock of the outer safe door—he'd instructed Nye to lock the safe before he left, or the painting wouldn't latch properly.

This time, the lock took him only one minute to pick. Lady Kingsley, who'd stood guard for Nye while Vere kept Miss Edgerton away, had the numbers for the combination lock. She turned the dial and pulled open the inner door.

And it was well worth the effort.

The contents of the safe documented Edmund Douglas's history of failure. The diamond mine was legitimate. But after his one remarkable find in South Africa, his subsequent business ventures—seeking to capitalize on his new fortune—had achieved nothing but massive losses.

"My goodness, he's a glutton for punishment, isn't he?" Lady Kingsley marveled.

He was and it did not make any sense to Vere. Why did Douglas persist in these investments? Ought not a man learn after five or seven times that he had been simply a lucky bastard where the diamond mine was concerned and stop trying to recapture the lightning?

"If you tally everything together, he might be in debt," Lady Kingsley whispered excitedly. "See, he does need money. There's our motive."

What excited Lady Kingsley even more was a dossier written in code, a far more complicated code than the mere shifting around of letters.

If one assumed that Edmund Douglas himself had committed his secrets in code, then he possessed a very fine penmanship indeed. The more Vere learned of Douglas, the more unlikely the man became. Understated home, refined appearance, elegant handwriting, not to mention educated speech—his niece's speech contained nothing of the Liverpool docks. Could a fortune in South Africa truly alter a man so much?

"A hundred quid says all the evidence we need is in here," said Lady Kingsley.

Vere nodded. He felt around in the interior of the safe. Ah, they had not exhausted its secrets yet. There was a false bottom.

The compartment beneath the false bottom contained only a drawstring pouch. Vere expected to find it full of diamonds; instead he found finished jewels.

"Rather ordinary, aren't they?" said Lady Kingsley, fingering a ruby necklace. "I would say a thousand pounds for everything inside, at most."

An image of Miss Edgerton suddenly came to him, Miss Edgerton with her bare throat, bare wrists, bare fingers. He'd never realized it before, but she wore not a single piece of jewelry, not even a cameo brooch. A singularly odd thing for the niece of a man who mined diamonds.

As he returned the pouch to the safe, however, he noted that he was mistaken. There was something else in the hidden compartment, a tiny key, less than an inch in length, with a great many notches along a spine as slender as a toothpick.

Lady Kingsley held the key up to the light. "If this is meant for a lock, then it's a lock I can snap in two with my bare hands."

They replaced everything except the coded dossier, which Lady Kingsley wanted to keep.

"Are you taking it to London in the morning?" Vere whispered, bypassing his exhausted vocal cords.

"I can't leave all my guests and go away for eight hours. And you'd best not either. Or Douglas's suspicion will fall squarely on you should he find it missing before we can get it back to the safe."

She left first with the dossier. Vere closed and locked the safe. When he'd pushed the painting back into place and latched it, he turned around—and froze.

Miss Edgerton, when she'd come to check on her aunt, must have added coal to the grate. In the firelight, Mrs. Douglas lay with her eyes wide open, staring at him.

Any other woman would have screamed. But she remained eerily quiet, even as her eyes bulged with terror.

Vere moved carefully, inch by inch toward the door. She closed her eyes, her whole person shaking.

He took a deep breath, slipped out the door, and listened. If Mrs. Douglas was going to recover her voice and scream, she would do so now. The service stairs were near, he'd escape that way to avoid the guests her bloodcurdling shrieks were sure to bring.

But no sounds came from Mrs. Douglas, not a gasp, not a wheeze, not even a whimper.

He walked back to his room, completely unsettled.

❧

The longcase clock gonged the hour, three brassy chimes that quavered in the dark, still air.

It was always three o'clock.

The ormolu banister was cold. The tall palm trees that his father was so proud of were now ghosts with long, swaying arms. One frond scratched against the back of his hand. He shook with fright.

Still, he kept descending, feeling his way down one step at a time. There was a faint light at the foot of the stairs. He was drawn to it, like a toddler to a deep well.

He saw her feet first, delicate feet in blue dancing slippers. Her gown shimmered, faintly iridescent in the light that came from nowhere. An arm, with its long white glove that reached past her elbow, lay across her torso.

Her white shawl curled slack about her shoulders. Her coiffure was ruined, feathers and combs embedded pell-mell in a tangle of dark knots. Her much-envied five-strand sapphire necklace had flipped itself and now draped her mouth and chin—a bejeweled muzzle.

Then, and only then, did he notice the impossible angle of her neck.

He was sick to his stomach. But she was his mother. He reached out to touch her. Her eyes suddenly opened, eyes empty yet petrified with fear. He reared back, his heel caught against the first rise of the staircase, and down he went.

Down, down, down—

Vere bolted upright in his bed, gasping. The dream recurred periodically, but never quite like this. He had somehow juxtaposed Mrs. Douglas's terrified eyes onto his old nightmare.

His door opened. "Are you all right, Lord Vere? I heard noises."

Miss Edgerton, a shadowed silhouette on the threshold.

For a moment he was seized with the mad desire to have her next to him, her hand caressing his cheek, telling him that it was only a dream. She would coax him to lie down, tuck him in, and smile—

"Oh, no, gosh, no, I'm not all right!" he said forcefully. "How I hate that dream. You know the one, where you are searching for a water closet high and low and there isn't one anywhere in the house— and no chamber pots and not even a proper bucket. And there are crowds in every room, and out in the gardens, on the lawn, and—Oh, good gracious, I hope I haven't—"

She made a choked sound.

"Oh, thank God," he continued. "Your beddings are safe. But if you will excuse me, I must—"

The door closed decisively.

❧

In the morning everyone drove over to Woodley Manor for a look at the disgusting mountain of dead rats. The rat catcher, with his exhausted rat dogs, a triumphant ferret, and an incomprehensible accent, proudly twirled his dark, luxuriant mustache as he posed for Lord Frederick's camera, commemorating the occasion.

"My staff is already hard at work," said Lady Kingsley to Elissande. "There is much to do, but they assure me the house will be fit for habitation by tomorrow. I promise you we shall remove ourselves the moment it is the case."

Elissande saw the handwriting on the wall. There was no more time left. Something must happen.

She must make something happen.

God helped those who helped themselves.

Chapter Seven

Elissande had inherited a few things from her parents: a set of her mother's silver combs, a bottle of perfume blended especially for Charlotte Edgerton by Parfumerie Guerlain, her father's shaving brush, a bundle of letters tied in lilac ribbon, and a small oil painting of a female nude.

She was sure Lord Frederick would appreciate seeing the painting. She hadn't shown it to him for one very significant reason: She was afraid that the subject might be her mother, and one simply did not go around letting gentlemen look at one's mother in such a state of exposure.

But now she was throwing all scruples to the wind.

"My goodness, but it's a Delacroix!" exclaimed Lord Frederick.

She was unfamiliar with the name; the books on art that the library had once housed had concentrated on the art of classical antiquity and that of the Renaissance. But judging by Lord Frederick's expression of delight and reverence, a Delacroix was nothing to sneer at.

"Do you really think so, Lord Frederick, that it is a Delacroix?"

"I am almost one hundred percent sure." He brought the small painting even closer to his eyes. "The signature, the style, the use of color—I would be shocked if it weren't a Delacroix."

His enthusiasm quite infected her. It must be a sign from above. How else could her treasure chest, which contained nothing of value—except the sentimental kind—prove so startlingly helpful on this very day?

"It is exquisite," Lord Frederick murmured, enraptured.

She stared at him, similarly enraptured by her sudden stroke of good fortune.

"How did you come to have a Delacroix?" Lord Frederick asked.

"I haven't the remotest idea. I suppose my father must have purchased it. He lived in Paris during the early seventies."

"I don't think so," scoffed Lord Vere.

Lady Kingsley had letters to write. Lady Avery and the young ladies had gone to Ellesmere. Most of the gentlemen had departed to shoot what grouse there was to be had at Woodley Manor. Lord Frederick had declined, citing a lack of interest in badgering the poor birds. Lord Vere, who had originally declared his intention to go, had, to Elissande's simmering exasperation, subsequently changed his mind to keep his brother company.

As a result, he sat at the other end of the morning parlor, playing solitaire. Elissande had done her best to ignore his presence, but now she had no choice but to turn her head his way. He did not look up from the cards he'd laid out—and they were *not* for a game of solitaire, but simply one long line from which he was now turning random cards faceup.

"I beg your pardon, sir? You don't think my father lived in Paris?"

"Oh, I'm sure he did, but I'm not so sure he came by his Delacroix honestly," said Lord Vere nonchalantly. "Lady Avery was chewing on my ears at dinner last night. She told me that your grandfather was a great lover of art and that your father stole some pieces from him before he ran away with your mother."

Elissande was overcome for a moment. Her uncle had said plenty of unpleasant things about her parents, but at least he had never accused her father of thievery.

"Please do not speak ill of the dead, my lord," she said, her voice tight with fury.

"Telling what happened in truth isn't speaking ill of someone. Besides, it's a fascinating story, what with your mother having been a kept woman and all. Did you know she was your great-uncle's mistress before she married your father?"

Of course she knew that. Her uncle had made sure she understood well the ignominy of her parentage.

But it was the worst breach of manners for Lord Vere to speak of it publicly, with such carelessness for the ramifications.

For the very first time Lord Frederick, red at the ears, spoke in censure of his brother. "Penny, that's enough."

Lord Vere shrugged and gathered his cards to reshuffle them.

There was a long, awkward silence. Lord Frederick broke it—lovely, lovely Lord Frederick. "I do apologize," he said softly. "Sometimes my brother gets his stories confused. I'm sure he's quite mistaken about your family."

"Thank you," she murmured gratefully.

"No, it is I who should thank you, for the chance to admire a Delacroix when I least expected it." He handed the painting back to her. "What joy such beauty brings."

"I found this among my father's things last night. We have trunks and trunks of my father's possessions. Perhaps I can unearth some more."

"I would *dearly* love to see what else you can find, Miss Edgerton."

"She's not wearing anything," said Lord Vere, suddenly next to her. She had not heard him get up from his chair at all.

"It's a nude, Penny," Lord Frederick explained.

"Well, yes, I can see that: She's not wearing anything." Lord Vere leaned in farther. "Except a pair of white stockings, that is."

His arm practically brushed her hair. She would

have expected his clothes to reek of tomato sauce—he'd had quite an incident with the sweetbread at luncheon. But he only smelled brisk and clean.

"It's a study of the female form. It's not prurient," said Lord Frederick. "It's not supposed to be prurient."

Oddly enough, Lord Frederick flushed. But he quickly gathered himself. "And thank you again, Miss Edgerton, for the privilege. I hope you find more hidden treasures. I cannot wait to see them."

"I will be sure to show you anything I find that very instant," she said, smiling and rising. There was still much, much to do.

Lord Vere called after her, "I'd like to see them too if they look like this, wearing only stockings!"

She did *not* throw a vase at his head. Her canonization was now assured.

❦

Miss Edgerton's movements and gestures intrigued Vere. The way she sometimes played with the ruches on her sleeves. The way she touched her hair, as if deliberately drawing attention to the soft, shining mass of it. The way she listened to Freddie, with one index finger along her jaw, her torso slanted at a slight angle, so that it gave a clear but still discreet impression that she wished to be closer.

But nothing incited Vere—and repelled him—quite as much as her smiles. When she smiled, despite everything, his heart skittered.

There was a science and an art to manufactured

smiles. He, too, was fairly accomplished at smiling, no matter what he truly felt. But she... she was the ceiling at the Sistine Chapel, the glorious, eternal, unsurpassable standard.

Where had she come by the ingénue charm and the virtuoso radiance? How did she manage to retain the honest naïveté in her eyes and the relaxed set to her jaw? Her smiles dazzled so much that sometimes he could not remember what she looked like otherwise.

But she had *not* smiled when she'd discovered that she'd sat on *his* lap. She had not smiled at any point during the ninety minutes his drunken antics had kept her away from her aunt's room. She had not smiled at him just now, as he reveled in her less-than-desirable parentage. And for her, not smiling was akin to another woman leaving the house without her petticoats.

It was what he wanted, wasn't it, to grate on her nerves enough to send her screaming to bedlam? Then why did it incense him so? He was even irked by Freddie, the object of her obvious affection, because Freddie didn't care about it one way or the other—and Freddie almost never rankled him.

"I'm going upstairs for a minute, Penny," said Freddie, rising from the desk where he'd been writing a letter since Miss Edgerton left. "I need my card case."

"I'll come with you," Vere answered. "I've nothing better to do."

He'd been working for hours on deciphering the

code used in Douglas's dossier, with letters marked at the corners of the cards he'd been arranging and rearranging, sifting for patterns. Or at least such had been his aim. He'd accomplished nothing on that front, his concentration flaccid the entire day.

Besides, Miss Edgerton still lurked somewhere in the house.

"Why do you want your card case? Are we calling on somebody?" he asked as they made their way up the stairs.

"No," said Freddie. "I'm writing a letter to Leo Marsden. He's on his way back from India."

"Who?"

"You remember him—we were all in the same house at Eton. I have his address in my card case."

Inside Freddie's room, Freddie opened the drawer of his nightstand and scratched his chin. "That's strange. My card case is not here."

"When was the last time you saw it?"

"This morning." Freddie frowned. "Perhaps I'm not remembering correctly."

Freddie was highly charitable: Most gentlemen would suspect the servants. Vere helped Freddie search around the room to no avail.

"You should tell Miss Edgerton that it's missing."

"I suppose I should."

They did not see Miss Edgerton again, however, until everyone had returned to the house for tea and chitchat on the day's events. Miss Edgerton expressed the appropriate mix of shock and dismay that such a thing should have occurred in her house and promised to do everything in her power to locate the card case and return it to Lord Frederick.

But as she gave her concerned reassurances, new lamb–pure and kitten-sweet, Vere suddenly suspected *her*. What she could possibly want with Freddie's card case he did not know. He knew only that when she didn't smile, there was a hardness to her eyes—a grimness, almost.

And that his instincts were almost always correct.

Lady Avery's demeanor at dinner elevated Vere's unease from mere disquiet to active alarm. He knew Lady Avery very well: A man of his profession would be foolish not to embrace such a fount of information. And he recognized her bloodhound look: eyes squinted, nostrils almost quivering, ready to pounce upon a meaty scandal if only she could follow its scent to the source of the delectable transgression.

Something was afoot. That in itself was not strange, but this something was *suddenly* afoot. For at tea Lady Avery had shown no sign of the hunt, content merely to tantalize Miss Melbourne and Miss Duvall with gossip too improper for their maidenly ears.

What could possibly have put Lady Avery on such alert? The girls, notwithstanding their youth and love of fun, were not a particularly scandal-prone group.

Miss Melbourne's main interest lay in her figure; Miss Duvall's in music. Miss Beauchamp nursed a strong tendresse for her second cousin, who was not present. And Miss Kingsley, despite her flirtation with Conrad, was keener on education than on marriage—she was due back at Girton in October.

Which left their hostess.

Vere stuck close to Freddie. Nothing happened. Dinner came and went. The evening's entertainment was staid and appropriate. The ladies retired at a decent hour. As the clock struck half past eleven, he was beginning to believe that perhaps, for once, he'd overreacted; that what he'd considered his own instinctual sensitivity to the undercurrents of the gathering had been but a raging case of paranoia.

And then, two minutes later, a sleepy-looking footman entered the drawing room bearing a silver salver upon which lay Freddie's card case and a sealed note.

Vere sprang to his feet and raced across the breadth of drawing room, stopping just in time to avoid knocking the footman backward, but not so soon that he didn't knock the silver salver to the ground.

"Sorry!" he cried, and crouched down to retrieve the things meant for Freddie. Then he straightened and patted the footman on the shoulder. "My apologies, my good man. I was too excited: We've been looking for the card case all day. Tell you what: You go on to bed, I'll take the case to my brother. That's who it was for, right?"

He pointed at Freddie.

"Yes, my lord. But I've orders to deliver everything into Lord Frederick's hands."

"Not a problem." Vere sauntered to Freddie and handed over the card case. "See, delivered into Lord Frederick's hands."

"Thank you, sir," said the footman, and left.

Freddie checked the contents of the case. "I wonder where she found it."

"Ask her tomorrow," said Vere. "At least now you can address your letter to Marsden."

He waited a few minutes before he left the room to read the sealed note that he'd pocketed with a sleight of hand.

> *Dear Lord Frederick,*
>
> *Here is your card case, which one of the maids found on the service stairs.*
> *And if I may please borrow a minute of your time, just now I have discovered, among my father's things, a sketch of such beauty and skill, signed by a name so majestic that I dare not set it down in writing for fear of making a fool of myself.*
> *May I trouble you for a look? My excitement refuses to let me wait. If you would please meet me in fifteen minutes in the green parlor, I would be much obliged.*
>
> *Elissande Edgerton*

Elissande. A beautiful name. Almost cutting, like a mouthful of sharply faceted gems. And lovely, clever Elissande wished to meet Freddie at close to midnight, well after the ladies had retired, far away from the drawing room and the billiard room, where the gentlemen still lingered.

A rendezvous alone, in a remote part of the house—with Lady Avery in an overexcited state of anticipation.

He had entirely underestimated Miss Edgerton's interest in Freddie, it would seem.

❧

Elissande trembled. This made her nervous. Her aunt was the trembler, not she. She had steady hands and eyes that remained unblinkingly limpid no matter how terrified she was.

Perhaps she could use the trembling to her advantage. A lady meeting a gentleman at an unorthodox hour ought to tremble a little, ought she not? It would give her suddenly unleashing passion a touch of authenticity, and that, in turn, might inspire Lord Frederick to a more heartfelt response.

She touched her shoulders. She'd unraveled the stitches that held the top of her nightdress together. Underneath her robe, it literally hung on by a thread. A tug with any force would split it in two and send the anchorless halves sliding toward the floor.

And what have you found this time, Miss Edgerton? Lord Frederick would ask.

And she would gaze upon him as if he were the

Second Coming itself. *Oh, forgive me, sir. I know I shouldn't have, but ever since we met, I haven't been able to stop thinking about you.*

At least that last part was mostly true.

She breathed deeply, out, in, out, in. It was time. She pulled her robe tight, prayed that she wouldn't rend her nightdress before its time, and left her bedchamber to head to the green parlor.

The light was on in the parlor. Japanese prints depicting the four seasons took up the walls. Vases and incense holders of jade echoed the lotus leaf hue of the silk wallpaper. Large, clear bottles, raised to chest level on custom-made stands, contained intricately crafted model ships—prisoners, just like her.

And she was alone in the room.

She blinked. She'd meant to arrive a few minutes after Lord Frederick. He should be here already, a little startled at her informal state of attire, perhaps, but eager and impatient to see exactly what too-good-to-believe treasure she'd uncovered.

No fire had been laid in the grate. After two minutes or so pacing madly about the room, she realized she was trembling far worse, as much from the chill in the air as from a sudden onset of panic—her plan was worth nothing without Lord Frederick.

Her hands inched near the flame of her handcandle, hungry for its meager heat. She breathed fast and shallow. The air smelled of turpentine, from the furniture paste the maids had applied.

The mantel clock striking the hour made her

jump. It was the time she'd stated in the unsigned note, with its wax seal already broken, that she'd left outside Lady Avery's door. *Midnight. The green parlor. My heart sighs for you.* And she knew Lady Avery had discovered the seemingly accidentally dropped note, because throughout the evening, she had scrutinized the gathering incessantly, trying to discover which love-demented pair dared set an assignation right beneath her nose.

And now it was all for naught.

Numbly, Elissande extinguished the light in the parlor and headed out toward her uncle's study—to avoid running into Lady Avery, who would most likely be coming from the direction of the front hall. Beyond the study were the service stairs. She would return to her room that way.

She came to a dead stop outside the study. She'd specifically informed her guests that the study was off-limits. But the study door was ajar and the light was on.

She pushed the door open the rest of the way. Lord Vere stood before the cabinets, opening them one after another, humming to himself.

"Lord Vere, what are you doing here?"

"Oh, hullo, Miss Edgerton," he replied cheerfully. "I'm looking for a book. I like to read before I go to sleep, you see. It's better than laudanum by far. Two pages—sometimes two paragraphs—and I sleep like a baby. Nothing like it, especially Latin verse. A bit of Latin verse and I won't get out of bed before ten o'clock in the morning."

She was surprised he could read at all, let alone read in Latin. "I'm sorry, sir, but you are in the wrong place. The books are in the library, not here."

"Ah, no wonder. I thought this was the library—was just telling myself what a bizarre sort of library it was." He stepped out into the passage. "I say, Miss Edgerton, what are you doing here? Haven't the ladies gone to bed already?"

"I forgot something."

"What is it? Can I help you find it?"

She was about to say she'd already found it when she realized that she had nothing on her except her hand-candle.

"I can find it myself, thank you, sir."

"Please do let me help."

This was the last thing she needed—to be possibly caught with *him* by Lady Avery. But Lady Avery had not yet arrived. Judging by the lack of footsteps anywhere near, she would not arrive for another minute or two, plenty enough time for Elissande to march back to the green parlor next door, pick up any old bric-a-brac, pronounce it found, and get rid of Lord Vere.

So that was what she did, Lord Vere in tow. Once in the green parlor, with only her hand-candle for illumination, she headed directly for the mantel, grabbed the nearest object, and said, "There. I have it."

"Oh, what a nice snow globe," said Lord Vere.

She could have picked up something else, anything else. The malachite candlestick, for example. The plain Chinese urn that held the spills for starting a fire in the grate. But she hadn't picked up anything else; she'd picked up the snow globe with a miniature village inside: church, high street, snow-covered cottages—the last Christmas present Aunt Rachel had given her, eight years ago.

It had snowed that Christmas Day. Her uncle, in one of his moods, had disappeared somewhere by himself. Elissande had persuaded Aunt Rachel, whose health had improved steadily under Elissande's care, to come outside for a walk in the snow. They'd made a topsy-turvy snowman. And then, somehow, they'd begun a snowball fight.

It had been a spirited battle. Aunt Rachel had good aim—who would have guessed? Elissande's overcoat had been full of the splattered remains of snowballs that had hit her straight and true. But she hadn't been so bad herself either. How Aunt Rachel had run screaming from her, and then laughed hysterically as she was hit squarely in the bottom.

She could see her aunt, her not-yet-graying hair escaping her bun, her face pink from exertion, bending down to form another snowball. Only to suddenly freeze, still crouched low, as she realized that her husband had returned.

Elissande never forgot her uncle's expression: anger, followed by a frightful flash of pleasure, of anticipation. By her laughter, her rosy cheeks, by the mere fact that she was at *play*, Aunt Rachel had betrayed herself. She had not been completely broken. There was still youth and vitality left in her. Her uncle, of course, could not allow this grave offense to pass unpunished.

Aunt Rachel had not left the house since.

Elissande glanced at Lord Vere, who seemed fascinated by the snow globe, which she herself could not bear to look at. He stood very close to her. She took in his broad shoulders, his strong neck, and the rather unbelievably perfect sweep of his brows. He did not smell of cigar smoke tonight, but only of foliage—belatedly she noticed his bouton-niere, a sprig of hard green berries pinned to a leaf of fir.

Could she bring herself to marry *him,* knowing there was nothing else to him, a pure void behind those already vacant eyes? Could she tolerate a life-time of his prattling and bosom staring? Could she smile at him for the rest of her days?

Her grip tightened on the snow globe. *I thought it would be a little grander,* her aunt had said as Elissande shook the globe for the first time. *I wanted something beautiful for you.*

Desperation. She thought she'd known it all her life. She'd never truly known it until this moment.

Distant footsteps. Lady Avery was coming.

She set down both her hand-candle and the snow globe, and smiled at Lord Vere. She was trembling again. Good. Trembling went well with the words that tumbled from her lips.

"Oh, dear sir, forgive me. I shouldn't. But ever since we met, I haven't been able to stop thinking about you," she said, undoing the sash at her waist and casting the dressing gown behind her.

Lord Vere's eyes widened. She wasted no time in stepping hard on the hem of her nightdress. The threads at her shoulder snapped. The nightdress whispered as it slid down her naked body.

Chapter Eight

For once in his life, Vere didn't need to *act* flabbergasted. He was struck dumb, his limbs turned to stone, his brain a pulped turnip.

His eyes, however, remained quite functional. She was ripe perfection, like a Degas nude, all curves and softness and shadowed mysteries. And then she came toward him, her lips parted, her skin smooth and lovely, her nipples the very points at which the darkness kissed the illumination of the candle flame.

Her arms raised and intertwined behind his neck. She smelled, as she always did, of honey and roses. Her mouth, cool and quivering, touched his.

Reaction jolted through him. Lust, an astonishing quantity of it, but not lust alone: He was finally shocked out of his paralysis.

How could he have missed it so badly? Her aunt was a broken woman who no longer knew how to scream even when terrified. Miss Edgerton herself could and did smile under almost all circumstances.

Everything pointed to her uncle being a monster. She didn't just want a husband. She wanted a way out of this house.

And she was desperate enough that even he would do.

He disengaged her arms and backed away from her. She followed him. Without thinking, he yanked the curtain next to him from its mooring and tossed ten yards of double muslin at her. She flailed inside the tent of fabric, a pornographer's idea of a girl mummy.

He ran. But encumbered as she was, she tackled him. Hard. Her weight crashing into him unbalanced him just enough to tumble them both over the curved, padded arm of a chaise longue, knocking down a stand in the process.

Something made of glass broke loudly—one of the ships in bottles. Something else crashed too—the hand-candle. The room plunged into darkness. He tried to heave her off him, but she was as demonically strong as one of Jules Verne's giant octopuses, her arms welded to him. He set one foot down on the ground, turned so that she was against the back of the chaise, and pushed.

Yes, her hold on him was loosening. He pushed harder. She emitted a muffled scream of frustration. Or was it pain? He didn't care. He had to be rid of her. She struggled with renewed vigor. Dear God, she almost kneed him in the groin.

He wasn't sure what happened, but suddenly the chaise longue overturned along its length, dumping the two of them onto the carpet. They rolled a turn and a half before coming to a stop, she again on top of him, but this time without the curtain.

Her hair had come entirely loose during the struggle. She panted. Her beautiful breasts rose and fell. And just visible behind the cascade of her hair, small, tightly budded nipples—

How could he see anything? Hadn't the candle gone out earlier? His eyes followed the source of illumination up and up, his gut already comprehending what his mind did not want to acknowledge.

There was someone else in the room.

"Oh, my. Oh, my, my, my," Lady Avery murmured. Then she giggled. "I must say, I did not expect the two of *you.*"

Now Miss Edgerton leaped off him. *Now* she wrapped herself in the muslin curtain. *Now* she stammered, "It's . . . it's not what you think."

"No? What do you think this is, Lady Kingsley?"

Bloody hell, not Lady Kingsley too.

Their eyes met. "I . . . ah . . ." Lady Kingsley stammered, her shock almost as strong as Vere's own. "It is certainly an inconvenient situation."

"Inconvenient, Lady Kingsley? Inconvenient is when your footman breaks his leg and you've no one but your parlor maid to serve tea to your callers. *This* is scandalous. And to think, Lord Vere, that your father was a schoolmate of Sir Bernard Edgerton, Miss Edgerton's uncle."

Until this mention of his late father, it had not occurred to Vere that being caught in Miss Edgerton's scheme would lead all the way to the altar. After all, he'd known her for only three days. He had not touched her in truth. And he was an idiot, for God's sake; surely some consideration must be given to that fact.

But that was apparently not the way Lady Avery's mind worked. He had compromised a young lady of good standing—never mind that the young lady had a loose-moraled mother; never mind that the young lady engineered the encounter herself—and therefore marriage must follow suit. And Vere, publicly at least, was a nice, docile idiot, not the sort to willingly stand by and watch a girl go to "ruin."

He put on his most thickly bovine expression, rose to his feet with a stumble and a grunt, and looked around. "Sorry for the nice ship-in-a-bottle, Miss Edgerton."

"It's quite all right," she said in a small voice.

"Arrangements, children, arrangements," chided Lady Avery. "Arrangements must be made. Isn't the archbishop of Canterbury your second cousin, Lord Vere? He will no doubt be glad to issue a special license to you."

"Oh, is he? My second cousin? I had no idea. Perhaps I shan't bother him, just in case he isn't."

"Banns then?" Miss Edgerton asked hesitantly.

She did it very well, this virginal timidity.

"Absolutely not. Very quaint, but not the thing to do at all, especially not under the circumstances," proclaimed Lady Avery. "You should ask your uncle to apply for a special license for you, Miss Edgerton."

"Oh, I don't know—"

"When your uncle comes home, you will explain the matter to him. He will meet Lord Vere. He will obtain the special license. Then we will all be delighted to attend your wedding."

Miss Edgerton said nothing.

"Very good. Now to bed," said Lady Avery, satisfied. "And no more secret meetings between the two of you. You are to be married. And that means your days of clandestine lovemaking are behind you."

❧

But the ordeal was far from over.

The other gentlemen had gathered outside the small parlor—no doubt drawn by the fearsome crashes Vere and Miss Edgerton had caused during their struggle. Lady Avery and Lady Kingsley, after putting Miss Edgerton back into her dressing gown, quickly whisked her away, leaving Vere behind to fend for himself.

"What happened?" Wessex asked, even though it couldn't be more obvious what had happened.

Vere ignored the question, walked past Wessex, marched out of the front door of the house, and did not stop until he was in the middle of the garden. And even then, it was only to pull out a cigarette and light it.

"I'm sorry," said Freddie, who had followed him out. "I should have said something."

Vere expelled a lungful of smoke. "What would you have said?"

"I was—I was thinking of telling you to be more careful."

The irony. "Me, be more careful?"

Freddie stuck his hands into his coat pockets. "Last night I was out walking late—and I saw the two of you, just the two of you, going back into the house. And in the morning, I thought you might be having your nightmare again. But when I opened my door I saw her coming out of your room."

Vere sucked hard on his cigarette. *Christ.*

"I thought at the time that surely there was an innocent explanation for everything—you know, that she'd heard your nightmare and come to check on you..."

Vere threw down his cigarette and crushed it under his heel.

Freddie sighed. He took the cigarette case and the matchbox out of Vere's pocket, lit another fag, and handed it to Vere. Vere sighed and accepted Freddie's offering. How could he be angry at Freddie?

"I'm sorry," Freddie said again.

Vere shook his head. "It's not your fault."

Freddie, who usually refrained from tobacco, lit a cigarette for himself. They smoked in silence.

"Will you be all right?" Freddie asked, after they'd had two cigarettes apiece.

Vere stared up at the starry sky. "I'll be fine."

"Well," Freddie said, hesitating, "I *have* seen the way you look at her. And since she does return your regard... I mean, you have been trying to find a wife for a while, haven't you?"

Had any man ever been so perfectly hoisted with his own petard? Next thing Vere knew, people would be genuinely delighted for him, that by hook or by crook he finally landed himself a wife. And once they'd had a look at her bosomy comeliness, he'd be the subject of a thousand congratulatory slaps on the back.

"She *is* very cheerful," Freddie continued. "And she listens when you speak."

When you *speak,* Vere wanted to retort.

He yanked off his necktie. "I think I'll go for a walk now, if you don't mind."

❧

As it turned out, one walk wasn't enough. Lady Kingsley was waiting for him in his room, nodding off, when he returned at two o'clock in the morning. The conversation she desired necessitated another trip out of the house.

He thought she wanted to speak of the ramifications concerning the investigation at hand. But that was not at all the case.

"Just now she came to my room and begged me to help her," said Lady Kingsley.

He glanced at her sharply.

"She said her uncle will kill her if he learns what happened. She wants to be gone from Highgate Court before he returns."

"And you *agreed* to help her?"

"I know you are not one, but the world is full of awful men who do unspeakable things to women who depend on them. I have no reason not to believe her. And since you must marry her anyway, I told her I would arrange for a special license for the two of you and that we will leave at first light for London."

"Is that all?" he asked coolly.

"She wants to bring her aunt along."

"Well, then, the more the merrier."

Lady Kingsley looked at him uncertainly, then placed a hand on his sleeve. "I don't know whether to console you or to congratulate you. I know you didn't quite have marriage in mind when you began your assignation, but if she gets you this carried away, marriage is not the most terrible outcome."

He'd expected better from Lady Kingsley. He'd expected her to know that it was entirely out of character for him to be *this* carried away and therefore to harbor at least *some* suspicion of foul play on Miss Edgerton's part.

Instead it was Freddie all over again, with the implication that Vere was largely, if not entirely, responsible.

"If you will excuse me," he said. "I'm quite exhausted."

Chapter Nine

Elissande packed, first in her own room, then in her aunt's. Aunt Rachel sometimes woke up in the middle of the night and took another dose of laudanum—which made her difficult to awaken in the morning—and Elissande needed to prevent that.

She finished packing at quarter to five. At five o'clock she began to rouse her aunt. Aunt Rachel was confused and sluggish. But Elissande was determined. She finished Aunt Rachel's usual morning ablutions, fed her a good portion of arrowroot pudding, and brushed her teeth.

It was not until she brought out actual clothes that Aunt Rachel first realized this was not to be another ordinary day in the Douglas household.

"We are leaving," Elissande said to Aunt Rachel's unspoken question.

"We?" Aunt Rachel croaked.

"Yes, you and I. I'm getting married and I need your help in setting up my new household."

Aunt Rachel clenched Elissande's hand in hers. "Married? To whom?"

"If you wish to meet him, dress and come with me."

"Where—where are we going?"

"London." Lady Kingsley had told her that she would help Elissande obtain a special license from the bishop of London.

"Does—does your uncle know?"

"No."

Aunt Rachel trembled. "What if—what will happen when he finds out?"

Elissande took Aunt Rachel into her arms. "My fiancé is a marquess. My uncle cannot harm me once I'm married. You come with me now and you need never see him again either: Lord Vere will protect us."

Aunt Rachel shook harder. "Are you—are you sure, Ellie?"

"Yes." She was a terrific liar: Her smiles were her best lies, but she was no slouch with words. "We may put our absolute confidence in Lord Vere. He is a prince among men."

She did not know whether she convinced Aunt Rachel completely. But Aunt Rachel became pliant enough that Elissande had no trouble dressing her in a pale green silk morning gown trimmed in white chiffon, and a hat of green velvet to match.

Unfortunately, real clothes only emphasized her aunt's grayish pallor, stick-thinness, and that particular shrinking quality she had, as if she yearned at all times toward invisibility—but she looked presentable enough. For Aunt Rachel's sake, Elissande could only pray that Lord Vere would appear half as formidable as she'd made him out to be.

Aunt Rachel started upon meeting her soon-to-be nephew-in-law. Elissande could well relate to that sense of delightful surprise. Inspecting him from the point of view of a stranger, she could not deny that he was a very impressive-looking man.

He was beautifully attired: all buttons properly aligned with their intended buttonholes, trousers free from food stains, and necktie not the least bit crooked. He spoke minimally—stunned into near silence by the enormity of the situation, she didn't doubt. And he dutifully proclaimed himself honored and delighted at the "bestowal of Miss Edgerton's hand."

When she had shoved that hand deep down his esophagus.

He gave her one look, a quick scan of her person. She was dressed demurely in gray chiffon broadcloth—not that she could fool Lord Vere anymore as to what kind of woman she was. The thought suddenly came to her that perhaps she hadn't needed to be entirely naked, that it might have been good enough to have been caught in his arms in her combination undergarment.

Instead he'd seen all of her.

She swallowed, looked down, and was glad when Lady Kingsley ordered everyone into the carriage.

Vere made sure he and Freddie traveled in a separate train compartment, away from the women. He slept while Freddie sketched next to him. Upon reaching London, Lady Kingsley warned him not to stray too far from his house, so she could inform him of the hour and location of his wedding.

The women left to do what women did when faced with imminent nuptials. Vere declined Freddie's offer of company and sent a note for Holbrook to meet him in the same hidey-hole where they'd last met.

The whorehouse—their sobriquet for this particular hidey-hole—had always amused Vere with its indelicate colors and its clumsy but wholehearted attempts at elegance. But today its faux tiger-skin rug and its purple lamp shades chafed his vision and chafed it badly.

Holbrook arrived in short order. Vere tossed down the coded dossier. "From Douglas's safe. It's yours for the day."

"Thank you, my lord. Well done, as always," said Holbrook. "I shall have it duplicated in no time."

He handed Vere a glass of Poire Williams—fruit brandies of all types fascinated Holbrook. "I understand that congratulations are in order."

Vere refrained from mentioning that Holbrook hardly had cause to offer another man matrimonial felicitations, since the late Lady Holbrook had once stuck a knife in him. "Thank you, sir."

"What happened?"

Vere lit a cigarette, took a drag, and shrugged.

"Not the proudest moment in an otherwise distinguished career, was it?" Holbrook commented lazily.

Vere flicked the barely forming ashes from his cigarette.

Holbrook played with the bead fringes of an antimacassar. "The suspect's niece, no less."

"My appeal is universal." Vere drained his glass. Enough chitchat. "There was a relative with whom Douglas lived for a while in London, wasn't there?"

"There was. Mrs. John Watts. London Street, Jacob's Island." Holbrook possessed an unerring memory. "But she's been dead a long time."

"Thank you." Vere rose from his seat. "I'll see myself out."

"Are you sure, sir? On your wedding day?"

What *else* was he to do on this day? Whore and carouse? Drink himself into a ditch? Form an opium habit?

"But of course," he said softly. "How better to enjoy this day and all that shall come with it?"

❧

"I still can't believe it. Penny, getting married," said Angelica Carlisle, Freddie's oldest friend, chortling.

She and Freddie were taking coffee—her new continental habit—in the drawing room of the town house that had once belonged to her mother.

Freddie had attended many a tea and dinner party here, read most of the books in the study, and regularly visited on Sundays, the day of the week strictly reserved for family and closest friends. Angelica had already mentioned the changes she intended to make to the interior of the house. But she was still settling in—she'd been back in England only a month. The house remained unaltered. And the very familiarity of the setting—comfortably faded rose-and-ivy wallpaper, lovingly preserved watercolors by long-perished spinster aunts, commemorative plates from Her Majesty's Silver Jubilee, thirty-five years ago—made the difference in her person all the more startling.

He'd always thought her handsome, strong boned and strong featured, remarkable rather than pretty. But during the years of her brief marriage and widowhood, she'd acquired a certain seductiveness to her person. Her eyes, instead of the wide-open alertness he recalled, were now heavy lidded and mysterious. Her smiles, usually just a slight upturn of one corner of her lips, somehow also radiated sultriness, as if while she conducted herself with perfect decorum, she'd been harboring very naughty thoughts beneath that façade of propriety.

And he, to his own dismay, began thinking of her as an object of desire for the first time in his life. *Angelica,* who'd always been like a sister to him, a pesky, too-honest, merciless younger sister who told him that his tailor was blind *and* incompetent, that he needed to brush his teeth at least three minutes longer, and that if he'd had more than two drops of champagne, he was not allowed to dance the waltz for the sake of public safety.

She took a sip of her coffee, chuckled again, and

shook her head. One coil of her hair, artfully loose, stroked the edge of her jaw, lending a new softness to the angularity of her features. As if aware of the fascination that one curl held over him, she pulled it straight between two fingers, then let go.

Somehow she imbued even such a minor motion with the full potency of her new powers, with the seduction of Eve.

He realized he hadn't answered and hastened to speak. "Penny is twenty-nine. He has to marry at some point."

"Of course that is the case. It's the scandal that shocks me. As much as I might roll my eyes at some of his antics, Penny isn't one to get himself into serious trouble."

"I know," said Freddie. "Perhaps I shouldn't have let my guard down."

He'd been fifteen when Penny's riding accident happened. It had been the rare summer week they'd spent apart: he with their late mother's cousin in Biarritz, Penny in Aberdeenshire with Lady Jane, their paternal great-aunt.

For the first few months after Penny's accident, Freddie had been worried sick. But after a while, it became clear that while Penny would never again lucidly trace the history of the Plebeian Council or make a devilishly persuasive case for granting women the right to vote, he also did not need a nursemaid all hours of the day. It had been a small mercy in a devastating turn of events, the unfairness of which still haunted Freddie. His brilliant, brave brother, who had claimed Freddie's mistakes as his own before their unkind father, and who could have had a significant career in Parliament, reduced to an expert in little more than his own daily schedule.

"You did say you didn't think Miss Edgerton was after Penny merely for his title and fortune."

"Her uncle has a diamond mine in South Africa and no children of his own. I don't think she is after him for his fortune, at least."

Angelica took a bite of her Madeira cake. He watched her absently wiping away the butter the rich cake left on her fingers, almost as if she were caressing the napkin. He imagined her fingers caressing *him* instead.

"So what do you think of this Miss Edgerton?" she asked.

He had to reel his mind back from the sensual, and sometimes shockingly explicit, thoughts it had a tendency to engage in these days—thoughts that never failed to involve Angelica in some state of undress. "Miss Edgerton, ah, well, she is very pretty, amiable, smiling. Doesn't have much to say, though, except to agree with whoever is speaking."

"That should suit Penny. He likes it when people agree with him."

What neither of them said, out of loyalty to Penny, was that a girl of middling intelligence and not many original thoughts was probably the most Penny could hope for.

"It's been thirteen years since his accident," said

Angelica. "He has managed remarkably well. He will manage this too."

Freddie smiled at her. "You are right. I should have more faith."

They said nothing for a minute or so, she nibbling on another piece of Madeira cake, he turning an almond biscuit in his fingers.

"Well," they said at nearly the same time.

"You first," he offered.

"No, no, you first. You are my visitor; I insist."

"I—I'd like to ask you for a favor," he said.

"In all my years of knowing you I don't remember a single instance of your ever asking me for favors. I will admit it might have had something to do with the fact that I was constantly thrusting my opinions and wishes on you." Her eyes twinkled. "But please, go ahead; I am resolutely intrigued."

He loved the shape of her mouth when she almost smiled. Why had he never noticed before the magnetic pull of her near-smile?

"I saw an interesting painting at Miss Edgerton's house. No one knows the identity of the artist. I believe I've seen a work in a similar style and vein. But I can't remember when or where," he said. "Your memory is far superior for such things, as is your knowledge."

"Hmm, compliments. I adore compliments— flattery will get you far, young man."

"You know I don't know how to flatter." Ten years ago Angelica had already been a singular connoisseur of art. These days she was formidable in her erudition. "I've taken some photographs of the painting. May I show them to you once they have been developed?"

She tilted her head to one side and played with the coil of hair at her jaw again. "But I have not agreed to help you yet. First, I think, I'd like to hear your answer to *my* request for a favor. I have been waiting on an answer for weeks, if you will recall."

And he'd been able to think of nothing else, for weeks.

He flushed despite his intention not to. "You speak of the portrait?"

The *nude* portrait she would like of herself. When he'd insisted to Penny that there was nothing prurient about a study of the female form, his head had been filled with the most carnal visions of Angelica.

"Yes, that's it."

She was direct and almost nonchalant, while he felt gauche, out of his element, and much too warm.

"You know I'm not an expert at the human form."

"You've always been too modest, Freddie dearest. I wouldn't have asked you if I didn't have faith in your abilities. I've seen the studies you've done: You do very well at the human form."

She was right, though it was his *preference* not to paint the human form very often. He had been a clumsy child prone to injuring himself, and as such was kept indoors when he most wished to be outside, running, spinning around and around, or simply lying in the grass and observing the changing color of the sky. Painting the human form meant his studio, when he'd much rather be *en plein air*, capturing the effusive pink cream of a cherry tree in blossom or the undercurrents of a tête-à-tête at a picnic party.

Yet as he looked at her, he already measured in his mind the proportion of Naples ochre and vermilion that he should add to silver-white to approximate the warm, healthy tone of her skin.

"You said it is for your private collection."

"That is my intention."

"So you won't have it exhibited?"

"So much concern for my modesty." She smiled teasingly. "Why can't I display half as much decorum?"

"I need a promise."

For the most part, he was an easygoing man. But he would not yield on this matter.

"I want it for a record of my youth, so that I may one day look back upon it and sigh over my own lost beauty. I promise you solemnly that not only will I not exhibit it anywhere, I will not even display it in my own house. Instead, it will go into a crate, and not be opened again until I see a hag in the mirror." She smiled again. "Will that satisfy you?"

He swallowed. "All right then. I'll do it."

She set down her teacup and gazed directly at him. "In that case, I find myself quite willing to help you track down the provenance of your mysterious painting."

Mrs. Watts had been dead a quarter of a century. Vere considered himself quite lucky to locate, in only a few hours, someone who had once known her.

His search took him from Bermondsey to Seven Dials. Barely a mile away from the spacious squares of Mayfair, Seven Dials had been notorious for its crime and poverty earlier in the century. In recent years, the character of the district had improved, although Vere was still disinclined to venture into its side streets alone at night.

But at the moment it was broad daylight. St. Martin's Lane, which led into the district, was raucous with birds, for it was here that London's bird fanciers gathered. He passed a shop full of songbirds in cages: bullfinches, larks, and starlings, all nervously twittering and chirping. Another shop brimmed with crates upon crates of plump, cooing pigeons. Hawks and owls and parrots amplified the cacophony. He was grateful to pass an occasional establishment specializing in aquatic creatures or rabbits, both blessedly silent.

Jacob Dooley lived on Little Earl Street, where crowds milled about a lively outdoor market, though Vere could not see much for sale that wasn't second- or third-hand goods. What use could any woman make of a set of crinoline hoops in this day and age, he did not know, but he saw not one, not two, but three being hawked as "Height o' fashion!"

Dooley's flat was on the top floor of a four-story building. The front of the building, grandly lettered, advertised the grocer on the ground floor—*Dairy*

Farmer, Family Butcher, Milk Contractor, Large Consumers Supplied. The narrow, dark staircase inside smelled intermittently of urine.

Vere's knock summoned a man in his mid-sixties, broad and hirsute, with a full head of salt-and-pepper hair and a beard of equally mixed shades. He stood behind his partially open door, warily examining Vere. Vere had changed into costume. He was now a burly drayman with a beard that almost rivaled Dooley's in luxuriance. His rough work clothes smelled as they ought: equal parts horse and brewery.

"Who are you? And why are you asking after Mrs. Watts?" Dooley's Irish origin was evident in his speech.

Vere had his answer and his Scouse accent ready. "Mrs. Watts was me dad's auntie, she was. That's how me mum told me. Me dad ran away to London to live with Mrs. Watts."

Dooley's eyes widened. "But Ned was only a lad when he came to live with her, sure he was. Me, I never saw him at all. But Mag—Mrs. Watts—she said he was fourteen when he came and sixteen when he left."

"Well, he had me in me mum before he left Liverpool. Least he had me mum fink so."

Dooley stepped back. "Come in then. I'll give you a cup of tea."

The flat consisted of only one room with a thin yellow curtain in the middle to separate the sitting and the sleeping areas. Dooley had a surprisingly heavy-looking table, two chairs, and a homemade set of shelves on which rested neat piles of newspapers and two large books—one of which looked to be a Bible, the other perhaps a devotional.

Dooley put water from a pitcher and a handful of tea leaves together into a pot and hooked the makeshift kettle over a spirit lamp. "You still have your mum?"

"Lost her December last. She told me before she died about me real dad. I been asking 'bout him since I buried her."

"You are in luck, lad," said Dooley, standing by the spirit lamp. "Last I heard of him, himself was a rich man in South Africa. Diamonds."

Vere stopped breathing for several seconds. He looked at Dooley with eyes full of hope. "You ain't funning me, are you, Mr. Dooley?"

"No. The last time I saw Maggie—your Mrs. Watts— she was after having a cable from him. He was stinking rich and coming home to make her a grand lady. Mind you, I was happy for her, but I was mighty sorry for myself. I was wanting her to marry me. She had a few years on me but she was a good woman, Maggie Watts, and sang real pretty, sure she did. But she wouldn't want a poor sailor like me when her nephew was going to build her a grand place in the country and have her presented to the queen, would she?

"I left on a steamer to San Francisco. And when I came back—" Dooley's jaw tightened. "When I came back she was already in the ground."

"I'm awful sorry." Vere did not need to manufacture his sympathy. He knew it all too well, the grief and bewilderment of loss.

Dooley did not answer for a while, but laid out two cups—the unchipped one for Vere—and sliced half a loaf of dark bread. Although the tea leaves had been boiled with the water, the tea Dooley poured was hardly darker than lemonade—like everything else for sale on the street below, the tea leaves too were secondhand.

"Thank you, sir," said Vere for his tea.

Dooley sat down heavily. "It bothered me all these years how she died—bothers me to this day."

"If you don't mind me asking, sir, how *did* she die?"

"The coroner's report said she died of too much chloral. Fell asleep and never woke up again. I tried to tell the coroner that she never had any such thing about. She was a hardworking woman who slept like the dead at night—you should have heard her snoring. 'Course, it didn't help me any that I said that, made her sound like a loose woman. The coroner—that fool—said that a woman would put that sort of thing away before she entertained a man in her 'place of domicile,' and I should leave the cause of death to men of science."

"You don't fink it was chloral?"

Dooley's face was troubled. "I asked all her neighbors. There were two young girls. They said she was cold—not stone-cold but real cool—and still breathing when they found her. They called for a doctor, but the doctor was a quack and didn't know anything."

He left his seat again and retrieved the book Vere had thought a devotional from the shelves. It was in fact titled *Poisons: Their Effect and Detection—A Manual for the Use of Analytical Chemists and Experts.* Dooley opened the book to a much dog-eared portion. "The way she was sleeping, going colder and colder, that was chloral. And if the doctor was himself a proper doctor, some strychnine could have saved her."

Strychnine caused otherwise deadly muscular convulsions. Yet it was for precisely that reason it was an antidote to an overdose of chloral, aiding the heart's function and putting a halt to the dangerous slide of body temperature. A shot of strychnine had been what the physician had administered in the Haysleigh case—for which Vere had needed much help from Lady Kingsley—to successfully save Lady Haysleigh.

"So it was chloral after all?"

"It was. I'd have sworn before a judge she never used any. But the coroner said she had a good thirty grams, even showed me the bottle." Dooley closed the book, his neck bent. "Maybe I didn't know her as well as I s'posed."

"I'm sorry," Vere said again.

As he took a sip of his hot but largely flavorless tea, he was suddenly reminded of a long dormant case concerning a man named Stephen Delaney. Delaney, too, had died from an overdose of chloral. But as Delaney had not been a poor woman carrying on an affair the coroner found distasteful, but an ascetic man of science—not to mention brother to a bishop—his death had received much more attention from the law when his family had strenuously protested that he had never kept any chloral.

Nothing had come of the investigation. By the time Vere had read the file, seven years ago, it had been thick with a decade of undisturbed dust. And even he had to concede, when he finished his reading, that there was nothing for anyone to go on.

"Here I go again," said Dooley, "getting caught up talking about my poor Maggie when you wanted to hear about your dad."

"If he's me dad, then she was me auntie too—me great-grandauntie."

"There's that. There's that." Dooley set his thick, calloused hands on the book of poisons. "But I can't tell you much more."

"Didn't you say he was going to come and see her and make her a grand lady?"

"He never did. His secretary came, but he never did."

Vere had to fight to make himself sound deflated. "His secretary?"

"That's what Fanny Nobb said. She said a real fine gentleman came to see Maggie a few days before she died. Your dad had to stay behind in Kimberley, in the diamond fields, so he sent his secretary to take care of things in London. The secretary was to look for a fancy house for Maggie and take her to buy everything she wanted. Maybe that was why she needed the chloral—too wound up to sleep."

Vere's heart thumped. Instead of the brawler Edmund Douglas, "a real fine gentleman" had come in his stead. And shortly afterward Mrs. Watts had died of a substance her lover was certain she had never used.

If his suspicions were right, if Douglas had not even come by the diamond mine by his own luck, then in a twisted way, his hunger for success in other arenas of business made sense. He was trying to prove that he did have what it took to thrive without the help of his criminality—except he didn't.

"Me dad, did he come for Mrs. Watts's funeral then?" Vere asked.

"Not enough time, was there? She died in July; had to put her underground real fast. But he did wire the money for her funeral expenses, Fanny said."

"The secretary, he didn't come to the funeral either?"

"I can't tell you. I was in San Francisco, drunk as a skunk. Sure I was." The old man sighed. "I thought about it a few times—looking up your dad and maybe telling him about my Maggie. But I never did. Never helped him any, and didn't want him to think I was after his money."

Vere nodded and came to his feet. "Thank you, Mr. Dooley."

"Sorry I couldn't tell you more."

"It was plenty what you did tell me, sir."

Dooley offered Vere his hand. "Good luck to you, young man."

Vere shook Dooley's rough hand, aware that this was where his disguise might fall apart: He didn't have the hands of a workingman. But Dooley, still in the grips of the past, did not notice.

For Dooley there would never be justice enough: He had already lost the woman he loved. But Vere might yet uncover the whole truth of what had happened to Mrs. Watts.

And that was what he would do.

Chapter Ten

The interior of the church was stone, the architecture Norman Romanesque. A gray, damp light fell from the windows of the clerestory. Here and there the cool gloom of the sanctuary was dispelled by the golden light of fat white candles, held aloft on candelabra as tall as Vere.

Freddie, who had been waiting outside, entered with Mrs. Douglas, helping her into a pew. Lady Kingsley came up to the altar and gave Vere a small nod—she would act the part of the matron of honor.

The church door opened and closed again, accompanied by a draft of humid, nippy air—the arrival of the woman who was to become Lady Vere in short order. Vere swallowed, agitated despite himself—and not merely with righteous indignation.

She was halfway down the aisle when he at last looked in her direction.

She wore the plainest wedding gown he'd ever seen,

unadorned by anything lacy, feathery, or glittery. Her accessories consisted of a bouquet of violets in her hands, a veil covering her hair, and her smile.

He did not like her but he had to admire her, for it was the most beautiful smile he'd ever seen on the face of a bride. Nothing gloating or boastful to it, only a simple and shyly serene joy—as if she were marrying the man of her dreams and could not believe her sheer good fortune.

He turned his head away.

The ceremony lasted and lasted—the clergyman was the wordy sort who saw no reason to abbreviate his homilies, even though the irregular nature of the proceedings must be obvious. The rain, which began at the same time as the ceremony, had intensified to a steady shower by the time Vere and his bride emerged from the church, arm in arm.

He handed her into the waiting carriage, then climbed in himself. She was surprised when the carriage door closed behind him. Her gaze flickered to him. In the sudden tightness of her posture he sensed her understanding—deep down—of what being married meant. That she would now be alone with him, and there would be no one to chaperone them.

No one to say what he could or could not do.

She smiled at him, a very proper, blissful-new-bride smile—it was her method of exerting control over any given situation. And yet he, who should—and did—know so much better, experienced once more an unwarranted flutter of happiness.

He tried to call to mind his once-constant companion, but he could no longer form an unpolluted image of her. Her simplicity had been spoiled by Lady Vere's complicity, her warm ease distorted by his wife's cold calculation.

He did not smile back at the woman he'd married. It occurred to him that there was quite enough time on the drive to the hotel—only two miles, but the rain was certain to cause delays in the traffic—for him to take her.

That would wipe the smile from her face.

Her fingers flicked away drops of rain that had landed on the glossy silk of her skirt. The material was heavy and chaste. She was swaddled, every single inch south of her chin. Even her hair was largely invisible beneath the veil. But he already knew what his sweet-faced liar looked like undressed, didn't he?

If he lowered the window shades, he could disrobe her this moment, from the top down—or bottom up, if he were so inclined. Actions had consequences. These would be her consequences: horror, revulsion, and eventually arousal; her nakedness separated from the elements by nothing but the black leather-padded walls of a Clarence brougham; the sounds she'd make, under him, muffled by the hard drumming of the rain on the roof, the clacking and grinding of a torrent of carriages, and the continual din that was London being London.

She turned and looked out the rear window. "Ah, they are right behind us."

As if it mattered.

He did not answer her, but turned his face toward the soggy world outside, while his bride sat still and breathed with quiet, meticulous care.

❧

Elissande stood on the balcony of her suite at the very top of the Savoy Hotel. London was a muted, distant murmur. Light from Victoria Embankment rippled on the dark waters of the River Thames. The great spires of the city rose tall and black against the shadows of the night.

She had been married four hours.

She'd describe her marriage thus far as hushed.

She'd also describe it as long.

His silence had been nerve-wracking on the drive back to the hotel. There she'd discovered that neither Lady Kingsley nor Lord Frederick would join them for dinner: The former was in a hurry to get back to her guests, the latter, having recently accepted a commission, needed to gather the necessary matériel to begin his work. After she'd seen to Aunt Rachel's dinner and put her to bed, she and Lord Vere had dined alone in a private room and he'd said not a word to her—*not a single word*—beyond a barely audible "Amen" at the end of grace. And now this interminable wait in their suite, which, while in terms of absolute time had yet to surpass the length of dinner, already had her in a state of head-throbbing tension.

Or perhaps that was the three glasses of champagne that she'd tossed back one after another.

Had she never read the book on matrimonial law

that had once been in her uncle's library, perhaps she would now be tentatively rejoicing that she was both married and blessedly left alone. But with knowledge came fear: an unconsummated marriage carried severe risks.

Had her uncle returned to Highgate Court yet? Had he learned what had happened and set out in pursuit? Was he even now hunting them in London?

And where was Lord Vere? Smoking? Drinking? Gone elsewhere by himself, even though a small suitcase of his had been delivered to the suite?

What if her uncle should locate her husband, sit him down for a talk, and point out all the obvious reasons why he did not want to be married to Elissande? Once he had Lord Vere convinced, it was only a short hop to an annulment, which would leave her with no husband, no protection, and not even the right to brag of having ever been married.

The height of the hotel was suddenly dizzying. She retreated into the relative safety of the sitting room, where on the table sat a small, beautifully iced cake, with pale blush marzipan roses blooming along deep green marzipan vines—her wedding cake, compliments of the hotel. With the cake had come a cake knife, napkins, plates, a bottle of champagne, and a bottle of Sauternes.

And no one to share any of it with.

She had been certain some mishap would erupt during the wedding ceremony. Lord Vere would mangle his vows. He would say the name of some other lady. Or, God forbid, he would decide at the last moment that he could not go through with the wedding, his reputation and her ruin be damned.

Instead he'd been solemn and steady. And she'd been the one to say his name wrong—Spencer Russell Blandford Churchill Stuart was quite a mouthful—and stumble over her vows not once, but twice.

Married.

She dared not understand it fully.

The door handle rattled lightly. She leaped to her feet. She'd locked the suite door out of fear of her uncle's sudden appearance.

"Who is it?" Her voice was wobbly. Breathless, almost.

"Is this Lady Vere's room?"

Lord Vere's—her husband's voice.

She squeezed her eyes shut a second, then moved forward.

Smile.

She had her smile in place before she opened the door. "Good evening, Lord Vere."

"Evening, Lady Vere."

He still wore the dark gray formal coat in which he'd been married—and which had somehow remained miraculously immaculate.

"May I come in?" he asked very politely, his hat in hand.

She realized that she had been standing in his way, staring at him. "Of course. I beg your pardon."

Would he notice her flushed complexion? He might, if he'd look at her. But he only walked past her into the middle of the sitting room and glanced about.

The suite had been furnished in the manner of a gentleman's home, the wallpapers a muted blue, the furniture sturdy yet unobtrusive. In Aunt Rachel's suite there had been Chinese vases painted in red ochre; here there were blue Delft plates displayed in a semicircle above a mahogany chiffonier.

"The cake is here," she said for something to say, locking the door again behind her.

He turned around, not so much at her words, but at the sound of the door locking—for that was where his gaze flicked before coming to rest on her face.

He had misunderstood what she meant by locking the door. He thought she signaled that she was ready to be his wife in truth: There was a tautness to his stare, a challenge almost.

She found she couldn't hold his gaze. Her eyes instead focused on the boutonniere on his lapel, a single blossom of blue delphinium, the color so deep and rich it was almost purple.

"The cake is here," she repeated herself. "Would you like me to cut it?"

"It would be a pity to eat it; it's too pretty."

She hurried to the table and reached for the cake knife. "Even something too pretty to eat will still spoil if no one eats it."

"How profound," he murmured.

Was that *irony* she heard in his voice?

She glanced at him and belatedly noticed that he

clutched a bottle of whiskey by its neck in his left hand.

She swallowed. Of course he was not happy. He'd been abused abominably. He knew quite well he had been entrapped.

Any idiot would know that.

She grimaced at the vocabulary of her thought, lowered her face, and attacked the cake, heaping his plate with an oversized slice. He set down the whiskey bottle, accepted the cake, and walked across the sitting room to the balcony.

She wished he'd revert to his blabbering ways. She could not have imagined that his silence would be so difficult to ignore—or to fill.

"Would you like something to drink with the cake?" she asked. "Some whiskey, perhaps?"

"Whiskey doesn't go well with cake." He sounded faintly impatient.

"Sauternes then?"

He shrugged.

She looked at the bottle of Sauternes. There was a cork underneath the wax seal. She believed it called for a corkscrew. And indeed, one had been supplied, between the bottles. She picked it up and turned it around in her palm. How did one use it? Uncorking bottles was the work of the servants at home.

"Should I call for assistance?" she asked timidly.

He returned to the table and set down his untouched cake. Taking the corkscrew from her, he inserted it into the cork. With a few deft turns of his wrist and one decisive pull, the cork emerged with a clean pop. He poured a full glass and set it before her, poured a full tumbler of whiskey for himself, and returned to the balcony with only that.

The rain had abated to a near-mist when she had returned to the suite after dinner. But now a strong, cold wind whipped, and the clouds looked ready to burst again. He drank slowly but steadily from his glass. The shaded electric light of the sitting room illuminated his profile against the dark, overcast sky beyond.

He was supposed to fidget, to tap his fingers against the glass or scrape his feet back and forth across the floor. He was not supposed to cut a stark, almost ominous figure ahead of an approaching storm.

She could not look away from him.

To distract herself, she raised her own glass. She didn't much care for wine or spirits, but the Sauternes was sweet, almost like a dessert on its own. She drank with a nervous thirst and, within a minute, stared at the bottom of her glass.

"It's been a long day," he said. He straddled the threshold between the balcony and the sitting room. "I think I'll retire early."

Was that her cue that he was taking her to bed? Her stomach felt as if someone took it by the ends and gave it a twist—though not as awful a twist as she would have expected. It must be the Sauternes and the champagne from dinner. She was only mildly panicked.

"You don't wish for a taste of the cake?" she said,

not sure what else she could say. *Good night? I'll join you shortly?*

"No, thank you." He set down his empty glass and ran his hand through his hair. She'd thought he had brown hair with strands of dark blond. She was quite mistaken. It was the other way around—he had mostly dark blond hair, and a few chestnut streaks here and there. "Good night, Lady Vere."

He disappeared into the en suite bathroom. She poured herself another glass of Sauternes. A few minutes later, as she was once more looking at her empty glass, he came out of the bathroom, headed directly into one of the two bedrooms, and closed the door.

Only to come out thirty seconds later, grab the whiskey bottle from before her, and leave again with a perfunctory nod.

She was flummoxed. She did not want to go to bed with him, but given the way he'd looked at her when they were at Highgate Court—and inside the Clarence brougham this afternoon—she had not considered the possibility that he would ignore her outright on their wedding night.

Well, this would not do. She could not possibly give her uncle such an easy opening as an unconsummated marriage. He was not going to stroll through the courts with some trumped-up invalidity concerning her wedding ceremony, and then wave this nonconsummation before the judges. He'd have to exert himself to prove that she was of unsound mind, at the very least.

This marriage would be consummated, and that was that.

&

Easier said than done.

Half an hour and the rest of the Sauternes later, Elissande was still where she was, alone in the sitting room.

Well, what was she waiting for? Consummation didn't happen by itself. If he wouldn't come to her, then she had to go to him.

She didn't move. She was so very ignorant of those things. And frankly, the thought of coming into renewed bodily contact with Lord Vere kept her bottom fastened firmly to the chair.

She had to use the sledgehammer on herself. She had to actually recall her uncle's image to mind, when her entire life she'd tried her best to banish it: the cold eyes, the aquiline nose, the thin lips, the soft-edged menace that lay at the root of her nightmares.

She took a few deep breaths and rose. And swayed so much she had to sit down again. Her uncle frowned upon women drinking. Until Lady Kingsley's guests arrived with their own supply, wine was never served at Highgate Court.

She'd completely underestimated the effect of an entire bottle of Sauternes—plus three glasses of champagne—on her balance.

Gripping on to the table, she rose again, this time with much greater caution. There, she was upright. She inched along the edge of the table, not quite looking as if she were an untried alpinist upon the north face of the Matterhorn.

The other side of the table was closer to Lord Vere's bedroom. She turned so that her back was to the table and carefully set off to negotiate the ten-foot distance to his room.

It was like walking on water. No wonder he had stumbled about when he'd had too much to drink; one really couldn't help it, not when the floor swelled and dipped without the least warning.

At the doorway she gratefully gripped the door handle and rested her weight, for a moment, against the jamb. Good gracious, the room was sliding back and forth—best get on before she became too dizzy. She turned the handle.

He was in bed already, naked from the waist up. She blinked, so that *he* would stop sliding back and forth in her vision. Who knew something as sweet as syrup would have such fascinating ophthalmological effects?

Slowly he came into focus. The periphery of his person became less blurred, his torso gained sharpness and definition. Goodness, he must be a Muscular Christian, for he was certainly muscular, his physique something Michelangelo would approve of, since the maestro never painted a young man who didn't have such a body.

And look, he had a book with him. Vaguely she remembered what he had said about using books as general anesthesia. No, that wasn't quite right. Laudanum, that was it. He used books as laudanum.

But it didn't matter just now. He looked halfway intelligent with that very big book in his lap.

She liked it.

"My lord," she said.

His eyes narrowed—or was that also an optic effect? "My lady."

"It's our wedding night." It was very important to state the obvious, lest he'd forgotten.

"So it is."

"Therefore I've come to oblige you," she said grandly. She felt at once brave, dutiful, and resourceful.

"Thank you, but it will not be necessary."

What silliness. "I beg to differ. It is absolutely necessary."

His tone was pointed. "Why?"

"For the flourishing of our marriage, sir, of course."

He closed the book and rose. Hmm, shouldn't he have risen as soon as she entered? She could not decide.

"Our marriage has come as a shock to both of us. I'm loath to impose myself on you when everything has been so rushed and . . . bizarre. Why don't we go on at a more leisurely pace?"

"No." She shook her head. "We don't have the time."

He gave her a look that was almost sardonic. "We've a lifetime—or so the clergyman said."

She needed to be mindful about her future consumption of Sauternes. Not only were her eyes functioning only questionably, her tongue had become thick and unwieldy. She had a coherent argument in her head concerning the urgency of the consummation. But she could not motivate her mandible to deliver that argument. It flatly refused.

So she tilted her head and smiled at him instead, not because she had to, but because she wanted to.

His reaction was to pick up the whiskey on his nightstand and take a swig directly from the bottle. Oh dear, but that was a very masculine thing to do. Very forceful and decisive.

Attractive.

Indeed, his whole person was attractive. Outstandingly handsome. That thick, slightly unruly hair that glinted like polished bronze. That bone structure. Those wide, tightly sinewed shoulders.

"I forgot what color your eyes are," she murmured.

How preposterous that after four days of acquaintance—and a wedding ceremony—she didn't remember the color of his eyes.

"They are blue."

"Really?" She was beguiled. "How wonderful. May I see?"

With that, she approached him and peered up. He was very tall, taller than she'd remembered, somehow, and she had to place her hands on his arms and stand on her tiptoes to see deeply into his eyes.

"Many people have blue eyes," he said.

"But yours are extraordinary." Truly they were. "They are the color of the Hope Diamond."

"Have you ever seen the Hope Diamond?"

"No, but now I know what it must look like." She sighed. "And you smell good."

"I smell like whiskey."

"Yes, that too. But"—she breathed in deeply—"better."

She could not define or describe it. It was a warm scent, like that of sheets freshly returned from the laundry. Or that of sunbaked stones.

"You've had too much to drink, haven't you?"

She stared at his mouth, firm yet enticing. " 'Thy lips, O my spouse, drop as the honeycomb: honey and milk are under thy tongue; and the smell of thy garments is like the smell of Lebanon.' "

"You've had too much to drink."

She smiled. He was so very amusing too. Her hands spread against his arms. So firm, they were, yet so smooth. She remembered the night of Squeak Piggy Squeak. She'd liked touching him even then. No wonder. He was marvelous to touch *and* he smelled like Lebanon.

She looked up into his eyes. He did not smile back at her. But he was very handsome this way, severe and judgmental.

" 'Let him kiss me with the kisses of his mouth,' " she murmured. " 'For thy love is better than wine.' "

"No," he said.

She wrapped her arms about his neck and touched her mouth to his. But only for an instant. He firmly removed her person. "You are completely inebriated, Lady Vere."

"No, not inebriated. Intoxicated," she declared proudly.

"In either case, you should go to your room and lie down."

"I want to lie down with you," she breathed. " 'He shall lie all night betwixt my breasts.' "

"Jesus," he said.

"No, Elissande. My name is Elissande."

"This is enough, *Lady Vere*. You may leave now."

"But I don't wish to."

"Then I will leave."

"But you cannot."

"Oh, can't I?"

Her tongue, which had been effortlessly lithe for quoting from the Song of Songs, again refused to cooperate here. "Please don't. We must, for my aunt. Please."

Surely he'd seen how shrunken and faded her aunt had become in her uncle's house. Surely he understood the importance of keeping her free from further oppression. Surely he was as compassionate and perceptive as he was handsome.

Gorgeous, really. She could not get enough of looking at him. God in Heaven, what a sensational jaw. Those magnificent cheekbones. And those Hope Diamond eyes. She could stare at him all day.

And all night.

"No," he said.

She threw herself at him. He was so solidly built. How she wished she'd had someone like him to hold on to in all the darkest days of her life—hugging Aunt

Rachel had always made her sadder, but Lord Vere made her feel safe. He was a fortress.

She kissed his shoulder—she loved the taste and texture of his skin. She kissed his neck, his ear, his jaw, which was not quite as smooth, but had a slight roughness that scraped her chin most deliciously.

She kissed him on the mouth, capturing those very seductive lips with her own, savoring the taste of whiskey that lingered just inside his mouth, running the tip of her tongue over his teeth.

Oh, dear. His—his—

They stood hip to hip and she felt it. Him. Hard and growing harder.

And then she felt it no more as she sailed through the air. Landing on the mattress rather knocked the breath out of her and made the room spin like a kaleidoscope. But, goodness gracious how strong he was. She weighed a solid nine and a half stone. But he'd picked her up and tossed her as if she were a bridal bouquet.

She smiled at him.

"Stop smiling," he said. It sounded as if he ground his teeth as he spoke.

Never smiling again was exactly what she aimed to do. For understanding her, she smiled at him with even greater abandon. Perhaps she ought to rethink the wholesale banning of smiles. They were quite enjoyable at times like this, when she was under no duress whatsoever, when she was relaxed and happy and at peace with the world.

She beckoned him with her index finger. "Come here."

For once, he obliged. He loomed above her for a moment, then leaned down and took her jaw between his fingers.

"Listen and listen well, if you can get anything into your barmy, addled head: *no*. You can force me into a corner and make me marry you. But you can't make me fuck you. Say one more word and I will have this marriage annulled tonight and send you back to the bedlam where you came from. Now shut up and get out."

She smiled at him some more. His lips moved in the most mesmerizing fashion when he spoke. She would have him read to her, so she could ogle him for long minutes at a stretch.

Then his words began to make an impression on her ear. On her mind. She shook her head. No, he could not have meant it. He was her fortress. He would not toss her over the rampart to her uncle.

"I mean it," he repeated. "Out."

She could not. She could only lie there and shake her head helplessly. "Don't make me go. Please don't make me go."

Don't make me go back to a place where I cannot take a single free breath, where never a moment passes without its share of fear and loathing.

He yanked her off the bed and to her feet, his fingers clamped about her arm to keep her upright. Without any mercy, he marched her to the still open door, then gave her a shove that sent her stumbling to the middle of the sitting room.

Behind her the door slammed shut.

❧

An hour later Vere came out of his room for the cake. He hadn't eaten much the entire day, and all the whiskey in the world couldn't mask the gnawing of his hunger anymore.

He was on his second slice when he realized that she was sobbing in her room. The sound was very faint—almost inaudible. He finished the cake on his plate and returned to his bed.

Five minutes later he was again in the sitting room. But why? Why did he care? What he'd said was expressly designed to make any woman cry. And feminine tears had absolutely no effect on him: Women who were criminally inclined or mentally disturbed—not to mention merely manipulative—tended to be terrific weepers.

He went back to bed and tilted the whiskey bottle for the last drop. But bugger it to hell if he wasn't back in the sitting room again three minutes later.

He opened her door but did not see her. He had to round the bed to the farther side to find her sitting on the floor, her knees drawn up to her chest, crying into her wedding veil, of all things.

The veil was a soggy wad. Her face was red and splotchy, her eyes puffy. She hiccupped convulsively. The front of her wedding gown, too, was damp from tears.

"I can't sleep when you are crying like this," he said crossly.

She looked up, a very dull expression on her face, no doubt waiting for his person to coalesce in her blurred vision. It did. She shivered.

"Sorry," she said. "I'll stop right now. Please don't send me away."

He couldn't decide which one he hated more: the devious and dementedly smiling Lady Vere, or the devious and abjectly sniveling one.

"Go to sleep. I won't send you away tonight."

Her lips quivered. With *gratitude,* for God's sake. In annoyance—and resentment and anger, which an ocean of spirits couldn't drown—he made the mistake of saying, "I'll wait till tomorrow morning."

She bit her lower lip. Her eyes filled with renewed tears. They rolled down her already wet face to disappear into the bodice of the wedding gown. But she made no sound at all, her weeping as silent as death.

Looking away from him, she began to rock back and forth, like a child trying to comfort herself.

He didn't know why it should affect him, why *she* should affect him—this woman had meant to force herself on *Freddie,* for God's sake—but she did. There was something about her wordless desperation that made him hurt.

She had no one else to whom she could turn.

It was partly the whiskey. But one bottle of whiskey wasn't enough to explain why he didn't march out of her room, now that he'd effectively silenced her. He fought it, the alcohol-fueled compassion, the onslaught of her bottomless misery, and the stupid sense that he of all people should do something about it.

She had brought it on herself, hadn't she?

❧

She gasped as he lifted her bodily. But this time he didn't toss her. Instead, he set her on the edge of her bed. He bent to remove her shoes. Then he reached behind her to unhook her dress. Her dress, her petticoats, her corset cover, and her corset itself fell from her.

Taking a handkerchief from his pocket, he wiped her face—carefully. Fresh tears swelled. For years she'd wiped away Aunt Rachel's tears. But no one had ever done it for her.

She caught his handkerchief when he would have put it back into his pocket and brought it before her nose. "It smells like Lebanon too," she said with wonder.

He shook his head briefly. "Let me tuck you in."

"All right," she said.

Their eyes met. Really, he had ridiculously beautiful eyes. And such unbearably alluring lips. She remembered kissing him. Even if she must take Aunt Rachel and go on the run, she would always remember kissing him.

So she kissed him again.

He let her kiss him, let her run her teeth lightly over his lower lip, nibble him on his jawline, and lick him, a tiny lick at the base of his throat. He emitted a small, strangled sound as she bit lightly where his neck joined his shoulder.

"Where did you learn to do that?" he asked, his breaths uneven.

Did such things have to be learned?

"I'm only doing what I want." And what she wanted was to sink her teeth into him, the way someone would bite a gold coin to ascertain its purity.

"You are a horny drunk, Lady Vere," he murmured.

"What does that mean?"

She didn't wait for an answer but kissed him again. There was such pleasure in kissing him, in touching him.

He exerted a gentle pressure against her shoulder. After a moment, she realized that he meant for her to lie down. She did, holding on to him, still kissing him.

"I shouldn't be here," he said, even as he stretched out beside her. "I might prove a horny drunk too."

Neither of them should be here. Lady Kingsley's house should never have been invaded by rats. And the Cumberland Edgertons should have had the decency to take her in after her parents' death.

She was inordinately remorseful. Of course he had every right to be angry with her. She'd manipulated—indeed, wrangled—him into this marriage. And he'd been very kind and very tolerant. Was it any wonder she looked to him for safety and guidance in such a confusing and uncertain time?

She lifted herself to her elbows and kissed him again, a straight trail down the center of his torso.

He stopped her, but only to unspool her hair. It

spilled in a long cascade over her right shoulder. "So much of it, but so light, like spun air."

She smiled at the compliment and lowered her head to his navel. He stopped her once more, his fingers sinking into her shoulder.

A question suddenly popped into her head. "What makes you grow hard?"

His gaze took on that peculiar tautness again. "Your kissing me and pulling me into bed, among other things."

"Why?"

"Arousal is necessary to performance."

"Are you aroused now?"

A beat of silence. "Yes."

"What is to be this performance then?"

"I really shouldn't," he said, even as his body turned in to hers and she felt his arousal very clearly. "I'm not thinking with my head."

"Is there anything else you can think with?" she wondered aloud.

He chuckled briefly. Then, at last, he touched her. He'd touched her before, of course, but always to do something else: escorting her to her seat at the dinner table or shoving her away from him, for example. This was the first time he'd touched her for the sake of touching her, for no other purpose than to feel her.

Before Aunt Rachel completely faded, sometimes she'd petted Elissande on her hair or her hand. But that was many years ago. Elissande had not known until this moment how desperately she missed it, the simple grace of being touched. He stroked her slowly, on her face, her shoulders, her arms, her back.

Still stroking her, he kissed her. She swam in pleasure. When he pulled away, she told him, "I want more."

"More what?"

"More you."

That was when he disrobed her, peeling away her combination, leaving her wearing only a pair of white stockings.

She should feel mortified to be so naked before him. But she did not. She felt only a little shy.

"What am I doing?" he murmured, even as he pressed kisses to her collarbone.

She shivered with the pleasure of it. "You are making me very happy," she whispered.

"Am I? Will you remember it in the morning?"

"Why won't I?"

He gave an enigmatic smile and kissed her down the center of her torso, as she had done with him. The air he exhaled teased her nipple. She tensed with the indescribable sensation of it, which grew a hundred times more indescribable when he took her nipple inside his mouth.

"It doesn't appear to be very difficult to make you happy," he said.

Indeed, it was not. A little freedom, a little security, a little love. It was all she'd ever wanted.

He continued to extract divine sensations from her. And she continued to be near teary eyed from happiness. When he removed his trousers at last, the size and weight of his arousal almost did not surprise her. She trusted that he would know what to do, even though she had trouble conceiving what he would do in relation to *her*.

"I shall regret this in the morning," he said, almost inaudibly.

"I shan't," she said earnestly, eagerly.

He kissed her chin. "Actually, I have a presentiment you will—very much. But I cannot seem to stop now."

He captured her mouth. His body settled over hers. He was hot and hard. And he—he—

She screamed. She hadn't meant to, but it hurt. It hurt so much.

All the kisses and caresses that led to this moment, then, were but to make it more palatable. But they did not. It was the most terrible burning in a most sensitive place.

Tears streamed anew down her face. Everything was always so difficult. Everything. Even this, so sweet and pleasurable, must turn out to entail such agony. But it was not his fault. Hadn't the Good Book declared "In sorrow thou shalt bring forth children"? No doubt this was what it had ominously prescribed.

"I'm sorry," she said shakily. "Quite sorry. Please, do go on."

He withdrew. She hissed at the pain of it and braced herself for more. But he left the bed altogether. She heard him dress. When he returned, it was with the handkerchief that smelled of Lebanon. He wiped away her newest tears.

"I'm quite done," he said. "You can go to sleep now."

"Really?" She could not believe her good fortune.

"Yes, really."

He pulled a cover over her and turned off the light by the headboard. "Good night."

"Good night," she said, trembling with relief. "And thank you, sir."

In the dark, he sighed.

Chapter Eleven

In the gray light of morning, she slept uneasily—and naked, the sheet twined about her like Eve's serpent. He touched her, her cheek, her ear, her hair. He should not touch her again. But that knowledge only made the illicit, forbidden sensation of her wholly and sharply arousing.

She shifted, revealing a small smear of blood on the bed, a sight that hit him with the force of a stone to the temple. He remembered very well what had transpired the night before, but to stare at the evidence, to know that she would see it too...

He covered her and stepped away from the bed. From her. What had happened to him? His plans had been simple: The marriage would exist in name only, until the time came for a convenient annulment. The execution of such a plan had promised to be equally simple: She wanted to be near him about as much as a fish wanted a walk.

And yet he had failed.

He'd meant only to put her to sleep. Instead, he'd allowed himself to be seduced by a Machiavellian virgin.

Her skin had been velvet, her hair silk, her body a geometrician's fantasy of curves. And yet her fleshly charms had not been his downfall. His undoing had been the pleasure she took in his company, her wholehearted, drunk-naïve delight—her inebriated infatuation.

Part of him had perceived perfectly that she was stewed, that she was not herself, and that the stars in her eyes were but reflections of the Sauternes flooding her veins. But ît had not been the clear-seeing part of him in charge last night. It had been the lonely, deprived, stupid him, the one who was still affected by her smiles, who was all too eager to let a mere bottle of whiskey be excuse enough. When she gazed at *that* him with wonder and marvel, when she murmured that he made her happy, when she touched him as if he were made of God's own sinews, nothing else had mattered.

Illusions, all illusions. He'd gladly succumbed to their seduction, to that false sense of intimacy and connection. And if it had not been for her cry of pain shattering the bubble—

He looked back at her. She stirred, whimpering as she did so.

I want more.

More what?

More you.

And he had believed her. More fool he.

The room he'd marched into the night before and marked for his own contained her belongings. Most of her things were in two large trunks, but there were walking boots, gloves, hats, and jackets scattered about.

On the writing desk sat her treasure chest, approximately fourteen inches wide, nine inches deep, and eleven inches high, with a lid that was curved on the top and flat on the bottom. Vere had already looked through its contents, which, except for the Delacroix, were souvenirs meaningful only to her.

He opened the chest again and looked at her parents' wedding photograph. Such antecedents—his father would have expired of an apoplexy. He had not even mentioned in front of Freddie the worst Lady Avery had told him; that given her birth date six months after the wedding, no one knew for certain whether her father was really Andrew Edgerton, her mother's husband, or Algernon Edgerton, Andrew Edgerton's uncle and Charlotte Edgerton's erstwhile protector.

Absently he ran his thumb down the underside of the edge of the lid. Something caught his attention— a tiny aperture, and then another one, and another. He turned on the electric light, opened the chest fully, and peered at it.

The chest was inlaid with ivory and mother-of-pearl on the exterior and padded with green velvet on the interior. The underside of the lid too was lined in green velvet, except around the edges, which were painted with scrolls and cartouches.

The slits, almost invisible, narrowly scored the left edge of the lid down the center of a black stripe. They were thin as a fingernail and little more than a quarter inch in length. He examined the right edge of the lid. The same, a line of tiny slits.

What were they, decorative grilles?

A knock at the suite's door startled him. Reluctantly he left the chest to answer the door: it was the arrival of his breakfast, along with a cable from Lady Kingsley.

My dear Lord and Lady Vere,

It is with much relief that I inform you all traces of the rats have been eradicated from Woodley Manor. And although we still have yet to discover the culprits behind the prank, the local constable is eagerly on the case.

Lady Vere will be relieved to know of my guests' orderly departure from Highgate Court yesterday, under Lady Avery's oversight. She will also perhaps be relieved to know that Mr. Douglas had yet to return as of this writing—a delivery boy I passed on my way into the village assured me that he'd just come from Highgate Court and that the master of the manor remained absent.

I enclose many more congratulations on your marriage.

Eloisa Kingsley

He stuck the telegram into his pocket, returned to the bedroom, and scrutinized the chest further. With the blade of his razor he sliced off a fraction of a calling card and folded that fragment into a thin, but still relatively stiff stem. The slits were not deep; most of them cut into the lid's edge by barely one-sixth of an inch. But there were two slits—one on either side of the lid—into which the card stem sank more than half an inch.

He suddenly remembered the minuscule key in the safe in Mrs. Douglas's room.

🐦

Elissande awoke to an epic clash in her head. Or rather, a titanic clash. For weren't the Titans defeated by Zeus? Her head, too, must have been split by a thunderbolt. She pried her eyelids apart, then squeezed them shut immediately. The room was unbearably bright, as if someone had shoved a torch directly into her eye socket. Her head splintered further in protest. Her innards, in contrast, decided to die in slow, roiling agony.

She moaned. The sound exploded in her ears, discharging shrapnel of pure pain deep into her brain.

How ironic that she was not even dead, when she was already fully in the embrace of hell.

Someone removed the blanket that covered her. She shivered. The person, careful not to jostle her, further disentangled her from more sheets that were twisted and bunched about her. She shivered again. She was vaguely aware that she was not wearing much—if anything. But she could not care; she was skewered on Beelzebub's spit.

Something cool and silky settled around her. Her unresponsive arms were lifted and stuffed into sleeves. A dressing gown?

Slowly she was turned around. She whimpered: The movement had intensified the pounding in her skull. Once she was facing up, her head was raised, causing her to cry out.

"Here," said a man's voice, his arm strong about her. "A cure for your bad head. Drink it."

The liquid that came into her mouth was the vilest concoction she'd ever tasted, swamp ooze and rotten eggs.

She sputtered. "No."

"Drink it. You'll feel better."

She whimpered again. But there was something at once authoritative and soothing about the voice, and something at once authoritative and soothing about the way he held her. She complied.

She stopped to gag after every swallow, but he kept tipping the cup at her lips and she, gasping and rasping, drank.

After she'd swallowed every last drop of the foul brew, he gave her water, and she'd never tasted anything so sweet. She gulped eagerly, thirstily, happy to feel the water spilling down her chin. When she'd at last had enough, she turned away from the glass and pressed her face into his chest.

His waistcoat was a very fine material, the linen of his shirt soft and warm. Her head still banged awfully, but she was—she was safe. She had a protector, for once, someone who cradled and looked after her and who smelled wonderful at the same time.

Lebanon, she thought, for no reason at all.

❧

This state of comfort and security, however, did not last long. Her protector set her back down on the bed, covered her again, and, despite her groan of disappointment and the hand she clutched at his waistcoat, left.

When footsteps once more came toward her, she opened her eyes and immediately closed them again.

Lord Vere.

No.

Not him.

"Come, Lady Vere," he chirped. "I know the temptation is strong to remain abed but you must stir. Your bath is waiting."

What was he doing in her room? She must still be dreaming.

Memories of the past week returned with a vengeance. Lady Kingsley's rat problem. A house full of bachelors. The lovely Lord Frederick. The tussle in her uncle's study. The wedding.

She was *married*. To *Lord Vere*.

She'd spent the night with him.

"Shall I sing you awake, then?" he said, all energetic eagerness. "I know just the song. 'Daisy, Daisy, give me your answer do. I'm half crazy all for the love of you'—"

She struggled upright. "Thank you. I'm quite awake now."

As she moved on the bed, the bedcover shifted to reveal a smear of red on the sheets. Her hand went to her throat as more memories spilled back into her head. She recalled his teeth against her tongue—what a bizarre, bizarre thing. She remembered being hurled onto his bed—dear God! And pain—awful, lacerating pain between her legs. She winced against the recollection.

But how trustworthy were those memories? She also remembered speaking of the Hope Diamond and a handkerchief that smelled like Lebanon. What could possibly have led her to allude to the Song of Songs?

"But I've just started," Lord Vere whined. "Let me finish the song."

She swallowed and determinedly swung her legs over the side of the bed. As she straightened, she realized that she was barely dressed, wearing only her silk dressing gown. Thankfully it was quite dim; only a faint halo of light framed the curtains—she didn't know why she'd thought the room unbearably bright before. "I'd be delighted to hear you sing another time. But you must excuse me now, sir. I believe my bath is waiting."

He ran before her and opened the bathroom door for her. "One piece of advice, my dear. Be very quick about it—or you'll melt."

She blinked. "Beg your pardon?"

"The water is hot. Don't stay much more than a

quarter of an hour, or you'll start to melt," he repeated, in all seriousness.

Such an assertion could only be met on its own level of absurdity. "But wouldn't the water have started to cool after a quarter of an hour?"

His jaw dropped. "My goodness, I've never thought of it. *That's* why we don't hear more about people dissolving in their tubs."

She closed the door, lowered herself into the tub, and stared at the tops of her knees. She would not cry. She refused to cry. She'd known perfectly well what she was getting into when she'd taken off her clothes before Lord Vere.

In precisely a quarter of an hour she emerged from her bath—to the sight of her husband at the table in the sitting room, staring at a fork in undiluted fascination. At the sound of her approach, he looked up, set down the fork, and smiled in that doltish way of his.

"How's your head, my dear? You drank a whole bottle of Sauternes."

Could he possibly be the person who had given her the bad head cure earlier? In whose arms she had lain so contentedly?

Best not to think of that. It would only spoil the sweetness of the memory.

"My head is better. Thank you."

"And your stomach? More settled?"

"I believe so."

"Come eat something then. I've ordered you tea and some plain toast."

Tea and plain toast did not sound as if they would send her stomach into renewed convulsions. She walked slowly to the table and sat down.

He poured tea for her, spilling enough to wet half the tablecloth. "I might have had a bit too much to drink myself, to tell you the truth, my dear. But it's not every day you get married, eh? Worth a bad head, I say."

She chewed on her toast and did not look at him.

"What do you think of the speaking tube, by the way? I think it's marvelous. I talk in this room right here and they hear it all the way in the kitchen. I was a little surprised, however, that a man came to deliver the tea and the toast. Thought they'd pop right out of the speaking tube. I didn't dare leave the spot. Wouldn't be quite the thing if the teapot made the trip all the way up here and then—splat—because I couldn't be there to catch it."

The throb in her head worsened; the place between her thighs also began to smart unpleasantly.

"I was reading the papers before you came," Lord Vere went on. "And I must tell you, I was shocked to read, in the pages of the *Times,* no less, the German Kaiser referred to as our dear sovereign's grandson. How can anyone besmirch Her Majesty so, to attach that Prussian bounder to her blameless family? I fully intend to write a letter to the paper requesting a retraction."

The Kaiser *was* the queen's grandson by her eldest daughter, the former Princess Royal. The House of Hanover was and had always been solidly German.

She smiled wanly. "Yes, you should."

She was determined to be a good wife to him: She owed him everything. Perhaps tomorrow, when her head no longer hurt, when listening to him talk didn't make her think longingly of a chorus of a thousand crows, she would sit down with him—and all the volumes of the *Encyclopaedia Britannica*—and correct some of his misconceptions.

But now, it was all she could do to smile at him and let him be as wrong as a broken clock.

❧

Elissande grunted in frustration. Her head was still not well enough for her to twist her neck and look into the mirror behind her. But without seeing her reflection, she fumbled with her corset, which laced in the back.

A light knock came at her door. "May I be of some help, my dear?"

"No, thank you. I'm fine." The last thing she needed was his help. The two of them would be tied together to a chair with the laces of her corset if he were to involve himself.

As if he hadn't heard her, he entered, clad in a blue lounge suit. Her uncle always wore a frock coat for going out, but gentlemen of her generation seemed to prefer less formal attire.

"Sir!"

She clutched the corset to her torso. She was *not* dressed—she had on only her combination—and he should not be anywhere in her vicinity. Then her gaze fell on the bed, where God only knew what had transpired during the night.

God and Lord Vere. Whatever it was that had taken place in this bed, it had certainly changed his mind about their marriage. Gone was the oppressive silence of yesterday; today he abounded with his usual bumbling zeal. She clutched harder at her corset.

"Really, I don't need any help," she reiterated.

"Of course you do," he said. "Lucky for you I'm an expert on ladies' undergarments."

Oh, he was, was he?

But he turned her around and, for once, demonstrated what might be considered real skill as he tightened the laces down her back efficiently and well.

She was astonished. "Where did you learn how to work a corset?"

"Well, you know how it is. If you help ladies out of their corsets, you have to help them back in."

There were ladies who let him help them out of their corsets without being compelled by vows of marriage? She couldn't tell whether she was shocked or appalled.

He yanked hard. All the air squeezed out of her—a daily necessity for fitting into her clothes.

"But that was before I met you. Now there is only you for me, of course."

A terrifying thought, that. But she did not have time to dwell on it as he proceeded with her corset cover and her petticoats.

"Hurry," he said. "We must make haste. It's already quarter past ten."

"Quarter past *ten*? Are you sure?"

"Of course." He took out his watch to show her. "See, precisely."

"And your watch is accurate?" She had no confidence in him at all.

"Checked it against Big Ben's chimes this morning."

She rubbed her still-tender temple. She was forgetting something. What was she forgetting?

"My aunt! My goodness, she must be famished." And frightened, all alone in strange surroundings, with Elissande nowhere in sight.

"Oh, no, she's fine. You left her room key about, so I visited with her earlier while you were still abed. We even had our breakfast together."

He had to be joking. This was a man who forgot that he needed to change his egg-stained trousers by the time he went from the breakfast parlor to his own room. How could he possibly have remembered her aunt?

"I invited her to come with us today, to call on your uncle. But she—"

"Excuse me?" Her head spun. "I thought...for a moment I thought you said we are going to call on my uncle today."

"Well, yes, that is the plan indeed."

She could not speak. She could only stare at him.

He patted her on the arm. "Don't you fret; your uncle will be thrilled to see you respectably married—you *were* getting a bit long in the tooth, my dear. And I *am* a marquess, you know, a man of considerable stature and influence."

"But—my—she—" Elissande stopped. In her fear she was stammering. "Mrs. Douglas, what did she say?"

He urged her into her blouse. "Well, I told her that we would be delighted if she could accompany us, but that I understood she must still be weary from her travels yesterday. She said she would prefer to rest today."

Elissande barely noticed that he was buttoning her blouse. "I thought she would," she said. "But don't you see, I can't leave her. She doesn't do well in my absence."

"Nonsense. I introduced her to my housekeeper and they are getting on famously."

"Your *housekeeper*?" She supposed he must have one, since he could scarcely be expected to keep his own house. But in the rush of the past thirty-six hours, she had not once thought about where he lived or what his household arrangements must be like. "Your housekeeper is in town?"

"Of course. I don't usually close my town house until early in September."

He had a house in town and they were at a hotel?

"I'd like to see my aunt," she said. She had little faith in his ability to hire good servants.

However, Mrs. Dilwyn, his housekeeper, turned out to be quite the pleasant surprise. She was a tiny dumpling of a woman in her late forties, soft-spoken and meticulous. In her notebook she had recorded everything that had transpired since her arrival at eight o'clock in the morning: the amount of fluid

Aunt Rachel had ingested, her visits to the water closet, even the precise number of drops of laudanum she had taken—Elissande noticed she'd taken three more drops than usual, no doubt to erase the horror Lord Vere had brought about by proposing to take her back to Highgate Court.

"See, I told you," said her husband. "Mrs. Dilwyn will quite pamper Mrs. Douglas. She spoils me extravagantly whenever I've the slightest sniffle."

"My mum was bedridden the last two years of her life—Lord Vere was kind enough to allow her to share my rooms, so I could care for her," said Mrs. Dilwyn.

"I quite enjoyed having her about. She used to tell me I was the handsomest man alive."

"Oh, you are, sir," said Mrs. Dilwyn with what appeared to be genuine fondness. "You are."

Lord Vere preened.

Mrs. Dilwyn leaned closer to Elissande and lowered her voice. "Mrs. Douglas, might she be a bit irregular? I know my mum was."

"Yes, unfortunately she is," said Elissande. "She does not like vegetables and she hates prunes."

"My mum hated prunes too. I will see if Mrs. Douglas might like a stewed apricot better."

"Thank you," said Elissande, half-dazed. She was not accustomed to having anyone share her burdens.

She did have a look at Aunt Rachel, who was dozing in bed. Then Lord Vere hurried her out of the bedroom and out of Aunt Rachel's suite.

"Quickly now, or we'll miss our train."

She made a last-ditch appeal as he marched her down the corridor toward the lift. "Must we? So soon?"

"Of course," he answered. "Don't you want the man who raised you to meet your very fine husband? I must tell you I'm quite excited. I've never met an uncle-in-law before. We shall get along splendidly, he and I."

❧

Freddie owed much of his development as a painter to Angelica. She was the one who had seen his pencil sketches and recommended that he try his hand at watercolor and, then later, oil painting. She'd read the daunting book on the chromatography of oil paints and summarized it for him. She'd introduced him to the works of the Impressionists, with the art journals she'd brought back from her family's holidays in France.

He had never been able to work with anyone next to him, except her. From the beginning she had been there with him, usually with a thick tome on her lap, absorbed in her own interests. From time to time she might read aloud from her book: the scientific reason why sugar of lead in paints resulted in the rapid darkening of the finished painting, a spicy sonnet from Michelangelo to a beautiful young man, an account of the infamous Salon des Refusés of 1863.

So in a way, it was inordinately familiar to work with her in proximity.

Except for her nakedness, that was.

She lay on her side on the bed he'd had his servants install in his studio, her back to him, her head propped up on one hand, reading *The Treasures of Art in Great Britain*.

Her hair fell loose, a tumble of umber locks interspersed with shades of raw sienna. Her skin gleamed, lit from within. The softness of her bottom made his fingers grip hard at his pencil. And that was before he even took into consideration her breasts and the shadowed triangle between her thighs reflected in the mirror she'd strategically placed on the far side of herself.

He had to remind himself every other minute that his purpose was art and the celebration of beauty. The comeliness of her body was as much a part of nature as the smooth bark of a birch or the sunlit ripples of a summer lake. He should have no difficulty appreciating it as form, color, interplay of light.

Yet he wanted nothing more than to throw down his pencil, walk up to this particular combination of form, color, and interplay of light, and—

He looked down at his sketchbook instead. Not that it was much help. He'd produced several drawings already, one a general outline of the entire tableau, one a study of her profile and her hair, one of her midsection, and one of what he saw in the mirror.

"Do you know, Freddie," she said, "before I returned to England, I thought surely your experience with Lady Tremaine would have left you brooding and resentful. But you are the same man you always were."

It was just like Angelica to raise unexpected topics. He looked at the empty canvas he had prepared.

"It's been a long time, Angelica. Four years."

"But are you completely recovered from her?"

"She wasn't an illness."

"From the loss of her then?"

"She was never truly mine." He took a sharper pencil from his box. "I think I knew from the very beginning that we were on borrowed time."

He'd been gloriously happy with Lady Tremaine. But there had always been an element of deep anxiety to his happiness. When she had reconciled with her husband, he'd been heartbroken but not bitter—because it had not been a betrayal, but only the end of a wonderful era of his life.

He flipped to a new page in his sketchbook and drew Angelica's shapely calves, wishing his hands were his pencils, that as the drawing took shape, he could slide his palms across her cool, soft skin.

Lady Tremaine had once told him that Angelica was in love with him. Freddie rarely questioned Lady Tremaine's pronouncements, but this particular one had come when Lady Tremaine had decided to reunite with her husband, when she no doubt wished that Freddie too would settle down with someone. Anyone.

If Angelica had been in love with him she had certainly said nothing of it, ever—and she had never been one to censor her words around him. And even if Lady Tremaine had been right, four years had passed, a long time for affections to remain constant from far away.

He glanced back at Angelica. Her head was bent, her attention absorbed in her book. She was even jotting down notations in the margins. A seduction this wasn't.

"I think that's enough for today," he said, closing his sketchbook. "I'll step outside."

❦

Angelica would not say that she had been in love with Freddie forever. Forever meant the mist of time, the blurred years of childhood. Her love had a definite moment of origin at a much later point, when she had been seventeen, he eighteen.

He'd come home following his first year at Christ Church. And she, set to join Lady Margaret Hall that autumn, had plopped herself down on a picnic blanket not far from him as he painted on the bank of the River Stour, to ask him as many questions about Oxford as it pleased her and to critique him as he worked. (She didn't paint herself, but she had an excellent eye. And she was exceedingly proud of the fact that she'd been the person who'd explained to him, four years prior, that one did not use pure white for highlights, but a paler shade of the color one wished to highlight.)

She had been eating a tangy, firm-fleshed peach,

tossing pebbles into the river—hardly wider than a bathtub—and telling him he needed to mix more blue into his green if he wanted to capture the proper deep hue of summer foliage. She was never sure whether he heard her on that particular tip, because he did not say anything, but instead clamped the filbert brush he was using between his teeth and reached for an angled brush.

Then and there lightning struck. She stared at him as if she'd never seen him before, her oldest friend all grown-up, and wanted nothing more than to be that filbert brush, to feel his lips on her, and his tongue, and the firm pressure of his teeth.

But whereas she'd been a confidently commanding friend, always certain that their friendship would gracefully weather all the advice and criticism she fusilladed his way, she'd proved completely hopeless as a seductress.

He did not notice the new frocks and hats she bought for enchanting him. He did not grasp that her effort to teach him to dance better was to give him an easy opening to kiss her. And when she talked excessively of some other man, in the hope of arousing jealousy on Freddie's part, he only looked at her quizzically and asked her was this not the same man whom she could not stand earlier.

The better approach would have been to confess her love and declare herself as a candidate for his hand. But the more her subtler efforts at winning his heart failed, the more cowardly she became. And just when she'd come to believe that perhaps he simply could not form a romantic attachment to an independent woman, he had to fall for the glamorous and audacious Lady Tremaine, who cared for no one's opinion but her own.

When Lady Tremaine had left Freddie to go back to her husband, Angelica's chance had finally come. He was distraught. He was vulnerable. He needed someone to take Lady Tremaine's place in his life. But when she'd gone to him, she'd stupidly said, *I told you so,* and he had asked her, in no uncertain terms, to leave him alone.

She finished dressing. He was outside the studio, waiting for her. During the four years she'd been away, he'd lost the baby fat that had still clung to him when he'd been twenty-four. And while he would never be quite as chiseled as Penny, she found him incredibly lovely, his features as gentle as his nature.

Even when he'd been chubbier, she'd still found him incredibly lovely.

"Can I offer you a cup of tea?" he asked.

"You may," she said. "But I'd like to return your favor first. Are the photographs you took of the painting ready?"

"They are still in the darkroom."

"Let's see them."

His studio was on the top floor, to take advantage of the light. His darkroom was one floor below, about eight feet by six feet in dimension, not much bigger than a closet. In the amber-brown glow of a safelight, the apparatuses for development were neatly laid out, with the sink, the baths, and the negative lamp along one wall, a worktable along another. Bottles of clearly labeled chemicals lined shelves built into the walls.

"When did you assemble a darkroom here?" He had taken up photography after her departure—after Lady Tremaine's departure, to be more precise. Once he'd sent Angelica a photograph of himself and she'd pasted it into her diary.

"I don't remember the exact date, but it was around the time your husband passed away."

"You sent a very kind condolence letter."

"I hardly knew what to say. You almost never mentioned him in your letters."

He applied a slight pressure on the small of her back to guide her deeper into the darkroom. She loved the warmth of his hand—he had large hands that could nevertheless paint the most extraordinarily delicate details. For years she'd gone to sleep thinking of caresses from those strong and skilled hands.

"It was a convenient marriage," she said belatedly. "We were leading separate lives well before he died."

"I worried about you," he said quietly, with that innate dignity for which she loved him so. "You used to say, when we were much younger, that you'd rather be a sufficient-unto-herself spinster than an indifferently married wife."

She'd sorely lacked the courage of her conviction, hadn't she? When it seemed that she could never have him, she'd married a virtual stranger and left England behind as swiftly as she could.

"I was fine," she said, more sharply than she'd intended. "I *am* fine."

He didn't say anything, as if he did not quite believe her reassurances but did not wish to say so outright.

She cleared her throat. "Well, Freddie, show me your photographs."

❧

The photographs, four inches by five inches in dimension, were affixed to a drying line.

"My goodness," Angelica said, stopping before the image of the rats. "How was that possible?"

She'd pinned her hair up, but it was a very soft knot and seemed in danger of spilling free. Or was it just him wishing to pull it free? The odor of the pyrosoda developer and the stop bath lingered in the air, but Freddie stood close enough behind her to smell the neroli of her toilette water, sweet and spicy.

"You should have heard the screaming. Penny had to slap one young lady to stop her."

"I can't see Penny slapping anyone."

"He was a very authoritative slapper," Freddie said dryly. That had rather surprised him too. "Here are the photographs of the painting."

He switched on another safelight. She squinted at the still-wet prints.

"I see what you mean," she said. "I *have* come across a painting very similar in style and execution. It had a lady angel in white—huge white wings, a white robe, a white rose in her hand. And there was a man on the ground, gazing up at her."

"My goodness, your memory *is* extraordinary."

"Thank you." She beamed at him. "When I go home, I shall consult my diary and see if I might have made a record of it. Sometimes I do, if an artwork strikes me in some way."

He wondered if she consulted her diary the same way she consulted *The Treasures of Art in Great Britain;* unclothed, with one strand of her unbound hair caressing her nipple, and one of her toes absent-mindedly tracing circles on the sheets.

Their gazes locked. Hers was bright and expectant.

"Were you really fine?" he heard himself ask.

The light faded from her eyes. "It was not actively painful. But it was not worthwhile either— having a husband merely for the sake of having a husband. I was already inquiring into an annulment when Giancarlo died. Never would I make that same mistake again."

"Good," he said, though he ached for the nearly two years she'd lost in her not-worthwhile marriage. He squeezed her hand briefly. "I'm glad you told me at last; you need never spare me any truthful answers."

"All right, then, I won't." She smiled a little. "Have you any other questions that you need answered honestly?"

He flushed. If she only knew. But how did one ask one's oldest friend whether she wanted to lie with him? He could already see her bursting out laughing. *Freddie, you silly, silly man. Where did you get* that *idea?*

"Well, yes," he said. "Would you care for some tea now?"

She cast her gaze down for a moment. When she looked back at him, her expression was very even. He wondered if he'd imagined the fleeting shadow in her eyes.

"Do you have coffee instead?" she asked.

Chapter Twelve

Vere had hoped to arrive at Highgate Court before Edmund Douglas: far easier that way to return the coded dossier to the safe and to take an impression of the key therein. Unfortunately, as he helped his wife out of the victoria Lady Kingsley had dispatched to fetch them from the train station, Edmund Douglas came striding out of the house.

Lines furrowed the corners of his eyes and mouth, and much of his dark hair had turned gray. But otherwise Douglas's appearance had changed little since the day of his wedding. He was still slender, still well dressed, still fine-featured and handsome.

He saw the Veres and stopped, his eyes as unreadable as those of a viper.

Vere glanced at his wife of less than twenty-four hours. For the first time in at least a decade, he'd been unable to sleep on a train. Instead, he'd observed her from underneath his lashes.

She'd kept the veil on her hat lowered, so he could

not see her expression. But for most of their journey, she'd sat with one hand at her throat, her other hand opening and clenching, opening and clenching. From time to time she shook her head slowly, as if trying to loosen her collar with that motion. And very, very infrequently, she let out an audibly uneven breath.

She'd been scared witless.

The moment Douglas appeared, however, it was as if the curtains had lifted, and her stage fright was now but a dim thought next to the all-consuming importance of her role.

"Oh, hullo, Uncle." She lifted her skirts, bounced up the steps, and kissed him on both cheeks. "Welcome home. When did you return? And did you have a good trip?"

Douglas stared at her coldly, a look that would have made grown men quail. "My trip was fine. However, instead of the joyful reunion I had anticipated, I came home ten minutes ago to find the house empty and my family disappeared, with Mrs. Ramsay recounting an *Arabian Nights* tale of revelry and destruction that concluded with your sudden departure."

She laughed as bubbly as a barrel of champagne. "Oh, Uncle. Mrs. Ramsay is such a stuffy old dear. There were no revelries: Lady Kingsley and her friends were delightfully civilized guests. Although I must admit that when Lord Vere proposed, in my burst of excitement I did knock over a ship in a bottle."

Lifting her left hand with its very modest wedding band toward him, she preened. "You are looking at the new Marchioness of Vere, sir. Allow me to present my husband."

She beckoned Vere. "Don't just stand there, my lord. Come meet my uncle."

She still believed him an inmitigated idiot. Had she been less distracted, less afraid, and less drunk, she might have noticed quite differently: He had been completely out of character for most of the previous day—and night. But he was lucky: She *had* been distracted, afraid, and much, much too drunk.

Vere took the steps two at a time and pumped Douglas's hand with the enthusiasm of a basset hound tearing into an old sock. "A pleasure, sir."

Douglas pulled his hand away. "You are *married*?"

The question was addressed more to his niece but Vere jumped in. "Oh, yes, church and flowers, and—well, everything," he replied, giggling a little.

She batted him on his arm. "Behave, sir."

Turning toward Douglas, she said more earnestly, "I do apologize. We are so much in love we could not bear to wait."

"But we rushed back to tell you the good news in person," Vere added. "Frankly, Lady Vere was a bit worried how you would receive me. But I told her I could not possibly fail to win your approval with my looks, address, and connections."

He bumped her lightly. "See, was I not right?"

She lobbed at him a smile brilliant enough to turn a field of sunflowers. "Of course you were, darling. I should not have doubted you. Never again."

"Where is your aunt, Elissande?"

Douglas's face had been impassive in the face of the Veres' smug bantering. His tone, however, was anything but. Something seethed beneath his words: a monstrous anger.

"She's at your favorite place in London, Uncle: Brown's Hotel, waited on hand and foot."

Vere could barely imagine the state of her nerves. She had no way of knowing that he would corroborate her lie. Yet nothing in her demeanor suggested the least nervousness or uncertainty.

"Indeed," he said. "I was the one who suggested that Mrs. Douglas should remain at the hotel and not tax her health too much by traveling again so soon. Lady Vere but acknowledged the wisdom of my recommendation."

Douglas narrowed his eyes, his silence ominous. Vere glanced at his wife. She gazed upon Douglas with enormous fondness, as if he'd just promised to take her to the House of Worth's showroom in Paris.

Vere had thought for a few days now that she was the best actress he had ever met. But as good as she had been during their brief acquaintance, before her uncle she was spectacular. Everything Vere had seen up to this moment had been but dress rehearsals; now she was the great thespian upon her stage, flooded in limelight, her audience at the edges of their seats.

"Well, let's not stand here," Douglas murmured at last. "We will sit down for a cup of tea."

No sooner had they taken their seats in the drawing room than Lord Vere started to squirm, obviously and embarrassingly. A minute later, he clamped his lips together, as if the integrity of his digestive system depended upon it. Finally, he wiped his brow and croaked, "If you will excuse me for a moment, I must—I fear—I must—"

He ran out.

Elissande's uncle said not a word, as if her husband were but a fly that had had the good sense to leave. Elissande, however, felt his absence keenly—a sign of just how utterly petrified she was that even his mindless presence buttressed her courage.

When she'd succumbed to the mad idea of marriage as a route of escape, a useless husband had not been what she'd anticipated, nor an encounter with her uncle bereft of protection. But now she was all alone before an anger that had hitherto been largely channeled toward her aunt.

"How do you like London, Elissande?" said her uncle silkily.

She'd scarcely paid any attention to London in the whirlwind of the past thirty-some hours. "Oh, big, dirty, crowded, but quite exciting, I must admit."

"You were at Brown's Hotel, you said, my favorite in London. Did you make it known to management that you are my close relation?"

Her heart beat as fast as a hummingbird's wings; her fear turned dizzying. Before her aunt became a complete invalid, when they, as a family, had taken afternoon tea together, he'd spoken to Aunt Rachel in precisely this same smooth, interested tone, asking her similarly mundane, harmless questions. And Aunt Rachel's responses would become shorter and slower with every question, as if each answer required her to knife herself in the flesh, until she fell silent altogether and the tears came again.

At which point he would escort her back to her room and Elissande would run to the remotest corner of the property, leap the fences, and run farther, pretending that she was not going back, that she was never going back.

"Oh, now I feel such a bumpkin," she moaned. *And don't wring your hands. Leave them still and relaxed on your lap.* "It never occurred to me that I would be treated differently by mentioning your name. How imbecilic of me."

"You are young; you will learn," said her uncle. "And your new husband, is he a good man?"

"The best," she avowed fervidly. "So very kind and considerate."

Her uncle rose from his seat and walked to a window. "I hardly know what to make of all this. My little girl, all grown-up and married," he said thoughtfully.

She clenched her toes in her kidskin boots. Her uncle sounding thoughtful always chilled her. This was the tone in which he said things such as *I do believe there are too many useless books in my library* or *Your aunt would not say it, bless her gentle soul, but she was most terribly in need of your company this afternoon, when you were away from the house. You should think more of her, and not always so much of your own pleasure.* The former pronouncement had preceded the purging of the library that had made her cry in her bed, under the covers, every night for a week, and the latter had turned Elissande almost as housebound as her aunt.

Tea was brought in. Elissande poured, breathing carefully so that her hand would not shake. The footman left, closing the door quietly behind him.

Her uncle approached the table. Elissande offered him his tea. The surface of the tea barely rippled: Her years under his tutelage were standing her in good stead.

She saw the teacup flying from her hand before she understood the burning pain on her cheek. Another slap came, even harder this time, and sent her careening from her chair. She lay where she'd fallen, stunned. She'd always suspected that he did unspeakable things to her aunt, but he'd never before raised his hand against *her*.

Her mouth tasted of blood. One of her molars moved. She could barely see for the liquid swimming in her eyes.

"Get up," he said.

She blinked back the tears and raised herself to her knees. Before she could get to her feet, he grabbed her by her collar, dragged her across the room, and slammed her into the wall.

Suddenly she understood that her skeleton was quite fragile. It was made of bones. And bones cracked under sufficient duress.

"You think you are so very clever. You think you can walk out of here with my wife—*my wife*."

His hand clutched her throat, shutting down her windpipe.

"Think again, Elissande!"

She would not. She was gladder than ever that she had finally taken Aunt Rachel away from him.

"You will return Mrs. Douglas to me and you will return her soon. If not—"

He smiled. She shuddered—she could not control it this time. He loosened his hold on her neck slightly. She gulped down air. He tightened his grip again.

"If not," he continued, "I fear something terrible might befall the handsome idiot you claim to love so much."

Her heart froze. She ground her teeth together so they would not chatter.

"Think of the poor overgrown dolt. You have already exploited him shamelessly, inveigling him into giving you his hand and his name. Does he truly need to lose an arm—and perhaps his eyesight—for you?"

She wanted to be haughty. She wanted to show him that she'd spit on his threats. But it was awfully difficult to appear strong and powerful when she could scarcely breathe. "You wouldn't dare," she managed to choke out.

"Wrong, my dear Elissande. For love, there is nothing I do not dare. Nothing."

For him to speak of love—the Devil might as well speak of salvation. "You don't love her. You have never loved her. You have only shown her cruelties great and small."

He drew back his hand and slapped her so hard

that for a moment she feared her neck had snapped. "You know nothing of love," he bellowed. "You know nothing of the lengths I've gone to—"

He stopped. She swallowed the blood in her mouth and stared at him. She had never, in her entire life, heard him raise his voice.

His outburst seemed to have surprised himself too. He took several deep breaths. When he spoke again, it was hardly more than a murmur. "Listen carefully, my dear: I will give you three days to bring her back. This is where she belongs; no court in the land will disagree with my prerogative as her husband.

"Bring her back, and you may enjoy your idiot for the rest of your days. Or you can look upon his blinded, maimed person for as long as you both shall live and know that you have been responsible for his mutilation. And remember—no matter what you decide, I will still have my wife back."

To mark his point, he put both of his hands on her throat. She struggled weakly. She must breathe. She wanted desperately to breathe. To be in the middle of a cyclone, high and loose in the sky, surrounded by nothing but air, air, and more air.

Air came as her husband yanked her uncle off and threw him—literally lifted him and flung him down. A plant stand crashed loudly: Her uncle skidded across the floor and knocked it over. Her husband pulled her into his arms. "Are you all right?"

She could not answer. She could only hold on tight—any port in a storm.

"Shame on you, sir," Lord Vere said. "This is your

niece, who has given up her youth to take care of your wife. Is this how you repay her devotion after all these years?"

Her uncle laughed softly.

"We left our honeymoon to call on you. I see now it was a mistake: You are not worthy of either our time or our courtesy," said her husband heatedly. "You may consider yourself cut from our acquaintance."

He kissed her on her forehead. "I'm sorry, my love. We should not have come. And you need never return here again."

❧

Vere had trouble calming himself enough to think properly.

He had sent three cables from the telegraph office: one to Lady Kingsley, alerting her to keep track of Douglas's movement at all times; one to Mrs. Dilwyn at the Savoy Hotel, for Mrs. Douglas's removal to Vere's town house; and one to Holbrook, requesting protection outside the house.

It would appear that he'd done all that was required of him at the moment. But something tugged at the back of his mind—something that just might yield an important connection if only he could clear his head for half an hour.

Which was exactly what he couldn't do. He turned around to look outside the window of the telegraph office, where the victoria sat with its hood up and his wife huddled inside the enclosure.

When he'd come upon Douglas with his strangle-hold on her, he'd known, rationally, that Douglas was not going to murder her then and there—it did not fit with the man's style of careful planning and even more meticulous execution. But rage had nevertheless exploded in him, and he had needed all his restraint to not pummel Douglas to within an inch of his life.

A very old rage that had never found its proper outlet.

He left the telegraph office and climbed back into the hooded victoria. She had her veil down; her fingers, white-knuckled, twisted her gloves. He lifted her veil and quickly lowered it: Her face still bore the imprints of Douglas's hand.

"I cabled my staff," he said by way of explanation. Turning to the coachman, he instructed, "The train station, Gibbons."

A few minutes later they were on the platform of the train station, out of hearing range of possibly curious servants.

"Does your uncle always do that?" he asked at last.

She shook her head; the pale gray veil fluttered. "He has never raised his hand to me before. I'm not so sure about my aunt."

"I'm sorry," he said.

He'd rather enjoyed dragging her back to Highgate Court against her wishes. He'd even enjoyed the panic that she'd done her best not to betray: She ought to suffer a little for what she'd done to him.

Now he felt awful. He had not forgiven her by any means, but his earlier glee had sharply evanesced.

Even that night in the green parlor he had not understood quite so vividly the true extent of her fear and desperation.

Her hands, now gloved, twisted a handkerchief. "He wants me to return my aunt to him in three days."

"And if you don't?"

She was silent a long time.

"He didn't promise to harm you or Mrs. Douglas, did he?" he prompted.

She began winding the twisted handkerchief along her index finger. "He promised to harm *you*."

"Me?" He was a little surprised to be dragged into this. "Hmm, I've never had people threaten harm to me before. I mean, ladies do occasionally kick me in the shin when I spill my drinks on them—and I don't blame them—"

"He said he would have you pay with a limb and your eyesight," she said flatly.

He was taken aback. "Well, that's not very nice of him, is it?"

"Are you afraid?" She certainly seemed to be. The way she was going, nothing would be left of the handkerchief but a few frayed threads by the time they reached London.

"Not afraid, precisely," he answered honestly for once. "But it hardly makes me happy that he chokes you one instant and menaces me the next."

She wrenched the handkerchief ever tighter—her finger must be blue inside her glove. "What should we do?"

He almost smiled—hard to believe the mightily

clever Lady Vere sought her idiot husband's advice. He reached for her hand and unwound the handkerchief. "I don't know, but we'll think of something. And you don't really think I'm so easy to harm, do you?"

"I pray not," she said. She was already twisting the handkerchief again. "But he is both cruel and subtle. He can harm you without leaving a trace of evidence—I've never been able to ascertain what it was he did to my aunt to make her so terrified of him."

Suddenly, the not-quite-thoughts in the back of Vere's head coalesced into a concrete theory. Edmund Douglas's ruthless finesse. The death of Stephen Delaney, so like Mrs. Watts's yet so removed from the current case. The decline of Douglas's diamond mine and his need for income, given both his insatiable appetite to prove himself in other avenues of investment and his dismal record.

He rubbed his hands together. "You know what we should do?"

"Yes?" she asked with both surprise and hope in her voice.

He almost hated to disappoint her. "We should not be hungry, that's what. I don't know about you but I'm a smarter and braver man when my stomach is full. You stay here. I'm paying a visit to the bakery. Anything I can bring back for you?"

Her shoulders slumped. "No, thank you, I'm not hungry. But be careful if you do go."

He went back to the telegraph office and sent out a fourth cable, this one to Lord Yardley, whom Holbrook half jokingly referred to as his overlord—the

Delaney case had been before Holbrook's time and Holbrook had always been more interested in the new than the old.

He asked only one question of Lord Yardley: Did Delaney's scientific inquiries have anything to do with the synthesis of artificial diamonds?

Lord Vere slept.

He seemed to have a special affinity for sleeping in trains, since he'd slumbered heavily on the way to Shropshire as well. But it mystified Elissande how anyone who had been threatened with such grievous harm could be so unconcerned about it—the way he'd reacted, as if she'd told him he stood to lose a cravat, instead of crucial body parts.

At least he hadn't blurted out that Mrs. Douglas was at the Savoy Hotel instead of Brown's. Perhaps he'd forgotten already at which hotel they'd spent the night, just as he seemed to have forgotten his earlier unhappiness about marrying her.

She rubbed her temple. Her uncle, ever insidiously clever, had chosen the perfect target for his threat. Elissande and Aunt Rachel knew the danger they faced in him; they were prepared to do everything to save themselves.

But how did she protect Lord Vere, who did not understand his imperilment? And yet protect him she must—it was only because of her action that he was embroiled in her troubles.

He'd returned with a box from the bakery just before they boarded the train and offered her the box's contents. And she'd shaken her head vigorously in refusal. But now she moved beside him and opened the bakery box. He'd left her two currant buns and a small Vienna cake.

Without quite intending to, she ate both the currant buns and half the Vienna cake. Perhaps he'd been right: She did feel less panicky with something in her stomach. And perhaps he had good cause not to be afraid of her uncle: Never in her life had she seen anyone put Edmund Douglas in his place the way her husband had.

He was so strong. She wished very much to be like him now, stalwart and unworried.

She sighed and laid her hand on his elbow.

❧

He did not expect her touch. He expected even less that it should feel as it did: infinitely familiar.

After a while, she removed her hat and rested her head along his upper arm. He opened his eyes to remind himself that it was only Lady Vere, who had become his wife by engaging in deceit and assault. But as he looked down upon her shining hair and listened to her soft, steady breaths, nothing, it seemed, could diminish the sweetness of her near-embrace.

There was what he thought of her. There was what he felt regardless. And there was very little middle ground.

To his surprise, the next thing he knew, the train

was decelerating into London and she was gently calling for him to wake up from a deep sleep.

They detrained, met the brougham that had been sent to fetch them, and drove to his town house, left to him by his late maternal grandfather, one of Britain's richest men while he lived.

Mr. Woodbridge had acquired the house with the intention to demolish it and build a bigger, taller mansion on the lot, but he had died before his architect completed the new plans. Vere, who saw no need for anything bigger or taller, had the plumbing modernized, electricity wired, and telephone service installed, but otherwise left the structure of the house unaltered.

The town house was situated exactly halfway between Grosvenor Square and Berkeley Square, an imposing classical edifice with soaring Ionic columns and a pediment that depicted a trident-wielding Poseidon on a hippocampus-drawn chariot. Lady Vere lifted her veil and swept her gaze over his impressive home—he was glad to see that the swelling on her face had already gone down.

"This is not the Savoy Hotel," she said.

"Well, no, this is my house."

"But my aunt, she is still at the hotel. We must retrieve her too if we are to stay here."

"She's already here. Don't you remember, in the morning I told you that when she'd had rest enough, Mrs. Dilwyn would bring her home?"

"You never told me any such thing."

Of course he never did. He hadn't even wanted to

put Mrs. Dilwyn at her aunt's disposal. Had, in fact, meant to keep his wife and her aunt well away from his house and separate from all the other spheres of his life. But now he had no choice but to take them into his home.

He patted her on the hand. "That's quite understandable, my dear. You were hardly yourself this morning—all that Sauternes. Come now, the staff will be waiting to meet you."

As soon as the servants had been presented to her, she asked to see her aunt. Mrs. Dilwyn accompanied her, giving a report of Mrs. Douglas's day as they started up the steps.

Vere remained behind and read the post that had come for him during his absence before he too took the stairs. By mutual agreement, he and Holbrook rarely met in public or called upon each other's residences. But they did belong to the same club. Tonight it would be quicker for Vere to find Holbrook at the club—and for that he needed to change into his evening clothes.

His wife and Mrs. Dilwyn were in the passage outside the mistress's room.

"Would you like me to bring back one of Mrs. Douglas's nightdresses for you to use tonight, ma'am?" asked Mrs. Dilwyn.

His wife frowned, an unusual expression for her.

"What seems to be the problem?" he asked. "Is everything all right with Mrs. Douglas?"

"She is very well, thank you. And there's not a problem at all," she said. "I forgot to pack nightdresses for myself—and I just had the maids take away all the rest of Mrs. Douglas's for laundering."

"What's the matter with Mrs. Douglas's night-dresses?"

"They smell of cloves. She doesn't like cloves and neither do I."

"You are right: That's not a problem," he said. "I'll lend you a nightshirt for tonight. My nightshirts absolutely do not smell of cloves."

It took two seconds before she beamed at him and said, "Thank you. But I don't wish to trouble you, sir."

Two whole seconds. When her smile was otherwise always instantaneous.

She was afraid he would touch her.

When she needed a little reassurance on the train, she'd felt quite free to touch him. And when she'd fallen asleep with her head against his person, her fragrance soft and sweet in his nostrils, he had thought—

He'd thought that he no longer quite repelled her. And the irony was, he was *not* going to touch her. His offer of a solution had not been in any way a ploy to take advantage of her. He would have sent Mrs. Dilwyn to fetch a nightshirt from his dressing room.

But her disproportionate reaction had his imaginary self reaching for one more chunk of rock.

"No, no, it would be no trouble at all," he said. "Come along."

He walked on into his bedchamber; she had no choice but to follow him. He stripped off his day coat and continued to his dressing room.

"How do you like your new house, by the way?" he asked as he discarded his waistcoat, looking back at her.

"Very well," she said, smiling. "It's a very fine house."

They managed quite a passable imitation of an ordinary marriage, he must concede.

"And Mrs. Dilwyn, has she been helpful?"

"Most helpful." Her smile persevered but she stopped well short of the door of the dressing room.

"Come in so you can choose one."

"Oh, I'm sure the one you choose will be perfectly fine."

"Nonsense, come inside."

She still maintained her smile, but needed a deep breath before she entered the dressing room.

He pulled his shirt over his head. Her smile deserted her.

He didn't always have this musculature throughout the year. But it was at the end of summer: Since the middle of April he had been based in London, which meant three miles every morning at his swimming club. He was in the best form he could possibly be in. And when he was in his best form he was, physically, a very intimidating man.

The dressing room was large. But it was also thickly populated with shelves, cabinets, and armoires, which made it secluded and isolated. She stood with her back against a chest of drawers. He walked up to her, braced his arm next to her shoulder, and did nothing else for a moment—he truly was not above tormenting her—before pulling off his signet ring and tossing it in a tray of accessories atop the chest of drawers.

"Come," he said softly.

She swallowed.

"You said you wanted to pick out the nightshirt you like best. So come."

He could see it in her eyes, the desire to correct him, to argue that she'd never wanted anything of the sort, that he was the one to impose the choosing on her. But she only said, "Certainly."

He had stacks of nightshirts, all white, in linen, flannel, silk, and merino wool. She snatched the uppermost nightshirt from the nearest stack.

"I'll take this one."

"But you haven't felt the others yet. Feel them."

He pressed the nightshirts into her hands, one after another, and offered accompanying treatises on fabrics and textures. Soon they stood in a knee-deep pile of discarded nightshirts. And he handed her yet another one to examine.

It was silk, lustrous, smooth, lavish, something that two thousand years ago would have been quite worth the walk from Chang'an to Damascus.

"So soft," he said. "Like your skin."

Her grip tightened on the nightshirt. "May I have this one then?"

"Indeed, have it. Took you long enough to find one you liked."

But she would not escape him so easily yet. He insisted she unclench her fingers, to avoid wrinkling the silk, and then he took hold of her hand and rubbed his thumb over her palm. Giving her his most thick-witted smile, he sighed. "Ah, yes, just as lovely as I remember it."

And remembered it. And remembered it.

It dawned on him that he tormented no one but himself with this little game of his.

He dropped her hand and stepped back. "Well, then, off you go."

She looked at him uncertainly. He began to undo the fastening of his trousers. She needed no more urging after that, her departure swift and resounding.

Chapter Thirteen

Holbrook sported a black eye.

Vere had to smile at the sight. "So Lady Kingsley did not forget to pay you a visit when she was in London."

Holbrook gingerly touched the bruises around his eye. "She should have delegated the task to you. You would have punished me more tenderly."

"Quite so." Vere pushed the cigarette case–size casting mold he'd used at Highgate Court across the table to Holbrook. "I need a key made from this."

They were seated at White's, as far away from the bow window as possible. It was more than permissible for mere acquaintances belonging to the same club to dine together, but there was no point advertising their contact to passersby on St. James.

"What does the key open?" asked Holbrook.

"Something of Edmund Douglas's."

"Hmm," said Holbrook, pocketing the casting

mold. "And what have you learned from your visit to Mrs. Watts's old neighborhood?"

"That Douglas probably murdered Mrs. Watts."

"His own great-aunt?"

"I don't think she was his great-aunt," said Vere, slicing his veal cutlet. "I don't think he is Edmund Douglas, in fact."

Holbrook's brows rose. "Where is the real Edmund Douglas, then?"

"My guess? Murdered, too."

"These are serious crimes to suspect of your uncle-in-law."

"I'm nothing if not a dutiful nephew-in-law." He almost wished his father were still alive. *I married the niece of a* murderer, *Pater. It's a spectacularly suitable match for me, don't you think?* "Any progress from your code breakers?"

"Some, but they haven't quite cracked it yet."

There was no doubt in Vere's mind that the Crown would nab Douglas sooner or later—not only was the noose tightening around the man's neck, but he was currently so distracted by his niece absconding with his wife that he had no idea his secret life was being peeled back layer by layer. From a strictly professional point of view, there was no hurry. On the extortion front, they did not yet have any diamond dealers willing to cooperate with the police. And if they wanted him prosecuted on charges of murder, they needed time to find old acquaintances of the real Edmund Douglas who were willing to travel from

South Africa to England to give their testimony in court.

But an Edmund Douglas at large was an Edmund Douglas capable of committing further atrocities. When he realized that Vere was a difficult man to hurt, he would no doubt turn his attention back to his wife and his niece. Vere had not left his house thinking the world of his wife. That did not, however, negate the fact that he was now responsible for her safekeeping.

"I want *you* to work on it," he said to Holbrook.

Holbrook was one of the best code breakers in the country, if not in the entire world. Like Lady Kingsley, Vere, too, believed instinctively that there was something in the coded dossier that would allow them to arrest Douglas immediately.

Holbrook, no doubt taking note of Vere's impatience, leaned against the back of his chair. "Why, Lord Vere, you know how much I hate real work."

Of course, Holbrook's help always came with a price. "What do you want?"

Holbrook smiled. "Remember the blackmailing of a certain royal I mentioned some time ago? I am still in need of a superior, dedicated agent to extract said royal from his troubles. But since you are a staunch republican and wouldn't lift a finger in the service of the monarchy, I have not brought it up."

Vere sighed. Under normal circumstances he'd have refused: He did not consider aiding useless royals a worthwhile endeavor. But just this once he would do it, if for nothing other than to appease his own conscience, which was still indignant that he'd so gleefully put his wife in harm's way.

"What do I need to know?"

❧

The blackmailer was a Mr. Boyd Palliser. According to Holbrook's intelligence, Palliser, in trouble with certain uncouth elements of society, feared for his safety. His house was tightly secured against intrusion and the only way to get in was to be let in.

"I want you to lose enough money to him at cards to be invited to his house. Once there, drink him insensate and abscond with the goods—and preferably with your gambling notes too," Holbrook said.

Vere rolled his eyes. "Someday you should give your own plans an implementation. I don't like drinking anymore."

"Nonsense. You can drink a rhinoceros under the table."

In his later adolescence and early twenties, Vere had been able to drink a herd of elephants under the table with no ill effects whatsoever. These days, however, his liver no longer cared for that sort of abuse. But on such short notice, there wasn't much else he could do.

He left White's and found Palliser at the latter's favorite gambling place. It took fantastical losses at the card table, enough rum to float the RMS *Campania*, and idiocy of an extent to impress even himself, but he was finally invited back to Palliser's house in Chelsea toward the end of the night.

They drank. They sang. They all but whored together. At one point, wobbling dangerously across the room, Palliser swung a curio cabinet away from the wall and revealed a safe behind it. Then, patting every pocket on himself, he eventually drew a chain from around his neck, opened the safe, and took out a jade statuette of such intricate lewdness that in Vere's state of advanced inebriation it took him nearly a minute to grunt in appreciation.

He also did not notice until Palliser opened the safe again to put the statuette back that the safe also contained a bundle of letters.

There was nothing to do now but drink Palliser to oblivion, then grab the packet of letters and run—a goal, however, that receded faster the more Vere imbibed, as Palliser had the vexing habit of staring at Vere until Vere emptied his glass, making it impossible to chuck his drink into the plant stand behind him.

Palliser reached across the table for the rum bottle and knocked over a pewter vase. The vase fell loudly to the floor.

"Did you hear that?" asked Vere.

"Of course I heard it."

"No, something else," said Vere. He rose unsteadily to retrieve the vase, only to upend a chair that had appeared out of nowhere.

The chair crashed.

"Did you hear that?" asked Vere again.

"Of course I heard it!" said Palliser, a little peeved now.

"No, something else."

Palliser grabbed hold of his walking stick and levered himself upright. He listened. Then he waved the walking stick in the air. "I don't hear nothin'."

The walking stick walloped a marble bust off a shelf, which promptly broke against the floor.

"Bugger!"

"Shhhhhhhhh," said Vere. "There is a scuffle going on."

"Where? I don't hear a thing."

Vere stepped backward and knocked over the entire side table. It fell with a terrific bang. "I think somebody's running this way."

"About time. This place is a disgrace. It needs to be tidied right now. In fact—"

The door opened and in rushed a stranger. A stranger with a revolver in his hand. He lifted the revolver with what seemed to Vere infinite slowness. Or was it that his perception and reflexes had become infinitely slow? Vere glanced at Palliser. The man hadn't even noticed the intruder yet; he was still staring with dumb fascination at the broken halves of the marble bust.

The intruder fired. The sound barely penetrated Vere's glue-like consciousness. He watched with a calm, distant appreciation as Palliser crumpled to the floor. The shot had gone in the left side of Palliser's chest, leaving a neat hole in the middle of the gaudy peony Palliser wore as a boutonniere.

The intruder turned toward Vere. He pulled the

trigger. Vere ducked. The sharp pain in his right arm abruptly revived all his rum-drowned instincts. His hand closed around the pewter vase on the floor.

That vase hurtled through the air and met the intruder squarely on the forehead. The man yelped and wobbled. Before he could recover, a chair hit him in the face. And then he was smashed with a side table, this time with Vere's weight behind it.

The man collapsed in a heap. Footsteps came pounding outside the room. Vere flattened himself against a wall. But it was only Palliser's servants—not his bodyguards, merely an excited and confounded pair of footmen.

"You, go fetch a doctor," he said to one of the footmen, though he'd be surprised if Palliser was still alive. The footman left running. To the remaining footman he said, "And you, the constable."

"But Mr. Palliser, he wants nothing to do with the police."

"Well, then go fetch whomever it is he would want to fetch when someone has shot him."

The footman hesitated. "I don't know, sir. I'm new here."

"Then fetch the constable!"

After he dispatched the second footman and made sure no more servants were arriving to witness the carnage, Vere slipped the chain from Palliser's lifeless head. Wrapping the key in his handkerchief—the police could do things with fingerprints these days—he opened the safe and retrieved the packet of letters. He glanced through the contents—yes, quite mortifying if made public—and counted the letters—seven, just what he was looking for.

He'd come prepared with a different packet of letters, also from said royal, but on entirely inconsequential matters. He made the switch, pocketed his loot, and returned the key to Palliser's corpse.

Only then did he glance down at his right arm. The bullet had grazed just below his shoulder. A fairly superficial wound. He would take care of it later, when he was in the safety and privacy of his own home.

Now he must vacate the premises before the doctor, the constable, or anyone else reached the scene.

❧

Outside his house Vere realized that he should have gone to one of Holbrook's hidey-holes instead. He had remembered to discard the wig, the mustache, and the spectacles he'd worn as part of the temporary identity he'd assumed for the evening, but forgot that he should never come home in a state of injury.

And now he was too disoriented and worn out to go anywhere else. He swayed and decided that bleeding arm or no, he'd best get inside.

He let himself in, grimacing as he did so. He was left-handed; a wound to the right arm did not overly inconvenience him. But that did not lessen the pain.

Somewhere a clock chimed quarter past four in the morning. He trudged up to his room and turned on the light just enough to see. The packet of letters immediately went into a locked compartment in his armoire—*immediately* meaning as soon as he could fit the key into the lock. His maids would find many scratches around the keyhole in the morning.

He grunted as he took off his evening coat. The waistcoat did not give him trouble. But the fabric of his shirt stuck to the wound and he grunted again as he ripped away the sleeve.

It was worse than he'd thought. The bullet had taken a chunk of his flesh. He would do what he could now and get himself to bed. When he woke up— assuming the bad head did not kill him outright—he would summon Needham, an agent of Holbrook's who also happened to be a practicing physician.

He soaked several handkerchiefs with water from the pitcher on his washstand and cleaned the blood from around the wound. There was a bottle of distilled alcohol among his shaving things. He doused another handkerchief with it.

The burn of the alcohol made him hiss. His head hurt. Now that the rush of action had worn off, the vast quantity of spirits he'd consumed was once again making its effect felt. He would be lucky if he didn't find himself on the floor shortly.

Suddenly he stilled. He wasn't sure what he'd heard, but he knew he was no longer the only person awake in the house.

He turned. The connecting door opened; his wife stood in his nightshirt, which on her dragged to the floor. Strange how his vision, otherwise quite impaired by the alcohol, wasn't so faulty as to not notice the way the nightshirt molded to her breasts, or the way her nipples peaked in the cool night air.

"It's so late. I was worried. I thought—" She gasped. "What happened? Did my uncle—"

"Oh, no, nothing of the sort. A hansom cab driver wanted my pocketbook. I wouldn't give it to him. He pulled out a pistol and waved it in the air. It accidentally went off, he bolted in a mad dash, and I had to walk the rest of the way home."

A coherent lie, something he'd have thought quite beyond him at the moment. He impressed himself.

She stared at him as if he'd said he'd come home naked, dancing all the way. Her reaction annoyed him—implicit in her look was the assumption that *he* must have perpetrated an act of unspeakable imbecility to cause his wound to materialize. Surely sometimes cabdrivers shot their passengers. Even a country bumpkin like her should be able to imagine such a scenario.

He returned his attention to his arm and dabbed more alcohol onto his wound. She approached him and took the handkerchief from his hand.

"I'll do it," she said.

It was quite charitable of her. But he'd left the house in a very uncharitable mood toward her and that mood hadn't improved in the subsequent hours.

I'm not so stupid I can't clean a simple bullet wound.

She left for her room and came back with a petticoat torn into strips. He handed her a jar of boracic ointment he'd found in the meanwhile. She looked at the jar, then at him, with something close to wonder— yet another sign that he was still indisputably an idiot in her eyes when a normal, reasonable act on his part brought forth such disbelief.

She turned on more lights, spread the ointment over a square of cloth, placed the anointed cloth over his wound, and bandaged him.

Working swiftly, she wiped away drops of his blood from the floor and then gathered his bloodstained garments.

"I know London is dangerous. But I was never given the impression that it was *this* dangerous—that law-abiding gentlemen are in danger from merely going about." She stuffed all the soiled items into his evening jacket and tied the bundle with the jacket's sleeves. "Where were you when you were shot?"

"I'm . . . not sure."

"Where were you then before you got into the hansom cab?"

"Ah . . . I'm not quite sure about that either."

She frowned. "Is this a common occurrence? You don't even seem alarmed."

He wished she would let him be. The last thing he needed now was a cross-examination "No, of course not." Most of the time—the vast, vast, overwhelming majority of the time—he did what he needed to do with a minimum of trouble and even less bloodshed. "I'm tiddly, that's all."

Her frown deepened. "What kind of cabbie carries a pistol?"

"The kind who drives at three in the morning?" he said, growing impatient with her questions.

She pursed her lips. "Please do not jest. You could have been killed."

Her sanctimonious concern angered him.

"You wouldn't have minded becoming a widow," he snapped, no longer able to censor his words.

Her expression changed, acquiring a guardedness that could not quite mask her shock and apprehension. "I beg your pardon?"

"It's Freddie you fancy, not me. I'm not *that* stupid."

She clamped her hands together. "I don't *fancy* Lord Frederick."

"Fancy. Prefer. What's the difference? And since we are on the topic, I do not appreciate what you did to force me into this marriage."

She bit her lower lip. "I'm sorry," she said. "I really am. I will try to make it up to you."

Pretty words. And as insubstantial as butterflies. He hadn't needed to swig all that vile rum this night. He'd done it for her, so that Holbrook would get off his indolent arse and decipher the coded dossier, so that her uncle could be arrested sooner, so that she and her aunt could live free of his menace.

And this was how she thanked him. *I will* try *to make it up to you.*

"Do it then. Make it up to me."

She recoiled.

He should have been too drunk to care. But the more she shuddered away from him, the more the memories of her sweet willingness seared.

"Take off your clothes," he said.

He was a dangerous drunk.

His body, by itself, was enough to force her to pay attention. She'd once seen, in a book on classical art, an etching of a statue of Poseidon. She had stared at it in fascination, at what the Greeks had considered the pinnacle of male form, and thought it nothing but a fantasy, a conjuration of the sculptor's mind that reality could never match.

Until him. He had that body, that impossibly ridged musculature. And just above the top of his trousers, the beginning of the deep, exaggerated indentations at the hips that—on Poseidon, at least—had left a long-lasting impression on her.

And the way he held himself: his head tilted back slightly, his body in one long, mouthwatering line.

Yes, mouthwatering. Physically he was strikingly fit and strikingly handsome. Something to salivate after.

She almost didn't hear what he said. "Pardon?"

"I would like you to take off your clothes," he repeated quite casually.

She was at a loss for words.

"It's not as if I haven't seen you before. We are married, if you will recall."

She cleared her throat. "Would it really make up for my taking advantage of you?"

"I'm afraid not. But it might make this marriage more bearable in the meanwhile—if I can remember to practice withdrawal."

"What—what is withdrawal?"

"Let's see, since you know your scripture so well, was that Onan? Yes, that bugger. What he did."

"Spilling his seed on the floor?"

"What a prodigious memory you possess. The whole of Song of Songs, and this too."

The Bible had been one of the few English-language books that her uncle had let remain in the house.

"And yes," continued her husband, "it would be lovely if I could take you and spill my seed somewhere else. Not on the floor, mind you. But perhaps on your very soft belly. Perhaps even on your splendid breasts. And perhaps, if I'm in a really terrible mood, I'll make you swallow it."

She blinked and did not ask if he was jesting. He probably wasn't.

He'd been quite decent to her and very nice to her aunt, after everything she'd done. He'd been most satisfactorily forceful with her uncle. And she had trusted implicitly in his solidity and strength as she slept next to him on the train.

But as he'd disrobed in the evening and beckoned her into the depth of his dressing room, she'd been afraid—the memory of the pain he'd inflicted on her was still fresh in her mind. Here again that fear rattled. And it seemed somehow wrong for him to demand that she remove her clothes when it was clear that he was not amorous, but angry.

"Surely," she mumbled, "surely you prefer to rest?"

He raised a brow. "Did I not just say I'd like to see you undress?"

"But you are hurt and it's five o'clock in the morning."

"You've much to learn about men if you think that a scratch on the arm will deter us. Go on, take off everything and lie down on the bed."

Her voice was growing smaller and smaller. "Perhaps this is not the best time. You've more rum in you than a pirate ship and you—"

"And I'd like to sleep with my wife."

She did not know he could speak this way, with force and weight behind his words. He did not threaten her, but she had been firmly reminded that she was in no position to deny him.

She exhaled very slowly, walked to his bed, and slid under the cover. Once there, she removed her nightshirt as discreetly as she could, and then, to signal that she'd complied, dropped the nightshirt to the side of the bed.

The first thing he did was to flick away the bedcover and expose her. She bit her lower lip and willed herself not to squirm.

His breaths were uneven. The way he looked at her—he devoured her already.

"Spread your legs," he murmured.

"No!"

He smiled and moved his left hand to the fastening of his trousers. "You will, someday."

She closed her eyes as his trousers fell. The

mattress dipped as he joined her in bed. Then the shock—their naked bodies aligned, touching everywhere.

Everywhere.

"Yes, keep your eyes closed very tightly and imagine that I'm Freddie," he whispered, the tickle of his breath sending hot, spiked signals along her nerves.

She shook her head, and then gasped as his lips brushed her ear. He kissed her where her shoulder and her neck joined. Then he set his teeth to the exact same spot. A sharp bite—possessive, angry.

But it didn't quite hurt. Instead, an inexplicable surge of pleasure curled her toes.

"Now imagine it's Freddie putting his mouth to your very superior bosom," he said, as he half licked, half bit his way past her collarbone.

She shook her head again. His caustic assertiveness did something to her. Some primordial part of her was all stirred up, responding to the power and command he radiated—sloshed, rude, and very much a man.

"Do you think Freddie lies awake at night thinking about your gorgeous titties?" he asked.

Her eyes opened in shock. Now this went too far. She stared into his eyes—good gracious, were they the reason she remembered talking excitedly about the Hope Diamond on their wedding night?

"No, I don't think so."

"Maybe he doesn't," said her husband very softly. "But I do."

And with that, he lowered his head and took her nipple into his mouth.

The pleasure was so sharp it was almost cruel.

He grazed her nipples with his teeth. She was reduced to arching her back and panting audibly. Finally he lifted his head and kissed the undercurve of her breasts instead. From there he went south, his mouth caressing her torso, her belly. He dipped his tongue into her navel, causing her to gasp.

She thought that was as far as he'd go, but he proved her wrong. He went lower. She clamped her thighs together in alarm. Surely he didn't mean to. Didn't God smite Sodom and Gomorrah for such wickedness?

But he did mean to. He pulled apart her thighs to nibble at the insides of them.

"No. Please don't."

"Shhh," he said, just before he put his mouth to her.

She'd never been more effectively shushed. He supped on her. He dined on her. He feasted on her. She was mortified, then aroused, then unbearably aroused. He agitated her on and on, sparing no consideration for her delicate sensibilities, no regard for her wish to maintain a decorous quiet.

He didn't stop until she thrashed wildly and bit down hard on the coverlet, so as not to wake the entire house.

But he wasn't finished. He pushed her thighs apart in a most indecent way, lifted her by her bottom, and came into her. God, the size and strength of him. For a moment she was paralyzed by the memory of her earlier agony. But there was not even discomfort. He was all patience and deftness and control. And she found out that she still wanted more. More of him, more pleasure, more of this mind-boggling coupling.

"Open your eyes," he ordered.

She had no idea she'd closed her eyes again—to feel more keenly what he did to her, the strange, addictive sensations of being filled to the brim by him.

"Open your eyes and look at me."

She did. He withdrew and reentered her, slowly, slowly, going deeper, deeper. And when she thought he couldn't come any farther into her, he did.

She gasped with the pleasure and depravity of it— his possession of her, while his eyes held hers.

"No pretending," he said softly. "Do you see who is fucking you?"

He thrust into her again. She could not answer. She could only gasp once more.

He was a god above her, powerful, beautiful, larger than life. The light brought out the latent gold of his hair. The shadows contoured the perfect form of his body. Light and shadows converged in his eyes, bright lust, dark anger, and something else. Something else entirely.

She recognized it because she'd seen it in the mirror so many times: a bleak, austere loneliness.

Her hands, which had been clutching at the sheets, moved up his arms. "I never pretended it was anyone but you."

Now he was the one to close his eyes, to gasp and grimace. She followed his example, and felt and felt and felt. Tides of chaos rose and gathered. An implosion came upon her. She was still in the grips of its after-tremors when his control broke at last. He ground into her with enough force to launch an ocean liner. And bucked and shook as if in pain, exquisite, breathtaking pain.

She opened her eyes again to see him looking down upon her, the way he would a cursed treasure. He lifted a hand and traced her brow.

"Now you are mine," he said softly.

She shivered.

❦

Belatedly she saw the blood on his bandage. The wound had started to bleed again.

From his exertion.

"Your arm," she said unsteadily.

He glanced at the dressing, then lowered himself and nipped her jaw. "If ever I can bring myself to leave you, my dear Lady Vere. Did you notice I forgot to withdraw? I didn't either. I don't think I could have had the fate of mankind hung in the balance."

She flushed. Who was he? This was not the bumbling, blabbering man she married. His words were sharp as knives, his lovemaking as dangerous as Waterloo.

"Your *arm*," she insisted, even as her cheeks scalded.

He sighed. "All right. Have it your way."

"Close your eyes," she said, once they'd separated. "Please."

He sighed again and obliged. She threw on her nightshirt and cut strips from another petticoat. From his armoire she retrieved a clean handkerchief, spread it with the ointment, and made him sit up so that she could dress his arm properly.

"Cleanse yourself with a solution of sterile water and red wine vinegar," he said as she tied the ends of the new bandaging. "You can buy what you need at a chemist's shop called McGonagall's, not far from Piccadilly Circus."

She looked up at him, not understanding what he meant.

"You don't want to procreate with a moron, do you?" he said amiably, but she did not miss his acerbic undertone.

The man she thought she knew would never have referred to himself as a moron. He'd been nothing if not consistent and fervent in his self-congratulations. Had it all been but an act then?

"Water and vinegar—is that what women do when they don't wish to conceive?"

"Among other things."

"You seem to know a great deal about such things."

"I know enough," he said, lying back down. "Hide everything under the bed and get me Eugene Needham in the morning. He has a practice on Euston Road. And he can see to the disposal of things."

She pushed the bundle under his bed and turned off the lights. Then she stood in the center of the very dark room and tried to understand what had happened, to pinpoint the exact moment her husband had turned into this potent and slightly terrifying stranger.

"Go," he said from the bed.

"Are you—are you still angry at me?"

"I'm angry at Fate. You are but a convenient substitute. Now go."

She hurried out.

Chapter Fourteen

"What a lovely garden," murmured Aunt Rachel.

Lord Vere's house was backed by a private garden to which only the residents in the surrounding houses had access, a situation that was both fortuitous and uncommon in London, according to Mrs. Dilwyn.

Several elegant plane trees grew in this enclosure, their wide canopies thrust sixty feet in the air to offer fine shade to those who strolled the flagstone path that bisected a smoothly clipped lawn. A three-tiered Italian fountain burbled agreeably nearby.

Mrs. Dilwyn had advised a daily intake of fresh air. Elissande, who was determined to do the right thing by her aunt, had steeled herself for a long bout of wheedling persuasion in order to extract Aunt Rachel from her bed. To her surprise, Aunt Rachel had agreed immediately to be put into a simple blue day dress.

Elissande had helped her into a chair and then, a

pair of impressively sized footmen had carried the chair, with Aunt Rachel in it, down to the garden.

A leaf floated down from the canopy above. Elissande caught it in her hand and showed it to Aunt Rachel.

Aunt Rachel stared reverently at the very ordinary leaf. "How beautiful," she said.

Elissande's reply was forgotten as a teardrop fell down Aunt Rachel's face. She turned toward Elissande. "Thank you, Ellie."

Panic engulfed Elissande. This shelter, this life, this green haven in the middle of London—the safety Aunt Rachel believed they'd found was as fleeting as a soap bubble.

For love, there is nothing I do not dare. Nothing.

Love was a petrifying word coming out of her uncle's mouth. He was quite ready to wage hell's own vengeance to regain his wife.

I fear something terrible might befall the handsome idiot you claim to love so much.

The handsome idiot who had claimed her thoroughly in the darkness before dawn.

Except he hadn't been at all an idiot, had he? He'd been angry, discourteous, and his language had been downright appalling. But he hadn't been stupid. He'd known very clearly what she'd done to him, which begged the question: Had he been, like her, pretending to be someone he wasn't?

The thought was a hook through her heart, yanking it in unpredictable directions.

The golden glow of his skin. The electric pleasure

of his teeth at her shoulder. The dark excitement of his flesh firmly embedded in hers.

But more than anything else, the raw power he exuded.

Take off your clothes.

She wanted him to say it again.

Her hand crept to her throat, her fingertip pressed into the vein that throbbed rapidly.

Was it possible—was it at all possible that she could come out of her most desperate choice with a man as clever as Odysseus who looked like Achilles and made love like Paris...?

And her uncle had threatened irreparable harm to him.

Only two days remained.

❦

Needham came, rebandaged Vere's arm, and left with both the packet of letters Vere had taken from Palliser and the bundle of bloodied clothes under Vere's bed. All without a single word. Good old Needham.

By the middle of the afternoon Vere was able to get up from his bed without immediately wanting to put a rifle to his head and pull the trigger. He rang for tea and toast.

When the knock came at his door, however, the person who entered was his wife, a smile on her face.

"How are you, Penny?"

No, *not* the person he wanted to see, not when the only thing he could remember of his predawn hours at home was his desperate release into her very willing body. He could deduce that she must have helped him with his wound, and that he must have instructed her to get Needham, but how had they gone from an activity as distinctly uncarnal as dressing a gunshot injury to the sort of untrammeled coupling the memories of which came near to making *him* blush?

Well, there was nothing to do but to brazen it out.

"Oh, hullo, my dear. And don't you look ever fresh and charming."

Her dress was white, a pure and demure backdrop for her guileless smile. The skirt of the dress, fashionably narrow, clung rather ferociously to her hips before dropping in a more seemly column to the floor.

"You are sure you feel well enough to eat?"

"Quite. I'm famished."

She clapped her hands. A maid came in and set down a tray of tea, bobbed a curtsy, and left.

His wife poured. "How is your arm?"

"Hurts."

"And your head?"

"Hurts. But better." He drank thirstily of the tea she offered, making sure to spill some on his dressing gown. "Do you know what happened to me? My arm, that is. My head always hurts after too much whiskey."

"It was rum you drank," she corrected him. "And you said a hansom cab driver shot you."

That was stupid of him. He should never have mentioned a gun. "Are you sure?" he asked. "I can hardly stand rum."

She poured herself a cup of tea. "Where *were* you

last night?" she said softly, with wifely interest. "And what were you doing out so late?"

She'd come to *interrogate* him.

"I can't quite remember."

Very deliberately she stirred in her cream and sugar. "You don't remember being shot at?"

Well, this would not do. He was much better on the offensive. "Well, you should know firsthand the deleterious effect the consumption of alcoholic beverages has on the retention of memory."

"I beg your pardon?"

"Can you recall anything from our wedding night?"

Her stirring stopped. "Of course I remember... some things."

"You told me my lips dripped beeswax. No one had ever told me before that my lips dripped beeswax."

To her credit, she raised her teacup and drank without choking. "Do you mean honeycomb?"

"Pardon?"

"Honeycomb, not beeswax."

"Right, that's what I said. Honeycomb. 'Honey and milk are under thy tongue,' you told me, 'and the smell of thy garments is like the smell of...' Hmm, let me think, what was it? Sinai? Syria? Damascus?"

"Lebanon," she said.

"Exactly. And of course, once we disrobed you"—he sighed in exaggerated contentment—"you were far better to look at than even the lady in the Delacroix your father stole. Do you suppose we could have you pose like that for Freddie? And not for a minuscule canvas either—life-size, I insist—and can we hang it in the dining room?"

"That would border on public indecency."

Her smile was beginning to assume that over-brightness he'd come to know so intimately. Good, he must be doing something right.

"Dash it. Would have been grand fun showing you off to my friends. How they would slobber over you."

He made moon eyes at her.

"Now, now, Penny," she said, her voice just the slightest bit tight. "We mustn't rub our good fortune in our friends' faces."

Happier, he ate four slices of toast. When he was finished, she said, "Dr. Needham told me your dressing should be changed in the afternoon, and again in the evening before bed. So shall we?"

He rolled up the sleeve of his dressing gown. She examined his wound and changed the bandaging. As he rolled down his sleeve, she stopped him and asked, "What are these?"

Her fingers pointed to a series of small half-moon marks just above his elbow.

"Look like nail marks to me."

"Did the cabdriver get his hand on you too?"

"Hmm, they seem more like they have been left by a woman. In the heat of passion, you see. She grabs on to the man's arms and her fingers dig into his sinews." He smiled at her. "Have you been taking advantage of me while I was mentally incapacitated, Lady Vere?"

She flushed. "It was you who wished it, sir."

"Was it? My, could have been disastrous, you know. When a man is that drunk, sometimes he can't get it up. And sometimes he can't finish it off."

She touched her throat. "Well, you didn't have any problem on either account."

He preened. "That is a testament to your charm, my lady. Although I must say, if we keep going at it like this, the family size will be increasing very soon."

A thought that rather petrified him.

"Do you wish to increase the family size?" she asked, as if it were an afterthought.

"Well, of course, what man doesn't? For God and country," he said, as he scanned the letters that had come with his tea and toast.

When he looked up again, she wore the oddest expression. He immediately worried he'd said something that had given his act away, but he could not think what.

"Oh, look, Freddie invites us for tea this afternoon at the Savoy Hotel. Shall we go then?"

"Yes," she said, with a smile he'd never quite seen before. "Do let us go."

❧

The terrace at the Savoy Hotel commanded a panoramic view of the Thames, with Cleopatra's Needle thrusting skyward just beyond the hotel's gardens. A steady traffic of steamships and barges traversed the water lanes. The sky was clear by London standards, but nevertheless seemed dirt-smudged to Elissande, who had yet to grow accustomed to the great metropolis's perpetually tainted air.

Lord Frederick had brought along Mrs. Canaletto, a childhood chum of the brothers, both of whom called her by her Christian name. She was several years older than Elissande, worldly, not given to the same sort of limitless enthusiasm as Miss Kingsley and her companions, but nevertheless friendly and approachable.

"Have you been to the theater yet, Lady Vere?" asked Mrs. Canaletto.

"No, I'm afraid I've not had the pleasure."

"Then you must have Penny take you to a performance at the Savoy Theatre right away."

Elissande's husband looked at Mrs. Canaletto expectantly, then said, "Only one recommendation, Angelica? You used to like to tell us how to do *everything*."

Mrs. Canaletto chuckled. "That's because I've known you since you were three, Penny. When I've known Lady Vere twenty-six years, rest assured I will tell her how to do everything too."

Elissande asked Mrs. Canaletto whether she'd visited the Isle of Capri during her stay in Italy. Mrs. Canaletto had not, but both Lord Vere and Lord Frederick had, on a continental jaunt the two had taken together after Lord Frederick had finished his studies at Oxford.

Lord Vere talked about the sights they'd seen on the trip, with Mrs. Canaletto correcting him good-naturedly alongside: the fabled Neuschwanstein Castle in Bulgaria, built by the mad Count Siegfried ("It's in Bavaria, Penny, built by King Ludwig II, who might or might not have been mad"); the Leaning Tower of Sienna ("Pisa"); and on Capri, the Purple Grotto ("The Black Grotto, Penny").

"It was the Black Grotto, really?"

"Angelica is teasing you, Penny," said Lord Frederick. "It's the Blue Grotto."

Undaunted, Elissande's husband went on. As he held forth, he dropped his handkerchief into the jam pot, knocked the contents of a slender flower vase onto the crumpet plate, and had one of his biscuits leap ten feet to land amidst the pink ostrich feathers of someone's extravagant hat.

Lord Frederick and Mrs. Canaletto seemed to think nothing of either Lord Vere's loquaciousness or his clumsiness. But his words and actions seemed excessive to Elissande, as if he were trying to make up for the flash of incisive intelligence he'd displayed during their predawn encounter by making himself appear especially inane.

And inept. To dilute the memory of his absolute mastery over her body, perhaps?

He had come to within an inch of convincing her that it had been a fluke—within an inch. And then he'd gone too far and directly contradicted himself— probably because he sincerely did not remember recommending, strongly, that she take measures against just such a possibility as the expanding of their family.

The lady in the pink ostrich hat, after recovering the biscuit from the depth of her millinery plumage, approached their table. For a moment Elissande thought she might have harsh words for Lord Vere, but Lord Vere and Lord Frederick rose, and both men plus Mrs. Canaletto greeted her familiarly.

"Lady Vere, may I present the Countess of Bourkes," said Lord Vere. "Countess, my wife."

It was the beginning of a parade. The Season was over, but London was still an important hub for the upper crust traveling between Scotland, Cowes, and the therapeutic spas of the Continent. Elissande's husband seemed to be acquainted with everyone who was anyone. And as Lady Avery must have lost no time in trumpeting her latest exposé, the whole world wanted to see what manner of woman had been caught with him in a most scandalous manner.

He introduced her with absurd pride. *Lady Vere has devoted herself to the well-being of her aunt. Lady Vere is as knowledgeable of modern art as Freddie. Lady Vere is certain to be one of London's great hostesses.*

It took her a minute to align her reaction with his. She discarded the moderately warm smiles she had thought appropriate for the situation and went for the full teeth-and-dazzle.

Lord Vere shines a precise and all-encompassing light upon the current Anglo-Prussian relationship. Lord Vere discusses the architectural history of Europe with aplomb and flair. Lord Vere's deep and detailed reading of Ovid has provided us with hours of enthralling conversation.

They made a stunning pair, in the most literal sense. People left their table agape, barely able to totter back to their own seats. Who'd have thought that the talents she'd honed to defend the integrity of her soul from her uncle would one day be put to such public theater? If it weren't so bizarre she'd almost find it funny.

"I rather enjoyed eloping, on the whole. I should have done it sooner. But of course I did it as soon as I could with Lady Vere," said her husband, once he was able to sit down again.

"Well, I do think we could have done it *one* day sooner," Elissande said with a giggle.

"That is true," he concurred. "I did not think of that. Why did I not think of that?"

"But that is quite all right. We are here and we are married and it couldn't be more wonderful."

Across from them, Lord Frederick and Mrs. Canaletto exchanged looks of good-natured incredulity, as if marveling that such a perfect match could and did exist for Lord Vere. Lord Vere leaned in for another slice of sultana cake and—what else?—overturned the creamer in the process.

Elissande was beginning to see an adroit choreography to his ungainliness, the carefully chosen angle of his arm, the precise path of his reach, the calculated sweep of the back of his hand.

There was no such thing as a man who was more lucid when drunk, only one who was less careful, and therefore less hidden. For him, who had expressed his potent displeasure only hours ago, to then take on the part of the dizzyingly happy husband—he was nothing if not a superb actor.

It took one to know one.

❦

There was a note for Vere from Mr. Filbert when he arrived back at his town house—Mr. Filbert being one of Holbrook's aliases. Vere changed into his evening clothes, told his wife he was going out to his club, met Holbrook and Lady Kingsley at the house behind Fitzroy Square, and worked feverishly. He did not return home again until nearly midnight.

His wife was waiting for him in his room. "This is much too reckless of you," she declared irately. "May I remind you that you were injured only last night from staying out too late?"

He paused in the removal of his necktie. "I, ah, well, I forgot," he answered with an appearance of sheepishness.

She came up to him, undid the buttons on his evening jacket, and pushed it off his shoulders. "You shouldn't be going about on your own in the dark. I don't trust my uncle; he doesn't play fair. When he says three days, he'd be quite happy to abduct you on the second day and then force me to trade my aunt for you."

"Would you?"

She glared at him. "Let's not talk about such unpleasant hypotheticals."

"But you brought it up just now," he said earnestly. "I thought you wished to talk about it."

She took a deep breath and two steps back. "May I ask you a favor?"

"Of course."

"Can we dispense with the pretenses?"

Alarm flooded him. He regarded her with wide eyes. "Beg pardon?"

"We are home. The servants are abed. There is no one else about but the two of us," she said impatiently. "You don't need to continue with your act. I know you are not as oblivious as you pretend to be."

Surely he hadn't given *that* much of himself away. "But this is preposterous. Are you implying that I come across as oblivious, madam? I will have you know that I have the brightest mind and the keenest wit. Why, people are often astounded by the perspicacity of my discourse and the subtlety of my insight!"

He'd done everything he possibly could this day to reinforce the impression of the idiot. Shouldn't that have been enough?

"This morning I visited the chemist's you recommended," she said. "Mrs. McGonagall taught me how to cleanse after lovemaking to minimize the chance of being in the family way. I did it after I came back home."

Christ. He told her all that? What else had he said to her? "But—but you can't do that. A woman is supposed to—she is *not* supposed to interfere with Nature in such matters."

"The whole history of civilization is one of interference with Nature. Besides, I was but following your instruction, sir."

"But I could never have given such instructions. Why, contraception is a sin."

She passed her hand over her face. He had never seen her in such an open state of frustration. It shocked him to realize what this meant: She had dropped *her* pretenses.

"Fine, then. Keep your charade," she said. "But tomorrow is the last day of grace my uncle allowed me. He is a dangerous man and I'm afraid. Is it possible for the three of us to vacate England for a while?"

"Good Lord. Where shall we go?"

She hesitated briefly. "I've always wanted to visit Capri."

At least he didn't seem to have told her anything about the investigation. "But there is absolutely nothing to do on Capri: It's a rock in the middle of the ocean. Minimal society, no sports, not even a music hall anywhere in sight."

"But it's safe. Come winter boats from the mainland will have a hard time getting to it."

"Precisely. The horror! I shall move us to my country house in a few days, but other than that, I've no intention of going anywhere else. This Season has been long enough already."

"But—"

"You should trust my luck," he pressed on. "Some people say I've a fool's luck. Of course, I take exception to that because I've always been a man of highly developed intelligence, but there is no denying my charmed luck. You've done well, Lady Vere. You've married me. Now my luck will rub off on you too."

She tightened the sash of her dressing gown, her motion ungentle. "It's maddening to talk to you."

He was only trying to reassure her. Things had been set in motion this night, but he could not tell her any more at the moment.

"But you insist on peppering me with such nonsense, my dear."

"In that case, don't be surprised to find yourself drugged and shanghaied. I *will* do whatever it takes to keep all of us safe."

He should be irked, since her whatever-it-takes stance was what had married them in the first place. But it was difficult to be too upset when it was *his* well-being that had her vexed and anxious.

"Ah, come, sweetheart," he coaxed. "We are only on the third day of our honeymoon and we are already bickering."

She threw up her hands. "Fine. Let's just change your bandage."

She assisted him in the removing of his waistcoat. He was only going to roll up the sleeve of his shirt but she wanted that gone too. "If I don't take off the shirt, how will I put your nightshirt on you?" she said, her ire still hot. "You will pull at the wound if you do it yourself."

Evidently the thought of his going to bed naked never occurred to her. He acquiesced.

After she changed his bandaging, she went into his dressing room and returned with a nightshirt. Something about his person caught her attention and made her frown. She pointed to the left side of his rib cage. "What are those?"

He looked down at the scars. "You've never noticed them before?"

"No. How did you get them?"

"They are from my riding accident." With his good arm he made the trajectory of someone being thrown high in the air and then falling sharply. "Everybody knows about my riding accident."

"I've never heard of it."

"That's very strange, considering that you are my wife. Well, it happened when I was sixteen, not long after I came into the title. I was at my great-aunt Lady Jane's summer place in Aberdeenshire. Went for a ride one morning, took a tumble off my horse, broke some ribs, suffered a concussion, and had to stay in bed for a few weeks."

"That sounds quite serious."

"It was. It was," he reassured her. "Of course, some stupid people believe that I fell directly on my head and damaged my brain. But that is an utter fabrication. I have been, if anything, a sharper thinker since my accident."

"Hmm, I wonder why they would believe that," she said. "Were there any witnesses?"

Smart woman. "Witnesses? What do you mean?"

"I mean, I can see you suffered an injury on your torso. But where is the evidence for the concussion? Who was your attending physician?"

His attending physician had been none other than Needham. But he was not about to tell her that.

"Ah..."

"So it's your word and your word alone that there was a severe concussion."

"Why would I lie about something like that?"

"To pass yourself off as a credible idiot if you hadn't been one before."

"But I just told you, I suffered no ill effects. I was a brilliant boy then and I am a brilliant man now."

She cast him a still-incensed look. "Indeed, your brilliance dazzles."

"Then don't worry when I tell you not to worry," he said softly.

She sighed and lifted her hand. Her fingers traced along one scar, her touch burning.

He yawned and walked away. "If you'll excuse me, I'm falling asleep on my feet."

Behind him she murmured, "You don't need me to make it up to you tonight?"

Her words went directly to his privates. He clenched his teeth against the upsurge of desire. "Pardon?"

"Never mind," she said after a moment. "Good night."

"Good night, my dear."

Chapter Fifteen

"Do you think, Ellie," said Aunt Rachel diffidently, "that there might be doctors who will know how to—how to distance me from laudanum?"

It took Elissande a moment to realize her aunt had spoken and another to understand what Aunt Rachel had said. She turned away from the window, where she'd been staring, unseeing, into the garden.

Aunt Rachel was having her breakfast in her bright, lovely room. She still had her meals brought to her bed. But after only a few days away from Highgate Court, she was already feeding herself.

The previous afternoon she'd requested her window be opened to let in a few notes of birdsong. Last night, after her dinner, she'd shyly inquired into the possibility of a tiny piece of chocolate, should such be available in the house. Elissande had had no idea, but Mrs. Dilwyn had been pleased to inform Mrs. Douglas that indeed, his lordship was very fond of French chocolate and there was always a supply on hand. Aunt Rachel's expression, as she placed the little morsel of chocolate in her mouth, had been one of such pure joy that Elissande had to turn aside to wipe at her eyes.

And this morning, as Elissande entered her bedroom, Aunt Rachel had said, "How pretty you look, my dear." The last time Aunt Rachel had been well enough to compliment Elissande had been eight years ago, before the snowball fight that fateful Christmas day, before the laudanum.

There was no doubt about it: Aunt Rachel was improving in every way. *Too fast.* Had she remained inert and unresponsive, perhaps it would not make such a difference. But to let her fall back into Edmund Douglas's clutches now—

"Ellie? Are you all right, Ellie?"

Elissande swallowed. She advanced to the edge of Aunt Rachel's bed and sat down. "I might have to hide you."

Aunt Rachel's fork fell. "Is it—is your uncle—"

"He's not here yet, but it's only a matter of time." Despite her husband's reassurance, Elissande had churned all night in her bed. "You are too easy to locate in this house. I've chosen a hotel for you. You will be only minutes away and I will come and see you as often as I can."

Aunt Rachel clutched Elissande hand. "Will you—will you and Lord Vere be all right?"

"We'll be fine. We are not afraid of him."

Though she wished her husband would be a little

more afraid. It was dangerous to underestimate her uncle.

"When you have dressed, I will take you to a dressmaker's. We will go in the front and come out the back, take a hack, and then head for the Langham Hotel. I will bring your things by later; first we secure your person. Do you follow me?"

Aunt Rachel nodded hard.

"Good, now—"

There was a knock on the door.

"Yes?" said Elissande.

"Your ladyship, Mrs. Douglas," said the footman, holding a silver salver before him. "Mrs. Douglas, there is a gentleman by the name of Nevinson calling for you. He asked me to deliver this note to you in person. And he wishes to know whether you are at home to him, mum."

Aunt Rachel, already too frozen to speak, looked to Elissande.

Elissande took the note and broke the wax seal on the envelope.

> *Dear Mrs. Douglas,*
>
> *This is Detective Nevinson of the Metropolitan Police, on urgent business with regard to your husband, Mr. Edmund Douglas. I pray you will receive me promptly.*
>
> > *Your servant,*
> > *Nevinson*

Elissande clenched her fist. Was it her uncle, sending the law after her aunt?

No, he had no cause for it. A man's wife was at perfect liberty to travel to London for a week.

Then it must be a ruse. The detective was an impostor, a Trojan horse sent to breach the defenses of this house when it could not otherwise be stormed.

"First give this note to his lordship and ask him to read it immediately," she said to the footman. "Then show Mr. Nevinson to the drawing room and make him welcome. We will receive him presently."

The footman left to do her bidding. Aunt Rachel gripped Elissande's arm.

"Are you sure?" Aunt Rachel's voice shook.

"*I* will receive him. *You* will enjoy your breakfast. Lord Vere is here and he is not going to let you be abducted from under his nose."

Or so she prayed. And locked Aunt Rachel's door just in case.

❧

"Thank you for seeing me, Lady Vere," said Nevinson.

He was dressed in a smart lounge suit of blue worsted, a man of early middle age, with sharp eyes and efficient movements—very much the competent and trustworthy officer of the law and precisely the sort of quality confidence artist she would have hired had she wanted her aunt stolen.

She pasted on her usual smile. "What may I do for you, Detective?"

"Will Mrs. Douglas be joining us, ma'am, if I may ask?"

"Mrs. Douglas is not at home. But I will be happy to relate your message to her."

Nevinson hesitated. "Forgive me, ma'am. What I am about to say is of an extraordinarily sensitive nature. Is it at all possible that I may speak to Mrs. Douglas face-to-face?"

"Alas," said Elissande, still smiling, "I'm afraid it is not possible."

The man regarded Elissande. "And why is that so, Lady Vere?"

Elissande cleared her throat and exaggeratedly looked about the empty drawing room. Then she said in a stage whisper, "You see, sir, for some time every month, she suffers. Oh, how she suffers. You could even say she is in the veriest of agony."

Nevinson obviously had not expected this particular answer. He flushed a deep red and struggled to regain his composure.

"In that case, I'd be grateful if you would pass on the message to Mrs. Douglas." He cleared his throat. "I hate to be the bearer of ill news, but Mr. Douglas has been arrested this morning on suspicion of murder."

Elissande blinked. "Is this a joke, Detective?"

"I'm sorry, ma'am. It is not. We have sufficient evidence to believe that he is responsible for the murder of one Stephen Delaney, a scientist whose unpublished method of diamond synthesis he stole."

Why would her uncle kill a man for a method of

diamond synthesis when he already had access to vast quantities of natural diamonds? The accusation was too ridiculous for words. This had to be a ploy. How long could she keep Nevinson in the drawing room? Could she get a message to her husband that he was to whisk her aunt away this moment?

She was breaking out in a cold sweat. She must not go into a panic. She needed to think clearly and effectively.

What was that? Someone was singing outside the drawing room—a familiar song.

" 'I've got a little cat. And I'm very fond of that. But I'd rather have a bow-wow. Wow, wow, wow, wow.' "

She had to conceal a smile as her husband opened the door and stuck his head inside. "Good morning, my dear. How lovely you are, as always," he warbled.

Thank God! She'd never been so happy to see anyone.

Lord Vere, sloppily dressed, his hair still sleep-mussed, turned toward Elissande's caller. "And is that you, Detective Netherby?" he exclaimed in a tone of surprise.

"Nevinson, my lord."

Had she caught a grimace on Nevinson's face?

"I knew it!" exclaimed Lord Vere, strolling into the room. "I never forget a face or a name. You were the lead detective on the Huntleigh case."

"The Haysleigh case."

"That's what I said. When Lady Haysleigh was discovered to have faked her own death in order to escape a prior marriage and marry Lord Haysleigh—and then she attempted to murder her first husband when he arrived at the Haysleigh estate."

"That, sir, would be the plot of a Mrs. Braddon novel. Lord Haysleigh's younger brother, Mr. Hudson, attempted to poison Lady Haysleigh in order to frame Lord Haysleigh for murder so that he himself would come into the title."

"Really? I always thought *that* was the plot of a Mrs. Braddon novel." Lord Vere sat down and accepted a cup of tea from Elissande. "Thank you, my dear. Now, Detective, I'm under the impression the Haysleigh case was settled several years ago."

"It was, sir."

"That's a bit odd to see you here then. I didn't know we were on calling terms."

Nevinson clenched his teeth. "Never fear, my lord. I'm here strictly on business."

"Ah, and what business would that be? I assure you, I have been nowhere near any suspicious activities."

"I'm sure you haven't, sir. I'm here to see Mrs. Douglas about her husband."

Elissande had been so entertained watching her husband toy with Nevinson that only upon the reference to her uncle did she suddenly understand the significance of what had transpired before her.

Nevinson was not an impostor. He was a real detective, here on official business.

And he was not lying to her.

As if to underscore that realization, Detective

Nevinson repeated to Lord Vere, almost word for word, what he had told Elissande.

Her uncle, a murderer.

Her head exploded piece by tiny piece. It was not a terrible sensation: bizarre and disconcerting, but not terrible. There would be an awful scandal, there was no avoiding that. But what a tremendous silver lining. Her uncle had been arrested: He was in no position to compel Aunt Rachel to return to him now.

Moreover, once he was tried and convicted, he would rot in jail for a long, long time. Perhaps he would even *hang*. And Elissande and Aunt Rachel would be free, completely, gloriously free.

She barely heard her husband when he said, "But of course you and your men are welcome to search the manor from top to bottom. Is that all right with you, my dear?"

"Beg pardon?"

"That is the express purpose of Detective Nevinson's visit. It is a courtesy on his part, as by now I believe he needs no permission from us to search Highgate Court."

"Well, yes, of course. We shall cooperate fully."

Nevinson thanked them and rose to leave.

She had to restrain herself from screaming in elation as she bade Nevinson good day. As soon as he left, she leaped high in the air, wrapped her husband in a hard embrace, then ran upstairs, tears streaming down her face, to inform her aunt of the news of their deliverance.

Stephen Delaney's main area of scientific interest had indeed been the artificial synthesis of diamonds, as amply demonstrated by the box of documents Lord Yardley had sent to Holbrook—apparently the file Vere had read had been a mere extract.

While Vere had slept off the rum, Holbrook had cracked the code used in Douglas's dossier. Last night, using Holbrook's guide, Vere had deciphered pages in the dossier, the text of which was identical to that in Delaney's spare laboratory notebook. (Apparently, Delaney had a system whereby he took his own notes in his primary notebook; then his assistant copied the notes and stored the duplicate notebook away from the laboratory for safekeeping.) So even though Douglas had stolen and, in all probability, subsequently destroyed Delaney's primary notebook, the existence of the duplicate still clearly and powerfully connected Douglas's dossier and Delaney's research.

And even better: a note written in the margins of a page in Douglas's dossier, which when deciphered read, *Should not have done away with the bastard before I could reproduce his results.*

Enough to arrest and charge Douglas. And enough, along with the ongoing investigation into his other crimes and strong pressure from Yardley—in response to Vere's request—to hold Douglas without bail.

Vere was suddenly tired. It always came, this

bone-deep weariness at the end of a case. But it seemed even more draining this time. Perhaps because above him his wife was literally jumping for joy, the impact of her landings reverberating through the ceiling.

Her purposes for this marriage had been served: She was safe and she was free, as was her aunt. He would let some more time elapse—for Douglas to be tried and convicted—and then he would demand an annulment.

It was still possible, or so he liked to think, to repair the damages she had wrought. When he'd had time and distance enough from her, her face and her smile would cease to intrude into his fantasies of tranquillity and peacefulness. Then, when he wanted simple companionship, he would have simple companionship, and all the easy comfort that came with it.

The emotions Lady Vere invoked were too dark, too sharp, too unnerving. He didn't want them. He didn't want the frustration, the lust, or the dangerous longings she incited. He wanted only for things to go back as they were, before their paths collided: an inner life that was soothing, consoling, placating, thickly buffered from the realities of his life.

Rather like Mrs. Douglas with her laudanum.

He poured himself two fingers of whiskey and downed it in a single gulp.

Upstairs she jumped again. No doubt she was laughing and crying at the same time, weightless with happiness and relief, her nightmare at last coming to an end.

His nightmares would just have to go on.

❧

"Allow me to read you a passage from my diary, dated twelve April 1884," said Angelica. She cleared her throat dramatically. "'On the bank of the trout stream, I read and Freddie drew. Penny struck up a conversation with the vicar, who was out on a walk— something about the Gnostics and the Council of Nicaea.'"

She looked up. "My goodness, remember how learned Penny used to be?"

"I remember," said Freddie.

But he never remembered it without an echo of sadness.

"At least he's happily married now. His wife seems to find him nothing short of miraculous."

"That does make me happy. I like the way she looks at him: There is so much that's good and admirable in Penny."

Angelica slid her finger along the edge of her leather-bound diary. "But?" she prompted him.

He smiled. She knew him too well. "I'll admit I am a little envious. I used to think that if I ended up an old bachelor, at least I'd have Penny for company."

"You can always have my company," she said. "It would be like being children all over again, except with fewer teeth."

He suddenly recalled an instance of fewer teeth. "Do you remember the time I accidentally broke my father's favorite pair of spectacles?"

"Was that the time when I stole my mother's specs to replace them and we were hoping he wouldn't find out?"

"Yes, that was it. My mother and Penny were both away somewhere and I was scared out of my wits. And you suggested that we pull your loose teeth to keep my mind off the specs."

"Really?" She chuckled. "I don't remember that part at all."

"Your new teeth had come out already. And your old teeth were so loose they were flapping about like a line of washing in the wind. Everyone was after you to get rid of the old teeth, but you were adamant that no one come near them."

"My goodness. Now I remember a little. I used to sleep with a scarf over my mouth, so that my governess couldn't have at them."

"I was so surprised that you'd let *me*, I forgot all about the specs. We pulled out four of your teeth that afternoon."

She bent over laughing.

"Listen, it gets better: My father dropped your mother's specs and stepped on them before he could put them on and realize they were the wrong ones. It had to be one of the few times when my clumsiness didn't get *someone* into trouble. The relief, my God."

"Well, one thing is certain: I will not let you pull out any of my teeth when I'm a crone."

He raised his coffee cup to her in salute. "Understood. All the same, I'd be thrilled to have your company when I'm a dotard."

She returned his salute, her eyes sparkling, and he suddenly realized, for the very first time, how privileged he was to have known her his entire life. Sometimes one took the best things in one's life for granted. He never fully understood how much he had wholeheartedly depended on Penny before Penny's accident changed everything. And he'd never considered the central role Angelica's friendship had played in his life, especially in those difficult, vulnerable years under his father—until now, when he was full of feelings that threatened to imperil that very friendship.

"Now, where were we?" She set down her coffee cup and found her place in the diary. "Here we go. 'The old dear, evidently delighted with the discussion, invited all of us to the vicarage for tea.'"

"We were at Lyndhurst Hall, weren't we?" he asked, beginning to have some recollection himself. "For the duchess's Easter house party?"

"Precisely. Now listen to this: 'The tea was very nice, as was Mrs. Vicar, but what caught my attention was the painting in the parlor of the vicarage. A beautiful angel, taking up most of the canvas, hovered above a man who was clearly in a state of worshipful ecstasy. The name of the painting was *The Adoration of the Angel*.' I asked Mrs. Vicar the name of the artist—he had signed only his initials, G. C. Mrs. Vicar did not know, but she said that they had bought the painting from the London art dealer Cipriani.'"

"Cipriani? The one who never forgets anything that passes through his hands?"

"That's the one," she said, closing her diary with much satisfaction. "He's retired now. But I wrote to him this morning. Who knows? He might welcome us to call on him."

"You are a marvel," he said, meaning every word.

"Of course I am," said Angelica, her black skirts rustling as she rose. "So you see, I've been upholding my end of the bargain. Now it's your turn."

His hands perspired. He dreaded seeing her naked again, even as he couldn't wait to walk into the studio and have her beautiful form spread like a feast before him—a feast for a man who must fast.

He had been working on the painting, his head overrun with carnal thoughts even as he analyzed color, texture, and composition. His dreams, full of erotic interludes ever since she'd broached the subject of the portrait, had by now taken on a disturbing vividness.

He cleared his throat rather ineffectually—and cleared his throat again. "I suppose you want to go up to the studio then?"

❧

Freddie had set the studio ablaze with light—too much light, in Angelica's opinion. Her skin would gleam unbearably bright under such lighting, and she always preferred the flesh tones in her paintings to look more natural.

There was a camera—not Freddie's No. 4 Kodak, which she had seen before, but a much more elaborate studio camera on a wooden tripod, with bellows for focusing and a black cloth draped behind. There was also a flashlamp, a screen of cheesecloth, and several white screens set at various angles.

"What is the camera for?" she asked, once he'd reentered the studio, after she'd disrobed and lain down.

"It must be a chore for you to pose for so long—and I'm not a fast painter. But once I have the photographs, I can work from them and you won't need to shiver in the cold."

"It's not cold." A fire had been laid in the grate and he'd supplied several braziers. He must be warm.

"Still."

"But photographs do not convey color!"

"Perhaps not, but they do convey shading and contrast, and I already know the exact hue of your skin," he said, disappearing behind the black cloth.

Disappointment gripped her. The nude portrait was her gambit for him to see her as a woman, and not just a friend. And she'd thought it more or less successful—he had looked at her strangely in the darkroom, as if he were on the verge of kissing her. But once he had the photographs, not only would he not need her naked, he wouldn't even need her in the studio anymore.

"What if the photographs are underexposed or overexposed?"

"Pardon?" The sound of his voice was muffled by the black cloth.

"What if the photographs don't come out well?"

He reemerged from behind the camera. "I've half a dozen plates. One of them is bound to turn out well."

He pulled the trigger on the flashlamp. It took a moment for the cartridge of magnesium powder to ignite, and for the controlled explosion to produce a burst of brilliant white light. He ducked again under the black cloth.

This time, when he came out, he raised the height of the flashlamp, moved the cheesecloth screen forward by a foot, and adjusted the angle of a white silk screen on the far side of the bed.

The screen was only two feet from the edge of the bed. As he lifted his head, he looked directly down at her, from what seemed a great height.

She licked her lips in nervousness. His hand tightened on the screen. And then he was walking away, back to the camera.

"I'm going to draw the slide," he said. "Make sure you are in the pose you want."

Her heart hammered, agitated by both his nearness and his refusal to succumb to her seduction. Her lips parted, her breaths shallow, she turned her head until she looked directly into the lens of his camera.

❧

It was late in the afternoon before Elissande noticed the oddity of Aunt Rachel's reaction.

In the morning she had been too joyful, too overwhelmed herself to mark Aunt Rachel's speechlessness as anything other than blissful stupefaction. She had jumped up and down like a monkey—though her landings had sounded more like those of a rhinoceros—and wept until she was a few pounds lighter.

She had thought nothing of her aunt's request for a bit of laudanum. Aunt Rachel was frail. The day's news was shocking. Of course she needed time and rest before she could properly cope with it.

When Aunt Rachel had fallen asleep, Elissande had sat next to her bed for some time, holding her hand, smoothing her hair, full of gratitude that Aunt Rachel had lived to see this day, and that she still had years ahead of her to be enjoyed, free of fear and shadows.

Then she'd gone to look for her husband, for no reason other than that she wanted to see him—he was the closest thing she had to an ally. And on this wonderful, triumphant day, who better to celebrate with than him?

But he had gone out already. So she contented herself with having his coachman drive her around town, and took pleasure in London for the first time since her arrival. She watched young people on bicycles in the park, walked every floor of Harrods, and then spent so long in Hatchards that her gloves were completely soiled with book dust.

She also visited Needham again and asked to be recommended a physician who was an expert on opiate addiction. As it turned out, Needham considered himself sufficiently versed in the matter to help her.

"He says it need not involve any suffering at all," she told Aunt Rachel when she reached home. "Each day you will take the same amount of a special tonic. But the amount of laudanum in each subsequent bottle of tonic will gradually be reduced. Your body will easily adjust to the new dosage until you no longer need any laudanum at all.

"And to think, all the torment my uncle put you through, when he could have—" She waved a hand in the air. "Never mind him. We need not think of him ever again."

Aunt Rachel didn't say anything. She shivered, as if she were cold. Elissande immediately draped another blanket on her, but Aunt Rachel only shivered again.

Elissande sat down at the edge of the bed. "What's the matter, my love?"

"I... I feel terrible for the man he murdered, Mr. Delaney. I wonder how many others there are in all."

"My goodness!" Elissande exclaimed. "Isn't one murder horrific enough?"

Aunt Rachel plucked at the top of her blanket. For no discernible reason, Elissande's hitherto bottomless ebullience suddenly reached a bottom.

"Is there something I should know?" she asked, hoping there wasn't.

"No, of course not," said Aunt Rachel. "You were telling me about the doctor, weren't you, the one who is going to treat me? Do go on."

Elissande looked at her aunt another moment, then smiled brightly. "Well, he's coming to see you tomorrow, and he seems a very kindly man."

Whatever it was Aunt Rachel was not telling her, Elissande did not want to know.

Chapter Sixteen

One of the first things Vere did when he came of age was to break entail on the marquessate's country seat. He had caused a minor scandal when he'd put the manor up for sale. But the world was changing. A grand house in the country, with land more and more ineffectual as a generator of wealth, had become an albatross around the necks of too many.

It was not the life he wanted, his destiny and choices chained to a pile of stones, however glorious and historical. Nor was it the life he wanted for Freddie and Freddie's heirs, since there was a good chance Vere would remain unwed and the title someday pass to Freddie.

But he did have a house in the country. Most of his long walks had been along the coast of the Bristol Channel. In the spring of 'ninety-four, however, he had hiked for two weeks around Lyme Bay. On the last day of his excursion, coming back from an inland jaunt to visit the ruins of the Berry Pomeroy Castle, he had stumbled upon the modest house and its immodestly gorgeous rose garden.

PIERCE HOUSE, the plaque on the low gate had said. He had gazed at it with a covetousness he did not know he could feel for a mere piece of property: the house, with its white walls and red trim; the garden, as fragrant and lovely as a long-lost memory. When he returned to London, he had instructed his solicitors to find out whether the house was for sale. It had been and he'd bought it.

On the day he brought his wife to Pierce House, she stood a long time before it, before the garden that still bloomed indefatigably, even though the peak months for roses had already come and gone.

"It's a wonderful place," she said. "So peaceful and..."

"And what?" he asked.

"Ordinary." She glanced up at him. "And I mean it as the highest compliment."

He understood her; of course he did. It was why the house and the garden had so enraptured him, why his heart always ached as he gazed upon it: the embodiment of all the sweet normalcy of which he had been robbed.

But he didn't want to understand her. He didn't want to find common ground.

He knew how to manage the life he had chosen. He had the perfect companion: one who would never hurt, anger, or disappoint him. He did not know how to cope with the pitfalls—or the possibilities—of a different life.

"Well, enjoy it," he said. "It's your home."

For now.

❦

Elissande found Devonshire beautiful, its climate warmer and sunnier than anything she'd ever known. And the sea, which had always fascinated her in her landlocked imprisonment, enchanted her utterly, even though she did not gaze upon it from the high, rocky cliffs of Capri, but only from the hills surrounding that stretch of coast known as the English Riviera.

But she would have found a barren rock in the middle of a desert beautiful, for it was freedom itself that truly intoxicated. Sometimes she had herself driven to the nearest village for no reason at all, simply because she could. Sometimes she rose early and walked until she reached the coast, and brought back a shell or a piece of driftwood for Aunt Rachel. Sometimes she took thirty books to her room, knowing that no one would take them away from her.

After the brief stutter of fear the day of Edmund Douglas's arrest, Aunt Rachel flourished too. Her consumption of laudanum had decreased by a quarter. Her appetite, still birdlike, was nevertheless ferocious for *her*. And when Elissande surprised her with a drive to Dartmouth, she had taken in everything with childlike amazement, as if discovering a world she never knew existed.

In short, they were as happy as they had ever been in Elissande's life.

If only she could be sure her husband shared their contentment.

He appeared much as he always had: cheerful, long-winded, and dense. She'd come to marvel at his ability to furnish lecture-length dissertations that were fantastically, almost deliciously misinformed, which he did every night at dinner, with just the two of them at the table. She tried it herself a few times and found that such speechifying required a surprisingly deep and wide knowledge of what was *right* and a remarkable nimbleness of mind to turn most everything on its head, with just enough content that was *not* wrong to drive a listener batty.

On her third attempt, she chose for her subject the art and science of jam making, on which she'd read extensively just that afternoon as it was the season for bottling the produce of the garden—and Pierce House had a walled garden with fruit trees espaliered all along the interior. She must have done rather well in mimicking his intricately unenlightening monologues, because at the end of her discourse, she caught him turning his face aside to hide a smile.

Her heart had lurched wildly.

But beyond that one instance, he never deviated from his role. And except for dinner, he was rarely to be found. Every time she would ask a servant for his whereabouts, the answer was invariably, "His lordship is out walking."

It seemed to be the norm. According to Mrs. Dilwyn, it was not unusual for his lordship to walk fifteen, twenty miles a day in the country.

Twenty miles of solitude.

For some reason, all Elissande could think of was the loneliness in his eyes when they'd last made love.

❧

She did not expect to run into him on her walk.

Her walks were much shorter than his. From the house, she went two miles northwest, to the ridge of the Dart Valley, where she usually needed a good long rest before trudging back.

She'd once thought nothing of a seven-mile trek. But her stamina had diminished during her years of near house arrest, and it would take months of regular exercise before she'd be strong enough to walk with him in the decidedly undulating countryside surrounding Pierce House.

That was what she wanted: to walk with him. They didn't need to speak much, but she would enjoy the pleasure of his nearness. And perhaps given time, he too might find something to like in her company.

She reached the top of the valley, breathing hard from her climb. And then her heart was racing from more than just the exercise. Halfway down the green slope toward the River Dart, he stood with one hand in his pocket, the other holding his hat, his height and breadth unmistakable.

As if she were stalking a wild Arabian that might bolt any moment, she stepped quietly and carefully. Still he turned around and saw her much too soon, when she was a good sixty feet away. She stopped. He gazed at her a moment, looked away briefly toward the hills, glanced at her again, and then turned back to the river.

No acknowledgment. But then again, no pretenses either.

She went to him, her heart full of a strange tenderness.

"Long walk?" she asked, when she stood next to him.

"Hmm," he said.

The sun went behind a cloud. The air stirred. A breeze ruffled his hair, the tips of which had become a great deal blonder from his long hours outdoors.

"You don't become fatigued?"

"I'm used to it."

"You always walk alone."

His response was a half grimace. She suddenly realized how tired he looked—not a purely physical exhaustion, but a weariness for which a good night's sleep would do nothing.

"Do you . . . do you ever wish for some company?"

"No," he said.

"No, of course," she mumbled, chastised.

They were silent for some time, he seemingly absorbed by the panorama of the gentle, verdant river valley, she wholly engrossed in the leather patches at the elbows of his brown country tweeds. She had a rather strong desire to touch those patches, to rest her hand where she could feel both the coarse warmth of the wool and the smooth coolness of the leather.

"I'll be off now," he said abruptly.

She gave in to her fascination for the leather patches and laid one hand on his sleeve. "Don't be too long. It might rain."

He stared at her, his look harsh, and then his gaze dropped to where she touched him.

She withdrew her hand hastily. "I just wanted to feel the patch."

He placed his hat on his head, nodded at her, and left without another word.

❦

It did not rain, but he did take too long: For the first time since their arrival in Devon, he did not appear at dinner.

Much later that night, she became aware that he'd returned to his room. She'd been listening, but she had heard nothing—for such a big man, when he wanted to, he moved with the silence of a ghost. She deduced his presence only by the light that had not been there before, under the connecting door between their rooms.

When she opened the door he was in his shirtsleeves, the tails of his shirt already pulled loose from his trousers.

He tossed aside his collar. "My lady."

She remained on her side of the door. "Have you had anything to eat?"

"I stopped by a pub."

"I missed you at dinner," she said softly.

She had. It hadn't been the same at all.

He glanced sharply at her but said nothing, instead picking up his already discarded tweed jacket and checking its pockets.

"Why do you do this?" she asked.

"Do what?"

"I smiled because my uncle demanded it. Why do you act in a way calculated for people not to take you seriously?"

"I don't know what you mean," he said flatly.

She hadn't thought he would address her question, but still his outright refusal disappointed her. "When Needham came to see my aunt at your town house, I asked him what he knew of your accident. He said he'd been your aunt's guest at the time of your fall and knew everything about it."

"There you go. It's not just my own word."

But Needham had also been the one he specifically named when he hadn't wanted news of his bullet wound to spread. Even to this day, none of the servants had any idea he had been injured. The bandaging had either been burned or smuggled out of the house.

"How's your arm, by the way?"

The last time he allowed her to change his dressing had been the night before her uncle's arrest.

"My arm is fine, thank you."

He crossed the room, opened the window, and lit a cigarette.

"My uncle never smoked," she murmured. "We had a smoking room but he never smoked."

He took a long drag. "Maybe he should have."

"You never say anything about your family."

And she had not felt comfortable asking Mrs. Dilwyn. She didn't want the housekeeper to wonder why she knew so little of her own husband, and yet she knew next to nothing besides the fact that he was no idiot.

"Freddie is my only family; you've met him already."

The cool air from the window was pungent with the smell of cigarette fume. "What about your parents?"

He blew out a thin stream of smoke. "They both died a long time ago."

"You said you came into your title at sixteen, so I suppose that was when your father passed away. What about your mother?"

"She died when I was eight." He took another long pull on his cigarette. "Any other question I can answer for you? It's late. I need to go to London early in the morning."

Her hand closed around the doorjamb. She did have another question, she supposed.

"Can you take me to bed?"

He went very still. "No, sorry. I'm too tired."

"Last time you had a river of rum in you *and* a bullet wound."

"Men do stupid things when they've had that much to drink."

He threw the remainder of his cigarette outside, walked to the connecting door, and closed it, gently but firmly, in her face.

❦

Angelica had to read Freddie's note three times.

He was inviting her to see the finished portrait. The *finished* portrait. Freddie was a slow and meticulous painter. She'd expected that he needed at least another four to six weeks.

When she arrived at his house, he clasped her hands briefly and greeted her with his usual warm smile. But she could tell he was nervous. Or were those her own nerves making themselves felt?

"How are you, Angelica?" he asked as they climbed up toward the studio.

They hadn't seen each other since he took the nude photographs to help with his painting: He hadn't called and she had been determined not to contact him until she'd heard something.

She'd already pushed herself at him plenty—too much—since her return.

"I've been well. Cipriani replied to my letter, by the way. He said we are welcome to call on him Wednesdays and Fridays in the afternoon."

"Then we can call on him tomorrow—tomorrow is Wednesday, isn't it?"

"No, Freddie, that would be today."

"Ah, excuse me. I've been working day and night," he said. "I thought today was Tuesday."

Freddie did not usually paint day and night. "I never knew you could work so fast."

He stopped two steps above her and turned around. "Perhaps I've just never been so inspired."

He said it very softly, but very properly, as if they were discussing something quite removed from her nakedness.

She rubbed her thumb against the banister. "Well, now I really can't wait to see it."

The bed was still in the studio, artfully rumpled, the canvas that was her nude portrait draped behind a large white cloth.

Freddie took a deep breath, then gripped the cloth and yanked it off.

She gasped. A goddess lay before her. She had dark hair that glimmered gold and bronze, warm-hued, flawless skin, and the figure of a courtesan—a very, very successful courtesan.

But as beautiful as her body was, what riveted Angelica was her unsmiling expression: She gazed directly at the viewer, her dark eyes burning with a desire that would not be suppressed, her parted lips full of agitated need.

Was this how she had appeared to Freddie?

She stole a glance at him. He was studying the floor rather attentively. She tried to look at the painting again and could not meet herself in the eyes.

"Well, what do you think?" Freddie asked at last.

"It's...it's rough around the edges." The edges being all she could manage to look at. The brush-strokes were not as fine as she was accustomed to seeing in a painting from Freddie. But there was such an intensity to the image, such a sexual charge, that if he questioned further, she would have to concede that the less polished style suited the raw, frustrated hunger the woman in the painting emanated.

He covered the painting again. "You don't like it?"

She smoothed her hair, hoping she was the very picture of decorum and propriety. "Did I really look like that?"

"You did to me."

"Perhaps you could repaint it and turn my face away."

"Why?"

"Because I look as if … as if …"

"As if you'd like me to make love to you?"

A surge of fearful anticipation nearly strangled her. They stared at each other. His throat worked. In the next heartbeat he had her in his arms, his kiss sweet yet forceful.

It was everything she had ever imagined—and more. They fell into the conveniently located bed. He pulled off her hat. She yanked loose his necktie.

"Just one moment," he whispered against her lips. "Let me lock the door."

He hurried to the door, but before he could turn the key in the lock, it was opened from the other side and in stepped Penny.

"Oh, hullo, Freddie. Hullo, Angelica. Two of my favorite people in the same place—excellent. Say, Freddie, your necktie is undone. What happened, a frenzy of artistic ecstasy?"

Freddie stood speechless as Penny reknotted his tie for him.

"And what's the matter, Angelica? You had to lie

down? Do you need me to find some smelling salts for you?"

She scrambled off the bed, where she'd sat frozen. "Ah, no, Penny, I'm much better already."

"Oh, look, Angelica, your hat is on the floor." He picked up her hat and handed it to her.

"My," she said. "I wonder how that happened."

Penny winked at her. "You are lucky it wasn't some nasty old gossip who walked in when you had to lie down for a spell, Angelica. Lady Avery would be marching the two of you to the altar already, like she did me!"

Freddie, flushed scarlet, cleared his throat. "What—what brought you to London, Penny?"

"Oh, the usual. Then I remembered I still had the key to your house and thought I'd come by and see you."

"It's always good to see you, Penny," said Freddie, belatedly embracing his brother. "I've hardly left the studio for days. But this morning my housekeeper told me some ghastly rumors. She said Lady Vere's uncle is awaiting trial for some terrible crimes. I already wrote you a letter. Is it true?"

Penny's face fell. "I'm afraid so."

"How are Lady Vere and her aunt taking the news?"

"As well as could be expected, I suppose. Although I suspect I've been a true bulwark to them in this awful time. But there's nothing any of us can do, so we might as well talk about happier things."

He looked about the studio, his gaze landing, to

Angelica's dismay, on the covered canvas. "Did you just say you've been spending a lot of time in the studio, Freddie? Is it for the commission you accepted right around the time of my wedding?"

"Yes, but I'm not quite finished yet."

"Is that it?" Penny walked toward the draped painting.

"Penny!" she cried, remembering that Penny was one of the few people Freddie allowed to see his works in progress.

He turned around. "Yes, Angelica?"

"Freddie and I were just about to leave to call on the art dealer Signor Cipriani," she said. "You want to come along?"

"That's right, Penny. Come along with us," Freddie echoed fervently.

"Why are you calling on him?"

"You remember the painting at Highgate Court, the one of which I took photographs?" Freddie rushed, his words stumbling over themselves. "Angelica has been helping me track down the painting's provenance. We think a painting by the same artist passed through Cipriani's hands—and Cipriani never forgets anything."

Penny looked briefly astonished. "There was a painting at Highgate Court? But sure, I will come. I love meeting interesting people."

They ushered Penny out. Angelica placed her hand over her heart in relief: She would have never been able to look at herself in the mirror again if Penny had seen her the way Freddie had.

Penny descended the stairs first. Freddie pulled her into a blind corner and quickly kissed her once more.

"Come back to my house later?" she murmured. Her servants had the afternoon off.

"I wouldn't miss it for the world."

Douglas had not talked while awaiting trial—set for five days hence—but progress had nevertheless been made on the case.

Based on information they had uncovered from the coded dossier, Lady Kingsley had tracked down a safety-deposit box in London that contained a thick stack of letters addressed to a Mr. Frampton. The letters were from the diamond dealers, each agreeing to look at Frampton's artificial diamonds.

"You see," Lady Kingsley had said excitedly at their meeting in the morning, "that's how he got the diamond dealers to cough up the money. I think in the beginning he might not have been thinking about extortion, but merely wanted to see if the synthesized diamonds were truly indistinguishable from the real thing. And then, once the synthesis process proved a failure, he looked at the few replies he'd received, and some of them were sloppily written and could be interpreted to mean the diamond dealer was willing to deal in artificial diamonds. Our man, ever the criminal mind, decided to contact even more diamond dealers. The letters were separated into two groups, and the ones who were not careful about how they responded became his targets."

For Vere, however, the most crucial piece of the puzzle still remained missing: the true identity of the man now known as Edmund Douglas. Until Freddie and Angelica mentioned their own investigation, he'd never thought to pursue that particular line of inquiry. Now he could have slapped himself for overlooking such obvious and important clues.

Sometimes it was better to be lucky than to be good.

Cipriani was about seventy-five years of age and lived in a large flat in Kensington. Vere had expected a place overflowing with art, but Cipriani was a ruthless curator of his own collection. The parlor where he received them had a Greuze and a Brueghel and nothing else.

Angelica described the painting she and Freddie had seen in the vicarage at Lyndhurst Hall—Vere had not paid any attention to it, apparently. Cipriani listened with his hands tented together.

"I do remember. I bought it from a young man in the spring of 'seventy."

Twenty-seven years ago.

"Was he the artist?" asked Angelica.

"He claimed that it had been a gift. But judging by his nervousness while I assessed his painting, I would say he *was* the artist. Of course, there was also the coincidence that the artist's initials were the same as his."

Vere hoped his best vapid expression was enough to hide his excitement. He further hoped either Freddie or Angelica would inquire after the young man's name.

"What was his name?" Freddie asked.

"George Carruthers."

George Carruthers. It might be a pseudonym, but at least it was a place to start.

"Have you ever come across him or his works again?" asked Angelica.

Cipriani shook his head. "I do not believe so. A shame, rather, as he had more than a modicum of talent. With proper instruction and dedication, he could have made some interesting art."

The subject of George Carruthers exhausted, Angelica and Freddie talked with the old man on the latest developments in art. Vere did not fail to notice the way they glanced at each other—he could only hope that he hadn't interrupted their very first instance of lovemaking.

He smiled inwardly. He had always wished fervently for Freddie's happiness: not only for Freddie's sake, but for his own, so that he could one day live vicariously through Freddie's domestic bliss.

Presupposing that he himself must always be on the outside looking in. That his own life would remain barren of the kind of contentment he so easily imagined for Freddie.

He remembered the way his wife had looked at him the day before, above the banks of the River Dourt: as if he were full of possibilities. As if *they* were full of possibilities.

But his mind was already made up. It was time she understood.

When they rose to bid Cipriani good-bye, Vere suddenly remembered that there was something more he wished to know, a question that no one else had asked.

So he did the asking himself. "Mr. Carruthers, did he say why he was selling his painting?"

"Yes, he did," replied Cipriani. "He mentioned he was raising funds for a venture to South Africa."

Chapter Seventeen

Her bed was crimson Italian silk. Against this sumptuous backdrop, Angelica stretched, immodestly, deliciously. Part of Freddie still felt he should avert his eyes. The rest of him not only could not look away, but reached out a hand to caress the underside of her breast.

"Hmm, that was splendid," she said.

His cheeks grew warm. He leaned in to kiss her again. "The pleasure was all mine."

And how.

"Can I make a confession?" he asked.

"Hmm, you never have confessions to make. This I must hear."

He cleared his throat, embarrassed now that he was about to volunteer the information. "I was not *that* interested in the provenance of the angel painting."

Her jaw went slack. "You *weren't*?"

"Your oldest friend asks you to paint her in the altogether. You are terribly tempted but not sure how to say yes. Wouldn't you find a seemingly legitimate inquiry so that you may exchange favors?"

She sat up straight, a rich cascade of crimson silk held to her breasts. "Freddie! I never guessed you to be so sneaky."

He flushed. "I'm not—not usually, in any case. I just wanted to be a little less transparent."

She hit him lightly on the arm. "Oh, you were opaque enough for me. I had quite despaired of how I would ever make myself understood."

"You could have just told me."

"If I could, I would have done it ten years ago." She kissed him where she'd hit him. "It was probably best I didn't: You viewed me as completely lacking in feminine attributes."

"That is not true. It was more the case that I never thought about your feminine attributes. I mean, you were—and are—my oldest friend. You didn't need breasts and buttocks to matter to me."

"That is a sweet thing to say, although my breasts and buttocks might dissent."

He smiled.

She snuggled closer to him. "Did you ever think that I was too critical? Or had too many ideas about how you should do things?"

"No, never. My father was too critical: He put me down because he enjoyed it, and because I didn't quite know how to fight back like Penny did. Your suggestions were always rooted in a sincere interest in me. And it was never a condition of our friendship that I must do as you said: You gave your advice and I was free to take it or not."

"Good," she said.

He hesitated.

She peered at him. "There is something else you want to say, isn't there? Go ahead; I'd like to hear it."

He kept forgetting how well she knew him. "I was thinking that there was a time when I felt you were too ambitious for me. You were constantly telling me that I needed to paint faster, and exhibit, and establish a large body of work."

"Ah, that. That was when I was unbearably jealous of Lady Tremaine. I was trying to make you see that she didn't know rose madder from crimson lake, while I was an expert in both art and the art world."

He truly had been blind. It never occurred to him that her seemingly frantic drive to propel him toward artistic prominence had anything to do with hidden desires of the heart. He lifted a strand of her hair. It would seem he had not done it justice in his painting: There were shades of auburn too.

"Before Lady Tremaine left for America, she'd hoped I would find solace in your arms. But when you came to comfort me, I all but chased you away."

"I don't blame you. I was very rude about it."

"When you married Canaletto out of the blue, I couldn't help but worry that my conduct that day had something to do with it. Just know I've always regretted my abruptness."

She shook her head. "My inability to handle my

disappointment without doing something stupid was not your fault, but my own shortcoming. In fact, this time, I was determined that should you turn me down, I was absolutely not going to do anything foolish—like sleeping with Penny, for instance—to soothe my bruised vanity."

"Penny would be traumatized. He still thinks of you as a sister."

She chuckled. "I would be traumatized, too."

She lifted her arm and set her hand down atop a small framed picture on her nightstand. Absently she twisted the frame this way and that, and he saw that the frame contained a pencil drawing of her face he had sketched many years ago and given her as a gift. The art critic in her should have found too many defects in the sketch, which lacked both technique and composition, and seemed to have only a great earnestness to recommend itself.

He'd always loved and cared about her, but now his heart was filled with tenderness, so much that it was almost painful. "I'm glad you came back," he said, tracing his hand across her cheekbone.

"So am I," she said, her gaze direct and clear. "So am I."

❧

It was very late at night, but her husband still had not returned from London.

Elissande lay awake in an unrelieved darkness, staring at a ceiling she could not see, thinking of the first time she laid eyes on him. She remembered every detail: the homburg he'd worn, the glimpse of blue waistcoat beneath his fawn jacket, the spark of sunlight on his cuff links, but most of all, the joyful buoyancy she'd experienced when he'd smiled at his brother.

If only they'd met a week later, when she no longer needed to entrap anyone. How different things would have been.

But she *had* entrapped him. And he was *not* happy with her. And if he would not talk to her—or make love to her—how would they ever be anything but strangers in this marriage?

Her door creaked slightly as it swung open. He was home. He had opened her door. He was on her threshold and had but to take one more step to enter her room.

Excitement shot through her, an excitement that was almost panic. Her heart pumped madly, like a steam-driven piston. She bit her lower lip to not breathe too heavily.

She must hold very quiet, and give the firm impression of being sound asleep. Then he might be more encouraged to approach her. To touch her. And from there, to forgive her, some day.

She willed him to come to her, to seek solace in her arms for his loneliness, his weariness.

But the door closed again and he sought his own bed instead.

❧

The longcase clock gonged the hour, three brassy chimes that quavered in the dark, still air.

It was always three o'clock.

He ran. The pitch-black corridor would not end. Something slammed into his calf. He cried out in pain, stumbling. But he must keep running. He must reach his mother and warn her of the mortal danger.

There, the hall. At the distant end of its Olympic length, the staircase that would be her undoing. He'd almost made it. He would save her; he would not let her fall.

He stumbled again, pain lancing deep into his knees.

He hobbled on.

But she was already there when he at last reached the foot of the staircase. Blood pooled under her head, blood the same black-red as her gown and the rubies glittering on her chest.

He screamed. Why could he not save her? Why was he never in time to save her?

Someone called his name. Someone shook his shoulder. It must be the person responsible for his mother's death. He threw the person down.

"Penny, are you all right?" she squeaked.

No, he was not all right. He would never be all right again.

"Penny, stop. *Stop.* You'll hurt me."

He very much wanted to hurt somebody.

"Penny, please!"

His eyes flew open. He was gasping, as if he'd been running from the hounds of hell. The room was pitch-dark, just like in his dream. He made a sound at the back of his throat, not yet free from the terror of the nightmare.

"It's all right," murmured the person in bed with him, someone warm and soft who smelled of honey and roses. "It was just a bad dream."

She caressed his face and his hair. "It was just a bad dream," she repeated. "Don't be afraid."

Ridiculous. He wasn't afraid of anything.

She kissed him on his jaw. "I'm here. It's all right. I won't let anything happen to you."

He was big, strong, and clever. He needed no one to protect him from something as flimsy as dreams.

She pulled him into her arms. "I have bad dreams too. Sometimes I dream I'm Prometheus, chained to the rock forever and ever. And then, of course, I can't go back to sleep afterward, so I think of Capri, beautiful, faraway Capri."

She had an exquisite voice. He'd never noticed before. But there in the dark, as she spoke, the sound of her words was as lovely as the sound of water to a desert tribe.

"I imagine that I have a boat of my own," she whispered. "When it's warm and breezy, I sail it into the open waters, sleep under the sun, and turn as brown as the fishermen. And when it's stormy, I stand atop the cliffs and watch the sea rage, knowing that an angry sea keeps me isolated—and keeps me safe."

His breaths no longer came in quite such huge gulps. He understood what she was doing. After the abrupt loss of their mother, he'd done the same for Freddie, his arm around Freddie's shoulders, talking about netting trout and catching fireflies until Freddie fell asleep again.

But he'd never let anyone do it for him.

"It was unlikely, of course," she continued. "I always knew that it was most unlikely. If ever I managed to get away from my uncle, I would need to work for a living, and nobody pays a woman much for anything. I'd have to scrimp to save for a rainy day, and count myself fortunate if I could someday spare the coin for a train ticket to Brighton." Her fingers traced his cheekbone. "But Capri made it possible to go on. It was my flame in the dark, my escape when there was no escape."

He tightened his arm about her—he hadn't even realized he had his arm about her.

"I know everything there is to know about Capri. Or at least everything people thought worth writing down in travelogues: its history, its topography, the etymology of its name. I know what grows in its interior and what swims in its waters. I know the winds that come with each season."

Her hand rubbed his back as she spoke. Her words were quiet, almost hypnotic. She might have successfully lulled him back to sleep were it not for the fact that her body was directly pressed into his.

"So tell me," he said.

She must have felt it, the physiological change on his part. But she did not pull away. If anything, she fitted herself more snugly to him.

"It is probably quite overrun these days. One book

mentioned that there is a colony of writers and artists from England, France, and Germany."

He could not stop himself anymore. He kissed her throat, his fingers unhooking her nightdress. Her skin, the smoothness of it, made his heart lose its beat.

"Of course," she went on, her voice increasingly unsteady, "I ignore their presence entirely so I may preserve my illusion of a sparsely populated paradise, empty except for the sea and the sky and me."

"Of course," he said.

He peeled her nightdress from her, pulled his own nightshirt over his head, and turned them so that she was on top of him.

"What do *you* think about when you wake up from nightmares?" she asked, her words barely audible.

He tugged off the ribbon at the end of her plait and loosened her hair. It fell, like a cloud, about his face and shoulders.

"This," he said. "This is what I think about."

Not the sexual act per se, but the presence of another. A closeness that would cocoon and shield him.

He had thought of her the last time he had the nightmare, at Highgate Court. As she ignored the presence of foreigners crowding the rugged shores of Capri, he had selectively forgotten her antagonism toward him—and his resentment toward her—and remembered only her sweetest smiles.

One did what one must to get through the night.

But now she was pliant and willing above him.

Now she not only permitted, but conspired for him to penetrate deep inside her. Now she whimpered and sighed with pleasure, her lips against his ear, her breaths invoking waves of almost violent desire.

And when his release came, it was heat, fury, and a powerful, almost rapturous, oblivion.

❦

Her breaths fluttered his hair. Her heart beat against his chest. Her hands sought his in the dark and laced their fingers.

A closeness that cocooned and shielded him.

Yet perfect peace eluded him in that drowsy warmth. Something was wrong. Perhaps everything was wrong. He did not want to think.

Night was now his refuge. Beyond dawn, chaos reigned. But in the dark there was only her embrace.

He murmured a thank-you, and let sleep overtake him.

❦

It dawned like any other morning in the country: birdsong, the lowing of dairy cows in the pasture behind the house, the snipping shears of his gardeners, already at work.

Even the sounds he himself made were peaceful and domestic. Water falling and splashing in a washbasin, drawers opening and closing softly, curtains pulling back, and shutters released for the day.

She was still comfortably ensconced in his bed. Her breaths were slow and even. Her hair, the color of sunrise, fanned out on the pillow. One of her arms was outside the bedspread; it was slung across the bed, as if reaching for him.

In her sleep she seemed entirely harmless, almost angelic, the kind of woman who inspired uncomplicated devotion. He lifted her exposed arm and tucked it back under the cover. She snuggled deeper into the bedding, her lips curving in contentment.

He turned away.

With his back to her, he snapped his braces into place over his shoulders and donned his waistcoat. He rummaged in the tray atop his chest of drawers and selected a pair of cuff links. Then, abruptly, he was aware that she was awake and that she was watching him.

"Good morning," he said, without turning around, his fingers busy with the fastening of his cuff links.

"Morning," she mumbled, her voice still thick with sleep.

He said nothing else for a while, but continued to dress. Behind him the bed shifted and creaked: She must be getting into her nightdress, which he'd found under his person this morning, along with her hair ribbon—a slender pastel reminder of what had transpired in the night.

"I'm going for a walk," he said, shrugging into a tweed coat—still without looking at her. "You are welcome to join me if you'd like."

What he was about to say to her he wanted said far from his home.

"Yes, of course," she answered. "I'd be delighted."

The barely suppressed excitement in her voice was a whiplash across his conscience. "I'll wait for you below."

"I won't be long," she promised. "I just need to dress and have a word with the nurse."

He paused at the door and glanced at her at last. After today, he would not see her again thus, glad and hopeful.

"Take your time," he said.

❧

Elissande dressed in record speed, looked in on her still sleeping aunt, and spoke to Mrs. Green, the nurse she'd hired on Mrs. Dilwyn's recommendation after coming to Devon. Mrs. Green assured her that she would see to Mrs. Douglas's breakfast and bath, and then have her take a turn in the garden for exercise and fresh air.

Mrs. Green was a very kind woman, but firmer than Elissande. Under her supervision, Aunt Rachel could already walk a short distance unsupported, a feat that was nothing less than miraculous.

Now, to complete Elissande's happiness, her husband had made love to her. *And* he'd invited her to come with him on his walk.

They didn't speak. But they did not need to. His company was enough. That she was by his side was enough. *This* was their new beginning.

They crossed the River Dart at the market town of Totnes, where they had tea and a quick breakfast, then continued north, walking along country lanes that were entirely new to her, past rolling fields and several tiny hamlets, into a dense copse, and emerged from the trees onto the grounds of a ruined castle.

It must have been a good five miles. She would have thought herself exhausted, but she was only exultant.

"Do you ever talk?" she asked finally, panting a little from the climb up to the castle.

"I believe the general consensus is that I talk and talk and talk."

She took off her hat and fanned herself. "I mean, when you are not playing your role."

He didn't answer, but looked east toward the sea—the castle was situated on a sharp rise of land that gave a panoramic view. She again wondered why he led this double life. But she'd had her reasons, and she assumed his reasons must be equally strong and compelling.

"Tell me something," he said.

She was terribly flattered. He so seldom asked her anything. "What would you like to know?"

"You inquired into Capri when you met Mrs. Canaletto. You mentioned Capri again when you wanted all of us to leave England and hide somewhere. And from what you said last night"—he thrust one hand into his pocket—"obviously you've thought a great deal about Capri your entire life."

"That is true."

"But I don't see you making any plans to visit Capri, now that you can. Why is that?"

She had never thought of it before. But the answer

seemed so obvious that she was surprised he had to ask.

"Because what I've loved all along is not Capri the physical entity—it could have been any beautiful, far-away place. What mattered was the hope and solace it gave me when I was a prisoner in my uncle's house."

He looked at her, his eyes very severe. Perhaps he did not understand her entirely.

She tried again. "Think of a raft, if you will. When a river is too wide and swift to cross by swimming, we need the raft. But once we have reached the farther shore, we leave the raft at the water's edge."

"And you have reached the farther shore."

She trailed her fingertips over the silk flowers ornamenting her hat. "I have crossed the river. As fond as I always shall be of my raft, I don't need it anymore."

He walked a few steps away. "So you are happy with your life and need no further bolstering?"

She bit the inside of her cheek. "Perhaps I could use just a little more bolstering."

"What would that be?" he said without inflection.

She'd thought she'd require more fortitude to confess her attachment. But when he'd kissed and held her at night, when he'd walked five miles beside her this morning, he'd made it easy to speak the word. "You," she said, her voice not at all hesitant or wobbly.

"How will I accomplish this admirable deed?"

"By doing what you have done already: walking with me and making love to me." She flushed only a little as she said those last few words.

He walked farther away. Skittish, her man.

She followed him into the keep. A mansion had once stood in the bailey but now only stone walls, archways, and empty window frames remained. The morning sun streamed through the breaks in the walls; the interior of the ruins was cool but not gloomy.

She laid her hand on his arm, the Harris tweed of his coat pleasantly woolly against her palm. When he did not remove her hand, she grew bolder and pressed a kiss on his cheek, and then another on his lips. There she lingered, until she coaxed him into parting his lips.

All of a sudden he kissed her back, hard, making her head spin.

And just as abruptly, he pushed her away.

❧

Never in his life had Vere botched anything so thoroughly as he had his should-have-been marriage in name only.

He didn't know what was wrong with him.

Or perhaps he did and simply couldn't bear to acknowledge it.

She was not the companion he wanted—hadn't the issue already been settled again and again? What he wanted was as different from her as the Isle of Capri was from Australia. He wanted milk and honey; nourishing, sweet, wholesome. She was laudanum; potent, addictive, occasionally helpful in forgetting his troubles, but dangerous in large dosages.

She was also a liar and a manipulator—he still had

the note she'd written Freddie that night, a physical manifestation of her intent to lure Freddie into her clutches, to deprive him of his happiness with Angelica for her own gains.

And yet here, out in the open, where at any moment an omnibus of tourists could pull up, he had nearly lost control once more. And this time without any excuses of tears, alcohol, or nightmares. It was a bright, brisk day, she was cheerful, and he'd thought himself grimly determined to speak the ugly but necessary truth.

He took several steps away from her.

If he didn't say it now, he would not be able to do it ever: She radiated such gladness he was on the verge of forgetting that she was the last thing from the sunny simplicity he needed to drive the darkness from his own soul.

He forced out the words. "Once your uncle has been sentenced, I would like an annulment."

She had been smoothing her sleeve and peering at him, her expression puzzled but still hopeful. She stilled; the color on her cheeks drained. She turned her gaze more squarely toward him.

"I'll make a generous settlement on you. You will have enough to live wherever you like in ease and luxury. On Capri itself, if you should desire."

"But an annulment is not possible," she said. His conscience contorted at the complete, almost naïve confusion in her voice. "Once the marriage has been consummated, it is not possible."

"With enough money and enough lawyers, it is not only possible, but has been achieved repeatedly."

"But . . . but we will have to lie."

She was so disproportionately bewildered that he considered for the very first time the likelihood that she was not as worldly as he'd thought. That she'd truly believed they were married for good.

"Both of us lie brilliantly. I don't see any problems at all."

She looked up into the rectangle of blue sky above them, framed by the manse's dilapidated walls. "Has this always been your intention?"

"Yes."

Her hand dug into her skirts. Her shoulders bunched tight. The ache in his heart turned into a sharp pain.

"I would like my own freedom," he said, intentionally heartless. "You should understand that."

Equating their marriage and her virtual imprisonment had the desired effect. A grim anger replaced the heartbroken bafflement in her eyes. Her gaze turned hard.

"So this is a straightforward transaction," she said. "You give me money for your freedom."

"Yes."

"Am I correct in assuming that because of what happened last night, your freedom costs more today than it did yesterday?"

"Perhaps."

"So I'm a whore in my own marriage."

Her words were a kick to his stomach.

"I'm paying for my lack of control."

"Oh, my, Lord Vere, why didn't you say so sooner?" she said bitingly. "Had I understood earlier that making you lose control more frequently was going to net me a larger fortune, I'd have devoted my days to your seduction."

"Be thankful that I have enough scruples to compensate you for the use of your body. And that I will keep silent on how you entrapped me—and how you meant to entrap Freddie."

She flinched. His callousness took his own breath away; he was using her one great act of desperation as justification for his utter selfishness.

She took a deep breath and slowly let it out. "I've always known that I'm no prize, but I thought you were," she said. "I thought the man behind the idiot would be fascinating. I thought he would understand what it is like to act a part all the time. And I thought he would have some sympathy for me, because it is not an easy life. I was wrong: You were a better man as the idiot you played. He was sweet, kind, and decent. I'm sorry I didn't properly appreciate him when I had the chance."

See, he thought. This was precisely why he needed a milk-and-honey companion, one who would never grasp that he was not sweet, not kind, and not always dependably decent, but only love him tenderly, blindly, unquestioningly.

It was as much a castle in the sky as her whimsy of a wild and empty Capri. Like her, he had held on to it through his darkest days, this unlikely vision of domestic haven. But unlike her, he was not ready to abandon something that had sustained him this many years, for a woman he did not want to love, except when he was drunk, lonely, or otherwise unable to control himself.

Chapter Eighteen

Her legs ached, her feet hurt, and her hands itched to slap him. For some time on the long road home she marched ahead of him, until she took a wrong turn and he had to call her back. After that she walked with him within her peripheral view, his silence steadily feeding the anger inside her.

Why had she believed she could find safety and contentment with someone who led a double life? No one embarked on such a path without duress. Had she thought about it, she would have realized that behind the idiot there must be a man as secretive and warped as herself.

She was *such* a fool.

Wrapped in a haze of fury, she almost did not see the footman running toward her until he stopped and then fell into step beside her.

"Milord, milady, Mrs. Douglas, she is gone!"

His sentence made no sense whatsoever. She passed her hand over her eyes. "Say it again."

"Mrs. Douglas, she is gone!"

"To *where?*"

"The station at Paignton, mum."

Why in the world would Aunt Rachel go to Paignton Station? She had no place to visit that required a train ride.

"Where is Mrs. Green?" No doubt the nurse would tell her that the footman was raving.

Mrs. Green, too, came running, her eyes wide, her face red. "Mum, Mrs. Douglas left by herself!"

Elissande walked faster. Surely by the time she arrived at Aunt Rachel's room, she'd see that the latter was safe and sound. "Why did you not go with her, Mrs. Green?"

"We took a turn in the garden in the morning. Afterward she said she wanted some rest. She looked unwell, so I took her back upstairs and tucked her in. I looked in on her an hour later and her room was empty."

"Then how do you know she's gone to Paignton Station?"

"That's what Peters says."

Peters, the coachman, had by now also come alongside Elissande. "Mrs. Douglas came to the carriage house herself and asked me to take her to Paignton Station. So I did, mum."

Elissande stopped at last. Her entire entourage, too, stopped.

"Did she say *why* she wanted to go to the train station?"

"Yes, mum. She said she was going up to London for the day. And when I came back, Mrs. Green and Mrs. Dilwyn and everyone else were up in a right panic."

The story overwhelmed Elissande. She could not make heads or tails of it, and part of her still believed that it was an elaborate April Fool's joke played on the wrong date.

Almost without thinking, she glanced at the man who was still her husband.

"Did any strangers come by the house today?" he asked, still his cool and competent self.

Her heart sank at his question.

Mrs. Dilwyn had by now joined them also. "No, sir, not that I know of."

The coachman and the footman both shook their heads. Mrs. Green, however, frowned. "Come to think of it, sir, there was this vagrant. He was loitering in the lane before the house when Mrs. Douglas and I were in the garden. I tried to shoo him away but Mrs. Douglas—her heart is too kind—she had me go to the kitchen and fetch a basket of foodstuffs. And when I brought out the basket, the vagrant, he fell to his knees and thanked her. I didn't like him clutching her hands, so I gave him a nice shove. He scampered off after that."

Elissande had thought her husband had driven a stake through her happiness. How wrong she had been. *This,* this could shatter the very foundation of her new life.

"The vagrancy law is too lenient these days, I

always say," declared Lord Vere, now fully back in character. "And was that when Mrs. Douglas started looking ill, Mrs. Green?"

"That's right, sir. It was."

"She is too delicate a lady to be in such rough company." He shook his head, then took Elissande by the elbow. "Come along, Lady Vere."

Back at the house, Aunt Rachel's room was as empty as a robbed tomb. Elissande swayed and caught herself on the doorjamb. A racket erupted downstairs. She took the steps down two at a time. Aunt Rachel had been sighted and everyone was clamoring in relief—it had to be that. It had to be.

But it was only a telegram addressed to Elissande that had been found, among the post that had arrived during the lord and the lady's absence from the house.

My Dearest,

I have experienced an unexpected yearning for the oyster au gratin served at the Savoy Hotel and have therefore decided to travel to London and stay overnight.

Please do not worry about me, Elissande. Just know that I love you very much.

Your loving aunt

Lord Vere took the cable from her numb hands and scanned its contents. He then read the telegram aloud for the gathered servants.

"See, nothing to worry about," he claimed. "She's gone to London, as she said was her plan—and she'll be back tomorrow. Return to your posts, everyone. Mrs. Green, you may have yourself a cup of tea and consider this a day off."

"But—"

Lord Vere gave Elissande a look. Elissande unclenched her hand and smiled reassuringly at Mrs. Green. "Her decisions do get a little erratic from time to time, Mrs. Green. We live with it. She will be back on the morrow if she says so."

Mrs. Green curtsied and went in search of her tea. The other servants also dispersed. Only Lord Vere and Elissande remained in the entry hall.

"Come with me," he said.

❧

He took her to his study, closed the door, and handed her another cable. "This one came for me. You might want to read it."

She glanced down at the telegram. The words lurched and staggered, refusing to coalesce into properly structured sentences. She had to close her eyes and then open them again.

Dear Sir,

It has recently come to our attention that Mr. Douglas has been reported missing. Neither his method of escape nor his current whereabouts have been determined. But the authorities would like to alert you to his fugitive status and request your assistance in returning him to custody.

Yours, etc.,
Filbert

"He was the vagrant," said Lord Vere, inexorably. "He must have instructed your aunt on how to meet him."

A vise closed over Elissande's chest. She could not breathe. Four days before his trial, her uncle had hunted down her aunt in broad daylight.

And what had Elissande been doing? Wearing her heart on her sleeve in a ruined castle, trying to woo her unfeeling bastard of a husband.

The same husband pressed a glass of whiskey into her hand. "Drink."

The whiskey burned a trail down her throat. She tilted back the glass again. It was already empty. "I need more."

"Not now. You don't have much capacity for liquor."

She rubbed the empty glass against her forehead. "I don't understand—none of this makes sense. She was not alone. My uncle did not grab her by the throat and abduct her outright. Why did she leave to meet him of her own volition?"

"He must have threatened your safety or mine, possibly both."

"He is a fugitive. He has the law after him. He can't do anything to harm any of us."

"You don't know him as she does."

She resented his assumption. "I've lived with him my entire life."

He gazed at her a long moment, as if she were some creature about to be led to slaughter. "Would you care for a seat? There is something I need to tell you."

He had something he needed to tell her. About *her* uncle?

Suddenly the events of the past few weeks flashed before her eyes. Hundreds of rats finding their way into Lady Kingsley's house, a very clever man coming to Highgate Court disguised as an idiot, skulking all around, and barely days later the police in possession of enough evidence to arrest her uncle. What were the chances that these had all been random events?

She sat down. Or perhaps her legs simply gave out from underneath her. "You had something to do with it, didn't you? You didn't come to my house because Lady Kingsley had a rat problem; you came because you were looking for evidence against my uncle."

"I see we may skip right over that part," he said lightly.

"Do you work for the police?"

He raised a brow. "Of course not—marquesses don't work. Although I might occasionally assist the police."

She pressed her fingers to the bridge of her nose. "What was it that you wanted to tell me?"

"Are you familiar with their courtship?"

"To hear him tell it, it was much charity and compassion on his part. He was a very rich man coming back from South Africa. She was a damsel in distress whose father had died in poverty after his bank failed and whose sister had run away to become a whore. My uncle, of course, swept in and rescued her from a life of drudgery and despair."

"They might have been introduced only after he returned from South Africa, but I believe he'd been fixated on her since long before."

Something in her tilted dangerously at his revelation. She had thought for certain that she knew everything she needed to know about her aunt and her uncle. "Why do you think so?"

"The paintings at Highgate Court. Freddie tracked down a sister painting, done possibly in the late sixties. Yesterday I went to Kent to see it. It too had an angel and a man: The angel was all in white and the man on his knees in rapture. The angel had Mrs. Douglas's face. The artist, whom I believe to be your uncle, sold the painting to finance his trip to South Africa."

"He went to South Africa for *her*?"

"Perhaps not *for* her, but it appears she loomed large in his mind. It was something close to an obsession."

She rose; she could remain seated no longer. "And then what happened?"

"He failed—your uncle lacks either luck or acumen in business, or perhaps both. But someone he knew found a rich vein and boasted to everyone who would listen. This man was going to voyage to England and glory in his newfound wealth. His name was Edmund Douglas."

The ugliness he implied—she did not want to hear any more. Yet she must know everything. "Go on," she croaked.

"I have cause to believe that your uncle murdered the real Edmund Douglas en route from South Africa to England. Upon his arrival in England, he established himself as Edmund Douglas, used the dead man's letters of credit, and married your aunt under false pretenses."

She had thought that she was prepared to hear the worst. But the whiskey glass still fell from her hand. It thudded softly onto the rug and rolled away.

"Inquiries have been sent to South Africa. People who knew Edmund Douglas before he left the mines remember him as a man who spoke with a strong Scouse accent, and had a scar slashing through his left eye from a pub fight gone wrong when he was still in England."

"Why—why has no one else ever suspected my uncle of being an impostor?"

"He is clever. He lives in a remote area and socializes rarely; he has never returned to South Africa; and it's possible he also murdered the real Edmund Douglas's sole remaining relative in England."

She shivered.

"But I think your aunt found out."

She gripped the back of a chair. "Are you sure I can't have any more whiskey?"

He fetched a new glass and poured her another finger. She downed it so fast she barely felt the burn. "How did my aunt find out?"

Her husband glanced at her. "I don't know. People find out all kinds of things in a marriage."

"That's your entire explanation?"

"That's my explanation for why your uncle behaves as he does. He believes himself a romantic hero, willing to go to any lengths for love."

She shivered again. "He said that to me when we were last at Highgate Court."

"So he committed the ultimate crime, possibly more than once, for the woman he considered his angel. He impressed himself. And yet once she discovered what he had done, like any sane person, she was not only not impressed, she was horrified and appalled. That was what he considered the angel's betrayal; that she had no appreciation for the sacrifices he'd made for her, and instead recoiled from him. That was why he painted her fleeing from him, having run him through with a sword."

"And that is what has driven his cruelty all these years," she murmured.

"I wouldn't have told this story to someone with less steely nerves—but you can handle it. And you need to know, so that you understand why your aunt is so frightened of him even when he is a fugitive. So that you recognize what we are dealing with here."

She pulled at her collar. "Will the police be any help?"

"We will, of course, need the police for his apprehension. But until then, I'm hesitant, especially to involve county constables—hostage rescue is not what they are trained to do. Besides, we have no evidence whatsoever of his involvement. As far as anyone knows, Mrs. Douglas has taken off by herself to London, which she is at perfect liberty to do."

She dropped into a stuffed chair and pressed her hands into her face. "So we just wait?"

"Your uncle will contact you."

"You sound very sure of it."

She heard him take the chair next to hers. "Would you say your uncle is vindictive?" he asked softly.

"Yes."

"Then trust that he is not finished yet. Merely getting his wife back is hardly vengeance enough. He will want to inflict something on you too."

She emitted a whimper. "How long will we have to wait?"

"My guess is you will hear from him by the afternoon post. After all, time is not on his side."

She didn't want to, but she moaned again in fear. She bent over and hid her face between her knees.

To Vere's relief, she did not remain hunched in defeat for long. She rose, walked the length and the width of the room, ignored the luncheon Vere asked to have brought in for her, stirred her tea without drinking it, and looked out the window every minute or so.

He'd dashed out several cables and had them sent. He'd had his luncheon and his tea. He even glanced through some of the other letters that had come for him in the morning. And now he, too, had nothing left to do, except to watch her in her agitation.

"Why do you keep a book in your underthings drawer?" he asked.

It was better to keep her mind from the worst possibilities for the remainder of their wait.

She'd been picking out and putting back random items from the mantel. At his question she spun around. "What were you doing mucking about in my things?"

"I had to search every room in the house. Yours was no exception."

But of course hers had been an exception. He'd rifled through any number of women's unmentionables in the course of his work, but he'd never lingered as he had among her soft, pristine linens. And that was after he'd already learned that her smiles were but tools.

"Just so you know, I didn't find anything of interest—except, as I said, I'd never seen a travelogue among a woman's undergarments before."

She sat down on the window seat, her entire person stiff and tense. "I'm delighted to have provided you a moment of diversion. And just so you know, the travelogue was only carelessly placed among my undergarments when my uncle was away. When he was in residence, it stayed hidden in a scooped-out volume of something Greek, on a shelf with three hundred other books in Greek."

He read five languages other than English and had thought nothing of the dearth of English books in Douglas's library. But to someone who had not been educated in continental languages, visiting that library must have been as tormenting as dying of thirst in the middle of an ocean.

Underneath every detail of her life was a history of oppression. And yet she'd emerged not only with her spirit intact, but with a capacity for joy that he had only begun to understand. That he would now never truly know.

The thought was a stab in his heart.

"The book in your drawer was a guide to Southern Italy. It had something on Capri, I imagine?"

"Not very much. There was a better book, but I lost it when my uncle purged the library."

Memories of the night came unbidden: her arms holding him, her lovely voice speaking of her faraway island. He realized he'd never given any thoughts as to what his milk-and-honey companion would do when faced with his nightmares. He had simply assumed they wouldn't exist anymore when he had his gentle, pure paragon.

She'd been looking out the window, but now her face turned toward him. "Why did you make me listen to you sing? You are a horrendous singer."

"There was a safecracker working in your aunt's room. Had to keep you away."

"You could have told me. I would have held the light for him."

"I couldn't tell you. You looked very pleased to be living in your uncle's house."

"More fool you. You could have saved yourself the ordeal of this marriage."

He tapped his pen against the desk. Suddenly all he could remember were the moments of surprising joy. Their nap together on the train; her outrageously erroneous soliloquy on jam making that had made him smile half the next day as he walked and walked; last night.

"I wouldn't quite classify this marriage as an ordeal. It's been more of a burden."

She threw a small potted plant clear across the breadth of the room. The glazed terra-cotta container shattered against the mantel. The soil and the orchid growing from it fell to the floor with a resounding *wump*.

"You have all my sympathies," she said. "And my sincere condolences."

His ideal companion did not know what anger was. Her voice would never drip with sarcasm. And, of course, since she was not real, it was easy for her not to have strong emotions, to be only smiles and cuddles and wholesale perfection.

He gazed at the very real woman on his windowsill, battered but unbroken. All her emotions were strong: her anger, her disillusion, her despair—and her love.

He picked up the plate of sandwiches on the desk and approached her. "Don't starve yourself. It won't help you and it certainly won't help your aunt."

She grimaced as if the plate were full of live scorpions. But just when he thought she'd knock it to the floor, she accepted it. "Thank you."

"I'll ring for a new pot of tea."

"You don't need to be so nice to me. I won't appreciate it."

Of this he knew better than she. "Wrong: I've never met a woman more grateful for a little kindness."

She glowered and turned her shoulders_more firmly toward the window.

❧

The afternoon post brought a letter from Aunt Rachel.

> *Dear Elissande,*
>
> *On my way to London, I met an old school friend of mine on the train. Imagine my delight! We have decided to stop at Exeter and take in the sights. Mrs. Halliday desires to meet you. She suggests that you take the 7:00 from Paignton tonight and detrain at*

the Queen Street station. Call for us at the Rouge-mont.

Your loving aunt

P.S. Come alone, as she is not fond of strangers.
P.P.S. Wear your best jewels.

Elissande handed the letter to Lord Vere. "I have no jewels."

It was the ultimate irony, as her uncle had made his fortune in diamonds. Jewels were an easily portable, highly liquid form of wealth; of course her uncle would not want her to have any.

"I have some of my mother's pieces. They should do."

She rubbed her temple. She hadn't even realized it, but her head had been throbbing for quite a while. "So I present myself at the Rougemont and meekly hand over your mother's jewels?"

"Not you, we. I'll be there."

"You saw what the note said. I'm to go alone."

"You will seem alone to him, but I'll be there. I'll watch out for you."

"But if we travel together—"

"You will take the seven-o'clock, as he instructed. I'm going to take an earlier train to Exeter and see what arrangements I can make."

She hadn't expected him to go before her. She did not want to be alone now. She wanted—she needed—

never mind what *she* wanted. If there was anything he could do in Exeter to help her retrieve Aunt Rachel safe and whole, then he must go to Exeter.

"Right."

He touched her lightly on her sleeve. "If anyone can handle him, you can."

"Right," she repeated, pushing away the memories of what had happened the last time she was alone with her uncle.

He looked at her a moment. "I have a few minutes before I must go. Let me help you prepare."

Chapter Nineteen

Elissande exited Queen Street station at two minutes past eight o'clock. Exeter was probably a nice, ordinary place. Tonight, however, its unfamiliar darkness harbored an all too familiar evil. And she wished nothing more than that she could run back inside the station and take the next train home.

She looked about, hoping to see her husband, her ally. But among the steady stream of people going into and coming out of the station, there was no one who had his height and size.

Then her heart seized. There, by the second lamppost from her, her uncle stood squinting at a rail schedule in the orange light. His brown lounge suit had been sized for someone two inches shorter and twenty pounds heavier. His hair had been dyed entirely gray, making him look ten years older. And he had a mustache when he had always been clean shaven before.

But she knew him by the way her blood congealed.

If anyone can handle him, you can.

She couldn't, but she must. She had no choice.

She looked around once more for Lord Vere—no sign of him. She uttered a silent prayer and walked toward her uncle.

"Pardon me, sir. You wouldn't happen to know where I can find the Rougemont?"

The man she'd known her entire life as Edmund Douglas stuffed the rail schedule into his pocket. "Good evening to you too, my dear Elissande. Did you truly come alone?"

"I would have liked to think I had a few more friends in the world. But you have seen to it that I have no one besides my aunt, sir."

"And what about your much adored husband?"

"Does it amuse you to see me married to an idiot?"

Her uncle laughed softly. "I can't deny there is, shall we say, a certain je ne sais quoi to the situation— he is no doubt the biggest cretin since Claudius himself, and you shall have a passel of moronic children. But other than that, I am delighted to see you so happily and profitably settled."

"You certainly do look pleased. The fugitive life seems to agree with you."

He looked faintly surprised by her biting tone. Then his expression hardened. "To the contrary, it irks me a great deal. I'm too old to be constantly on the move, and your aunt likewise—we should be settled down in peace and comfort. And this is where you will play your dutiful role, my dear niece, and supply us with that dignity that at our age we cannot do without."

"That would depend." Her unyielding tenor astonished even herself. If anything, she'd thought she would fall back on her falsely smiling ways. "Is my aunt well?"

"Of course. And overjoyed to see me."

"I very much doubt that. Shall we go see her then?"

Her uncle's gaze turned harsh; his voice grew even softer. "Such concern. You need not worry: Who could better care for a woman than her devoted husband of twenty-five years?"

She said nothing, her fingers clutching hard at her reticule.

"Do let us go someplace more cordial to talk," murmured her uncle.

❧

The Rougemont was practically across the street from the railway station. But Edmund Douglas hailed a hansom cab. They drove away from the center of the city, descended toward the River Exe, and turned onto a bedraggled-looking street.

The houses were old here; the entire street smelled of mildew and ill-maintained plumbing. He took Elissande into a narrow three-story house that must have sat vacant for a while. The light of a single candle revealed thick layers of dust on mantels and windowsills—though the floor seemed to have been recently swept.

Behind her the door locked. Now no one would

hear her scream when he pummeled the stuffing out of her. She perspired.

But her voice, for the time being, held steady. "Where is my aunt?"

"You think of her so." Her uncle ambled across the narrow entry hall, his shadow long and stark behind him. "One wonders what she has ever done for you. Has she devoted herself to your welfare? Has she instructed you in the womanly arts? Has she actively sought you a good match? No, she has done nothing for you—other than making you a slave to her invalidity, that is. Yet you come running when she leaves you for a few hours.

"I, on the other hand, have supplied you with a beautiful home and a fortunate life. But you did not bestir yourself to visit me once the entire time I was in custody."

"I have been on my honeymoon," she said. "I would have come to your trial, though."

He gave her a smile that made the hairs on the back of her neck stand on end. "I hope you have brought proper jewels."

"I want to see my aunt first."

"But *I* need a token of good faith first."

She handed over the diamond-and-emerald necklace her husband had given her. It was the most extravagant thing she'd ever seen in her life, the emeralds bigger than sovereigns, the diamonds as numerous as stars in the sky.

Douglas, accustomed to gems, merely took the necklace from her and slipped it into his pocket.

She was on a heart-ripping state of alert. But still she did not react in time. Her uncle's punch sent her reeling backward. Had he broken her jaw? She could not tell. The entire left side of her face was on fire.

"Get up, you treacherous bitch."

She rose unsteadily to her feet. His next punch made her see black. She crumpled again.

"Get up, you worthless chit. You thought you could leave me rotting in jail, didn't you? You thought you could repay my kindness by turning your back on me. And you thought I wouldn't notice? Get up!"

She remained on the grubby floor, limp as a piece of waterlogged paper.

Her uncle bent down and gripped the front of her dress. "You don't learn, do you? A lifetime and you still haven't learned the kind of love and respect you owe me."

This was as good a chance as she was going to get. She swung her reticule at his head with all her strength. He screamed—for they had prepared well, she and her husband, and the seemingly delicate reticule held nothing less than a one-pound disk of iron from her husband's dumbbell set. She had spent her entire train journey reinforcing the reticule's seams and straps.

He stumbled, bleeding from his temple. But she did not stop: She swung again, hitting him squarely on the other side of his face.

He grunted. Her third swing he blocked with his arm. She hoped she'd broken a bone in his forearm, but he came at her, his face contorted with anger.

"How dare you? You stupid girl!"

Suddenly she too boiled with rage. Of course she dared—did he not know, stupid man who thought himself so clever, that she dared almost anything, when it was her freedom and her aunt's well-being that were at stake?

She swung her reticule at him hard and fast, at an angle, so that it caught him on the chin. He staggered backward. Now she swung it high, with all her revulsion and loathing behind it. For everything he had done to Aunt Rachel and herself, robbing them of the best years of their lives, keeping them confined and suffocated, and feasting on their fear and anguish like a vampire at an open vein.

Never again.

Never again.

❧

Vere walked toward the house. In a window on the opposite side of the street, a curtain lifted, and a woman looked out from a grubby, dimly lit parlor. He swayed drunkenly, banging into a lamppost, laying his head down on a postbox, and finally, before the house into which his wife and her uncle had disappeared, he turned his back to the street, and made as if to urinate—judging by the smell in the air, he wouldn't have been the first man to do so.

Thirty seconds later, the woman had not only closed her curtain but pulled her shutters tight.

He crept up to the door of the house and listened.

Elissande and Douglas were talking, their voices too faint for him to make out their words.

His heart pounded in a way it never did during his normal investigations: with fear. That nothing seemed to have erupted yet only rubbed his nerves rawer. Inside his coarse driving mittens, his palms perspired: something else that never happened to him.

He tugged off the mittens, wiped his hands on his trousers, and pulled out his lock picks. Douglas would not place his wife by the door. For Elissande to see her, they must move deeper into the house. And when they did, he would get to work.

He glanced behind him. Damn it, someone else was looking out of her window. The light of the street lamp was hazy, almost brown, but still enough for any unlawful action on his part to be seen. He took two steps, gripped the post that supported the shoddy-looking portico before the house, and proceeded to rub himself against it. The curtain shut quickly.

As he turned back toward the door, there came a cry of pain. A man's cry of pain. Good girl: She'd listened with unwavering attention as he'd demonstrated the best way to wield a weighted reticule.

Douglas shrieked again. Excellent.

And then *she* screamed.

He fumbled for the lock picks. It wasn't until the third time he attempted to insert the pick that he realized his hand was shaking.

His hands never shook.

She screamed again.

Sod it.

He pulled back the pick and kicked the door. It didn't give immediately. He kicked again. The hinges splintered. His shin felt as if it had splintered too. He couldn't care less.

One more kick and the door swung open.

❧

Her uncle went down as the straps of her reticule broke. The weight thudded heavily against the floor and rolled a little distance away. A dent marked where it had fallen.

She panted, still seeing red, hardly able to get enough breath into her lungs.

Behind her the door burst open in a thunderous crash. A big, burly stranger with unruly black hair and a handlebar mustache rushed toward her.

Who was this man? Some ruffian hired by her uncle? No, wait. He was the driver of the hansom cab that had brought them to this house.

"Elissande, my God, are you all right?"

She barely recognized her husband's voice before he enfolded her in a painfully tight hug. She buried her face in his rough woolen jacket that smelled of horse and some sort of strong, foul drink.

He had been here, as he'd promised. And she had not been alone.

He pulled away and checked her uncle's pulse. "He's plenty alive. I'll stand guard over him. There are rope and lanterns in the boot of the cab. Turn left when you get out of the house."

She picked up her skirts and ran. Outside she experienced a moment of confusion, as there were not one, but two hansom cabs on the street. But one of them still had the driver perched behind, so she went to the empty one, retrieved the rope and two lanterns, and rushed back. Vere took the rope from her, checked her still-unconscious uncle for weapons—pocketing a derringer and the necklace—and bound him hand and foot.

Now he hugged her much longer. "My God, you scared me. All I could hear from the door was this awful ruckus, your uncle howling and you screaming. I feared the worst."

"Was I screaming? I had no idea." Perhaps the refrains of *Never again!* had not been only in her mind.

He cradled her face in his hands. "You will look awful tomorrow morning. We need to get you an ice compress as soon as we can."

"My aunt!" she suddenly remembered. "We must find her."

The house had a spiral staircase. Vere dragged her uncle near the foot of it, so that they could keep an eye on him from any part of the stairs. They searched through the largely empty house, each giving a brief recitation of what they had done since arriving in Exeter. He had visited a gin house and made a lonesome independent cabbie very happy by overpaying for his horse and his carriage. The cabbie was so delighted he hadn't even asked for more when Vere wanted his jacket too.

They located Aunt Rachel in the attic—in a servant's tiny bedchamber—by the muffled sounds she made in response to their shouts. Lord Vere swiftly picked the lock. Aunt Rachel lay on her back on the hard, dusty floor, bound and gagged, but very much conscious. Her eyes filled with tears as Elissande ran toward her.

It was Vere who freed her—he had the foresight to carry a sharp pocketknife on his person. Elissande kissed Aunt Rachel, who wept softly and clung to her, and rubbed Aunt Rachel's arms and legs to restore their circulation.

"Are you hungry, Mrs. Douglas? Or thirsty?" Vere asked. He had ripped off his black wig and thick black mustache, which had quite startled Aunt Rachel at first.

Aunt Rachel shook her head. She looked too embarrassed to speak. He understood right away. "Let me go check on your uncle again, Elissande," he said.

Elissande helped her aunt to the chamber pot. After she had relieved herself, Elissande pinned her hair as best she could, smoothed her wrinkled clothes, and put on her shoes for her. Then with Aunt Rachel's arm about Elissande's shoulder and Elissande's arm around the older woman's middle, they shuffled out of the room and slowly started down the stairs.

Her husband met them one flight of steps down. "May I?" He gave his lantern to Elissande and gently lifted Aunt Rachel into his arms.

He waited for Elissande to precede him down the stairs, lighting the way. She gazed at him a moment, this striking, complicated man. In the blaze of happiness that had come with her aunt's successful rescue, she'd forgotten that she'd lost him—or rather, that he had never, not remotely, been hers.

One could not have everything. It was enough, today, that she had Aunt Rachel back.

&

As they reached the ground floor, Elissande was again glancing back at her husband and her aunt, as she had done numerous times during their descent. So it was Vere who first saw the inevitable.

"Lady Vere, I believe your uncle has come to," he said.

In his arms, Aunt Rachel trembled. Elissande laid a hand on her shoulder to calm her. Her joy at finding her aunt safe and sound diminished: Her uncle was still alive, still capable of hurting them and haunting them.

He certainly appeared so: In the flickering light of the lanterns, his gaze was chilling, his bloodied face as ominously arrogant as ever.

They were now at the bottom of the staircase. "Which way should I turn, my dear?" Vere asked.

His tone alerted Elissande that she should be the one giving directions. She touched him on the elbow to let him know she'd understood. "I'd like you to go to the police station and fetch the chief inspector and as many constables as you can convince to come with you. I will remain here to keep an eye on . . . things."

"Right away, my lady."

"And Mrs. Douglas will go with you. She has been in this house long enough."

"Of course." He set down Aunt Rachel carefully. "We'll just be heading toward the door then, Mrs. Douglas."

"And so you will gleefully hand me over to the police, when I've taken such trouble to come and see the two of you?" said her uncle. He spoke with an uncharacteristic slur—Elissande hoped she'd done serious and lasting damage to his jaw—but as ever his menace was there, a poison that destroyed slowly but inexorably.

"Yes," she said, with immense satisfaction.

"All these years being the father you've never had, and this is the gratitude I receive."

She smiled, the first time she'd meant it before her uncle in "all these years." "You will receive exactly as much gratitude as you deserve."

"No mercy then?" The icy, pure malice in his eyes would have frightened her if he hadn't been bound tighter than Ebenezer Scrooge's purse. "Will you come to see me hang also?"

"No," she said. "I have no desire to ever see you again."

She turned to Vere. "Please hurry."

"I will," he said. He offered his arm to Aunt Rachel. "Mrs. Douglas?"

Aunt Rachel cast a quick, apprehensive glance toward her husband, then placed her hand on Vere's arm.

"I see vows of marriage mean no more to you than

a game of charades, Rachel," said Douglas. "But then, they never did, did they?"

Aunt Rachel hesitated. Elissande decided there was no more point in keeping up the lie. "Do not listen to anything he says, Aunt Rachel. I know he married you under false pretenses; he is in no position to chastise anyone on the solemnity of vows."

Aunt Rachel stared at her. "How...how do you know?"

"False pretenses." Her uncle sneered. "You have perpetrated your share of false pretenses too, haven't you, Rachel? I know your lies. I know the truth of what happened to Christabel."

Aunt Rachel swayed. Vere caught her. "Are you all right, Mrs. Douglas?"

She breathed hard and fast. "If I may—if I may rest for a moment."

Vere helped her sit down on one of the lower steps. Elissande sat down next to her and hugged her tight. "Shhh. It will be all right."

Her uncle laughed softly. "You think so? Why should she be all right when I haven't been in twenty-four years?" He gazed at Aunt Rachel. "Everything I've done in my life, I've done for you. To be worthy of your hand, to keep you in the style befitting a princess. I worshiped you. *I worshiped you!*"

Aunt Rachel began to shake.

Elissande bit into her lower lip. Her hand itched for her reticule. Instead she rose. "Can we gag him?" she said to Vere. "We've heard enough from him today."

"I've some chloroform with me," he answered.

She clasped his arm briefly. He was ever to be relied upon in a situation like this.

"Don't be rash, my dear," said her uncle. "I am willing to offer you a deal. If you don't wish to hear from me again, then let me go with the necklace."

She laughed out of incredulity. "Such bargains you offer, sir. Allow me to remind you that when you are swinging from the gallows, I won't ever hear from you again either. *And* we'll keep the necklace."

Douglas chuckled. "Perhaps you would listen to a word of advice from your aunt? Mrs. Douglas, won't you say that our beloved niece, with her contempt and loathing for me, should give much to purchase my silence?"

Aunt Rachel stared blankly at her feet, still shaking.

"Rachel!" her uncle said sharply.

Aunt Rachel jerked and looked reluctantly at him.

"Would you not say, Rachel, that some secrets are better left…buried?"

Aunt Rachel recoiled.

Elissande had had enough of his cat-and-mouse games. "My lord, the chloroform, please."

"Then I shall divulge it now," said her uncle, no doubt imagining that he was still the master of Highgate Court and that his merest utterings shook the earth.

"No!" Aunt Rachel cried. "No. Ellie, he's right. Let him go."

"Absolutely not!" Elissande's voice rose with

frustration. Aunt Rachel could not possibly be this easily manipulated, with her erstwhile tormentor bound and helpless, and herself surrounded and protected. "We cannot trust him. We let him go today and he will be back in six months. And think of everyone he murdered: Do those poor souls not deserve some justice?"

"The real Edmund Douglas did atrocious things to and with the natives," her uncle said smoothly. "So don't imagine you are avenging some pure, blameless innocent."

"It doesn't matter. I am going to silence you. I am going to the police station to turn you in. And I am going to hire private guards, so you will not escape again."

Her uncle sighed. "Listen to her, Rachel. I should have taken more of an interest in her, don't you think? The decisiveness, the ruthlessness, the willingness to ride roughshod over all obstacles in her way: She quite reminds me of myself at that age."

"Don't you dare compare us," Elissande snapped.

"Why not? You are my flesh and blood. Why shouldn't I compare us?"

A terrible premonition tingled her spine. But she ignored it. "Your daughter died when she was an infant. I am not related to you except by marriage."

Her uncle smiled, a smile that would make a glacier of the Mediterranean. "No, my child, your cousin died. My *daughter* never did."

It was as if Goliath had struck her on the head with her very own reticule.

"You are lying!" she shouted reflexively.

"You see, your mother found me out," he said calmly. "And I wept and begged her not to leave, if only for the sake of our unborn child. And she lied to me—oh, how sweetly she lied. She vowed that of course she would always be mine, till her dying day."

"You said you'd kill me if I left," Aunt Rachel said, almost inaudibly.

Douglas turned toward his wife. "Did you expect me to simply let you go? To give up my wife and my child? I believed your lies of faithful love, until you spit in my face and told me it was *my* daughter who had died, instead of your niece.

"You would rather my daughter grew up thinking that her father was a wastrel and her mother a whore. You would rather that she believed herself a penniless orphan. I should have killed you then, but I loved you too much."

Elissande felt faint, but curiously calm, as if surrounded by thick castle walls, as if the din and mayhem outside those walls—Genghis Khan and his ransacking army—had nothing to do with her. She was not there. She was somewhere else entirely.

Her husband placed his hand on her back and murmured words of concern. She only extended her palm for the chloroform. He gave her the bottle and a handkerchief. She soaked the handkerchief, walked to her uncle, and pressed it into his face.

Chapter Twenty

"W ill Lord Vere be able to handle everything?" asked Aunt Rachel, as the train pulled out amidst much whistling and steaming.

Vere remained on the platform, watching their departure. Still in his cabbie guise, he had driven Elissande and Aunt Rachel to the rail station, so they could leave Exeter and its ordeal behind. *Much better that Mrs. Douglas recuperate at home than at a police station,* he'd said.

But his home was not *theirs,* was it?

"He will be fine," said Elissande.

He receded farther and farther from view, his absence a sharp emptiness within her. Finally the train station became only a buoy of light in the darkness and he was lost from her sight.

"I suppose...I suppose you will want to know everything," said her aunt.

No, not her aunt, her *mother*. Elissande turned her gaze to that familiar face, less gaunt than before but still aged far before her time, and felt a wave of terrible sadness.

"Only if you feel strong enough for it, ma'am."

She didn't know if *she* was strong enough for it.

"I can manage, I think," said Aunt Rachel with a weak smile. "But I don't quite know where to start."

Elissande thought back to what her husband had recounted earlier. It was an effort not to shudder. "I've been told that my uncle—my father—had painted you as a good, kind angel long before you were married. You did not know who he was?"

"He said he first saw me in Brighton, on the West Pier, and was so taken with me that he bribed the owner of the studio where we had a family portrait taken to tell him the address we'd written down for our portraits to be sent to—and also to sell him a photograph of me. I never saw him before he called on me. He claimed to be an acquaintance of my late father's and I did not doubt him. I was in reduced circumstances and Charlotte had run away from home—people lied about why they no longer wished to receive me; it didn't occur to me that anyone would lie to get *close* to me."

Elissande's heart pinched: her gentle, trusting mother, all alone in the world and utterly vulnerable to a monster like Douglas.

"When did you learn the truth?"

"Shortly before you were born. I found his old diary when I was looking for quite something else—I don't remember what. Had I known the diary belonged to him, I wouldn't have opened it. But it had the initials G. F. C. embossed on the cover and I was curious."

Mrs. Douglas sighed. "I was so naïve, so stupid, and so completely thrilled with my handsome, clever, rich husband—even his jealousy I'd thought romantic. When I realized that George Fairborn Carruthers's handwriting looked just like my husband's, and some of the events from this stranger's life were identical to what Edmund had recounted from his, I asked *him*, of all people, about it.

"He must have panicked. He could have fobbed me off with some cock-and-bull story, but he told me terrible things. That was when I first saw his true nature—when I first became afraid of him."

That was why she had been so distressed by the news of Stephen Delaney's murder, Elissande realized: Douglas must have vowed to her that he would never take another life.

"When you were one month old, your cousin was delivered to our doorstep by a Salvation Army sergeant. I'd lost touch with Charlotte over the years. I had no idea she'd died in childbirth or that her husband had perished already. The sergeant said that she tried to give the baby to the Edgertons, but they absolutely refused. I was terrified of admitting another child into my house—under my husband— but there was nothing else I could do.

"The baby was adorable. She was only a week older than you, and you two could have easily passed for twins. But less than ten days after she came to live with us, you both caught a fever. She had seemed stronger, while I feared for your life. The jubilation I felt when your fever broke...you could not imagine. But only a few hours later, in the middle of the night, your cousin died in my arms. The shock of it—I could not stop crying. I thought surely she wouldn't have died had she been with the Edgertons. I was petrified that the Edgertons had realized their mistake and would arrive in the morning to claim her. What would I tell them then?

"That was when it occurred to me. Your uncle—your father—was away on business in Antwerp, and the nursemaid had been dismissed because the house-keeper had caught her with the footman. If I claimed that you had died instead of your cousin, nobody would be the wiser. Then when the Edgertons came, you could go with them and live free of your father, the way I could not. Once I made my decision, I sent out death notices to everyone I knew—it was before your uncle moved us to the country, and I still had some friends and acquaintances. That made it official. No one doubted that a mother wouldn't know her own child."

She dabbed a handkerchief at the corners of her eyes. "I must say the Edgertons disappointed me terribly. I sent letters. I sent your photographs. They never even wrote back."

Elissande had to wipe at her own eyes. "It's all right, ma'am. You did your best."

"I did not. I have been an awful mother, a useless burden to you."

Elissande shook her head. "Please don't say that.

We both know what kind of man he is. He *would* have killed you had you tried to leave."

"I should have made you leave. He didn't need to have dominion over both of us."

Elissande reached across the narrow space between their seats and touched her mother on the cheek. "I wasn't altogether a prisoner: I had Capri. I always imagined myself there, far away from him."

"Me too," said Mrs. Douglas, tucking her handkerchief into the cuff of her sleeve.

Elissande was astonished. "You also imagined yourself on Capri?"

"No, I imagined *you* there. There was this passage you used to read to me that I dearly loved. I still remember bits and pieces of it: 'Like Venice, Capri is a permanent island in the traveler's experience—detached from the mainland of Italian character and associations,'" Mrs. Douglas recited, her eyes wistful, "'a bright, breezy pastoral of the sea, with a hollow, rumbling undertone of the Past, like that of the billows in its caverns.'

"I imagined you exploring those caverns—I'd read about the discovery of the Blue Grotto when I was a girl; it seemed enchanting. When you had had your fill of grottos, you would dine at a farmhouse and eat robust peasant food full of herbs and olives. And when evening came, you would return to your villa high above the cliffs and watch the sun set over the Mediterranean."

Tears rose again in Elissande's eyes. "I don't believe

I ever thought about what I'd eat or where I'd live on Capri."

"That is quite all right. But I'm your mother. When I imagine you far away, I'd like to think that you are well fed and safely housed."

But I'm your mother. The words were as disconcerting and beautiful as the first sight of stars.

"And I imagined this easily navigable path between your villa upon the ramparts of the island and the hostel where all the English visitors were gathered. So that when you were bored or lonely, you could go there for tea or dinner. And perhaps a nice young man could call on you."

Mrs. Douglas smiled hesitantly. "I'd imagined an entire life for you, in a place I've never seen."

Elissande had always known that the woman before her loved her, but never how much. "It sounds like a lovely life," she said, a catch in her throat.

"Almost as lovely as the life you have with Lord Vere." Mrs. Douglas took hold of her hands. "You are a fortunate woman, Ellie."

Her marriage was a sham, her husband willing to pay large sums of money to never see her again. And the man she despised the most had turned out to be her father—the ramifications of which she was still too numb to understand. But Mrs. Douglas was not wrong. Elissande *was* fortunate: She had her mother, safe and sound.

She leaned forward and kissed her mother on the forehead. "Yes, and how well I know it."

Vere watched the train that carried his wife disappear into the night.

He'd thought he'd known everything there was to know about the twists and turns of the Douglas case. But tonight's revelations had shocked him to the core.

Was she reeling? Was she in denial? Had she even understood everything that had transpired?

Instead of allowing himself to be mesmerized by the unfolding secrets, he should have sensed imminent calamity. He should have been quicker with the chloroform. Had he acted a minute sooner, he would have preserved her state of ignorant bliss.

There had been such joy to her—this ugly, faded world was fresh and beautiful in her eyes. Once, at dinner, she had recounted her aunt's amazement at their visit to Dartmouth. And he had almost commented on the amazement he saw on *her* face each day, the incredulous pleasure she took in the least things.

He had said nothing, in the end. Her joy had unsettled him: It was a flame, a dangerous flame that he feared would burn him if he were foolish enough to embrace it. He had not known until this moment how beautiful he thought it. How much he cherished it.

He did not dare such happiness for himself—he did not deserve it—but he wanted it for her. Hers had been a hard-won innocence. And he felt its shattering deep inside him, shards of pain puncturing his every breath.

When he arrived back at the house Douglas had chosen for his scheme, Holbrook, also dressed the part of a cabdriver, stood guard in the meager streetlight.

"Our man has already come to," he said by way of greeting.

Vere nodded. "I will change into my own clothes and we'll take him."

He changed inside the house. Then together he and Holbrook carried Douglas, still bound tight, into Holbrook's hansom cab. Holbrook mounted the driver's perch; Vere climbed inside the cab and took a seat next to Douglas.

"So, you are my son-in-law," said Douglas.

As the man spoke, Vere felt something crawl on his skin. "Eh?" he said. "No, no, I married your wife's niece."

"Didn't you understand a single thing that has been said tonight? She is not my wife's niece. She is my daughter."

Vere looked at Douglas blankly. "Cracked in the head, aren't you?"

Douglas laughed. "I must say, part of me is more than a little delighted that she married an idiot."

"I'm not an idiot," Vere said quietly, experiencing a great and terrible regret at not having thrashed the man more systematically when he'd had the chance.

"No? Then beware. She is my daughter. I know her.

I know she entrapped you. Clever as the devil himself, she is, and just as ruthless. She will use you until you've nothing more to give, and who knows, maybe she will get rid of you."

The vileness of the man never failed to astonish. Vere's fingers tightened into a fist. "How can you say such things about your own daughter, as you keep insisting?"

"Because it's true. She has learned a great deal from me, an opportunist if ever there was one. Why do you think—pardon me—you don't think; I forgot. Well, I feel sorry for you, you cretinous lummox."

"Pardon?" said Vere.

"You stupid half-wit."

Vere punched him in the face, almost breaking his own hand with the force of his violence. Douglas screamed in pain, his entire body shuddering.

"Sorry," Vere said, smiling to see Douglas flinch at his voice. "I do that when people call me stupid. You were saying?"

❧

"Let me make sure I understood you correctly, Lord Vere. You were in Dartmouth at a pub. The gentleman sat down and bought you a drink. After which drink you found yourself lighthearted and silly, and agreed with him to come look at a nice piece of property in Exeter. You woke up on the floor of an empty house, realized you'd been abducted, subdued your abductor when he came to give you your bread and water, and brought him in?" asked Detective Nevinson, who, as a result of one of the cables Vere had sent from Paignton, was at the police station.

This damnable, never-ending role. Vere ached to be home—his wife should not be alone tonight.

"Yes," he said. "I am what you would call, well, not an heiress—I know that's a woman—but what is a man heiress?"

"You are a rich man," said Nevinson, with a roll of his eyes.

"That's right. And as such, I know when I've been mugged for my money. And the bastard there—pardon my language, gentlemen—the bounder there had the audacity to suggest he'd keep me so that my wife would continually hand over thousands of pounds. Doesn't even know the proper etiquette for a ransom, does he? Ah, thank you, sir," he said to the chief inspector of the Exeter City Police, who had handed him a cup of dark, overbrewed tea. "Good stuff this is, Inspector. Can hardly taste the fancy Ceylon the missus likes."

Nevinson shook his head. "Do you know, sir, who you've brought in?"

" 'Course not. Told you, never laid eyes on him before."

"His is name is Edmund Douglas. Sound familiar?"

"Good Lord, I've been had by my tailor!"

"No!" Nevinson cried. He took a deep breath and swallowed a mouthful of his own tea. "That man is your wife's uncle."

"That's not possible. My wife's uncle is at Holloway."

"He was found missing from Holloway."

"He was?"

"That's why he wanted you. Not because you are a random rich bloke, sir, but because you are his nephew-in-law."

"Then why didn't he introduce himself?"

Nevinson bit hard into a rock biscuit.

"Well, in any case," said the chief inspector, "you've brought him in, my lord, and saved everyone from a prolonged manhunt. I, for one, think this calls for more than tea. A bit of whiskey, perhaps, Detective?"

"Please," said Nevinson fervently.

A police sergeant rushed into the chief inspector's office. "Sorry to disturb you, sir, but the man his lordship just brought in, he's dead."

Nevinson gasped. Vere jumped up, knocking over his chair. "I didn't kill him."

"Of course you didn't kill him," Nevinson said impatiently. "What happened, Sergeant?"

"We aren't sure, sir. He was perfectly fine. Then he asked for some water. Constable Brown gave him the water. Five minutes later, when Constable Brown went to get the mug back, he was lying in his cot, dead."

They all rushed out to Douglas's cell. Douglas lay on his side, seemingly asleep, but entirely without a pulse.

"How did this happen?" Vere cried. "Did he just drop dead?"

"This looks like either cyanide or strychnine." Nevinson patted Douglas's person. "Nothing on him but a bit of money and a watch."

"Do you think he kept his cyanide pills in his watch?" Vere asked, eyes wide.

"That's lud—" Nevinson stopped. He fiddled with the watch; the face slid open to reveal a secret compartment. "You are right: There are more pills. Enough to kill three people—*if* these are cyanide pills."

A chill shot down Vere's spine. Perhaps Douglas had envisioned poisoning his wife along with himself. Or perhaps they'd all been meant for Mrs. Douglas, his long-delayed, ultimate vengeance.

And perhaps there was enough to do in Elissande as well. Vere's blood turned cold, even though the danger was now well past.

"I suppose he knew that this time there would be no more escaping," said Nevinson. "We have enough evidence; he was headed for the gallows."

For a man who sought to master his fate through whatever means necessary, the thought of having his death imposed upon him must have been unbearable. At least he could never again hurt Elissande or her mother.

A thought that did not bring nearly the relief Vere had hoped. For the damages Douglas had wrought this day—and over the entirety of his worthless life— he should have suffered every last agony the human body could comprehend before dying in public ignominy.

"And look." Nevinson set the watch on the floor

and showed them a tiny pouch. "There are still two diamonds inside. That's how he must have bribed the prison guards to make his escape."

While the detective and the chief inspector examined the diamonds, Vere took the watch in hand and unobtrusively fiddled with it some more. There, a second hidden compartment, and inside, another tiny key.

He pocketed the key and handed the watch back to Nevinson. "Really, he didn't need to kill himself. I would have said a word to the judge for leniency. Rich men are tempting targets. And he's my uncle, after all."

❦

Suddenly Elissande could not breathe.

She had inhaled and exhaled tolerably on the journey home. She'd not lacked for air as she put her mother to bed. Even when she was at last by herself, reclined on the chaise longue in the parlor, a compress on her face, another waiting in a basin of water made cold by a block of ice from the ice cellar, her lungs had expanded and contracted as they ought to.

But now she bolted upright, throwing the compress to the floor. Now she yanked at her collar. Now her uncle's hands were clenched about her throat again, pitilessly, inexorably closing her airway.

She panted and gasped. She opened her mouth wide and gulped down what little oxygen remained in the room.

But she was still not getting enough air. Her head spun; her fingers were numb; her lips tingled strangely. She breathed ever faster, deeper. Her chest hurt. Her vision dotted with points of light.

Sounds came from outside. Was it a carriage? Was that someone opening the front door? She could not make sense of anything. She could only bend over and tuck her head between her knees, fighting not to lose consciousness.

Footsteps—she was no longer alone.

"Slow your breathing, Elissande," he instructed, sitting next to her. "You must control your breathing."

He stroked her hair, the warmth of his touch as lovely as that of a cashmere scarf. But his words made no sense—she needed air.

"Inhale slowly, and not too deep. Same when you exhale." His hand was now on her back, a subtle pressure that calmed her.

She did as he asked. Soon it became apparent that he was right. Controlling her intake of air, a course of action that ran entirely counter to her intuition, soothed her nerves. The numbness and tingling went away; the tightness in her chest dissipated, as did the wobbliness in her head.

He helped her sit straight. Her eyes still hurt slightly at the corners, but she no longer saw dancing spots—only him. He looked worn, his expression a slight frown, but his gaze was steady and kind.

"Better?" he asked.

"Yes, thank you."

His fingers barely touching her, he turned her face to inspect it. "The bruises will be ugly. You should be in bed—it's been a very long day."

Was it only *this* morning she'd awakened full of boundless optimism for the future, certain that every piece of her life had at last fallen into place? How could so much be destroyed in so little time?

"I'm all right," she muttered mechanically.

"Are you?"

She could not hold his gaze. Her eyes dropped to her own hands. "Is he back in custody?"

"He was."

Her chin jerked up. *"Was?"*

He hesitated.

Her hand gripped the scroll arm of the chaise longue. "Has he escaped again? Please tell me he has not escaped again!"

Her husband glanced away briefly. When he looked back at her, there was a certain emptiness to his eyes. "He is dead, Elissande. He committed suicide at the police station. Some sort of poison pills—cyanide, most likely. We'll have to wait for the coroner's report to know exactly what he died of."

Her jaw dropped. Her breaths once more turned wild and uneven.

"Slowly," he had to tell her, his hand on her arm. "Or you might get dizzy again."

She counted as she breathed. She could force her diaphragm to obey, but inside her rib cage, her heart pounded away in shock.

"You are—you are sure it was not a ruse?"

"I was there in person. He is as dead as any of his murder victims."

She rose; she could no longer remain seated. "So he couldn't bear to face the consequences of his own actions," she said, her voice sounding infinitely bitter in her own ears.

"No, he couldn't. He was a coward in every way."

She pressed two fingers to the place between her brows—hard. It hurt. But nothing hurt as much as the truth. "And he was my father."

Everything she believed of herself had been turned on its head.

Something was pressed into her hands—a generously filled glass of whiskey. She wanted to laugh: Had Vere forgotten her limited capacity for liquor? Instead she had to bite her lip to force back tears.

"He abused Andrew and Charlotte Edgerton to me every chance he had. I understood that even were the two judged kindly, most people would still see Charlotte Edgerton as loose and her husband foolish. Yet—"

She blinked hard. "Yet I loved them—I believed them dashing and larger-than-life. I imagined that as they drew their last breaths, their greatest regret was that they could not watch me grow into womanhood."

Instead, when her father drew *his* last breath, his greatest regret must have been that he could no longer torment Elissande and her mother to his heart's content.

The thought seared her. Instead of generous,

affectionate, if overly impulsive Andrew Edgerton, her father was a man who laughed gleefully at the possibility of her having to raise a passel of moronic children.

She saw her reflection in the mirror on the wall. Her husband was wrong. It was not that her bruises were *going* to be ugly, they already *were:* red welts turning purple, a cut across her lips, one of her eyes swollen nearly shut.

Her own father had done this to her, with distinct pleasure at her pain and injury.

She had believed freedom was as easy as physically escaping Highgate Court. But how did she escape *this*? For as long as she lived, Edmund Douglas's blood would pulse in her, a daily reminder of the unbreakable ties of kinship that now forever bound her to him.

She turned away from the mirror, pushed the glass of whiskey back into her husband's hand, and made for the door. Up the stairs, down the corridor, into her room. She opened the treasure chest and took out all the mementos she had so cherished over the years.

"Elissande, don't do anything rash," said Vere.

She had not even heard him, but he was in her room with her.

"I'm not going to damage them." Even if the mementos no longer held the same meaning for her—it was a knife in the heart to look upon them and remember the life she believed she could have had if only Andrew and Charlotte Edgerton had lived—her mother would still wish to have a few keepsakes by which to remember her sister. "I only want to burn this chest."

"Why?"

"There is a secret compartment in the lid. When I was a little girl he showed me the key slots and told me that one day I would find the keys. I know now what's in it." She had to clench her teeth against an upsurge of disgust; she felt entirely unclean. "It must be his diary."

And the painting that had hung in her room at Highgate Court, with the thorny red rose arising from a pool of his blood, that had been his hint to her all along, hadn't it?

"This chest would produce a great deal of fume in the grate," said her husband. "I have the keys for the compartment. Why don't I open it instead?"

She stared at him; she'd forgotten his field of expertise. "When and where did you find the keys?"

"One in the safe at Highgate Court, when we visited after our wedding, the second tonight on Douglas's person."

He left briefly to retrieve the other key from his room. She set the chest on top of her dresser. He fitted in the keys and turned both at the same time. The bottom of the lid sprang open half an inch or so. He carefully pulled it down until a small, cloth-wrapped package slid into his palm.

Opening the square of blue broadcloth revealed a leather-bound volume, with the initials G. F. C. embossed in a corner.

"There is a note here for you."

"What does it say?" She did not want to touch anything that had been in Douglas's hands.

" 'My Dear Elissande, Christabel Douglas never died. Ask Mrs. Douglas what happened to her. And—' " Her husband stopped and glanced at her. " 'And may I live forever in your memory. Your father, George Fairborn Carruthers.' "

It was as if Douglas had punched her again. At least he need no longer regret not silencing him sooner with the chloroform. He always meant to have the last laugh from beyond the grave.

She grabbed the diary from Vere's hands and threw it across the room. "God *damn* him!"

The tears that she'd tried to keep back streamed down her face. They burned where Douglas had hit her.

"Elissande—"

"That's not even my name."

She'd always loved her name, which combined Eleanor and Cassandra, the names of Charlotte and Andrew Edgerton's mothers. She'd relished the care and thought that had gone into its creation, the exotic, musical syllables, the aspirations that Charlotte and Andrew Edgerton must have had for their daughter to bestow such a grand name on her, one not every girl could carry off.

Much of her life she had seethed in powerlessness. But never had she felt as powerless as she did this moment—stripped of everything that had ever mattered to her.

Behind her, her husband placed his hands on her arms. Then, very gently, he wrapped his arms about her middle and held her against him.

And she wept for all her broken dreams.

❧

When she had no more tears, he disrobed her and changed her into her nightdress. Then he lifted her, carried her to her bed, and tucked her in.

He extinguished the light and left her room. She lay with her eyes open, staring into the shadows, wishing she hadn't been too proud to ask him to remain with her for a little longer. But to her relief—and a bittersweet moment of happiness—he came back in the next minute.

"Are you thirsty?" he asked.

She was. He pressed a glass of water into her hand—that must have been what he'd left to get. She drank almost the entire glass and thanked him. He pulled a chair next to her bed and sat.

Perhaps he was right. Perhaps she *was* grateful for every little kindness shown her. But this was no little kindness on his part, to stay with her on the darkest night of her life.

He took her hand in his. "Elissande."

She was too worn-out to remind him that Elissande was not her name.

As if he'd heard her, he said, "It's beautiful, this name with which your mother rechristened you."

Her heart skidded. She had not thought of it that way.

"It's beautiful for all the hope with which she endowed it, the bravest moment in an otherwise timid life. That she dared to hide her daughter in plain sight is testament of her love for you."

She'd believed that she had no more tears. Yet her eyes prickled hotly again as she remembered her mother's desperate valor.

"Do not forget it, Elissande."

Tears spilled from the corners of her eyes, past her temples, into her hair. "I won't," she murmured.

He gave her a handkerchief. She held on tight to it—and with her other hand she held on tight to him.

He skimmed the back of her hand with his thumb. "When I did my reading on the artificial synthesis of diamonds, every article I came across mentioned the fact that a diamond consists solely of carbon, which makes it kin to both blacklead and coal. Douglas is your father—I don't dispute that. But whereas he is nothing but a lump of coal, you are a diamond of the first water."

She was hardly that. She was a liar and a manipulator.

"Your mother would not have lived to this day were it not for you—of that I have no doubt. When she was defenseless, you defended her."

"How could I not? She needed me."

"Not everyone watches out for the powerless. You would have profited far more by flattering Douglas—or you could have left by yourself. It takes moral fiber to do the right thing."

She bit the inside of her lip. "Keep talking and soon I will believe myself a paragon of virtues."

He chortled. "That you are not, and probably never will be. But you have both strength and compassion, neither of which Douglas understood or possessed in the least."

He smoothed away the wetness at her temple, his touch as light and careful as a miniature painter's brushstrokes.

"I have watched you these past days. A life under Douglas could easily have made you brittle, anxious, and resentful. But you have been incandescent. Don't let him take it away from you. Laugh at him instead. Have friends, have books, have a ball with your mother. Let him see your days suffused with pleasure. Let him see that even though he devoted his life to it, he'd failed to ruin yours."

More tears tumbled into her hair. Mrs. Douglas was right: Elissande *was* a fortunate woman. The man she'd wronged the most had turned out to be a true friend.

She thought of her mother, safe and sound in her room, never to be mistreated again. She thought of herself: still her own mistress—that would not change. She thought of the coming morning—even the darkest night did not last forever—and surprised herself with a desire to see the sunrise.

"You are right," she said. "I will not let him diminish me from beyond the grave, just as I never allowed him to take a piece of my soul while he yet lived."

When Vere was sixteen, he and Freddie were summoned from Eton to attend their father on the latter's deathbed.

Being a dying man had not rendered the marquess any less vitriolic than usual. With Freddie in the room, he had instructed Vere to marry soon and reproduce fast, so that there would be no chance for the title and the estate to pass on to Freddie.

Vere had held his tongue because of the presence of a physician and a nurse. But he'd grown angrier and angrier as the evening progressed. Finally, deep in the night, he could stand it no more. His father might be at Death's door but he needed to be told that he was a despicable man and a wretched excuse for a father.

He made for the marquess's bedchamber. The nurse had nodded off in the next room but the door to the marquess's bedchamber was ajar, leaking both light and voices into the passage. He peeked in and recognized the rector by the man's vestment.

"But—but—but, my lord, that was murder," stammered the rector.

"I knew bloody well it was murder when I pushed her down the staircase," said the marquess. "Had it been an accident, I wouldn't need you here."

Vere saw black. He gripped a wall sconce for support. Eight years before, his mother had died of what everyone believed to be an unfortunate fall from the grand staircase of the marquess's London town house. She'd stayed out too late, had a little too much to drink, the heels of her dancing slippers had caught, and down she had gone.

Her death had devastated Vere and Freddie.

Her blood had had nothing of the Norman purity her husband so prized in himself; her father, despite his superlative wealth, had ranked in the marquess's eyes as little more than a peddler. But she had been no wilting flower. The only child of an extraordinarily wealthy man, she'd known very well that her dowry paid the marquess's debts and kept the estate afloat. And she'd protected her children, especially Freddie, from the marquess's unpredictable and often virulent temper.

The marquess and the marchioness's mutual loathing had been common knowledge. The spendthrift marquess had already depleted the considerable dowry his wife had brought into the marriage and was in debt again. Vere's maternal grandfather, Mr. Woodbridge, no fool, provided for his daughter's needs directly: her gowns, her jewels, her trips abroad so she and her children could get away from her husband.

Yet despite all the domestic tension, no one had ever suspected foul play in her death. Or at least, no one had ever dared to accuse the marquess himself of it. Six months later the marquess married again, a lesser heiress this time, but one who had already come into her inheritance—no pesky father-in-law this time.

While the record was firmly set that the first marchioness's death had been an accident, pure and simple.

And so Vere had believed, until that heinous moment. He wanted to hide. He wanted to run. He wanted to kick open the door and stop the proceedings. But he was frozen in place, unable to move a single muscle.

"I assume you have repented, my lord?" asked the rector, his voice squeaking.

"No, I would do it again if I had to—I couldn't stand her another minute," said the marquess. He laughed, a wheezing, horrible laugh. "But I suppose we must go through the formalities, mustn't we? I tell you that I'm sorry and you tell me all is well on God's green earth."

"I can't!" the rector cried. "I cannot condone either your action or your unrepentant ways."

"You will," said the marquess, his spite inexorable. "Or the world would finally learn why you are the confirmed bachelor you are. For shame, Reverend Somerville, carrying on with a married man, damning his eternal soul to hell even as you damn your own."

Vere turned and walked. He could not stand to listen to the marquess have his way one last time, not after he already got away with murder.

The marquess's funeral was a dreadful occasion, thickly attended, his lofty character and good deeds lauded to the rafters by those who either didn't know or didn't care what he truly had been: a fiend.

The night after the funeral, Vere had his nightmare for the very first time. Never mind that he'd never seen the scene of his mother's death; he would now find her cold and broken at the foot of the staircase again and again and again.

❧

Three months later, Vere broke down and confided in his great-aunt Lady Jane.

Lady Jane listened with sympathy and sensitivity. And then she said, "I'm so sorry. It devastated me when I learned of it from Freddie. And yet it devastates me no less to hear it again from you."

Her revelation shocked Vere almost as much as the truth behind his mother's death.

"*Freddie* knew? He knew and he didn't tell me?"

Lady Jane realized her mistake but it was too late. Vere refused to allow her to retract her knowledge. Eventually she gave in.

"Freddie was worried about your reaction. He feared you might kill your father if you knew—not an unjustified concern, based on what I've seen so far," said Lady Jane. "Besides, he believes your father already adequately punished."

When Freddie was thirteen, so the story went, he had gone to their father's room one night, after the marquess had confiscated one of his favorite sketches, in the hope of stealing it back. Apparently the marquess, believing the sounds Freddie made to indicate the presence of his first wife's ghost, had been terrified.

Vere was beside himself. How dense could Freddie be, to think that their father suffered any twinge of regret, let alone fear? The man who'd threatened to expose the rector's homosexuality had been no penitent and deserved no one's forgiveness.

Two years Freddie had known it, two years during which Vere could have made his father's life a living hell. That, to him, would have been Justice, or at least some measure of it. To have been denied it…to have been denied it by Freddie of all people…

Perhaps Lady Jane saw true potential in Vere. Perhaps she only wished that he would stop with his rants on Truth and Justice. In any case she returned his confidence with one of her own: She was an agent of the Crown whose life's work had been to unearth truth and restore justice. It was too late for Vere's mother. But might he find some solace in helping others?

He said yes immediately. Lady Jane advised that in order to turn himself into someone no one took seriously—an enormous asset to a covert agent—he should adopt a pose. She suggested the guise of a hedonist. Vere balked. He'd never been one to overindulge his senses. More important, despite his loneliness, he did not want to be near crowds any more than he must. And who'd ever heard of a secluded hedonist?

"I'd rather be an idiot," he said.

Little did he realize that as a hedonist, at least he'd have been able to express his own opinions on a range of issues. The role of the idiot permitted no such relief. And the more skillfully he played the fool, the more he isolated himself.

Lady Jane recommended that he not make a decision right away. Exactly two days later, however, he was thrown from his horse. He immediately resolved to exploit the very serious accident, and to take advantage of Needham's presence as Lady Jane's houseguest. Once the physician stamped the cachet of his considerable medical expertise on Vere's condition, nobody would be able to say he *didn't* suffer a severe, life-changing concussion.

The physical requirements for his sudden transition to idiocy established, he had a choice to make: What to tell Freddie?

Had Lady Jane's slip of the tongue never happened, he might have made a very different decision. He and Freddie had always been close. While Freddie couldn't lie, in this instance he didn't have to: Vere's own act was going to spread the news. Should Freddie be asked, he could simply give Needham's diagnosis verbatim. And Freddie's loyalty to Vere was so well-known that even if he continued to speak of his brother's assorted cleverness, his listeners would only conclude that he had trouble accepting the new reality.

But as Freddie had seen fit to rob Vere of any chance of avenging their mother, Vere returned the favor and kept his new secret to himself.

❦

When Vere had wholeheartedly disliked his wife, in a way it had been because she, with her thespian skills and her facile lies, reminded him too much of himself.

But those had been mere surface similarities. Underneath, he was a man who had been fractured at sixteen and never been made whole again, while she, as imperfect as she was, possessed a resilience that left him breathless.

Her hand remained in his, her fingers slack with slumber. He'd meant only to stay with her until she fell asleep, but he was still here at the break of dawn, guarding against her nightmares.

He wanted always to be a bulwark against her nightmares.

The thought didn't surprise him as much as he imagined it would, now that he'd stopped denying that he loved her. But he wasn't worthy of her—at least, not as he was, now with all the deceit and cowardice that still blighted his character.

He knew what he had to do. But did he have the courage and humility for it? Was his desire to walk beside her and protect her stronger than his instinct to shy away from the repercussions of truth and continue the fraud that was his life?

He felt as if he stood at the very top of a high cliff. Take a step back and all was safe and familiar. But going forward required a singular leap of faith—and he was a man of little faith, particularly when it came to himself.

But he wanted her to look at him again as if he were full of possibilities. As if *they* were full of possibilities.

And for that he would do the right thing, whatever his shortcomings.

Chapter Twenty-one

A death in the family, especially a death under such strained circumstances, required much to be done in its wake.

Edmund Douglas's body had to be claimed and buried, his solicitors consulted with regard to his will and his estate. Had things been different, Elissande would have taken care of matters. But with her battered face—the bruises had turned a cringe-inducing mélange of purple, green, and darkish yellow—Mrs. Douglas had insisted that Elissande remain home to recuperate. She would go in Elissande's stead.

It was time she took a greater interest in matters of her own life, said Mrs. Douglas. Vere, who had anyway needed to go to London, volunteered to accompany her. They also brought along Mrs. Green, who would see to it that Mrs. Douglas was comfortably put up and meticulously looked after.

And now Mrs. Douglas dozed in their rail compartment, her weight against Vere's arm as insubstantial as that of a blanket.

Memories surfaced of her daughter sleeping next to him on the train. He remembered his resentful bewilderment that he could have been drawn to someone of such questionable character. His intellectual self had yet to recognize what a deeper, more primal part of him already sensed at first sight: her integrity.

Not integrity in the sense of unimpeachable practice of morality, but a personal wholeness. Her trials under Douglas had not left her unmarked, but neither had they lessened her.

Whereas he had been both scarred *and* diminished.

He had always used the language of Justice to relate to his work. True justice was motivated by an impartial desire for fairness. What underlay *his* entire career had been anger and grief: anger that he could not punish his father, grief that he could not bring back his mother.

That was why he derived only negligible satisfaction from even his greatest successes: They reminded him of his impotence in his own life, of what he could never accomplish.

And that was why he had been so livid at Freddie: part of it had been envy. By the time he had spoken to Lady Jane, his father had been three months dead. And yet Vere's obsession had only grown. He could not understand how Freddie could let go and move on, while he remained stuck between the night of his mother's death and the night of his father's.

Thirteen years. Thirteen years of chasing after

what could never be had in the first place, while his youth fled by, his erstwhile ambitions lay forgotten, and his life grew ever more isolated.

A single snore in the compartment brought his attention back to his fellow traveler. Mrs. Douglas fidgeted, then slept on. On the way to the rail station, she had shyly confided that before she'd met him, she'd already seen him in a laudanum-fueled dream—he'd rather wondered what she'd made of his presence in her room. One day, when he had his life in order, he would tell her the truth and apologize for frightening her.

She fidgeted again. Vere studied her: the cheeks, still pale, but now with a whisper of color; the neck, still thin, but no longer sticklike. When he'd first met her, he'd assumed her permanently broken. She had instead proved herself a dormant seed that needed only a less hostile environment to come alive.

He turned to the window again. Perhaps he too was not as permanently broken as he'd believed.

❧

This time, instead of using his own key, Vere rang Freddie's bell.

He was shown into Freddie's study, where Freddie was checking a book of rail schedules, his finger moving down a column, searching for what he needed. Freddie looked up and dropped the book.

"Penny! I was just coming to see you." He rushed up to Vere and embraced him anxiously. "If you arrived fifteen minutes later I'd have left to Paddington Station already. I heard the most bizarre rumors this morning: Lady Vere's uncle escaped jail and abducted you—and you had to fight for your life. What happened?"

The words were on Vere's lips—*Oh rubbish, don't people know how to gossip properly anymore? I didn't have to fight for my life. I subdued that toothpick of a man with one finger*—and an expression of thick satisfaction was already rising to his face.

The temptation to fall back on the idiocy he played so expertly was enormous. Freddie didn't expect anything else of him. Freddie had long become accustomed to the idiot. They were still brothers—loving brothers. Why change anything at all?

He crossed the study, poured himself a measure of Freddie's cognac, and tossed it back. "What you heard was a lie I told," he said. "Mr. Douglas had abducted Mrs. Douglas, in truth. But once we rescued Mrs. Douglas, we decided that it was better for her to go home to recuperate rather than talk to the police. So I took Mr. Douglas to the police station and made up a cock-and-bull story."

Freddie blinked. And blinked again several times. "Ah—so, is everyone all right?"

"Lady Vere has some bruises; she won't be able to receive callers for a few days. Mrs. Douglas had quite a fright, but she came with me today and is currently enjoying herself at the Savoy Hotel. Mr. Douglas, well, he's dead. He decided that he was better off swallowing cyanide than taking his chances in court."

Freddie listened attentively. When Vere had finished speaking, he looked at Vere for some more time, then gave his head a small shake. "Are *you* all right, Penny?"

"You can see I'm perfectly fine, Freddie."

"Well, yes, you are in one piece. But you are not acting like yourself."

Vere took a deep breath. "This is who I've always been. But it's true that sometimes—most of the past thirteen years, in fact—I haven't *acted* myself."

Freddie rubbed his eyes. "Are you saying what I think you are saying?"

"What do you think I'm saying?" Vere asked. He thought he'd made himself clear, but Freddie hadn't reacted as he'd expected.

"One moment." Freddie reached for a small encyclopedia and opened it to a random page. "In what year was the first plebeian secession?"

"In 494 B.C."

"Dear Lord," Freddie muttered. He turned the encyclopedia to a different section, then looked up with an expression of such singular hope that Vere's stomach wrenched. "Who were Henry the Eighth's six wives?"

"Catherine of Aragon, Anne Boleyn, Jane Seymour, Anne of Cleves, Catherine Howard, and Catherine Parr," Vere said slowly. He could have recited the list much faster, but he dreaded finishing answering the question.

Freddie set down the book. "Do you support women's suffrage, Penny?"

"New Zealand granted unrestricted voting rights to women in 'ninety-three. South Australia granted voting rights *and* allowed women to stand for Parliament in 'ninety-five. The sky hasn't fallen in either place, last I checked."

"You have recovered," Freddie whispered, tears already coursing down his face. "My God, Penny, you have recovered."

Vere was suddenly crushed by Freddie's embrace.

"Oh, Penny, you have no idea. I have missed you so *much*."

Tears rolled down Vere's cheeks: Freddie's joy, his own shame, regret for all the time they had lost.

He pulled away.

Freddie did not notice his distress. "We must tell everyone right away. Too bad the Season is finished. My goodness, won't everyone be in for a genuine shock next year. But we can still go to our clubs and make the announcements. And you are not leaving town right away, are you? Angelica is up in Derbyshire visiting her cousin, but she should be back tomorrow. She will be thrilled. *Thrilled*, I tell you." He spoke in such a rush his words were shoving one another out of the way. "Let me ring for Mrs. Charles. I think I have a bottle or two of champagne lying around. We must celebrate. We must celebrate properly."

Freddie reached for the bellpull. Vere grabbed his arm. But what he needed to say stuck in his throat like wet cement. He'd steeled himself to face Freddie's wrath, not this overwhelming joy. To speak more on the subject would annihilate the happiness that flushed Freddie's face and glistened in his eyes.

But Vere had no choice. If he allowed himself to

stop here, it would be another Big Lie between the two of them, where there were piled too many lies already.

He dropped his hand from Freddie's arm and clenched it into a fist. "You misunderstood me, Freddie. I haven't recovered from anything, because there was nothing to recover *from*. I never had a concussion. It has been my choice to act the idiot."

Freddie stared at Vere. "What are you saying? You were diagnosed. I talked to Needham myself. He said you suffered a personality-altering traumatic injury to the head."

"Ask me again about women's suffrage."

Some of the color drained from Freddie's cheeks. "Do you…do you support women's suffrage?"

For some reason, the role did not immediately come to Vere, as if he were an actor who had already left the stage, stripped off his costume, wiped clean his makeup, and fallen half-asleep, and then was suddenly asked to reprise his performance.

He had to take several deep breaths and imagine strapping a mask over his face. "Women's suffrage? But what do they need it for? Every woman is going to vote the way her husband tells her to, and we will still end up with the exact same idiots in Parliament! Now if dogs could vote, that would make a difference. They are intelligent, they are loyal to the Crown, and they certainly deserve more of a say in the governance of this country."

Freddie's mouth dropped open. He flushed with embarrassment. And then, as Vere watched, his expression slowly darkened into anger. "So all these years, all these years, it was just an *act*?"

Vere swallowed. "I'm afraid so."

Freddie stared at him another minute. He drew back his fist. It landed on Vere's solar plexus with an audible thwack. Vere stumbled a step. Before he could recover, another punch landed. And another. And another. And another. Until he was pinned to the wall.

He'd had no idea Freddie was capable of violence.

"You bastard!" The words exploded in a roar. "You swine! You bloody sham!"

He'd had no idea Freddie was capable of swearing, either.

Freddie stopped, his breaths hard and heavy.

"I'm sorry, Freddie." Vere could not meet his eyes. He stared at the desk behind Freddie's back. "I'm sorry."

"*You* are sorry? I used to cry like a frigging fountain whenever I thought of you. Did you ever think of that? Did you even care about the people who loved you?"

His words were shards of glass in Vere's heart. He had tried to spend as much time away from Freddie as possible in the months following his accident, but there had been no mistaking Freddie's devastation, the tentative hope at the beginning of each new meeting fracturing into splinters of despair.

And now the moment of reckoning had come. Now Freddie saw him for what he truly was.

"And I have *never* let anyone call you an idiot," Freddie snarled. "I almost came to blows with Wessex over that. But my God, you are. You are such a sodding idiot."

He was. God, he was. A sodding idiot and a selfish bastard.

"It was as if you had died. The person who was you was gone. And I had all this grief that I couldn't even speak of, except maybe to Lady Jane or Angelica, because everyone kept telling me that I should be thankful you were still alive. And I was, and then I would look at this stranger who had your face and your voice and miss you desperately."

Fresh tears rolled down Vere's face.

"I'm sorry. I was fixated on Mater's murder and Pater's guilt and I was furious you didn't tell me anything—"

Freddie clamped his hand on Vere's arm. "How do you know about them?"

"I heard Pater on his deathbed, trying to bully the rector to absolve him of the murder."

Freddie's expression changed. He walked away, poured himself a full glass of cognac, and emptied half the glass in one gulp. "For a moment I thought Lady Jane or Angelica told you."

"Angelica knows too?"

"I would have told only Angelica, but she was away that summer with her family." Freddie thrust his hand into his hair. "But I don't understand. What does your knowing what happened to Mater have to do with your act?"

"I've been an investigative agent for the Crown, as Lady Jane had been in her day. I thought that was how I would be able to find a measure of peace. And the idiocy was a guise, so nobody would take me seriously."

Freddie spun around. "My God! So when you saw

Mr. Hudson injecting Lady Haysleigh with the chloral, you didn't stumble upon it by accident."

"No."

"And Mr. Douglas, you were investigating him too?"

"Yes."

Freddie emptied the rest of his cognac. "You could have told me. I would have taken your secret to my grave. And I would have been so proud of you."

"I should've. But I was still seething at you for not telling me—for depriving me of any chance I had to punish Pater." Vere cringed at the rampant immaturity his words revealed—and the narrowness of his views. Anger and obsession had been for him the only acceptable reactions to the truth. "I seethed for weeks. Maybe months. And when I'd finally calmed down some it seemed that you'd already made your peace with the new me."

Most of the angry red had faded from Freddie's cheeks. He shook his head slowly. "I never completely made my peace with the not-you. And I wish you'd come to me; then I could have told you that Pater didn't need you to punish him: He was in hell already. You should have heard him that night. He begged for three hours, cowering under his counterpane all the while. I had to sit down because I got so tired of standing."

"But he never showed the slightest remorse."

"It was his tragedy: He stewed in so much fear without the least understanding that he could and should repent. That he even brought this up with the rector tells me he was terrified of eternal damnation. I pity him."

Vere braced his hand against the side of a bookcase. "Did you know that I envied you, Freddie? You were able to move on, whereas I wouldn't and couldn't let go. I've always prided myself on my cleverness—but it is an empty cleverness. How I wish I had some of your wisdom instead."

Freddie sighed. When he looked at Vere again, there was a deep sympathy in his eyes. Vere almost had to look away; he didn't deserve Freddie's sympathy.

"What has it been like for you all these years, Penny?"

Vere blinked back further tears. "It's been all right and it's been terrible."

Freddie was about to say something, then he started. "My God, does Lady Vere know?"

"She does now."

"And does she still like you?"

The anxiety in Freddie's voice made Vere's throat tighten once more. He didn't deserve Freddie's concern either.

"I can only hope."

"I think she will," said Freddie, his eyes once again shining with that clear earnestness Vere loved so well.

Vere caught his brother in an embrace. "Thank you, Freddie."

He didn't deserve Freddie's forgiveness today, but one day he hoped to. One day he would make himself equal to it.

Mrs. Douglas sent Elissande telegrams. She dispatched one upon arriving at each new destination to assure Elissande of her well-being. An enthusiastic paragraph arrived after Vere took her to the Savoy Theatre to watch a comic opera called *The Yeomen of the Guard*, which she adored even though she was strong enough to sit through only half of the first act. And one very brief cable simply said, *Mrs. Green allowed me a spoonful of ice cream. I had forgotten how divine it is.*

Her telegrams also brought news. The first significant piece of news came after she and Vere had met with Douglas's solicitors. In a will that dated to the beginning of the decade, Douglas had left nothing to his wife and his niece and had instead bequeathed everything to the Church. Elissande had chuckled. Truly, he was nothing if not consistent in his spite.

A companion cable came from Vere, explaining that not inheriting Douglas's estate might be a blessing in disguise—Douglas had borrowed heavily against the worth of the diamond mine and could prove to have nothing but debts to bequeath. The Church's lawyers would have a trying time with this particular gift horse.

A cable the next day was much more jubilant: Vere had located the jewels that Charlotte Edgerton had bequeathed to Mrs. Douglas, but which Douglas had immediately confiscated. A thousand pounds' worth of jewels.

Elissande reread the cable several times. *A thousand pounds.*

The morning after Exeter, when she woke up, both Douglas's diary and the chest were gone from her room. Where the chest had been, there was an elegant ebony box, in which the mementos from Charlotte and Andrew Edgerton were neatly stowed. In her dressing gown, Elissande had stood before the box, her fingertip grazing its edges, and hoped that the gift of the box meant what she wanted it to mean. But her husband had left soon thereafter, with only a solemn word to her to look after herself.

She had not been able to do much in the two days since his departure, except to try to come to terms with the fact that he had not changed his mind. The last time she had been furious; this time she only grieved. She did not want to lose the man who had held her hand when she most needed him.

There were ways she could justify remaining longer at Pierce House: She herself first must recover; then the news must be broken very gently to her mother; after that they must take their time and choose where to go.

But she had already begun to turn on those reasons. If she must leave—and she must—this was as good a time as any, with *you are a diamond of the first water* still echoing faintly in her ears, rather than tarrying until they wore out their welcome.

Now, with a thousand pounds at her disposal, they could ponder their eventual destination from anywhere—an inn, a house for let, the Savoy Hotel itself, if they were so inclined. And there was no gentle way of breaking it to her mother, was there? No matter how long she beat about the bushes, the truth of the matter would not dismay Mrs. Douglas any less.

She directed the maids to pack their belongings—it was less painful to delegate the task—while she tried to cheer herself. A new place, new people, and a brand-new life—those were the things that would have thrilled her during her captive days at Highgate Court. But one look out of the window to the fading but still beautiful garden and her heart would pinch with how much she loved this place, this life, and this man who had taken her mother to see *The Yeomen of the Guard* at the Savoy Theatre.

Without quite thinking, she left the house and walked to the spot above the River Dart where she had come across her husband on his long hike. She supposed when they were long gone, he would still walk these acres of rolling countryside, still stop occasionally on a slope to gaze down at the river, his hat by his side, leather patches on the sleeves of his tweed coat.

And she ached for his long miles of loneliness.

When she returned to the house, she went to her husband's study.

Within the first few days of her arrival in Devon, she had seen a book in the study entitled *How Women May Earn a Living*. Then it had seemed a bizarre tome to come across among the collection of a man who never needed to earn a living; now she'd become accustomed to the broad, deep, and eclectic compilation of knowledge he had at his fingertips.

As she searched the shelves for the book, her eyes landed on the corner of a postcard that had become wedged between two books. She pulled out the postcard and gasped. The sepia-toned image was all pounding ocean and high cliffs. Capri, her mind immediately decided, before she saw the words at the bottom left corner of the postcard: *Exmoor Coast.*

She called in Mrs. Dilwyn to help her find Exmoor Coast on the detailed map of Britain that hung on the wall of the study. It wasn't that far, a little more than fifty miles away on the north shore of Devon. She showed Mrs. Dilwyn the postcard. "Do you think I will be able to find this particular spot if I am on the Exmoor Coast?"

"Oh, yes, ma'am," said Mrs. Dilwyn after one look. "I've been there. It's the Hangman Cliffs. Lovely place, that."

"Do you know how to get there then?"

"Indeed, ma'am. You take the train from Paignton to Barnstaple, then you take the local branch line and go to Ilfracombe. The cliffs are a few miles more to the east."

She thanked Mrs. Dilwyn and spent some more time gazing wistfully at the postcard. Such a place as the Hangman Cliffs was difficult to visit: Her mother would not be able to navigate the steep paths that led to the top.

The idea came suddenly: She could go by herself. Her mother was not expected home until day after tomorrow. If she left first thing in the morning, she would be back by tomorrow evening, in plenty of time to greet her mother the next day, all the while having experienced what she had dreamed of for so many years: standing atop a precipice above a temperamental sea.

If she must begin a new era in her life for which she was less than enthusiastic, she might as well end this one on an extraordinarily high note.

❧

"Still thinking of Penny?" Angelica asked.

"Yes—and no," said Freddie.

Freddie had been waiting outside her house when she returned from Derbyshire. And for the past hour and a half they'd talked of nothing but Penny's revelations, recalling dozens of instances where some words or actions of Penny's could be reinterpreted in the light of his service to the Crown.

She had been outraged at first. She and Freddie had always been closer, but Penny had been the god-like elder-brother figure of her childhood. There had been times when she and Freddie had cried together, mourning the young man they both loved, not gone but lost all the same.

But because Freddie already forgave him, she was, given some time, willing to forgive him too.

She rang for a fresh pot of tea. All the talking had made her thirsty. "How can you be thinking about him and not be thinking about him at the same time?"

Freddie looked at her a long moment. "I was glad Penny came clean. And we talked a good hour before he left to take Mrs. Douglas to see her husband's solicitors. But I was still plenty unsettled after he left and I wanted to speak to you"—he stopped for a second—"and no one else but you. Those were some of the longest twenty-four hours of my life, waiting for you to come back."

It was most gratifying to hear. After all the time and effort she'd expended to take them from friends to lovers, now ironically she sometimes worried that their lovemaking—delicious as it was—had taken over everything. Silly of her—of course they were still best friends.

She smiled at him. "I'd have returned sooner if I'd known."

He didn't quite return her smile, but reached for the teapot instead.

"There's no more tea in there," she reminded him.

He reddened slightly. "Well, of course not. You rang for a new pot just now, didn't you?"

Fresh tea arrived. She poured for both of them. He raised his teacup.

"Don't you want some milk and sugar?" He never drank his tea black.

He reddened further, set down his teacup, and rubbed his fingers across his forehead. "I still haven't answered your question, have I?"

She'd already forgotten what question she'd asked. Somehow his sudden nerves made her tense too.

But he seemed to have made up his mind, whatever

it was. He gazed directly at her, his voice firm. "I've struggled for a while now to characterize what it is I feel for you, which is so much more potent than friendship, yet nothing like what I have experienced of love."

She had been reaching for a biscuit. Her hand stopped in the air. She had to force her fingers to close around the biscuit. They'd yet to bring up the word *love* in conversation—at least not with regard to the two of them.

"With Lady Tremaine, I was always the humble worshiper. Every time I walked into her drawing room, I felt as if I were an acolyte approaching the altar of a goddess. It was electrifying and unnerving at the same time. But your drawing room has been more like an extension of my own home. And I didn't know how to interpret that."

Their eyes met. She had no idea, she realized, not a single one, what he would say next. Her heart struggled to contain her dread—and a rising anticipation.

"And then this wait for you to come back. As I walked up and down the street outside, I realized at some point that I never went to Lady Tremaine unless I felt I had something to offer. When I called on her just because I wanted to see her, I always feared that I'd wasted her time.

"But you I want to see in all my moods. When I'm particularly pleased, when I'm simply going about my day, when I'm utterly overwhelmed, as I was yesterday and today. And it honors me that when I bring myself, I seem to have brought enough for you."

Her hand unclenched from the biscuit, which she'd crushed into several pieces in her palm. She let the pieces drop onto the tablecloth and breathed again.

"In doing what he did, Penny took me for granted. But he wasn't alone in it: I took him for granted also, before his 'accident.'" He smiled slightly, his eyes deep and warm. "Like Penny, you too have been a pillar of my life, which would have been far less meaningful without you. And yet I've taken you for granted too."

He came out of his seat. It seemed only natural that she should rise also—clasp his hands in hers.

"I don't want to take you for granted ever again, Angelica. Will you marry me?"

She drew back one hand and covered her mouth. "You have become full of surprises, Freddie!"

"Whereas you have been the best surprise of my life."

A surge of pure happiness nearly knocked her over. And of course he meant every word—he never said anything he didn't wholeheartedly mean.

"I can't imagine a better way to go through life than with you beside me," he continued.

"Constantly reminding you not to take me for granted?" she jested. She might start blubbering otherwise.

He chuckled. "Well, maybe not constantly. Quarter days should be fine." Placing his hands on her arms, he gazed into her eyes. "Does this mean you have said yes?"

"Yes," she said simply.

He kissed her, and then held her tight a long time. "I love you."

The words were sweeter than she'd thought possible—and she had exorbitant expectations, having wanted to hear them for so many years.

"I love you, too," she said. She pulled back a few inches and winked at him. "A second nude portrait to commemorate our engagement?"

He laughed and crushed her to him for another kiss.

❧

Ilfracombe was a severe disappointment. A fog as thick as old porridge had come to make chill, damp love to the coast. Visibility was so reduced street lamps had to remain lit during the day, faint rings of mustard-colored light amidst gray vapors that hid everything farther than five feet from Elissande's person.

She did derive *some* pleasure from being on the coast: the smell of the sea, bracing and salty; the surf crashing wild and harsh upon unseen cliffs, nothing like the gentle tides of Torbay; the deep tenor of foghorns from passing ships in the Bristol Channel, forlornly romantic.

She decided to stay the night. Should the fog clear, there would be enough time in the morning to see the cliffs and return to Pierce House—she was schooling herself to stop thinking of it as home—ahead of her mother and her husband.

And then she must break the news to her mother and bid adieu to her marriage.

❧

At the sight of the suitcases in his wife's room, a fist closed around Vere's heart.

He and Mrs. Douglas had arrived in London in mid-afternoon. There was no question of further travel the rest of the day for the exhausted older woman. Vere put her and Mrs. Green up at the Savoy Hotel, then rushed home by himself. Now that he'd spoken to Freddie, there was so much he needed to tell his wife: how stupid he'd been, how badly he missed her, and how eager he was for their marriage to begin anew.

He pulled open her drawers—empty. He yanked open the doors of her armoire—empty. He glanced at her vanity table, empty except for one single comb. And then a sight that made his stomach lurch: a book on her nightstand entitled *How Women May Earn a Living*.

She was leaving.

He sprinted downstairs and grabbed Mrs. Dilwyn. "Where's Lady Vere?"

He could not disguise his distress, his voice loud and brusque.

Mrs. Dilwyn was taken aback by his abruptness. "Lady Vere has gone to the Hangman Cliffs, sir."

He tried to digest this information and failed. "Why?"

"She saw a postcard in your study yesterday and thought the view marvelous. And since you and Mrs.

Douglas weren't expected until tomorrow, she decided to go first thing today."

It was almost dinnertime. "Shouldn't she have returned already?"

"She cabled an hour ago, sir. She has decided to stay the night. It was foggy on the coast today and she wasn't able to see anything. She hopes for better weather in the morning."

"The Hangman Cliffs—so she would have gone to Ilfracombe," he said, as much to himself as to Mrs. Dilwyn.

"Yes, sir."

He was out of the house before she'd finished speaking.

The sun seared her eyes, the sky so harshly bright it was nearly white. An arid mountain gale blasted. She was desiccated, her skin as fragile as paper, her throat sandy with thirst.

She tried to move. But her wrists were already bloody from her struggles against her chains, chains sunk deep into the bones of the Caucasus.

The piercing cry of an eagle made her renew her struggle, a frenzy of pain and futility. The eagle glided closer on dark wings, casting a shadow over her. As it plunged into her, knife-sharp beak gleaming, she twisted her head back and thrashed in agony.

"Wake up, Elissande," whispered a man, something at once authoritative and soothing about his voice. "Wake up."

She did. She sat up, panting. A hand settled on her shoulder. She wrapped her own fingers around it, reassured by its warmth and strength.

"Do you want some water?" asked her husband.

"Yes, thank you."

A glass of water found its way into her hand. And when she had quenched her thirst, he took the glass away.

Suddenly she remembered where she was: not in her room at home—Pierce House—but at a hotel in Ilfracombe—a hotel that looked out to the harbor, but from the windows of which she had barely been able to see even the street outside.

"How did you find me?" she asked, amazed and baffled, while an excitement, so hot it singed, began pulsing through her veins.

"Rather easily—there are only eight hotels in Ilfracombe listed in the travel handbook I bought on my way. Of course, no reputable hotel would give out a lady's room number—I had to use slightly underhanded means to gain that information once I found out where you were staying. And then it was just a matter of picking your lock and dealing with the dead bolt."

She shook her head. "You *could* have just knocked."

"I have a bad habit: After midnight I don't knock."

She heard the smile in his voice. Her heart thudded. She dropped her hand, which had been clasped about his. "What are you doing here?"

He did not answer her, but only spread his fingers on her shoulder. "Was it the same nightmare you told me about—the one in which you are chained like Prometheus?"

She nodded. He would have felt her motion, for his hand had moved to just below her ear.

"Would you like me to tell you about Capri, to help you forget it?"

He must have stepped closer to her; she became aware of the scent of the fog that still clung to his coat. She nodded again.

"'Looking seaward from Naples, the island of Capri lies across the throat of the bay like a vast natural breakwater, grand in all its proportions, and marvelously picturesque in outline,'" he spoke softly, his voice clear and beguiling.

She started. She recognized those lines: They were from her favorite book on Capri, which she had lost when her uncle purged his library.

"'Long ago, an English traveler compared it to a couchant lion,'" he continued. "'Jean Paul, on the strength of some picture he had seen, pronounced it to be a sphinx; while Gregorovius, most imaginative of all, finds that it is an antique sarcophagus, with bas-reliefs of snaky-haired Eumenides, and the figure of Tiberius lying upon it.'"

He eased her back down on the bed. "Do you want to hear more?"

"Yes," she murmured.

He undressed, tossing down one garment after another, the clothes landing with the softest of plops that made her throat hot and her heart wild.

"'Capri is not strictly a byway of travel.'" He

removed her nightdress and skimmed his fingers down her side. "'Most of the tourists take the little baysteamer from Naples, visit the Blue Grotto, touch an hour at the marina, and return the same evening via Sorrento.'"

He kissed the crook of her elbow, the pulse of her wrist, and gently bit the center of her palm. She shivered in pleasure.

"'But this is like reading a title-page, instead of the volume behind it.'"

His hand moved up her arm and kneaded her shoulder. His other hand cradled her face. Lightly, ever so lightly, disturbing not at all the bruises that had mostly faded from their unruly colors but were still sensitive to pressure, he traced the outline of her cheekbone.

"'The few who climb the rock, and set themselves quietly down to study the life and scenery of the island, find an entire poem, to which no element of beauty or interest is wanting, opened for their perusal,'" he recited, as his thumb pulled down her lower lip.

She emitted a whimper of need. His breath caught.

"But you are more beautiful than Capri," he said, his voice at once fervent and wistful.

She crushed him to her and kissed him fiercely. From there, Capri was forgotten and they had lips and hands and minds only for each other.

"What are you thinking?" Vere asked, his head in his palm, lying on his side.

He could not see her. She was only the rhythm of her breaths and the warmth of her skin.

Her hand traced the scars on his rib cage. "I was thinking that, one, I have never, ever, not once in all my years of reading travelogues, realized that they could also serve as tools of seduction. And two, that this must be the first time we've both stayed awake afterward."

He made the sound of snoring.

She chortled.

"If you are not too sleepy, I'd like to tell you a story," he said.

It was time.

"I'm not sleepy at all."

He wanted to give her some warning. "My story, it isn't always happy."

"No story is. Or it wouldn't be a story; it'd be a paean."

Very true. So he recounted for her the events that had led to the creation of his double life, starting with the night of his father's death. Despite his warning, her whole body turned rigid with dismay. Her hand clutched hard at his arm. But she listened quietly, intently, if with breaths that caught and trembled.

"And perhaps my life would have continued indefinitely on that path—it was a well-worn path, after all— if I'd never met you. But you came along and you changed everything. The better I knew you, the more I had to ask myself whether things I thought were immutable were truly set in stone, or simply seemed so because I was afraid of changes."

As his story moved away from the initial devastation, her person had gradually relaxed too. Now his hand upon her shoulder no longer detected as much tension.

"Two days ago I confessed everything to Freddie. It was a terribly difficult conversation going in, and yet afterward I felt light and free, as I haven't been in the longest time. And for that I have you to thank."

"I'm very, very glad you and Lord Frederick had your talk, but I don't see what I have to do with it," she said, her befuddlement genuine.

"Remember what you said a few nights ago about Douglas? 'I will not let him diminish me from beyond the grave, just as I never allowed him to take a piece of my soul while he yet lived.' Those words shattered me. Until that moment I had not understood that I *had* let a piece of my soul be taken from me. And until I recognized that I was no longer whole, I could not begin to put myself together again."

He was full of gratitude toward her. But it was yet another sign of how secretive he'd become that *she* had no idea of the changes she'd wrought in him.

"It's wonderful that I could be of some help," she said, sounding both pleased and embarrassed. "But I must protest that I don't deserve nearly the credit you give me. You saw it: Just now I had another nightmare. I'm nobody's shining example."

"You are mine," he said firmly. "Besides, I came equipped for the nightmare, didn't I?"

"I was just going to ask! How did you happen to know one of my favorite books by heart?"

"I asked your mother if she remembered any books on Capri you liked. She quoted me a passage, but she couldn't recall the name of the book, only that you loved it. So I set to work."

He had seven bookshops deliver to his hotel every single travel guide they stocked that so much as mentioned Italy. After he and Mrs. Douglas returned from the Savoy Theatre, he stayed up most of the night perusing any and all pages that dealt with Capri, until he came upon the passage Mrs. Douglas had recited.

"I found the book with the intention of reading it to you until you fell back asleep, should you have your nightmare again. But then I realized that reading would require a light. Better just to commit it to memory, which was what I did on the train going back to Devon."

"That is—that is incredibly sweet." The bed creaked. She pushed a little off the mattress and kissed him on the lips.

"I have only two more paragraphs of text left in me. But had I known that travelogues had such erotic properties, I'd have memorized the whole thing."

She chortled. "Oh, you would, would you?"

He combed his fingers through her cool hair. "If you want me to, I would—even if I'm banned from ever seducing you with Capri travelogues again."

She leaned her cheek against his, a simple gesture

that almost caused his gratitude to spiral out of control.

"Would this be a good time to apologize to you for my having been a complete ass when we were in the castle ruins?"

His conduct that day had chafed his conscience ever since.

She pulled back slightly, as if to look him in the eyes. "Only if it's also a good time to apologize to you for having forced you to marry me."

"So I'm forgiven?"

"Of course," she said.

He used to believe that to forgive was to allow an offense to go unpunished. Now he finally understood that forgiveness was not about the past, but the future.

"And me, am I forgiven?" she asked, a note of anxiety in her voice.

"Yes, you are," he said, and meant every word.

She exhaled unsteadily, a sound of relief. "Now we can go on."

Now they could look forward to the future.

Chapter Twenty-two

"What does 'Pedicabo ego vos et irrumabo' mean?" Elissande asked, as they hiked up the steep path that led to the top of the Hangman Cliffs.

The day had dawned sunny and beautiful. And the coast had been a revelation of untamed headland and feral sea. She had been instantly captivated.

After breakfast, they'd hired a coach and driven to Combe Martin, the closest village to the Hangman Cliffs, and from there they had set out on foot, tramping across the green moors on a path dotted with surprisingly white goats.

Her husband had been taking a sip from the canteen of water he carried. At her question, he choked, as badly as his brother had the night he'd brought up the phrase as the family motto for the Edgertons of Abingdon. Elissande had to forcefully smack his back to help him clear his airway.

He panted and laughed at the same time. "My God, you still remember it?"

"Of course I do. It is not anyone's family motto, is it?"

"No!" He doubled over with mirth. "Or at least, I hope not."

She adored his laughter. All the more so for the long, lonely path he'd trudged to reach this day, when they could enjoy the coast of the West Country arm in arm. She picked up his hat, which had fallen onto the trail.

"What is it then?" She smoothed his hair with her fingers and put the hat back on his head, adjusting the angle for it to sit properly—she was largely unfamiliar with a man's toilette.

"It's from a poem by Catullus, probably the rudest poem you could ever hope to read in your life," he said, playfully lowering his voice, "so rude I don't think a translation has ever been published in English."

"Oh?" This she must hear. "Do tell."

"A nice young lady like you shouldn't ask," he teased.

"A nice young gentleman like you shouldn't withhold—or the nice young lady might be driven to ask your brother."

"Ooh, blackmail. I like it. Well, if you *must* know, the first verb refers to buggery." He burst out laughing again, this time at her expression. "Don't look so shocked; I already told you it's rude."

"Clearly I've led a sheltered life. My idea of rudeness is calling someone ugly and stupid. Is there a second verb?"

"Indeed there is. It refers also to a sexual act, one of somewhat lesser infamy—but would still have roomfuls of ladies braying for their smelling salts if it were ever mentioned."

She gasped. "I think I know what it is."

He drew back in astonishment. "No, you most certainly do not know what it is."

"Yes, I do," she said smugly. "The night you were drunk as a skunk, you mentioned withdrawal. And you said that if you were in a really terrible mood, you'd make me swallow your seed."

His jaw dropped. "I take it back. You do know what it is then. My God, what all did I say to you that night?"

A young shepherd appeared on the path, walking toward them with his flock.

"On second thought," said her husband, "let's wait until tonight. I have a presentiment that speaking of my precise words and actions that night might lead us to activities that would get us arrested."

She giggled. He gave her a mock glare. "Be serious. It's *your* reputation I'm worried about."

She cleared her throat and set her face. "Was this the sort of Latin verse you were looking for to put yourself to sleep when you were at Highgate Court?"

"Indeed not. This is the sort of Latin verse I read when I want to choke on my water, obviously."

She chortled. "Speaking of looking for Latin verse, what *were* you doing in my uncle's study that night?"

His expression turned sheepish. "It was right next door to the green parlor. I was hoping to come in on you after Lady Avery had caught you all by yourself. I thought it would be amusing." He sighed. "See, my own vengefulness led to my downfall."

She patted him on the arm. "You are still a good man."

"You think so?"

He had probably meant for the question to be nonchalant, but it had emerged laden with both hope and doubt.

She understood him. She'd never thought of herself as particularly good—how could anyone good be so adept at lies and deceit? But she did not doubt *his* goodness: She needed only to look at the way he took care of her mother.

And he gave himself too little credit. To recognize the change he needed required insight; and to confess before Freddie, after all these years, took true courage.

"I know so," she said.

He was silent. The path turned. He held out his hand to help her over a rock that jutted from the ground. She gazed upon him, her strapping, handsome man, golden and pensive, and felt a ferocious protectiveness.

They walked on for almost five minutes before he touched her shoulder and said, "Thank you. I'll live up to it."

She had no doubt he would.

❧

The top of the Hangman Cliffs gave onto a stunning vista: miles of verdant headlands towering hundreds of feet high, a twilight-blue sea upon which the sun glimmered like silver netting, and in the distance a pleasure boat, all its sails unfurled, gliding across the water with the leisurely grace of a swan.

She could not take her eyes off the views. And he could not take his eyes off her. Her face was flushed, her breath still slightly uneven from the strenuous climb, and her smile, ah, her smile—he would have crawled across broken glass for it.

"It's even more beautiful when the heathers are in bloom," he said. "Then the slopes turn a glorious purple."

"We must come back then, when the heathers are in bloom."

Her skirts whipped in the fresh, briny breeze. A particularly lively gale almost blew her hat away. She laughed as she clamped onto the crown of the hat with one hand. Her other hand slipped into his, her grip warm and light.

His heart lurched: It was her. It was always her for whom he'd waited all these years.

"I used to have this idea of a perfect companion," he said.

She glanced at him, a mischievous look in her eyes. "I'm going to bet she is nothing like me."

"Actually, she was nothing like *me*. I made her my opposite in every way. She was simple, content, with no deceit to her—no darkness, and no history."

She turned more fully toward him, her expression now a solemn curiosity. "Was she your Capri?"

Of course she would understand, but his heart still

swelled with gratitude. "Yes, she was my Capri. But whereas your Capri was an aspiration, mine had become a crutch. Even after I'd fallen in love with you, I tried to cling to her. In fact, I opted to drive you away and lose any possibility of a future together rather than acknowledge that perhaps my Capri had a limited life span and the end of its time had come."

Her hand squeezed his. "Are you sure you are ready to let it go?"

"Yes." At long last. "And I'm going to let go of far more than that. I think it's time I had another 'accident.'"

Her jaw dropped. "You are resigning your service as an agent to the Crown?"

"I'd always wanted a seat in the House of Commons until the day came when I had to take my father's in the Upper House instead. And then I learned the truth about my mother's death. My own plans became irrelevant. Instead, I devoted myself to a vengeance that could never be mine. But with another 'accident,' I could claim that I'd recovered and go from there."

She only gazed at him, wide-eyed.

Doubt suddenly assailed him. "Do you think it's too extravagant an idea, to take my seat in the House of Lords?"

"No, absolutely not. I'm only amazed at all the changes that have been and will be taking place in your life." She touched a hand to his brow. "Will you be happy in the House of Lords?"

"No. It's full of self-important reactionaries: I was ever so incensed when they vetoed the Irish Home

Rule bill in 'ninety-three." He smiled at her. "But somebody should be there to tell them that they are nothing but a ragtag collection of self-important reactionaries."

"In that case, I shall act appropriately mystified in the beginning, as my husband abruptly metamorphoses from the idiot I much esteemed to a man whose intellect and learning are quite beyond my grasp. And then, under his patient, obliging tutelage, I shall discover hidden cerebral prowess of my own." She nodded. "Yes, I think it's doable. When is this new 'accident' of yours to take place?"

He was torn between mirth and admiration at how she planned to handle the demands of this, her last great role.

"The timing and the precise tactics we can decide later. There is something much more urgent I must take care of first. Now, in fact."

She tilted her face up. "What is it?"

The bruises were still faintly visible, but they did not distract from her beauty: He only loved her more for her valor.

"As much as I subsequently tried to deny it, I have loved you from the moment I first saw you. Lady Vere, would you do me the immense honor of remaining married to me?"

She gasped softly, then giggled. "Is this a *proposal*, Lord Vere?"

"It is." He hadn't expected it, but his heart was beating fast. "Please say yes."

"Yes," she said. "Yes, I would. Nothing would make me happier."

He took off her hat, then his own, and kissed her, this one woman he loved the most, in his favorite place in the entire world.

❧

When they returned home they found not only Mrs. Douglas back from London—she proudly presented her sister's jewels to Elissande as her dowry—but also Freddie and Angelica, who had come in person to announce their engagement.

Angelica, who looked radiant, punched Vere symbolically on the chest as his penance for lying to her all these years.

"Punch me more," he said. He had told Freddie that he could share everything with Angelica, understanding that Freddie needed that.

"I should," said Angelica, "but I have decided to forgive you."

He was moved to embrace her. "Thank you."

It never failed to astonish him, the generosity of those who loved him—and whom he loved—best.

Together they chatted for a while with Mrs. Douglas. After Mrs. Douglas left to take her nap, the four of them congregated in the study and made good-natured fun of Vere as they plotted his return to form.

"We can say you came upon a bear in the woods," said Angelica, "and the bear smacked you on the head the way I should have!"

"Wild bears have been extinct in Britain since the

tenth century," Vere pointed out. "We will have trouble with that story."

"How about an accident during a cricket game?" said Freddie. "I can hit you very gently."

"After having been thoroughly pummeled by you, Freddie, I think you underestimate your own strength. One gentle hit from you might shear off my head."

"I can smack you with a frying pan," suggested his wife, joining the fun. "Domestic strife is always believable."

"Excellent idea!" exclaimed Angelica.

"But you are a marchioness, not a farmer's wife." Vere shook his head. "What lady of your station would run five minutes from her drawing room to her kitchen for a skillet? She's much more believable using a Ming vase."

"Or his walking stick," said Freddie, with a wink to Elissande.

They all cackled at that.

Freddie and Angelica stayed for dinner, during which they drank many toasts: to the newly engaged couple's future happiness, to Mrs. Douglas's health, to Vere's upcoming "miraculous" recovery, and to his wife's saintly patience with the unbearably pedantic man Vere was certain to become, now that he was free to exploit his intellect again.

Vere offered his brother and sister-in-law-to-be lodging for the night, but they declined. He did not press too hard, knowing that the new lovers were eager for their privacy. The four of them made plans to meet again soon, then Vere and Elissande were standing before the house, waving good-bye to Freddie and Angelica as the latter left for the rail station.

When the carriage had disappeared from sight, Vere placed his arm around his wife's shoulder. She leaned into him.

"I love you," he said, kissing her on her hair.

"I love you too." She lifted his hand from around her shoulder and kissed his palm. "And I want to take long walks with you, many, many of them."

He smiled. "Your wish is my command, my lady."

"Good," she said. "Now let's retire upstairs and talk at *great* length—if you know what I mean—about Latin verse."

They were still laughing as they closed the bedroom door.

Author's Note

The electric hand torch was invented toward the end of the nineteenth century. Patents for various designs, aimed at commercial application, date from 1896 to 1898. While they were probably not quite as portable and inconspicuous as the one Vere used in this book, I feel quite confident that given the available technology, a talented and dedicated engineer working for the Crown could easily have made just such a James Bond–ish gadget.

The passages on Capri are quoted from *A Handbook for Travellers in Southern Italy and Sicily,* and *By-ways of Europe.* Both books are now in the public domain.

Acknowledgments

Caitlin Alexander, for her tireless dedication and absolute brilliance, and for always knowing what needs to be done.

Kristin Nelson and Sara Megibow, for their support and wisdom.

Janine, for staying up with me all night, and for sound advice when I most needed it.

Tracy Wolff, for food and gossip and laughter.

Courtney Milan, for preventing me from going down a completely inaccurate path.

Jo, for helping with English criminal law.

My readers, for their emails and letters.

My family, my bulwark in life.

And as always, if you are reading this, thank you from the bottom of my heart.